THE EVOLUTION ~~OF~~ THE AMERICAN SHORT STORY...

In the decades since the end of World War II, the American short story has become a good deal more literary—with less emphasis on plot, for example, and much more focus on characterization and the possibilities of form and language. And it is the short story, rather than the novel, that has become, in a sense, the literary barometer of our time. Major authors—John Cheever, Flannery O'Connor, Saul Bellow, and others—are included alongside such innovative stylists as Stanley Elkin and Grace Paley. With the younger authors—Jayne Anne Phillips and Ann Beattie, for example—this collection reveals the prevailing trend toward a dispassionate narrative voice, but it also shows fascinating exceptions.

Just as *The Signet Classic Book of American Short Stories* covered the genre up until World War II, *The Signet Classic Book of Contemporary American Short Stories* reflects the extraordinary blooming of the form since 1945. This book offers some of the best writing in all of American literature—and voices that cannot be ignored.

THE SIGNET CLASSIC BOOK OF CONTEMPORARY AMERICAN SHORT STORIES

BURTON RAFFEL, Professor of English at the University of Denver, is the translator of *Sir Gawain and the Green Knight* (Mentor), author of *How to Read a Poem* (Meridian) and editor of *The Signet Classic Book of American Short Stories*.

The Signet Classic Book of Contemporary American Short Stories

EDITED AND WITH AN
INTRODUCTION BY
Burton Raffel

A SIGNET CLASSIC

NEW AMERICAN LIBRARY

A DIVISION OF PENGUIN BOOKS USA INC., NEW YORK
PUBLISHED IN CANADA BY
PENGUIN BOOKS CANADA LIMITED, MARKHAM, ONTARIO

Introduction copyright © 1986 by Burton Raffel

Grateful acknowledgment is made to the following for permission to reprint
these stories:

"First Heat," by Peter Taylor, from THE COLLECTED STORIES OF
PETER TAYLOR. Copyright © 1968, 1969 by Peter Taylor. Reprinted
by permission of Farrar, Straus and Giroux, Inc.

"A Modest Proposal," by Jean Stafford, from THE COLLECTED STO-
RIES OF JEAN STAFFORD. Copyright © 1949, 1969 by Jean Stafford.
Reprinted by permission of Farrar, Straus and Giroux, Inc. Chatto and
Windus, The Hogarth Press, and the author.

"The Hartleys," by John Cheever, from THE STORIES OF JOHN CHEEVER,
by permission of Random House, Inc., and International Creative
Management.

"Mosby's Memoirs," by Saul Bellow, from MOSBY'S MEMOIRS AND
OTHER STORIES. Copyright © 1951, 1954, © 1955, 1957, 1967, 1968 by
Saul Bellow. Reprinted by permission of Viking Penguin Inc. and Harriet
Wasserman Literary Agency.

"The Dumb Waiter," by Walter Miller, Jr. Copyright 1952 by Walter
Miller, renewed in 1980 by Walter Miller. Reprinted by permission of
Don Congdon Associates, Inc.

"A Good Man Is Hard To Find," by Flannery O'Conner from A GOOD
MAN IS HARD TO FIND. Copyright 1953 by Flannery O'Connor;
renewed 1981 by Mrs. Regina O'Conner. Reprinted from A GOOD MAN
IS HARD TO FIND by Flannery O'Connor by permission of Harcourt
Brace Jovanovich, Inc., and Harold Matson Company, Inc.

"You May Safely Gaze," by James Purdy, from DREAM PALACES.
Copyright © 1956, 1957, 1959, 1960, 1980 by James Purdy. Reprinted
by permission of Viking Penguin Inc., and the William Morris Agency,
Inc. on behalf of the author.

"The Pale Pink Roast," by Grace Paley, from THE LITTLE DISTUR-
BANCES OF MAN. Copyright © 1956, 1957, 1958, 1959 by Grace
Paley. Reprinted by permission of Viking Penguin Inc. and Grace Paley.

"The Conversion of the Jews," by Philip Roth from GOODBYE, COLUM-
BUS. Copyright © 1959 by Philip Roth. Reprinted by permission of
Houghton Mifflin Company.

"The Jewbird," by Bernard Malamud, from IDIOTS FIRST. Copyright ©
1963 by Bernard Malamud. Reprinted by permission of Farrar, Straus &
Giroux, Chatto & Windus, The Hogarth Press, and the author.

Library of Congress Catalog Card Number: 85-63514

SIGNET TRADEMARK REG. U.S. PAT. OFF. AND FOREIGN COUNTRIES
REGISTERED TRADEMARK—MARCA REGISTRADA
HECHO EN DRESDEN, TN, U.S.A.

SIGNET, SIGNET CLASSIC, MENTOR, ONYX, PLUME, MERIDIAN and NAL BOOKS are published *in the United States* by New American Library, a division of Penguin Books USA Inc., 1633 Broadway, New York, New York 10019, and *in Canada* by Penguin Books Canada Limited, 2801 John Street, Markham, Ontario L3R 1B4

First Printing, June, 1986

3 4 5 6 7 8 9 10 11

PRINTED IN THE UNITED STATES OF AMERICA

CONTENTS

INTRODUCTION

In the decades since the end of World War Two there have been two major developments in the American short story. First, many of the largest and best-paying magazine markets have disappeared, including such longtime bastions as *The Saturday Evening Post* and *Colliers*. Secondly, and to some extent as a result of the first development, the story form itself has become a good deal more literary. That is, not only has its style become less and less sharply distinguishable from the style of poetry, but form and structure too have become more episodic, more tangential, much less plot-centered, and in the end a good deal less resolved. (Appropriately, stories by well-known writers have begun to appear with greater frequency in literary and "little" magazines, magazines that the likes of Howells and O. Henry, Sherwood Anderson and John Dos Passos, or Fitzgerald and Hemingway had little to do with, once their careers were well established.) Many of these changes involve larger, more basic shifts in esthetic, affecting novels as well as stories. But the longer, more complex novel form has of necessity held such changes to a minimum: it is the short story rather than the novel that has become, in a sense, the literary barometer of our time.

The thirty-four stories here included are about as representative a record of the American short story during the past four decades as one could put together, evenly apportioned among those decades and among the various and shifting approaches and styles writers have employed. Beginning with

the very earliest of them, Peter Taylor's "First Heat," there
is no mistaking the sharp change from earlier styles and
approaches. Introspective, analytical, owing perhaps more to
Kafka than to the famous Americans of the nineteenth century,
Taylor's story deals with a common enough theme in American literature—the corrupting effects of a political life—but
gives that theme a subjective, personal slant distinctly identi-
fiable as a post-war phenomenon. For example, the story's
unnamed protagonist (his wife is also unnamed) is expressing
moral anxiety in physical form: he is sweating. "The flow of
perspiration was quite extraordinary. . . . He had never been
one to sweat so. It was rather alarming. It really was." But
he is also self-tormenting, perversely wishing that there might
be "something else . . . to hide," something other than
himself to keep hidden from his wife's eyes. "Oh, if only, if
only—if only there were a woman, herself covered with
sweat, . . . for him to hide. What an innocent, simple thing it
would be." His sense of himself, now that he knows he has
been conclusively caught up in the corruption of politics, now
that he knows he has betrayed something, though he is not
yet sure just what, is that he has become "utterly empty." He
envisions his wife and himself, leaving for a reception, as
"the tuxedo and the evening gown," and has no conviction
left about who "would be in them" when the reception was
over and the clothes "rode back across town to their empty
hotel room." That question, expressed in a single word, is
the story's final sentence: "Who?"

Taylor not only does not give us his characters' names, he
tells us almost nothing about their backgrounds, their families, their training, even their fiscal condition. We assume
that the man has money; we do not know for sure. We
assume that the woman has certain social graces; we cannot
be sure here either. He is an unlikely politician, his father has
told him. His father has also once taken him on a fishing trip.
And that is all we know of his family, and more than we
know of hers. He has friends, but we know literally nothing
of them. He has children, for they have been married fifteen
years, but we do not know how many children, of what sex
or age. His wife hires a baby-sitter, we are told in passing, in
order to free herself to come to the reception: that is about as

much family financial information as Taylor wants us to have.

What the story is after, plainly, is no longer the full social analysis that engaged earlier American writers like Howells, nor the full personal analysis that engaged writers like Henry James. Omission of the factual record on which such analyses could be based is the farthest thing from accidental. Taylor wants us to feel the man's mood, but without knowing exactly why the man himself is experiencing it. We are told just enough of the political background to understand that there has been a vote change, and that the vote change has created a problem. "As if he didn't *have* a problem, as if he needed to make one up!" There are suggestions of political ambition, but only suggestions. "Wasn't the state Senate as far as he would go and farther than he should have gone?" The author has arranged matters so that the character is entitled to interrogate himself, but we are not enabled to go behind his question. Our only concern, once again by the author's careful arrangement, is with the character's concern— the fact of that concern, but not with its substance. *Whatever* he thinks or feels, indeed, all we are enabled to do is follow along in his wake, observing without understanding, dealing with effects rather than with causes. The only dialogue in the entire story is a brief exchange, toward the end, between husband and wife, and it is telephonic rather than face to face. By the time they are actually in one another's presence there is apparently nothing to be said, everything is as it must and will be.

This actively concerned but insistently dispassionate stance is one of the hallmarks of the contemporary short story, visible time and again both in this volume and in the many stories for which, unfortunately, room could not be found here. The stance is neither morally or humanly neutral, but nor is it as socially engaged as Mark Twain or Howells or Kate Chopin, nor so humanly engaged as Ambrose Bierce or Henry James or Edith Wharton. It would be untrue to maintain that all contemporary American stories present so cool, so abstract, so intricately self-absorbed a front, but surely a great many do, and American short fiction tends to become more and more cool and abstract and self-absorbed as the decades roll by.

Donald Barthelme is in many ways the epitome, and even in some ways the archetype, of this cool, abstract approach. The story here reprinted, "Rebecca," is perhaps not fully representative of these aspects of his work. It does however contain a good many of its essential features, notably a compressed, almost telegraphic structure and narrative movement, and an insistent mocking of traditional values. "Are you a homosexual lesbian? Is that why you never married?" asks a judge, and it is the author himself who immediately replies. "Christ, yes, she's a homosexual lesbian, as you put it. *Would you please shut your face?*" We are informed that our homosexual lesbian protagonist "of course . . . has a classic and sexual figure which attracts huge admiration from every beholder." We hear of her that "she thought about sticking her head in the oven. But it was an electric oven." Plainly, bad jokes are permitted, and freely indulged in; so too are resonant platitudes. "They love each other—an incredibly dangerous and delicate business, as we know. . . . Human love . . . remains as grisly and golden as ever . . ." Even the act of writing is itself mocked, freely and frequently. The phrase just quoted, for example, runs in its entirety: "One should never cease considering human love, which remains as grisly and golden as ever, no matter what is tattooed upon the warm tympanic [i.e., resonant? as in the ear's tympanic bone?] page." Style in the usual, the traditional sense is no more important, in this view, than are other traditional values. Indeed, everything traditional is to be attacked, and with every available means. The writer therefore can, and Barthelme does, employ whatever stylistic levels he chooses, mixing them as he happens to desire, and employing words as he prefers to employ them. "Tympanic" (which as I have indicated I do not entirely understand, in this context) is a plain example of this arbitrary freedom—and Barthelme himself has assured us that his practice is both a deliberate and a principled one. "We like books that have a lot of *dreck* [feces] in them," he has written, "matter which presents itself as not wholly relevant (or indeed at all relevant)." John Hawkes, whose approach is closely similar, speaks for both

Bartheleme and for others when he explains that "As a writer I'm concerned with innovation . . . , and *obviously* I'm committed to nightmare, violence, meaningful distortion, to the whole panorama of dislocation and desolation in human experience [emphasis added]." And Hawkes also sets the approach in its full literary context:

> Of course I think of myself as an experimental writer. But it's unfortunate that the term "experimental" has been used so often by reviewers as a pejorative label intended to dismiss as eccentric or private or excessively difficult the work in question . . . I should think that every writer, no matter what kind of fiction writer he may be or may aspire to be, writes in order to create the future. Every fiction of any value has about it something new. At any rate, the function of the true innovator or specifically experimental writer is to keep prose alive and constantly to test in the sharpest way possible the range of our human sympathies and constantly to destroy mere surface morality.

Robert Alter's 1975 study of "the novel as a self-conscious genre," *Partial Magic*, neatly sets this approach in its historical context. "Over the past two decades, as the high tide of modernism ebbed and its masters died off, the baring of literary artifice has come to be more and more a basic procedure—at times, almost an obsession—of serious fiction in the West." Leslie Fiedler's *What Was Literature?* (1982) refers, with equal trenchancy, to Barthelme's "long-drawn-out experimentation with terminal fiction," adding that such work is "redeemed variously by political indignation, an infatuation with pop culture, a kind of cutesy charm, or an obsession with the middle of the middle of our country."

From a strictly literary perspective, it is often difficult to know the precise genre these writers are working in. The story "Margins," from Barthelme's 1964 collection, *Come Back, Dr. Caligari*, seems to have three principal objectives: (1) to pass along assorted information on calligraphy, (2) to offer us specifically literary judgments, as for example that "John Hawkes also wrote *The Beetle Leg* and a couple of

other books . . . I think he's one of the best of our younger
American writers,'' and (3) to inform us that poor is good
and very poor is better still: under the signboards hung over
the shoulders of the two down-and-out protagonists beat hearts
of pure gold. Or are they in truth just as malicious and
mean-spirited as the rest of us? ''When Carl returned the two
men slapped each other sharply in the face with the back of
the hand—that beautiful part of the hand where the knuckles
grow.'' It is hard to tell; plainly, Barthelme does not want us
to be sure. In any event, the thrust of the story, to the extent
that it is a story and that it has a thrust, is deliberately
obscured, making genre identification difficult. What is the
story up to? what is the author up to? And when we come to
the ending of the story entitled ''Alice,'' from Barthelme's
1968 *Unspeakable Practices, Unnatural Acts*, how are we to
know whether we are still reading prose at all?

> but I do know where I am I am on West Eleventh Street
> shot with lust I speak to Alice on the street she is
> carrying a shopping bag I attempt to see what is in the
> shopping bag but she conceals it we turn to savor rising
> over the Women's House of Detention a particularly
> choice bit of ''sisters'' statistics on the longevity of life
> angelism straight as a loon's leg conceals her face
> behind *pneumatiques* hurled unopened scream the place
> down tuck mathematical models six hours in the confes-
> sional psychological comparison scream the place down
> Mars yellow plights make micefeet of old cowboy airs
> cornflakes people pointing to the sea overboots nasal
> contact 7 cm. prune the audience dense car correctly
> identify chemical junk blooms of iron wonderful lofti-
> ness sentient populations

This sort of verbal explosion seems a good deal more like
poetry than like what has usually been considered prose. And
when Mark Helprin titles a piece in his 1975 volume *A Dove
of the East*, ''On 'The White Girl' by James Whistler,'' does
the title signal us that we are to be given a story or an essay?
Helprin's ''On 'The White Girl' by James Whistler'' is itself
not as helpful as one would like. ''Without sacrifice the

world would be nothing," it begins. We meet, more or less, a female figure who is married to a husband who is a painter and "who painted her . . . standing in a white dress by a white marble fireplace." Is he Whistler? Is she Whistler's wife? Are we supposed to know? Is it supposed to matter? "He painted and she loved him, loved him, loved him, as much as he loved her, for the gentle arching of her eyebrows and her mortality made him a man." Love is indeed an oddly insistent theme in these abstract, dispassionate tales which have few human handles by which we can grasp the characters, if there are any characters to grasp, if indeed there is not simply a set of ideologies, quasi-embodied principles.

These are serious confusions. In the work of Barthelme and Robert Coover and Mark Helprin and others, we are over and over again cast away from our usual moorings, left floundering in an alien, unreal sea. Richard Elman will allow us, at most, "hope for a postcard back now and then." In his "Crossing Over," all ties to reality are either stretched out of shape or destroyed. "By now I was nearly forty-eight and Joseph who had once been my younger brother was at least fifty-six." The relationship between the brothers has been several times compared to that between and among "gnomes and midgets," which is more or less clear. But then suddenly we are told that "the crowd of midgets and gnomes congregating every day outside my window was truly getting fierce." Why are they out there, what is their purpose? Where have they come from? Why are they so regular, why are they so fierce? We are not told, but we do hear, with equal suddenness, that "their leader was a certain Julia Pierce." Who then is Julia Pierce, where does *she* come from and what is her role in this story? We are not told, though the narrator pleads "with her not to make me do a thing like that . . ." What thing? "But when I did it again she said it's too late already, now you'll have to do it like this." Julia Pierce disappears, to the extent she was ever there, as the narrator thinks to himself: "I guess that's how I got to be such a student of human nature, though if you ask me I prefer building bridges any day of the week, especially next Tuesday, when I'm scheduled to be five years old again."

On the other hand, the unreality employed by Walter Miller,

in "Dumb Waiter" as also in most of his work (which includes the magnificent novel *A Canticle for Leibowitz*), is of a very different order.

> The bombers came out of the east. The ram-jet fighters thundered upward from the outskirts of the city. They charged, spitting steel teeth and coughing rockets at the bombers. The sky snarled and slashed at itself. The bombers came on in waves, occasionally loosing an earthward trail of black smoke. The bombers levelled and opened their bays. The bays yawned down at the city. The bombers aimed. Releases clicked. No bombs fell. The bombers closed their bays and turned away to go home. The fighters followed them for a time, then returned to land. The big guns fell silent. And the sky began cleaning away the dusky smoke.

As Miller makes perfectly clear, this is not in truth a fierce war scene, because what we are seeing is nothing more than the reflex action of blindly, automatically functioning machines. There are no people flying any of the planes, or shooting any of the guns, just as there are no more bombs for the bombers to drop. But this unreality is unreal only because it has not yet happened, not because it cannot happen. Miller's unreality is a prophecy, and it is a warning. There is an enormous distance between the interior worlds crookedly and sometimes randomly displayed by Barthelme, and the bent and broken external worlds displayed by Miller. Fantastic gargoyles operating in the real world, which is what Bartheleme gives us, are wholly unlike sane, rational men and women operating in a world gone overtly mad. Bartheleme is hostile to the world he sees; Miller is terrified of the world he might have to see, one day. I do not propose to choose between them, as to passion and sincerity. But it is very apparent that Barthelme's attitudes tend inevitably to radicalism of all sorts, while Miller's tend with equivalent inevitability toward conservative stances. Barthelme wants to destroy a world that considers itself sane. Miller wants to preserve what he sees as civilization's and humanity's only and final hope, a clear, conscientious rationality, in the face of the brutal irrationality in man which always struggles to destroy civilization. Both writers, and those who think and write like them, are fantasists, but worlds apart.

Logically enough, as classical realism has faltered and to a degree withered, explicit fantasy (as distinguished from Barthelme's essentially implicit sort) has increasingly gained favor. Although only one story here is in usual terms labeled fantasy, and that is of course Miller's "Dumb Waiter," two others are overt and explicit tales of fantasy, Bernard Malamud's "The Jewbird" and Layle Silbert's "A Hole in California." But there is an extraordinary amount of fantasizing in other stories, too. Mark Helprin's "The Schreuderspitze," for example, has almost as many pages describing the central character's dreams as it has pages that deal with externally visible realities. Time itself seems hardly to exist in Richard Elman's "Crossing Over," and while there are significant strands of realism in Stanley Elkin's "In the Alley," the terminally ill central character acts out a series of fantasies, from one of continued good health to one of morbid and declining health, ending his life on a fantastic journey to (literally) the "end of the line." Elkin plays fair with us. The very first paragraph ends with the assertion, less mocking than it seems, that "as soon as the implications of the word 'malignant' had settled peaceably in his mind, Feldman decided he must . . . become a hero." And the last paragraph ends with Feldman smiling and thinking "sadly of the dying hero"—though he himself has just been beaten to the point of death and left to die, as die he does, in an alley, "by the waiting garbage, by the coffee grounds in their cups of wasted orange hemispheres, by the torn packages of frozen fish, by the greased, ripped labels of hollow cans, by the cold and hardened fat, by the jagged scraps of flesh around the nibbled bones, and the coagulated blood of cow and lamb." The fantasy could not be more grimly in conflict with reality—and that, to be sure, is Elkin's intent. The point is that the generation or two of American writers who preceded him would not have used precisely these literary tools in precisely this way, any more than they would have employed the tools of Donald Barthelme or of Walter Miller.

—BURTON RAFFEL

Peter Taylor

Peter Taylor was born in Nashville, Tennessee, in 1917. Educated at Vanderbilt, Southwestern College, and Kenyon College (where he became a friend to both Robert Lowell and Randall Jarrell), he has spent virtually his entire life in the South, as a teacher of writing, notably at the University of North Carolina and the University of Virginia. He has written plays and a novel, but most of his literary work has been in the story form. His first collection appeared in 1948; others have followed at regular intervals. All have been extremely well received critically, though they have had no great popular success. Collected Stories *appeared in 1969.* The Old Forest and Other Stories *was published to great critical acclaim in 1985.*

A supple, vigorous, yet subtle stylist, Taylor's strengths are a wry but friendly understanding of the inner psychology of Southern families and a singularly deft but rarely barbed humor. His plots are clear and strong but never the basic motivating force of his fiction. Rather, he focuses on an immensely careful, detailed, and somehow always balanced consideration of morals and motives. One does not initially read Taylor for excitement, but readers find themselves coming back to his stories, sometimes over and over. These are tales that not only linger in the mind but seem to become continually more satisfying, more perceptive, and in the end more powerfully true.

FIRST HEAT

He turned up the air conditioning and lay across the bed, wearing only his jockey shorts. But it didn't stop. Two showers already since he came in from the afternoon session! Showers had done no good. Still, he might take another presently if it continued. The flow of perspiration was quite extraordinary. Perhaps it was the extra sleeping pill he took last night. He had never been one to sweat so. It was rather alarming. It really was. And with the air conditioner going full blast he was apt to give himself pneumonia.

What he needed of course was a drink, and that was impossible. He was not going to have a single drink before she arrived. He was determined to be cold sober. She would telephone up from the desk—or from one of the house phones nearby. He always thought of her as telephoning directly from the desk. Somehow that made the warning more official. But she did always telephone, did so out of fear he might not have his regular room. So she said. He knew better, of course. Married for nearly fifteen years, and at home she still knocked on doors—on the door to his study, on the door to the bathroom, even on the door to their bedroom. She even had the children trained to knock on doors, even each other's doors. Couldn't she assume that since he knew she was on the way, knew she was by now wheeling along the Interstate—doing seventy-five and more in her old station wagon—couldn't she assume that whatever kind of fool, whatever kind of philanderer she might suspect him of being, he would have the sense to have set matters right by the time she got there? But what rot! As if he didn't *have* a problem, as if he needed to make one up!

He could hear his own voice in the Senate Chamber that afternoon. Not his words, just his guilty voice. Suddenly he got up off the bed, pulled back the spread, the blanket, the top sheet. He threw himself down on his back, stuck his legs in the air, and pulled off his shorts. They were wringing wet

with his damnable perspiration! He wadded them into a ball
and, still lying on his back, still holding his legs in the air, he
hurled the underwear at the ceiling, where it made a faintly
damp spot before falling to the carpeted floor. And she—she
would already know what his voice in the Senate Chamber
had said. (His legs still in the air.) And knowing how the
voting went, know who betrayed whom, who let whom down,
who let what bill that was supposed to go through intact be
amended. It would all have been reported on the local six
o'clock state news, perhaps even with his taped voice uttering
the words of betrayal. She would have picked it up on the
radio in the station wagon just after she set out, with her
evening dress in a suitbox beside her. Maybe she would even
have turned back, feeling she just couldn't face certain people
at the mansion reception tonight . . . or couldn't face him.

Now—only now—he let his legs drop to the bed, his feet
coming down wide apart on the firm, first-rate-hotel mattress.
And he threw out his arms, one hand palm upward landing on
each pillow of the double bed. He *would* relax, *would* catch a
quick nap. But a new charge of sweat pressed out through
every pore of his skin, on his forehead, on his neck, in the
soft area just above his collarbone, from the exposed inner
sides of his thighs and his ankles, from the exposed armpits
and upper arms and forearms, from the palms of his hands
and the soles of his feet. He felt he was aware of every
infinitesimal modicum of sweat that was passing through
every pore of every area of his body. Somehow it made him
feel more utterly, thoroughly naked than he had ever before
felt in his entire life. Yes, and this time the sweat came
before the thought—just a little before the thought this time.
The thought of what he had done and left undone concerning
the amendment, said and left unsaid concerning the amendment, the thought of the discrepancy between his previously
announced position and the position he finally took on the
floor, all thought of *that* seemed something secondary and
consequential to the sweat. Perhaps he was ill, really ill!
Perhaps it was only a coincidence that this sickening sweat
had come over his body. But no, he was not that sort—to
claim illness. One thing for certain, though, the sweat was
already like ice water on his skin.

Now he would have to get up and dry himself off again. There was a scratching sensation in his throat. He even coughed once. He would have to turn *down* the air conditioner. And he would have to find something else to focus his mind on. After all, he had not betrayed his country or his family. And not, God knew, his constituents. Was it only old man Nat Haley he was worrying about? He had agreed to support Nat Haley's waterways bill, had been quite outspoken in favor of it. The newspapers all over the state had quoted him. And then, yesterday, he had received promises from other sources, promises so much to the interest of his constituents that he could not resist. By God, it was the sort of thing he—*and* she—had known he would have to do if he stood for the legislature and got elected, the sort of thing he would have to face up to if he went into politics, where everybody had said *he* ought not to go. He and she had looked each other in the eye one day—before he ever announced—and said as much . . . Well, at the last minute he had agreed to support the very amendment which Nat Haley had said would be ruinous, would take all the bite out of his bill. But Nat Haley was, himself, the damnedest kind of double-dealer. Even *he* had observed that. Ah, he was beginning to know politics. And he was beginning to understand what "everybody" had meant. Old Nat Haley was well known for the deals he arranged and didn't live up to. Everyone knew about Nat Haley. Nat Haley wouldn't have hesitated to fight this bill itself if he had discovered, even at the last minute, that that was to his advantage.

Who, then, was he betraying? And it wasn't a bill of any great import, either.

He sat up and swung his feet over the side of the bed. His hand came down briefly on the moisture his body had left on the otherwise starchy hotel sheet. He glanced backward and saw the wet shadow of himself that his perspiration had left there, and he turned away from it. But as he turned away from his silhouette on the sheet, there he was, in all his nakedness, in the large rectangular mirror above the dresser. And there he was in the mirror on the open bathroom door. He reached to the floor and took up a bath towel he had dropped there earlier and began drying himself—and hiding himself. He stood up and went over his body roughly with the towel; then, his eyes lighting on the mirror on the bathroom door, he wadded up the towel, just as he had the jockey shorts, and hurled it at the door. It came right up against his face there! And when it had fallen, he realized that this time it wasn't—as so often—his face in the mirror that offended him. He didn't care about the face. He knew it too well and what its every line and look meant. The body interested him as never before, or as it had not in years. For a moment, it was like meeting someone from the past, someone he had almost forgotten—an old friend, and old enemy. It was— almost—a young man's body still; he was not forty yet and he exercised as much as he ever had and ate and drank with moderation. The body in the door mirror and in the large mirror over the dresser had good tone, was only a little heavier about the hips than it had once been, and the arm muscles were really better developed than when he was twenty. Taking in the different views he had of the body in the two mirrors he recalled that as late as his college days he had sometimes shadow-boxed before mirrors, usually wearing his ordinary boxer shorts and imagining they were made of silk, with his name, or some title, like *The Killer*, embroidered on them in purple or orange letters. He didn't smile over the recollection. But neither did he take any such stance before the mirrors now. The body in the mirrors was tense, as if prepared to receive a blow; and he looked at it objectively as a painter or a sculptor might, as a physician might. He observed features that particularized it: the modest island of dark hair on the chest, which narrowed into a peninsula pointing down below the navel and over the slightly rounded belly, almost joining the pubic hair above the too-innocent- looking penis; the elongated thighs; the muscular calves; the almost hairless arms; the shoulders, heavy and slightly stooped. Presently, his interest in himself seemed entirely anatomical. And all at once it was as though his eyes were equipped with X-rays. He could see beneath the skin and under the flesh to the veins and tendons and the ropelike muscles, the heart and lungs, the liver, the intestines, the testicles, as well as every bone and joint of the skeleton. And now it was as though a klieg light—no, a supernatural light—shone from behind him and through him. Only when at last he moved one foot, shifting his weight from one leg to the other, did the flesh and the covering skin return. Had it been a dream? A vision? It seemed to him now that he was not naked at all, or that this was not the nakedness he had sought when he removed his clothes. At any rate, his body had ceased to sweat.

He stepped back to the bed and lay down on his side, his back to the mirrors. He experienced momentary relief. It was as though he had seen beyond mere nakedness of body and spirit, had looked beyond all that which particularized him and made his body and his life meaningful, human. Was that the ultimate nakedness? Why, it could just as well have been old Nat Haley's insides he had seen. And he did relax now. He closed his eyes . . . But then it came on again. Only this time there was no sweat. There was just the explicit dread of that moment—soon now, soon—when he would open the door to her. And he thought of how other, older politicians would laugh at his agonizing over so small a matter. *They* would know what a mistake politics was for him. Or perhaps they would know that, like them, he was *made* for politics. Wasn't this merely his baptism—in betrayal? In politics the ends were what mattered, had to matter. In politics that was the only absolute. If you were loyal to other men, you were apt to betray your constituency. Or did he have it all backward? No, he had it right, he was quite sure. And for that very reason, wasn't the state Senate as far as he would go and farther than he should have gone? Friends had warned him against state politics especially. His father had said to him: "You are the unlikeliest-looking political candidate I have ever seen." But it was a decision she and he had made together, and together they had agreed that one's political morality could not always coincide with one's private morality. They had read that somewhere, hadn't they? At any rate, one had to be prepared to face up to that morality . . . And now, though he felt chilled to the bone, the sweat came on again. He rolled over and reached for the towel on the floor, forgetting he had thrown it at the mirror. As he got off the bed, the same hand that had reached for the towel reached out to the wall and turned down the air conditioner. He went into the bathroom and got a dry towel and came back drying

himself—or those two hands were drying him. He stopped
before the long mirror on the bathroom door, the hands still
drying him. He remembered something else his father had
said to him once when they were on a fishing trip at Tellico
Plains. He had gone for a swim in the river and stood on a
rocky slab beside the water afterward, first rubbing his chest
and his head with a towel and then fanning his body with it
before and aft. His father, watching the way he was fanning
himself with the towel, said, "You do cherish that body of
yours, don't y'?" But what mistaken notions his father had
always had about him. Or perhaps it was only wishful thinking on his father's part. Perhaps he had only *wished* that kind
of concern for him. Ah, if only his body *had* been his great
care and concern in life—his problem! And no doubt that's
what his sweating meant! He *wished* it were only a bodily
ill!

He wasn't, as a matter of fact, a man who was given to
lolling about this way with no clothes on—either at home or
in a hotel room. And it occurred to him now that it wasn't the
sweat alone that had made him do so today. As soon as he
had walked into the room and closed the door after him he
had begun pulling off his clothes. It seemed to him almost
that the sweat began *after* he had stripped off his clothes. But
he couldn't definitely recall now whether it had begun before
or after he got to the room. At any rate, he wasn't *sure* it had
begun before. Had it? Else, why had he undressed at once?
. . . He lay down on the bed again and his eye lit on the
black telephone beside the bed. The first thing some men did
when alone in a hotel room, he knew, was to take up the
telephone and try to arrange for a woman to come up. Or that
was what he always understood they did. The point was, he
should have *known*. But he—he would hardly know nowadays how to behave with such a woman. He would hardly
know what to say or do if one of those hotel creatures came
into the room. Or would he know very well, indeed! Yes,
how simple it all would be. What a great satisfaction, and
how shameful it would seem afterward. How sinful—how
clearly sinful—he would know himself to be. There the two
of them are, in bed. But suddenly there comes a knock on the

door! He will have to hide her. His wife is out there in the passage. The baby-sitter came a little early. And the traffic was not as bad as she had anticipated. With the new Interstate, a forty-mile drive is nothing. He has no choice. There isn't anything else he can do: he will have to hide the creature. She will have to stand naked, her clothes clutched in her arms, behind the drapery or in the closet, while he and his wife dress for the reception at the governor's mansion. If only—But the telephone, the real, black telephone was ringing now, there on the real bedside table.

He let it ring for thirty seconds or so. Finally, he took up the instrument. He said nothing, only lay on his side breathing into the mouthpiece.

"Hello," she said on the house phone. He could hear other voices laughing and talking in the lobby.

"Hello," he managed.

"I'm downstairs," she said, as she always said, waiting for him to invite her to come up. He invited her now, and she replied, "Is everything all right? You sound funny."

"Everything's fine. Come on up," he said. "You've heard the news?"

"I listened in the car, on the way over."

"I changed my mind about the bill," he said.

"Is Mr. Haley pretty angry?"

"He cut me cold on the Capitol steps afterward."

"I thought so," she said. "He was icy to me when I passed him in the lobby just now. Or I imagined he was."

"Do you still want to go to the reception?"

She laughed. "Of course I do. I'm sure you had good reasons."

"Oh, yes, I had good reasons."

"Then, shall I come on up?"

"Do," he said. But then he caught her before she hung up. "Wait," he said. He sat on the bed, pulling the sheet up about his hips. "Why don't you wait down there? Why don't we go somewhere and have a drink and something to eat before we dress for the reception? I'm starved."

"I'm starved, too," she said. "I had only a very small snack with the children at four-thirty."

"I'll be right down," he said.

"Well—" She hesitated and then said, "No, I have my dress with me in a box—my dress for tonight. I want to put it on a hanger. I'll be right up—that is, if you don't mind."

"Good," he said.

"And why don't we have our drink up there? It might be easier."

"Good," he said.

As soon as he had put down the telephone, he sprang from the bed, ran to pick up his sweaty shorts and the sweaty hotel towels. He began straightening the room and pulling on his clothes at the same time, with desperate speed. She must not find him undressed, this way. It would seem too odd. And if he should begin the sweating again, he was lost, he told himself. He would have to try to ignore it, but she would notice, and she would know . . . She would be on the elevator now, riding up with other members of the legislature and their wives, wives who had also come to town for the reception at the mansion. He felt utterly empty, as though not even those veins and tendons and bones and organs were inside him. Wearing only his shirt and fresh shorts and his black socks and supporters, he stopped dressing long enough to give the bed a haphazard making up. He yanked the sheet and blanket and spread about. Fluffed the pillows. But if only there were something besides his body, something else tangible to hide. Catching a glimpse of himself in the mirror, he blushed bashfully and began pulling on his trousers to cover his naked legs. While slipping his tie under his collar, he was also pushing his feet into his shoes. As he tied the necktie and then tied the shoe strings, he was listening for her footsteps in the passage. Oh, if only, if only—if only there were a woman, herself covered with sweat, and still—still panting, for him to hide. What an innocent, simple thing it would be. But there was only himself . . . When the knock came at the door, he was pulling on his jacket. "Just a second," he called. And for no reason at all, before opening the door he went to the glass-topped desk on which lay his open briefcase and closed the lid to the case, giving a quick snap to the lock. Then he threw open the door.

It was as though only a pair of blue eyes—bodiless, even lidless—hung there in the open doorway, suspended by invisible wires from the lintel. He read the eyes as he had not been able to read the voice on the telephone. They were not accusing. They had done their accusing in the car, no doubt, while listening to the radio. Now they were understanding and forgiving . . . He bent forward and kissed the inevitable mouth beneath the eyes. It too was understanding and forgiving. But if only the mouth and eyes would not forgive, not yet. He wanted their censure, first. She entered the room, with the suitbox under her arm, and went straight over to the closet. He held his breath, his eyes fixed on the closet door. She paused with her hand on the doorknob and looked back at him. Suddenly he understood the kind of sympathy she felt for him. Is it the lady or the tiger? her hesitation seemed to say. If only, she seemed to say with him, if only it *were* the lady, naked and clutching her bundle of clothing to her bosom. But he knew of course, as did she, it would be the tiger, the tiger whose teeth they had drawn beforehand, whose claws they had filed with their talk about the difference between things private and things political. The tiger was that very difference, that very discrepancy, and the worst of it was that they could never admit to each other again that the discrepancy existed. They stood facing each other well and fully clothed. When, finally, she would open the closet door, they would see only his formal evening clothes hanging there, waiting to be worn to the governor's mansion tonight. And while he looked over her shoulder, she would open the cardboard box and hang her full-length white evening gown beside his tuxedo. And after a while the tuxedo and the evening gown would leave the hotel room together and go down the elevator to the lobby and ride in a cab across town to the governor's mansion. And there was no denying that when the tuxedo and the evening gown got out of the taxi and went up the steps to the mansion and then moved slowly along in the receiving line, he and she, for better or for worse, would be inside them. But when the reception was over and the gown and the tuxedo came down the steps from the mansion, got into another taxi, and rode back across town to their empty hotel room, who was it that would be in them then? Who?

(ca. 1948)

Jean Stafford

Jean Stafford was born in California in 1915. She grew up and went to school in Colorado, and later studied in Germany. Her fiction includes strong, rather Jamesian novels like Boston Adventure *(1944) and the somewhat more loosely constructed and much more popular* The Mountain Lion *(1947), set largely in rural Colorado. Her shorter fiction, assembled as* Collected Stories *(1969), exhibits a remarkable range and great power; she is a singularly accomplished stylist. Stafford wrote one nonfictional work,* A Mother in History *(1966), about the mother of President Kennedy's assassin, Lee Harvey Oswald.*

Stafford married Robert Lowell in 1940; the marriage lasted eight years. She was at the time a zealous convert to Catholicism and exerted a large influence on Lowell's beliefs and poetry. From 1959 to 1963 she was married to the journalist A. J. Liebling. Memoirs and other writing make it clear that she lived a distinctly tormented existence, both alone and when married.

Much of her shorter work appeared first in The New Yorker, *but it does not suffer from the obvious weaknesses of a great deal of that magazine's fiction. Never less than graceful, she is also direct, trenchant. She does not avoid genuine confrontation; she rarely settles for superficial, merely graceful poignancy. And in part because of the great diversity of her interests, Stafford's stories, taken as a whole, preserve a freshness and sense of surprise that make for deeply satisfying reading.*

She died in 1979.

A MODEST PROPOSAL

The celebrated trade winds of the Caribbean had, unseasonably, ceased to blow, and over the island a horrid stillness tarried. The ships in the glassy harbor appeared becalmed, and nothing moved except the golden lizards slipping over the pink walls and scuttering through the purple bougainvillaea, whose burdened branches touched the borders of the patio. The puny cats that ate the lizards slept stupefied under the hibiscus hedges. Once, a man-o'-war bird sailed across the yellow sky; once, a bushy burro strayed up the hill through the tall, hissing guinea grass and, pausing, gazed aloft with an expression of babyish melancholy; now and then, the wood doves sang sadly in the turpentine trees behind Captain Sundstrom's house.

The Captain's guests, who had been swimming and sunning all morning at his beach below and then had eaten his protracted Danish lunch of multitudinous hors d'oeuvres and an aspic of fish and a ragout of kid and salads and pancakes, now sat on the gallery drinking gin-and-Schweppes. Their conversation dealt largely with the extraordinary weather, and the residents of the island were at pains to assure the visitors that this unwholesome, breathless pause did not presage a hurricane, for it was far too early in the year. Their host predicted that a rain would follow on the heels of the calm and fill the cisterns to the brim. At times, the tone of the talk was chauvinistic; the islanders asked the outlanders to agree with them that, unpleasant as this might be, it was nothing like the villainous summer heat of Washington or New York. Here, at any rate, one dressed in sensible décolletage—the

Captain's eyes browsed over the bare shoulders of his ladies—
and did not shorten one's life by keeping up the winter's
fidgets in the summertime. Why people who were not obliged
to live in the North did, he could not understand. It was a
form of masochism, was it not, frankly, to condemn oneself
needlessly to the tantrums of a capricious climate? Temperate
Zone, indeed! There was no temperance north of Key West.
The visitors civilly granted that their lives were not ideal,
they were politely envious of the calm and leisure here, and
some of them committed themselves to the extent of asking
about the prices of real estate.

If the talk digressed from the weather, it went to other local
matters: to the municipal politics, which were forever a bear
garden; to the dear or the damnable peccadilloes of absent
friends; to servant-robbers from the States; to the revenue the
merchants and restaurateurs had acquired in their shops and
bars when the last cruise ship was in, full to her gunwhales of
spendthrift boobs. And they talked of the divorcées-to-be who
littered the terraces and lounges of the hotels, idling through
their six weeks' quarantine, with nothing in the world to do but
bathe in the sun and the sea, and drink, and haunt the shops
for tax-free bargains in French perfume. They were spoken of
as invalids; they were said to be here for "the cure." Some
of them did look ill and shocked, as if, at times, they could
not remember why they had come.

It was made plain that the divorcées who were among the
gathering today were different from the rest; *they* were not
bores about the husbands they were chucking; they did not
flirt with married men, or get too drunk, or try anything fancy
with the natives (a noteworthy woman from Utica, some
months before, had brought a station wagon with her and
daily could be seen driving along the country roads with a
high-school boy as black as your hat beside her); and they
fitted so well into the life of the island that the islanders
would like to have them settle here or, at least, come back to
pay a visit. Mrs. Baumgartner, a delicious blonde whose
husband had beaten her with a ski pole in the railroad station
at Boise, Idaho (she told the story very amusingly but it was
evident that the man had been a beast), and who meant to
marry again the moment she legally could, announced that

she intended to return here for her honeymoon. Captain Sundstrom reasonably proposed that she not go back to the States at all but wait here until the proper time had passed and then send for her new husband. It would be droll if the same judge who had set her free performed the ceremony. Crowing concupiscently, the Captain invited her to be his house guest until that time. A lumbering fourth-generation Dane, and now an American citizen, he had a face like a boar; the nares of his snout were as broad as a native's and his lips were as thick and as smooth. By his own profession to every woman he met, he was a gourmet and a sybarite. He liked the flavor of colonial argot and would tell her, "My bed and board are first-chop," as he slowly winked a humid blue eye. He had never married, because he had known that his would be the experience of his charming guests; it was a nuisance, wasn't it, to assign six weeks of one's life to the correction of a damn-fool mistake? Who could fail to agree that his was the perfect life, here on a hillside out of the town, with so magnificent a view that it was no trouble at all to lure the beauties to enjoy his hospitality. Mufti for the Captain today consisted solely of linen trunks with a print of crimson salamanders; below them and above them his furred flesh wrapped his mammoth bones in coils. At the beach that morning, he had endlessly regretted that there were no French bathing suits, and privily he had told Sophie Otis that he hoped that before she left, he would have the opportunity of seeing her in high-heeled shoes and black stockings.

To Mrs. Otis, who had left the rest of the party and was sitting just below the gallery on a stone bench in the garden in front of the house, this two-dimensional and too pellucid world seemed all the world; it was not possible to envisage another landscape, even when she closed her eyes and called to mind the sober countryside of Massachusetts under snow, for the tropics trespassed, overran, and spoiled the image with their heavy, heady smells and their wanton colors. She could not gain the decorous smell of pine forests when the smell of night-blooming cereus was so arrogant in her memory; it had clung and cloyed since the evening before, like a mouthful of bad candy. Nor was it possible to imagine another time than this very afternoon, and it was as if the clocks, like the winds, had been arrested, and all endeavor were ended and all passion were a *fait accompli,* for nothing could strive or love in a torpor so insentient. She found it hard to understand Mrs. Baumgartner's energy, which could perpetrate a plan so involving of the heart. She herself was nearly at the end of her exile and in another week would go, but while she had counted the days like a child before Christmas, now she could not project herself beyond the present anesthesia and felt that the exile had only just begun and that she was doomed forever to remain within the immobile upheaval of this hot, lonesome Sunday sleep, with the voices of strangers thrumming behind her and no other living thing visible or audible in the expanse of arid hills and in the reach of bright-blue sea. It was fitting, she concluded, that one come to such a place as this to repudiate struggle and to resume the earlier, easier indolence of lovelessness.

On the ground beside her lay, face down, a ruined head of Pan, knocked off its pedestal by a storm that had passed here long ago. A bay leaf was impaled on one of the horns and part of the randy, sinful grin was visible, but the eyes addressed the ground and the scattered blue blossoms from the lignum vitae tree above. Prurient and impotent, immortalized in its romantically promiscuous corruption, the shard was like the signature of the garden's owner, who now, sprawled in a long planter's chair, was telling those who had not heard of it the grisly little contretemps that had taken place the night before aboard the Danish freighter that still lay in the harbor. Twelve hours before she entered, a member of her crew, a Liberian, had fallen from the mast he was painting and had died at once, of a fractured skull. Although it was the custom of the island to bury the dead, untreated, within twenty-four hours, the health authorities, under pressure from the ship's captain, agreed, at last, to embalm the body, to be shipped back to Africa by plane.

"But then they found," said Captain Sundstrom, "that the nigger's head was such a mess that the embalming fluid wouldn't stay in, so they had to plant the bugger, after all. We haven't got enough of our own coons, we have to take care of this stray jigaboo from Liberia, what?" He appealed to little Mrs. Fairweather, a high-principled girl in her middle twenties, who had fanatically learned tolerance in college, and who now rose to his bait, as she could always be counted on to do, and all but screamed her protest at his use of the words "nigger" and "coon" and "jigaboo."

"Now, now," said the Captain, taking her small ringless hand, "you're much too pretty to preachify." She snatched away her hand and glared at him with hatred and misery; she was the most unhappy of all the divorcées, because it had been her husband's idea, and not hers, that she come here. She spent most of her time knitting Argyle socks for him, in spite of everything, the tears falling among the network of bobbins. She took the current pair out of her straw beach bag now, and her needles began to set up a quiet, desperate racket. Half pitying, half amused, the company glanced at her a moment and then began their talk again, going on to other cases of emergency burials and other cases of violent death on these high seas.

Mrs. Otis had brought the Captain's binoculars to the garden with her, and she turned away from the people on the porch to survey the hills, where nothing grew but bush and, here and there, a grove of the gray, leafless trees they called cedars, whose pink blossoms were shaped like horns and smelled like nutmeg; they did what they could, the cedar flowers, to animate the terrain, but it was little enough, although sometimes, from a distance, they looked beautifully like a shower of apple blossoms. She peered beyond the termination of the land, toward the countless islands and cays of the Atlantic, crouching like cats on the unnatural sea. They were intractably dry, and yet there was a sense everywhere of lives gathering fleshily and quietly, of an incessant, somnolent feeding, of a brutish instinct cleverer than any human thought. Some weeks before, from a high elevation on another island, through another pair of glasses, she had found the great mound of the island of Jost Van Dykes and had just made out its two settlements and its long, thin beaches, and she had found, as well, a separate house, halfway up the island's steep ascent, set in a waste as sheer as a rain catchment, where only one tree grew. And the tree was as neat and simple as a child's drawing. She had quickly put the glasses down, feeling almost faint at the thought of the terrible and absolute simplicity with which a life would have to be led in a place so wanting in shadow and in hiding places, fixed so nakedly to the old, juiceless, unloving land. Remembering that strident nightmare, she turned now to the evidences on the gallery of the prudent tricks and the solacing subterfuges of civilization; even here, as in the cities of their former days, the expatriates had managed to escape the aged, wickedly sagacious earth. See how, with optimism, gin, jokes, and lechery, they could deny even this satanic calm and heat!

Mr. Robertson, the liquor merchant, was explaining the activities of the peacetime Army here to a Coca-Cola salesman who had stopped off for a few days on the island en route from Haiti to the Argentine. Robertson, a former rumrunner and Captain Sundstrom's best friend, was as skinny as one of the island cats, and his skeleton was crooked and his flesh was cold. His eyes, through inappropriate pince-nez, mirrored no intellect at all but only a nasty appetite. He was a heliophobe and could never let the sun touch him anywhere, and so, in this country of brown skins and black ones, he always looked like a newcomer from the North and, with that fungous flesh, like an invalid who had left his hospital bed too soon. On the beach that morning, he had worn a hat with a visor and had sat under an enormous umbrella and had further fended off the sun by holding before his face a partially eviscerated copy of *Esquire*. In spite of his looks, he was a spark as ardent as the Captain, and lately, while his wife had been ailing, he had cut rather a wide swath, he claimed; all day he had giggled gratefully at his friends' charges that he had been stalking the native Negro women and the pert little French tarts from Cha Cha Town.

Rumor had it, he told the salesman, that a laboratory was presently to be set up on an outlying cay for the investigation of the possible values of biological warfare. The noxious vapors would be carried out to sea. (To kill the fancy, flashy fish weaving through the coral reefs, wondered Mrs. Otis, half listening.) Captain Sundstrom, who was connected with the project, turned again to Mrs. Fairweather, a born victim, and prefacing his sally with a long chuckle, he said, "We're hunting for a virus that will kill off the niggers but won't hurt anybody else. We call it 'coon bane.' " One of the kitchen boys had just come out onto the gallery with a fresh bucket of ice, but there was no expression at all on his long, incurious face, not even when Mrs. Fairweather, actually crying now, sobbed, "Hush!" The Coca-Cola man, in violent embarrassment, began at once to tell the company the story of an encounter he had had in Port-au-Prince with an octoroon midget from North Carolina named Sells Floto, but his heart was not in it, and it was clear that his garrulity was tolerated only out of good manners.

Mrs. Otis picked up the binoculars again and found the beach. For some time, she watched a pair of pelicans that sat on the tideless water, preposterously permanent, like buoys, until their greed came on them and they rose heavily, flapped seaward for a while, then dived, like people, with an inexpert splash, and came up with a fish to fling into their ridiculous beaks. The wide-leaved sea grapes along the ivory shingle were turning brown and yellow, a note of impossible autumn beside that bay, where the shimmer of summer was everlasting. Mrs. Otis shifted her focus to the grove of coconut palms that grew to the north of the curve of the ocean, and almost at once, as if they had been waiting for her, there appeared, at the debouchment of one of the avenues, a parade of five naked Negro children leading a little horse exactly the color of themselves. The smallest child walked at the head of the line and the tallest held the bridle. But a middle-sized one was in command, and when they had gained the beach, he broke the orderly procession and himself took the bridle and led the horse right up to Captain Sundstrom's blue cabaña. If her ears had not been aided by her eyes, Mrs. Otis thought she would not have heard the distant cries and the distant neigh, but the sounds came to her clearly and softly across the stunted trees. The children reconnoitered for a while, looking this way and that, now stepping off the distance between the cabaña and the water, now running like sandpipers toward the coconut grove and back again. Then the smallest and the tallest, helped by the others, mounted the horse; it was a lengthy process, because the helpers had to spin and prance about to relieve their excitement, and sometimes they forgot themselves altogether for an absent-minded minute and ran to peer through the cracks of the closed-up cabaña; then they returned to the business at hand with refreshed attention. When the riders were seated, one of the smaller children ran back to the grove and returned with a switch, which he handed up to the tall child. The horse, at the touch of the goad, lifted his head and whinnied and then charged into the water, spilling his cargo, only to be caught promptly and mounted by two others who had run out in his wake. They, in their turn, were thrown. Again and again, they tried and failed to ride him more than a few yards, until, at last, the middle-sized ruler managed to stick and to ride out all the way to the reef and back again. The cheers were like the cries of sea birds. The champion rested, lying flat on the sand before the cabaña, and for a while the others lay around him like the spokes of a wheel, while the horse shuddered and stomped.

On the gallery, the Captain had noticed the children. "Cheeky little beggars, muckering around on my beach, but I'll let them have it. I'm a freethinker, what?" he said; then, turning to Mrs. Fairweather, "I'm going to give you a fat little blackamoor to take back with you, to remind you of our island paradise, what?"

Mr. Robertson said, "Don't let him ride you, honey. For all his big talk, he's softer about them than you are." He leaned over to sink his fist into the Captain's thigh. "Get me?" he cried.

The Captain laughed and slapped his leg. "The whole thing's a lie, that's what it is, you outlaw!"

"It's a lie if the gospel truth's a lie," said Robertson. Mrs. Fairweather did not look up from her knitting, even though he was as close to her as if he meant to bite or kiss her. "Listen, kiddo, when I first knew him, he used to be all the time saying what he wanted most of all in the world to do was eat broiled pickaninny. All the time thinking of his stomach. So one day I said to him, 'All right, damn it, you damned well *will* one of these fine days!' "

Mrs. Baumgartner gasped, and one of the other women said, "Oh, really, Rob, you're such a fool. Everyone knows that our slogan here is 'Live and let live.' "

But Robertson wanted to tell his story and went on despite

them. He said, "Well, sir, a little while after I made that historic declaration, there was a fire in Pollyberg, just below my house, and I moseyed down to have a look-see."

"Let's not talk about fires!" cried Mrs. Baumgartner. "I was in a most frightful one in Albany and had to go down a ladder in my nightie."

Captain Sundstrom whistled and blew her a noisy kiss.

"They had got it under control by the time I got there, and everyone had left," pursued the liquor merchant. "I took a look in the front door and I smelled the best goddamned smell I ever smelled in my life, just possibly barring the smell of roasting duck. 'Here's Sundstrom's dinner,' I said to myself, and, sure enough, I poked around a little and found a perfectly cooked baby—around ten and a half pounds, I'd say."

The Coca-Cola salesman, who, all along, had kept a worried eye on Mrs. Fairweather, leaped into Robertson's pause for breath and announced that he knew a man who had his shoes made of alligator wallets from Rio.

Robertson glanced at him coldly, ignored the interruption, and went on speaking directly to Mrs. Fairweather. "It was charred on the outside, naturally, but I knew it was bound to be sweet and tender inside. So I took him home and called up this soldier of fortune here and told him to come along for dinner. I heated the toddler up and put him on a platter and garnished him with parsley and one thing or another, and you never saw a tastier dish in your life."

The Coca-Cola man, turning pale, stood up and said, "What's the matter with you people here? You ought to shoot yourself for telling a story like that."

But Robertson said to Mrs. Fairweather, "And what do you think he did after all the trouble I'd gone to? Refused to eat any of it, the sentimentalist! And *he* called *me* a cannibal!"

Robertson and the Captain lay back in their chairs and laughed until they coughed, but there was not a sound from anyone else and the islanders looked uneasily from one visitor to another; when their reproachful eyes fell on their host or on his friend, their look said, "There are limits."

Suddenly, Mrs. Fairweather threw a glass on the stone

floor and it exploded like a shot. Somewhere in the house, a dog let out a howl of terror at the sound, and the kitchen boy came running. He ran, cringing, sidewise like a land crab, and the Captain, seeing him, hollered, "Now, damn you, what do *you* want? Have you been eavesdropping?"

"No, mon," said the boy, flinching. There was no way of knowing by his illegible face whether he told the truth or not. He ran back faster than he had come, as if he were pursued. The Captain stood up to make a new drink for Mrs. Fairweather, to whom speech and mobility seemed unlikely ever to return; she sat staring at the fragments of glass glinting at her feet, as if she had reached the climax of some terrible pain.

"Oh, this heat!" said Mrs. Baumgartner, and fanned herself gracefully with her straw hat.

Something had alarmed the children on the beach below, and Mrs. Otis, turning to look at them again, saw them abruptly immobilized; then, as silently and as swiftly as sharks, they led the horse away and disappeared into the palm grove, leaving no traces of themselves behind. Until she saw them go, she had not been aware that the skies were darkening, and she wondered how long ago the transformation had begun. Now, from miles away, there rolled up a thunderclap, and, as always in the tropics, the rain came abruptly, battling the trees and lashing the vines, beheading the flowers, crashing onto the tin roofs, and belaboring the jalousies of Captain Sundstrom's pretty house. Blue blossoms showered the head of Pan. Wrapping the field glasses in her sash to protect them from the rain, Mrs. Otis returned to the gallery, and when the boy brought out a towel to her—for in those few minutes she had got soaked to the skin—she observed that he wore a miraculous medal under his open shirt. She looked into his eyes and thought, Angels and ministers of grace defend you. The gaze she met humbled her, for its sagacious patience showed that he knew his amulet protected him against an improbable world. His was all the sufferance and suffering of little children. In his ambiguous tribulation, he sympathized with her, and with great dignity he received the towel, heavy with rain, when she had dried herself.

"See?" said Captain Sundstrom to his guests, with a gesture toward the storm. "We told you this heat was only an interlude." And feeling that the long drinks were beginning to pall, he set about making a shaker of martinis.

(1949)

John Cheever

———————————◆———————————

John Cheever was born in Massachusetts, in 1912. Expelled from private school in his teens, he never completed his formal education, though later in life he served briefly as a teacher of creative writing at Barnard College and at Boston University. He began to make his living as a free-lance writer before he was old enough to vote, first turning out limpid, quintessentially New Yorker-style stories, and then a number of novels. Cheever's fiction, long and short, revolves around suburban people, usually with money, often with serious moral and characterological shortcomings, and frequently with drinking problems. His first novel, The Wapshot Chronicle, appeared in 1958 and won the National Book Award. The novel Falconer (1977) was both a critical and a commercial success, as was Collected Stories (1978), a massive assemblage of almost 700 pages. The latter volume also won the Pulitzer Prize.

There has been a great deal of posthumous scandal associated with Cheever's personal life. His life seems plainly to have had significant connections to his fiction; the scandal, equally clearly, is largely irrelevant. At his best, Cheever has a rare gift for the dramatic, for the almost O. Henry-like ending and for the pitiless exposure of neuroticisms and subtle immoralities of all sorts. In his lesser tales (and he is a stronger, more enduring writer of stories than of novels), the style sometimes seems smoothly pointless, rather fliply wry and over-sophisticated. But in the best of his work the prose achieves genuine and lasting power.

He died in 1982.

THE HARTLEYS

Mr. and Mrs. Hartley and their daughter Anne reached the Pemaquoddy Inn, one winter evening, after dinner and just as the bridge games were getting under way. Mr. Hartley carried the bags across the broad porch and into the lobby, and his wife and daughter followed him. They all three seemed very tired, and they looked around them at the bright, homely room with the gratitude of people who have escaped from tension and danger, for they had been driving in a blinding snowstorm since early morning. They had made the trip from New York, and it had snowed all the way, they said. Mr. Hartley put down the bags and returned to the car to get the skis. Mrs. Hartley sat down in one of the lobby chairs, and her daughter, tired and shy, drew close to her. There was a little snow in the girl's hair, and Mrs. Hartley brushed this away with her fingers. Then Mrs. Butterick, the widow who owned the inn, went out to the porch and called to Mr. Hartley that he needn't put his car up. One of the men would do it, she said. He came back into the lobby and signed the register.

He seemed to be a likable man with an edge to his voice and an intense, polite manner. His wife was a handsome, dark-haired woman who was dazed with fatigue, and his daughter was a girl of about seven. Mrs. Butterick asked Mr. Hartley if he had ever stayed at the Pemaquoddy before. "When I got the reservation," she said, "the name rang a bell."

"Mrs. Hartley and I were here eight years ago February," Mr. Hartley said. "We came on the twenty-third and were here for ten days. I remember the date clearly because we had such a wonderful time." Then they went upstairs. They came down again long enough to make a supper of some leftovers that had been kept warm on the back of the stove. The child was so tired she nearly fell asleep at the table. After supper, they went upstairs again.

In the winter, the life of the Pemaquoddy centered entirely on cold sports. Drinkers and malingerers were not encouraged, and most of the people there were earnest about their skiing. In the morning, they would take a bus across the valley to the mountains, and if the weather was good, they would carry a pack lunch and remain on the slopes until late afternoon. They'd vary this occasionally by skating on a rink near the inn, which had been made by flooding a clothesyard. There was a hill behind the inn that could sometimes be used for skiing when conditions on the mountain were poor. This hill was serviced by a primitive ski tow that had been built by Mrs. Butterick's son. "He bought that motor that pulls the tow when he was a senior at Harvard," Mrs. Butterick always said when she spoke of the tow. "It was in an old Mercer auto, and he drove it up here from Cambridge one night without any license plates!" When she said this, she would put her hand over her heart, as if the dangers of the trip were still vivid.

The Hartleys picked up the Pemaquoddy routine of fresh air and exercise the morning following their arrival.

Mrs. Hartley was an absent-minded woman. She boarded the bus for the mountain that morning, sat down, and was talking to another passenger when she realized that she had forgotten her skis. Her husband went after them while everyone waited. She wore a bright, fur-trimmed parka that had been cut for someone with a younger face, and it made her look tired. Her husband wore some Navy equipment, which was stenciled with his name and rank. Their daughter, Anne, was pretty. Her hair was braided in tight, neat plaits, there was a saddle of freckles across her small nose, and she looked around her with the bleak, rational scrutiny of her age.

Mr. Hartley was a good skier. He was up and down the slope, his skis parallel, his knees bent, his shoulders swinging gracefully in a half circle. His wife was not as clever but she knew what she was doing, and she enjoyed the cold air and the snow. She fell now and then, and when someone offered to help her to her feet, when the cold snow that had been pressed against her face had heightened its color, she looked like a much younger woman.

Anne didn't know how to ski. She stood at the foot of the

slope watching her parents. They called to her, but she didn't move, and after a while she began to shiver. Her mother went to her and tried to encourage her, but the child turned away crossly. "I don't want *you* to show me," she said. "I want Daddy to show me." Mrs. Hartley called her husband.

As soon as Mr. Hartley turned his attention to Anne, she lost all of her hesitation. She followed him up and down the hill, and as long as he was with her, she seemed confident and happy. Mr. Hartley stayed with Anne until after lunch, when he turned her over to a professional instructor who was taking a class of beginners out to the slope. Mr. and Mrs. Hartley went with the group to the foot of the slope, where Mr. Hartley took his daughter aside. "Your mother and I are going to ski some trails now," he said, "and I want you to join Mr. Ritter's class and to learn as much from him as you can. If you're ever going to learn to ski, Anne, you'll have to learn without me. We'll be back at around four, and I want you to show me what you've learned when we come back."

"Yes, Daddy," she said.

"Now you go and join the class."

"Yes, Daddy."

Mr. and Mrs. Hartley waited until Anne had climbed the slope and joined the class. Then they went away. Anne watched the instructor for a few minutes, but as soon as she noticed that her parents had gone, she broke from the group and coasted down the hill toward the hut. "Miss," the instructor called after her. "Miss . . ." She didn't answer. She went into the hut, took off her parka and her mittens, spread them neatly on a table to dry, and sat beside the fire, holding her head down so that her face could not be seen. She sat there all afternoon. A little before dark, when her parents returned to the hut, stamping the snow off their boots, she ran to her father. Her face was swollen from crying. "Oh, Daddy, I thought you weren't coming back," she cried. "I thought you weren't ever coming back!" She threw her arms around him and buried her face in his clothes.

"Now, now, now, Anne," he said, and he patted her back and smiled at the people who happened to notice the scene. Anne sat beside him on the bus ride back, holding his arm.

At the inn that evening, the Hartleys came into the bar

before dinner and sat at a wall table. Mrs. Hartley and her daughter drank tomato juice, and Mr. Hartley had three Old-Fashioneds. He gave Anne the orange slices and the sweet cherries from his drinks. Everything her father did interested her. She lighted his cigarettes and blew out the matches. She examined his watch and laughed at all his jokes. She had a sharp, pleasant laugh.

The family talked quietly. Mr. and Mrs. Hartley spoke oftener to Anne than to each other, as if they had come to a point in their marriage where there was nothing to say. They discussed haltingly, between themselves, the snow and the mountain, and in the course of this attempt to make conversation Mr. Hartley, for some reason, spoke sharply to his wife. Mrs. Harley got up from the table quickly. She might have been crying. She hurried through the lobby and went up the stairs.

Mr. Hartley and Anne stayed in the bar. When the dinner bell rang, he asked the desk clerk to send Mrs. Hartley a tray. He ate dinner with his daughter in the dining room. After dinner, he sat in the parlor reading an old copy of *Fortune* while Anne played with some other children who were staying at the inn. They were all a little younger than she, and she handled them easily and affectionately, imitating an adult. She taught them a simple card game and then read them a story. After the younger children were sent to bed, she read a book. Her father took her upstairs at about nine.

He came down by himself later and went into the bar. He drank alone and talked with the bartender about various brands of bourbon. "Dad used to have his bourbon sent up from Kentucky in kegs," Mr. Hartley said. A slight rasp in his voice, and his intense and polite manner, made what he said seem important. "They were small, as I recall. I don't suppose they held more than a gallon. Dad used to have them sent to him twice a year. When Grandmother asked him what they were, he always told her they were full of sweet cider." After discussing bourbons, they discussed the village and the changes in the inn. "We've only been here once before," Mr. Hartley said. "That was eight years ago, eight years ago February." Then he repeated, word for word, what he had said in the lobby the previous night. "We came on the

twenty-third and were here for ten days. I remember the date
clearly because we had such a wonderful time.''

The Hartleys' subsequent days were nearly all like the first.
Mr. Hartley spent the early hours instructing his daughter.
The girl learned rapidly, and when she was with her father,
she was daring and graceful, but as soon as he left her, she
would go to the hut and sit by the fire. Each day, after lunch,
they would reach the point where he gave her a lecture on
self-reliance. ''Your mother and I are going away now,'' he
would say, ''and I want you to ski by yourself, Anne.'' She
would nod her head and agree with him, but as soon as he
had gone, she would return to the hut and wait there. Once—it
was the third day—he lost his temper. ''Now, listen, Anne,''
he shouted, ''if you're going to learn to ski, you've got to
learn by yourself.'' His loud voice wounded her, but it did
not seem to show her the way to independence. She became a
familiar figure in the afternoons, sitting beside the fire.

Sometimes Mr. Hartley would modify his discipline. The
three of them would return to the inn on the early bus and he
would take his daughter to the skating rink and give her a
skating lesson. On these occasions, they stayed out late. Mrs.
Hartley watched them sometimes from the parlor window.
The rink was at the foot of the primitive ski tow that had been
built by Mrs. Butterick's son. The terminal posts of the tow
looked like gibbets in the twilight, and Mr. Hartley and his
daughter looked like figures of contrition and patience. Again
and again they would circle the little rink, earnest and serious, as if he were explaining to her something more mysterious than a sport.

Everyone at the inn liked the Hartleys, although they gave
the other guests the feeling that they had recently suffered
some loss—the loss of money, perhaps, or perhaps Mr. Hartley
had lost his job. Mrs. Hartley remained absent-minded, but
the other guests got the feeling that this characteristic was the
result of some misfortune that had shaken her self-possession.
She seemed anxious to be friendly and she plunged, like a
lonely woman, into every conversation. Her father had been a
doctor, she said. She spoke of him as if he had been a great
power, and she spoke with intense pleasure of her childhood.
''Mother's living room in Grafton was forty-five feet long,''

she said. "There were fireplaces at both ends. It was one of
those marvelous old Victorian houses." In the china cabinet
in the dining room, there was some china like the china Mrs.
Hartley's mother had owned. In the lobby there was a paperweight like a paperweight Mrs. Hartley had been given when
she was a girl. Mr. Hartley also spoke of his origins now and
then. Mrs. Butterick once asked him to carve a leg of lamb,
and as he sharpened the carving knife, he said, "I never do
this without thinking of Dad." Among the collection of canes
in the hallway, there was a blackthorn embossed with silver.
"That's exactly like the blackthorn Mr. Wentworth brought
Dad from Ireland," Mr. Hartley said.

Anne was devoted to her father but she obviously liked her
mother, too. In the evenings, when she was tired, she would
sit on the sofa beside Mrs. Hartley and rest her head on her
mother's shoulder. It seemed to be only on the mountain,
where the environment was strange, that her father would
become for her the only person in the world. One evening
when the Hartleys were playing bridge—it was quite late and
Anne had gone to bed—the child began to call her father.
"I'll go, darling," Mrs. Hartley said, and she excused herself
and went upstairs. "I want my daddy," those at the bridge
table could hear the girl screaming. Mrs. Hartley quieted her
and came downstairs again. "Anne had a nightmare," she
explained, and went on playing cards.

The next day was windy and warm. In the middle of the
afternoon, it began to rain, and all but the most intrepid skiers
went back to their hotels. The bar at the Pemaquoddy filled
up early. The radio was turned on for weather reports, and
one earnest guest picked up the telephone in the lobby and
called other resorts. Was it raining in Pico? Was it raining in
Stowe? Was it raining in Ste. Agathe? Mr. and Mrs. Hartley
were in the bar that afternoon. She was having a drink for the
first time since they had been there, but she did not seem to
enjoy it. Anne was playing in the parlor with the other
children. A little before dinner, Mr. Hartley went into the
lobby and asked Mrs. Butterick if they could have their
dinner upstairs. Mrs. Butterick said that this could be arranged. When the dinner bell rang, the Hartleys went up, and
a maid took them trays. After dinner, Anne went back to the

parlor to play with the other children, and after the dining room had been cleared, the maid went up to get the Hartleys' trays.

The transom above the Hartleys' bedroom door was open, and as the maid went down the hall, she could hear Mrs. Hartley's voice, a voice so uncontrolled, so guttural and full of suffering, that she stopped and listened as if the woman's life were in danger. "Why do we have to come back?" Mrs. Hartley was crying. "Why do we have to come back? Why do we have to make these trips back to the places where we thought we were happy? What good is it going to do? What good has it ever done? We go through the telephone book looking for the names of people we knew ten years ago, and we ask them for dinner, and what good does it do? What good has it ever done? We go back to the restaurants, the mountains, we go back to the houses, even the neighborhoods, we walk in the slums, thinking that this will make us happy, and it never does. Why in Christ's name did we ever begin such a wretched thing? Why isn't there an end to it? Why can't we separate again? It was better that way. Wasn't it better that way? It was better for Anne—I don't care what you say, it was better for her than this. I'll take Anne again and you can live in town. Why can't I do that, why can't I, why can't I, why can't I . . ." The frightened maid went back along the corridor. Anne was sitting in the parlor reading to the younger children when the maid went downstairs.

It cleared up that night and turned cold. Everything froze. In the morning, Mrs. Butterick announced that all the trails on the mountain were closed and that the tramway would not run. Mr. Hartley and some other guests broke the crust on the hill behind the inn, and one of the hired hands started the primitive tow. "My son bought the motor that pulls the tow when he was a senior at Harvard," Mrs. Butterick said when she heard its humble explosions. "It was in an old Mercer auto, and he drove it up here from Cambridge one night without any license plates!" The slope offered the only skiing in the neighborhood, and after lunch a lot of people came here from other hotels. They wore the snow away under the tow to a surface of rough stone, and snow had to be shoveled onto the tracks. The rope was frayed, and Mrs. Butterick's son had planned the tow so poorly that it gave the skiers a strenuous and uneven ride. Mrs. Hartley tried to get Anne to use the tow, but she would not ride it until her father led the way. He showed her how to stand, how to hold the rope, bend her knees, and drag her poles. As soon as he was carried up the hill, she gladly followed. She followed him up and down the hill all afternoon, delighted that for once he was remaining in her sight. When the crust on the slope was broken and packed, it made good running, and that odd, nearly compulsive rhythm of riding and skiing, riding and skiing, established itself.

It was a fine afternoon. There were snow clouds, but a bright and cheerful light beat through them. The country, seen from the top of the hill, was black and white. Its only colors were the colors of spent fire, and this impressed itself upon one—as if the desolation were something more than winter, as if it were the work of a great conflagration. People talk, of course, while they ski, while they wait for their turn to seize the rope, but they can hardly be heard. There is the exhaust of the tow motor and the creak of the iron wheel upon which the tow rope turns, but the skiers themselves seem stricken dumb, lost in the rhythm of riding and coasting. That afternoon was a continuous cycle of movement. There was a single file to the left of the slope, holding the frayed rope and breaking from it, one by one, at the crown of the hill to choose their way down, going again and again over the same surface, like people who, having lost a ring or a key on the beach, search again and again in the same sand. In the stillness, the child Anne began to shriek. Her arm had got caught in the frayed rope; she had been thrown to the ground and was being dragged brutally up the hill toward the iron wheel. "Stop the tow!" her father roared. "Stop the tow! Stop the tow!" And everyone else on the hill began to shout, "Stop the tow! Stop the tow! Stop the tow!" But there was no one there to stop it. Her screams were hoarse and terrible, and the more she struggled to free herself from the rope, the more violently it threw her to the ground. Space and the cold seemed to reduce the voices—even the anguish in the voices—of the people who were calling to stop the tow, but the girl's cries were piercing until her neck was broken on the iron wheel.

The Hartleys left for New York that night after dark. They were going to drive all night behind the local hearse. Several people offered to drive the car down for them, but Mr. Hartley said that he wanted to drive, and his wife seemed to want him to. When everything was ready, the stricken couple walked across the porch, looking around them at the bewildering beauty of the night, for it was very cold and clear and the constellations seemed brighter than the lights of the inn or the village. He helped his wife into the car, and after arranging a blanket over her legs, they started the long, long drive.

(ca. 1950)

Saul Bellow

Saul Bellow was born in Quebec, Canada, in 1915; his family, newly emigrated from Russia, moved to Chicago in 1924, and Bellow was educated at the University of Chicago and Northwestern University. After teaching at a number of colleges and universities, including Princeton, New York University, and the University of Minnesota, in 1963 he became a professor at the University of Chicago, where he has taught ever since.

Bellow's critical reputation was immediate and has been large; it has grown steadily larger. The award of the Nobel Prize for Literature, in 1976, surprised no one and outraged no one: if there was ever an American writer who thoroughly deserved such recognition, it was Bellow. His first novels, The Dangling Man *(1944),* The Victim *(1947), and the immensely successful* The Adventures of Augie March *(1953), show the richly fascinating prose, the sweeping narrative impetus, and the intricate understanding of human nature that continue to ripen and dazzle in all his later books, whether novels, collections of stories, or plays.* Henderson the Rain King *(1959) shows Bellow making splendid use of exotic terrain.* Herzog *(1964), a partially autobiographical novel, shows Bellow able to penetrate with singular skill and humor into the soul of modern urban man.* Humboldt's Gift *(1975), based in part on the life of the poet Delmore Schwartz, similarly shows Bellow able to blend narrative and dense philosophical thought, stunning dialogue and exciting action.*

The comic strain in his work has become somewhat more ironic, as he has grown older. In all other respects, he has remained the same truly major figure he has been for over forty years, turning everything he touches into profound and deeply moving fiction. Many critics consider him the foremost American writer of fiction in the postwar years.

MOSBY'S MEMOIRS

The birds chirped away. Fweet, Fweet, Bootchee-Fweet. Doing all the things naturalists say they do. Expressing abysmal depths of aggression, which only Man—Stupid Man—heard as innocence. We feel everything is so innocent—because our wickedness is so fearful. Oh, very fearful!

Mr. Willis Mosby, after his siesta, gazing down-mountain at the town of Oaxaca where all were snoozing still—mouths, rumps, long black Indian hair, the antique beauty photographically celebrated by Eisenstein in *Thunder over Mexico.* Mr. Mosby—Dr. Mosby really; erudite, maybe even profound; thought much, accomplished much—had made some of the most interesting mistakes a man could make in the twentieth century. He was in Oaxaca now to write his memoirs. He had a grant for the purpose, from the Guggenheim Foundation. And why not?

Bougainvillaea poured down the hillside, and the hummingbirds were spinning. Mosby felt ill with all this whirling, these colors, fragrances, ready to topple on him. Liveliness, beauty, seemed very dangerous. Mortal danger. Maybe he had drunk too much mescal at lunch (beer, also). Behind the green and red of Nature, dull black seemed to be thickly laid like mirror backing.

Mosby did not feel quite well; his teeth, gripped tight, made the muscles stand out in his handsome, elderly tanned jaws. He had fine blue eyes, light-pained, direct, intelligent, disbelieving; hair still thick, parted in the middle; and strong vertical grooves between the brows, beneath the nostrils, and at the back of the neck.

The time had come to put some humor into the memoirs. So far it had been: Fundamentalist family in Missouri—Father the successful builder—Early schooling—The State University—Rhodes Scholarship—Intellectual friendships—What I learned from Professor Collingwood—Empire and the mental vigor of Britain—My unorthodox interpretation of John Locke—I work for William Randolph Hearst in Spain—The personality of General Franco—Radical friendships in New York—Wartime service with the O.S.S.—The limited vision of Franklin D. Roosevelt—Comte, Proudhon, and Marx revisited—De Tocqueville once again.

Nothing very funny here. And yet thousands of students and others would tell you, "Mosby had a great sense of humor." Would tell their children, "This Mosby in the O.S.S.," or "Willis Mosby, who was in Toledo with me when the Alcázar fell, made me die laughing." "I shall never forget Mosby's observations on Harold Laski." "On packing the Supreme Court." "On the Russian purge trials." "On Hitler."

So it was certainly high time to do something. He had given it some consideration. He would say, when they sent down his ice from the hotel bar (he was in a cottage below the main building, flowers heaped upon it; envying a little the unencumbered mountains of the Sierra Madre) and when he had chilled his mescal—warm, it tasted rotten—he would write that in 1947, when he was living in Paris, he knew any number of singular people. He knew the Comte de la Mine-Crevée, who sheltered Gary Davis the World Citizen after the World Citizen had burnt his passport publicly. He knew Mr. Julian Huxley at UNESCO. He discussed social theory with Mr. Lévi-Straus but was not invited to dinner—they ate at the Musée de l'Homme. Sartre refused to meet with him; he thought all Americans, Negroes excepted, were secret agents. Mosby for his part suspected all Russians abroad of working for the G.P.U. Mosby knew French well; extremely fluent in Spanish; quite good in German. But the French cannot identify originality in foreigners. That is the curse of an old civilization. It is a heavier planet. Its best minds must double their horsepower to overcome the gravitational field of tradition. Only a few will ever fly. To fly away from Descartes. To fly away from the political anachronisms of left, center, and right persisting since 1789. Mosby found these French exceedingly banal. These French found him lean and tight. In well-tailored clothes, elegant and dry, his good Western skin, pale eyes, strong nose, handsome mouth, and virile creases. *Un type sec*.

Both sides—Mosby and the French, that is—with highly developed attitudes. Both, he was lately beginning to concede, quite wrong. Possibly equidistant from the truth, but lying in different sectors of error. The French were worse off because their errors were collective. Mine, Mosby believed, were at least peculiar. The French were furious over the collapse in 1940 of *La France Pourrie*, their lack of military will, the extensive collaboration, the massive deportations unopposed (the Danes, even the *Bulgarians* resisted Jewish deportations), and, finally, over the humiliation of liberation by the Allies. Mosby, in the O.S.S., had information to support such views. Within the State Department, too, he had university colleagues—former students and old acquaintances. He had expected a high post-war appointment, for which, as director of counter-espionage in Latin America, he was ideally qualified. But Dean Acheson personally disliked him. Nor did Dulles approve. Mosby, a fanatic about *ideas*, displeased the institutional gentry. He had said that the Foreign Service was staffed by rejects of the power structure. Young gentlemen from good Eastern colleges who couldn't make it as Wall Street lawyers were allowed to interpret the alleged interests of their class in the State Department bureaucracy. In foreign consulates they could be rude to D.P.s and indulge their country-club anti-Semitism, which was dying out even in the country clubs. Besides, Mosby had sympathized with the Burnham position on managerialism, declaring, during the war, that the Nazis were winning because they had made their managerial revolution first. No Allied combination could conquer, with its obsolete industrialism, a nation which had reached a new state of history and tapped the power of the inevitable, etc. And then Mosby, holding forth in Washington, among the elite Scotch drinkers, stated absolutely that however deplorable the concentration camps had been, they showed at least the rationality of German political ideas. The Americans had no such ideas. They didn't know what they were doing. No design existed. The British were not much better. The Hamburg fire-bombing, he argued in his clipped style, in full declarative phrases, betrayed the idiotic emptiness and planlessness of Western leadership. Finally, he said that when Acheson blew his nose there were maggots in his handkerchief.

Among the defeated French, Mosby admitted that he had a galled spirit. (His jokes were not too bad.) And of course he drank a lot. He worked on Marx and Tocqueville, and he drank. He would not cease from mental strife. The Comte de la Mine-Crevée (Mosby's own improvisation on a noble and ancient name) kept him in PX booze and exchanged his money on the black market for him. He described his swindles and was very entertaining.

Mosby now wished to say, in the vein of Sir Harold Nicolson or Santayana or Bertrand Russell, writers for whose memoirs he had the greatest admiration, that Paris in 1947, like half a Noah's Ark, was waiting for the second of each kind to arrive. There was one of everything. Something of this sort. Especially among Americans. The city was very bitter, grim; the Seine looked and smelled like medicine. At an American party, a former student of French from Minnesota, now running a shady enterprise, an agency which specialized in bribery, private undercover investigations, and procuring broads for V.I.P.s, said something highly emotional about the City of Man, about the meaning of Europe for Americans, the American failure to preserve human scale. Not omitting to work in Man the Measure. And every other tag he could bring back from Randall's *Making of the Modern Mind* or *Readings in the Intellectual History of Europe*. "I was tempted," Mosby meant to say (the ice arrived in a glass jar with tongs; the natives no longer wore the dirty white drawers of the past). "Tempted . . ." He rubbed his forehead, which projected like the back of an observation car. "To tell this sententious little drunkard and gyp artist, formerly a pacifist and vegetarian, follower of Gandhi at the University of Minnesota, now driving a very handsome Bent-

ley to the Tour d'Argent to eat duck *à l'orange*. Tempted to
say, 'Yes, but we come here across the Atlantic to relax a bit
in the past. To recall what Ezra Pound had once said. That
we would make another Venice, just for the hell of it, in the
Jersey marshes any time we liked. Toying. To divert ourselves in the time of colossal mastery to come. Reproducing
anything, for fun. Baboons trained to row will bring us in
gondolas to discussions of astrophysics. Where folks burn
garbage now, and fatten pigs and junk their old machines, we
will debark to hear a concert.' "

Mosby the thinker, like other busy men, never had time for
music. Poetry was not his cup of tea. Members of Congress,
Cabinet officers, Organization Men, Pentagon planners, Party
leaders, Presidents had no such interest. They could not be
what they were and read Eliot, hear Vivaldi, Cimarosa. But
they planned that others might enjoy these things and benefit
by their power. Mosby perhaps had more in common with
political leaders and Joint Chiefs and Presidents. At least,
they were in his thoughts more often than Cimarosa and
Eliot. With hate, he pondered their mistakes, their shallow-
ness. Lectured on Locke to show them up. Except by the will
of the majority, unambiguously expressed, there was no legitimate power. The only absolute democrat in America (perhaps in the world—although who can know what there is in
the world, among so many billions of minds and souls) was
Willis Mosby. Notwithstanding his terse, dry, intolerant
style of conversation (more precisely, examination), his
lank dignity of person, his aristocratic bones. Dark long
nostrils hinting at the afflictions that needed the strength
you could see in his jaws. And, finally, the light-pained
eyes.

A most peculiar, ingenious, hungry, aspiring, and heartbroken animal, who, by calling himself Man, thinks he can
escape being what he really is. Not a matter of his definition,
in the last analysis, but of his being. Let him say what he
likes.

> Kingdoms are clay: our dungy earth alike
> Feeds beast as man; the nobleness of life
> Is to do thus.

Thus being love. Or any other sublime option. (Mosby knew his Shakespeare anyway. *There* was a difference from the President. And of the Vice-President he said, "I wouldn't trust him to make me a pill. A has-been druggist!")

With sober lips he sipped the mescal, the servant in the coarse orange shirt enriched by metal buttons reminding him that the car was coming at four o'clock to take him to Mitla, to visit the ruins.

"Yo mismo soy una ruina," Mosby joked.

The stout Indian, giving only so much of a smile—no more—withdrew with quiet courtesy. Perhaps I was fishing, Mosby considered. Wanted him to say I was *not* a ruin. But how could he? Seeing that for him I *am* one.

Perhaps Mosby did not have a light touch. Still, he thought he did have an eye for certain kinds of comedy. And he *must* find a way to relieve the rigor of this account of his mental wars. Besides, he could really remember that in Paris at that time people, one after another, revealed themselves in a comic light. He was then seeing things that way. Rue Jacob, Rue Bonaparte, Rue du Bac, Rue de Verneuil, Hôtel de l'Université—filled with funny people.

He began by setting down a name: Lustgarten. Yes, there was the man he wanted. Hymen Lustgarten, a Marxist, or former Marxist, from New Jersey. From Newark, I think. He had been a shoe salesman, and belonged to any number of heretical, fanatical, bolshevistic groups. He had been a Leninist, a Trotskyist, then a follower of Hugo Oehler, then of Thomas Stamm, and finally of an Italian named Salemme who gave up politics to become a painter, an abstractionist. Lustgarten also gave up politics. He wanted now to be successful in business—rich. Believing that the nights he had spent poring over *Das Kapital* and Lenin's *State and Revolution* would give him an edge in business dealings. We were staying in the same hotel. I couldn't at first make out what he and his wife were doing. Presently I understood. The black market. This was not then reprehensible. Postwar Europe was like that. Refugees, adventurers, G.I.s. Even the Comte de la M.-C. Europe still shuddering from the blows it had received. Governments new, uncertain, infirm. No reason to respect their authority. American soldiers led the way. Flamboyant

business schemes. Machines, whole factories, stolen, treasures shipped home. An American colonel in the lumber
business started to saw up the Black Forest and send it to
Wisconsin. And, of course, Nazis concealing their concent-
ration-camp loot. Jewels sunk in Austrian lakes. Art works
hidden. Gold extracted from teeth in extermination camps,
melted into ingots and mortared like bricks into the walls of
houses. Incredibly huge fortunes to be made, and Lustgarten
intended to make one of them. Unfortunately, he was
incompetent.

You could see at once that there was no harm in him.
Despite the bold revolutionary associations, and fierceness of
doctrine. Theoretical willingness to slay class enemies. But
Lustgarten could not even hold his own with pushy people in
a *pissoir*. Strangely meek, stout, swarthy, kindly, grinning
with mulberry lips, a froggy, curving mouth which produced
wrinkles like gills between the ears and the grin. And perhaps, Mosby thought, he comes to mind in Mexico because
of his Toltec, Mixtec, Zapotec look, squat and black-haired,
the tip of his nose turned downward and the black nostrils
shyly widening when his friendly smile was accepted. And a
bit sick with the wickedness, the awfulness of life but, re-
spectfully persistent, bound to get his share. Efficiency was
his style—action, determination, but a traitorous incompe-
tence trembled within. Wrong calling. Wrong choice. A bad
mistake. But he was persistent.

His conversation amused me, in the dining room. He was
proud of his revolutionary activities, which had consisted
mainly of cranking the mimeograph machine. Internal Bulle-
tins. Thousands of pages of recondite examination of fine
points of doctrine for the membership. Whether the American
working class should give *material* aid to the Loyalist Government of Spain, controlled as that was by Stalinists and
other class enemies and traitors. You had to fight Franco, and
you had to fight Stalin as well. There was, of course, no
material aid to give. But *had* there been any, *should* it have
been given? This purely theoretical problem caused splits and
expulsions. I always kept myself informed of these curious
agonies of sectarianism, Mosby wrote. The single effort made
by Spanish Republicans to purchase arms in the United States

was thwarted by that friend of liberty Franklin Delano Roosevelt, who allowed one ship, the *Mar Cantábrico*, to be loaded but set the Coast Guard after it to turn it back to port. It was, I believe, that *genius* of diplomacy, Mr. Cordell Hull, who was responsible, but the decision, of course, was referred to F.D.R., whom Huey Long amusingly called Franklin de la *No!* But perhaps the most refined of these internal discussions left of left, the documents for which were turned out on the machine by that Jimmy Higgins, the tubby devoted party-worker Mr. Lustgarten, had to do with the Finnish War. Here the painful point of doctrine to be resolved was whether a Workers' State like the Soviet Union, even if it was a *degenerate* Workers' State, a product of the Thermidorian Reaction following the glorious Proletarian Revolution of 1917, could wage an Imperialistic War. For only the *bourgeoisie* could be Imperialistic. Technically, Stalinism could not be Imperialism. By definition. What then should a Revolutionary Party say to the Finns? Should they resist Russia or not? The Russians were monsters but they would expropriate the Mannerheim White-Guardist landowners and move, painful though it might be, in the correct historical direction. This, as a sect-watcher, I greatly relished. But it was too foreign a subtlety for many of the sectarians. Who were, after all, Americans. Pragmatists at heart. It was *too* far out for Lustgarten. He decided, after the war, to become (it shouldn't be hard) a rich man. Took his savings and, I believe his wife said, his mother's savings, and went abroad to build a fortune.

Within a year he had lost it all. He was cheated. By a German partner, in particular. But also he was caught smuggling by Belgian authorities.

When Mosby met him (Mosby speaking of himself in the third person as Henry Adams had done in *The Education of Henry Adams*)—when Mosby met him, Lustgarten was working for the American Army, employed by Graves Registration. Something to do with the procurement of crosses. Or with supervision of the lawns. Official employment gave Lustgarten PX privileges. He was rebuilding his financial foundations by the illegal sale of cigarettes. He dealt also in gas-ration coupons which the French Government, anxious to obtain dollars, would give you if you exchanged your money

at the legal rate. The gas coupons were sold on the black
market. The Lustgartens, husband and wife, persuaded Mosby
to do this once. For them, he cashed his dollars at the bank,
not with la Mine-Crevée. The occasion seemed important.
Mosby gathered that Lustgarten had to drive at once to Munich. He had gone into the dental-supply business there with
a German dentist who now denied that they had ever been
partners.

Many consultations between Lustgarten (in his international intriguer's trenchcoat, ill-fitting; head, neck, and shoulders sloping backward in a froggy curve) and his wife, a
young woman in an eyelet-lace blouse and black velveteen
skirt, a velveteen ribbon tied on her round, healthy neck.
Lustgarten, on the circular floor of the bank, explaining as
they stood apart. And sweating blood; being reasonable with
Trudy, detail by tortuous detail. It grated away poor Lustgarten's patience. Hands feebly remonstrating. For she asked
female questions or raised objections which gave him agonies
of patient rationality. Only there was nothing rational to begin
with. That is, he had had no legal right to go into business
with the German. All such arrangements had to be licensed
by Military Government. It was a black-market partnership
and when it began to show a profit, the German threw
Lustgarten out. With what they call impunity. Germany as a
whole having discerned the limits of all civilized systems of
punishment as compared with the unbounded possibilities of
crime. The bank in Paris, where these explanations between
Lustgarten and Trudy were taking place, had an interior of
some sort of red porphyry. Like raw meat. A color which
bourgeois France seemed to have vested with ideas of po-
tency, mettle, and grandeur. In the Invalides also, Napoleon's
sarcophagus was of polished red stone, a great, swooping,
polished cradle containing the little green corpse. (We have
the testimony of M. Rideau, the Bonapartist historian, as to
the color.) As for the living Bonaparte, Mosby felt, with
Auguste Comte, that he had been an anachronism. The Revolution was historically necessary. It was socially justified.
Politically, economically, it was a move toward industrial
democracy. But the Napoleonic drama itself belonged to an
archaic category of personal ambitions, feudal ideas of war.

Older than feudalism. Older than Rome. The commander at the head of armies—nothing rational to recommend it. Society, increasingly rational in its organization, did not need it. But humankind evidently desired it. War is a luxurious pleasure. Grant the first premise of hedonism and you must accept the rest also. Rational foundations of modernity are cunningly accepted by man as the launching platform of ever wilder irrationalities.

Mosby, noting these reflections in a blue-green color of ink which might have been extracted from the landscape. As his liquor had been extracted from the green spikes of the mescal, the curious shárp, dark-green fleshy limbs of the plant covering the fields.

The dollars, the francs, the gas rations, the bank like the beefsteak mine in which W. C. Fields invested, and shrinking but persistent dark Lustgarten getting into his little car on the sodden Parisian street. There were few cars then in Paris. Plenty of parking space. And the streets were so yellow, gray, wrinkled, dismal. But the French were even then ferociously telling the world that they had the *savoir-vivre*, the *gai savoir*. Especially Americans, haunted by their Protestant Ethic, had to hear this. My God—sit down, sip wine, taste cheese, break bread, hear music, know love, stop running, and learn ancient life-wisdom from Europe. At any rate, Lustgarten buckled up his trenchcoat, pulled down his big hoodlum's fedora. He was bunched up in the seat. Small brown hands holding the steering wheel of the Simca Huit, and the grinning despair with which he waved.

"*Bon voyage*, Lustgarten."

His Zapotec nose, his teeth like white pomegranate seeds. With a sob of the gears he took off for devastated Germany.

Reconstruction is big business. You demolish a society, you decrease the population, and off you go again. New fortunes. Lustgarten may have felt, *qua* Jew, that he had a right to grow rich in the German boom. That all Jews had natural claims beyond the Rhine. On land enriched by Jewish ashes. And you never could be sure, seated on a sofa, that it was not stuffed or upholstered with Jewish hair. And he would not use German soap. He washed his hands, Trudy told Mosby, with Lifebuoy from the PX.

Trudy, a graduate of Montclair Teachers' College in New Jersey, knew French, studied composition, had hoped to work with someone like Nadia Boulanger, but was obliged to settle for less. From the bank, as Lustgarten drove away in a kind of doomed, latently tearful daring in the rain-drenched street, Trudy invited Mosby to the Salle Pleyel, to hear a Czech pianist performing Schönberg. This man, with muscular baldness, worked very hard upon the keys. The difficulty of his enterprise alone came through—the labor of culture, the trouble it took to preserve art in tragic Europe, the devoted drill. Trudy had a nice face for concerts. Her odor was agreeable. She shone. In the left half of her countenance, one eye kept wandering. Stone-hearted Mosby, making fun of flesh and blood, of these little humanities with their short inventories of bad and good. The poor Czech in his blazer with chased buttons and the muscles of his forehead rising in protest against *tabula rasa*—the bare skull.

Mosby could abstract himself on such occasions. Shut out the piano. Continue thinking about Comte. Begone, old priests and feudal soldiers! Go, with Theology and Metaphysics! And in the Positive Epoch Enlightened Woman would begin to play her part, vigilant, preventing the managers of the new society from abusing their powers. Over Labor, the supreme good.

Embroidering the trees, the birds of Mexico, looking at Mosby, and the hummingbird, so neat in its lust, vibrating tinily, and the lizard on the soil drinking heat with its belly. To bless small creatures is supposed to be real good.

Yes, this Lustgarten was a funny man. Cheated in Germany, licked by the partner, and impatient with his slow progress in Graves Registration, he decided to import a Cadillac. Among the new postwar millionaires of Europe there was a big demand for Cadillacs. The French Government, moving slowly, had not yet taken measures against such imports for rapid resale. In 1947, no tax prevented such transactions. Lustgarten got his family in Newark to ship a new Cadillac. Something like four thousand dollars was raised by his brother, his mother, his mother's brother for the purpose. The car was sent. The customer was waiting. A down payment had already been given. A double profit was expected. Only, on the day the car was unloaded at Le Havre new regulations went into effect. The Cadillac could not be sold. Lustgarten was stuck with it. He couldn't even afford to buy gas. The Lustgartens were seen one day moving out of the hotel, into the car. Mrs. Lustgarten went to live with musical friends. Mosby offered Lustgarten the use of his sink for washing and shaving. Weary Lustgarten, defeated, depressed, frightened at last by his own plunging, scraped at his bristles, mornings, with a modest cricket noise, while sighing. All that money— mother's savings, brother's pension. No wonder his eyelids turned blue. And his smile, like a spinster's sachet, the last fragrance ebbed out long ago in the trousseau never used. But the long batrachian lips continued smiling.

Mosby realized that compassion should be felt. But passing in the night the locked, gleaming car, and seeing huddled Lustgarten, sleeping, covered with two coats, on the majestic seat, like Jonah inside Leviathan, Mosby could not say in candor that what he experienced was sympathy. Rather he reflected that this shoe salesman, in America attached to foreign doctrines, who could not relinquish Europe in the New World, was now, in Paris, sleeping in the Cadillac, encased in this gorgeous Fisher Body from Detroit. At home exotic, in Europe a Yankee. His timing was off. He recognized this himself. But believed, in general, that he was too early. A pioneer. For instance, he said, in a voice that creaked with shy assertiveness, the French were only now beginning to be Marxians. He had gone through it all years ago. What did these people know! Ask them about the Shakhty Engineers! About Lenin's Democratic Centralism! About the Moscow Trials! About "Social Fascism"! They were ignorant. The Revolution having been totally betrayed, these Europeans suddenly discovered Marx and Lenin. "Eureka!" he said in a high voice. And it was the Cold War, beneath it all. For should America lose, the French intellectuals were preparing to collaborate with Russia. And should America win they could still be free, defiant radicals under American protection.

"You sound like a patriot," said Mosby.

"Well, in a way I am," said Lustgarten. "But I am getting

to be objective. Sometimes I say to myself, 'If you were
outside the world, if you, Lustgarten, didn't exist as a man,
what would your opinion be of this or that?' "

"Disembodied truth."

"I guess that's what it is."

"And what are you going to do about the Cadillac?" said
Mosby.

"I'm sending it to Spain. We can sell it in Barcelona."

"But you have to get it there."

"Through Andorra. It's all arranged. Klonsky is driving
it."

Klonsky was a Polish Belgian in the hotel. One of
Lustgarten's associates, congenitally dishonest, Mosby thought.
Kinky hair, wrinkled eyes like Greek olives, and a cat nose
and cat lips. He wore Russian boots.

But no sooner had Klonsky departed for Andorra, than
Lustgarten received a marvelous offer for the car. A capitalist
in Utrecht wanted it at once and would take care of all excise
problems. He had all the necessary *tuyaux*, unlimited drag.
Lustgarten wired Klonsky in Andorra to stop. He raced down
on the night train, recovered the Cadillac, and started driving
back at once. There was no time to lose. But after sitting up
all night on the *rapide*, Lustgarten was drowsy in the warmth
of the Pyrenees and fell asleep at the wheel. He was lucky, he
later said, for the car went down a mountainside and might
have missed the stone wall that stopped it. He was only a foot
or two from death when he was awakened by the crash. The
car was destroyed. It was not insured.

Still faintly smiling, Lustgarten, with his sling and cane,
came to Mosby's café table on the Boulevard Saint-Germain.
Sat down. Removed his hat from dazzling black hair. Asked
permission to rest his injured foot on a chair. "Is this a
private conversation?" he said.

Mosby had been chatting with Alfred Ruskin, an American
poet. Ruskin, though some of his front teeth were missing,
spoke very clearly and swiftly. A perfectly charming man.
Inveterately theoretical. He had been saying, for instance,
that France had shot its collaborationist poets. America, which
had no poets to spare, put Ezra Pound in Saint Elizabeth's.
He then went on to say, barely acknowledging Lustgarten,

that America had had no history, was not a historical society. His proof was from Hegel. According to Hegel, history was the history of wars and revolutions. The United States had had only one revolution and very few wars. Therefore it was historically empty. Practically a vacuum.

Ruskin also used Mosby's conveniences at the hotel, being too fastidious for his own latrine in the Algerian backstreets of the Left Bank. And when he emerged from the bathroom he invariably had a topic sentence.

"I have discovered the main defect of Kierkegaard."

Or, "Pascal was terrified by universal emptiness, but Valéry says the difference between empty space and space in a bottle is only quantitative, and there is nothing intrinsically terrifying about quantity. What is your view?"

We do not live in bottles—Mosby's reply.

Lustgarten said when Ruskin left us, "Who is that fellow? He mooched you for the coffee."

"Ruskin," said Mosby.

"*That* is Ruskin?"

"Yes, why?"

"I hear my wife was going out with Ruskin while I was in the hospital."

"Oh, I wouldn't believe such rumors," said Mosby. "A cup of coffee, an apéritif together, maybe."

"When a man is down on his luck," said Lustgarten, "it's the rare woman who won't give him hell in addition."

"Sorry to hear it," Mosby replied.

And then, as Mosby in Oaxaca recalled, shifting his seat from the sun—for he was already far too red, and his face, bones, eyes, seemed curiously thirsty—Lustgarten had said, "It's been a terrible experience."

"Undoubtedly so, Lustgarten. It must have been frightening."

"What crashed was my last stake. It involved family. Too bad in a way that I wasn't killed. My insurance would at least have covered my kid brother's loss. And my mother and uncle."

Mosby had no wish to see a man in tears. He did not care to sit through these moments of suffering. Such unmastered emotion was abhorrent. Though perhaps the violence of this abomination might have told Mosby something about his own moral constitution. Perhaps Lustgarten did not want his face to be working. Or tried to subdue his agitation, seeing from Mosby's austere, though not unkind, silence that this was not his way. Mosby was by taste a Senecan. At least he admired Spanish masculinity—the *varonil* of Lorca. The *clavel varonil*, the manly red carnation, the clear classic hardness of honorable control.

"You sold the wreck for junk, I assume?"

"Klonsky took care of it. Now look, Mosby. I'm through with that. I was reading, thinking in the hospital. I came over to make a pile. Like the gold rush. I really don't know what got into me. Trudy and I were just sitting around during the war. I was too old for the draft. And we both wanted action. She in music. Or life. Excitement. You know, dreaming at Montclair Teachers' College of the Big Time. I wanted to make it possible for her. Keep up with the world, or something. But really—in my hospital bed I realized—I was right the first time. I am a Socialist. A natural idealist. Reading about Attlee, I felt at home again. It became clear that I am still a political animal."

Mosby wished to say, "No, Lustgarten. You're a dandler of swarthy little babies. You're a piggyback man—a giddyap horsie. You're a sweet old Jewish Daddy." But he said nothing.

"And I also read," said Lustgarten, "about Tito. Maybe the Tito alternative is the real one. Perhaps there is hope for Socialism somewhere between the Labour Party and the Yugoslav type of leadership. I feel it my duty," Lustgarten told Mosby, "to investigate. I'm thinking of going to Belgrade."

"As what?"

"As a matter of fact, that's where you could come in," said Lustgarten. "If you would be so kind. You're not *just* a scholar. You wrote a book on Plato, I've been told."

"On the *Laws.*"

"And other books. But in addition you know the Movement. Lots of people. More connections than a switchboard. . . ."

The slang of the forties.

"You know people at the *New Leader?*"

"Not my type of paper," said Mosby. "I'm actually a political conservative. Not what you would call a Rotten Liberal but an out-and-out conservative. I shook Franco's hand, you know."

"Did you?"

"This very hand shook the hand of the Caudillo. Would you like to touch it for yourself?"

"Why should I?"

"Go on," said Mosby. "It may mean something. Shake the hand that shook the hand."

Very strangely, then, Lustgarten extended padded, swarthy fingers. He looked partly subtle, partly ill. Grinning, he said, "Now I've made contact with real politics at last. But I'm serious about the *New Leader*. You probably know Bohn. I need credentials for Yugoslavia."

"Have you ever written for the papers?"

"For the *Militant*."

"What did you write?"

Guilty Lustgarten did not lie well. It was heartless of Mosby to amuse himself in this way.

"I have a scrapbook somewhere," said Lustgarten.

But it was not necessary to write to the *New Leader*. Lustgarten, encountered two days later on the Boulevard, near the pork butcher, had taken off the sling and scarcely needed the cane. He said, "I'm going to Yugoslavia. I've been invited."

"By whom?"

"Tito. The Government. They're asking interested people to come as guests to tour the country and see how they're building Socialism. Oh, I know," he quickly said, anticipating standard doctrinal objection, "you don't build Socialism in one country, but it's no longer the same situation. And I really believe Tito may redeem Marxism by actually transforming the dictatorship of the proletariat. This brings me back to my first love—the radical movement. I was never meant to be an entrepreneur."

"Probably not."

"I feel some hope," Lustgarten shyly said. "And then also, it's getting to be spring." He was wearing his heavy moose-colored bristling hat, and bore many other signs of interminable winter. A candidate for resurrection. An opportunity for the grace of life to reveal itself. But perhaps, Mosby thought, a man like Lustgarten would never, except with supernatural aid, exist in a suitable form.

"Also," said Lustgarten touchingly, "this will give Trudy time to reconsider."

"Is that the way things are with you two? I'm sorry."

"I wish I could take her with me, but I can't swing that with the Yugoslavs. It's sort of a V.I.P. deal. I guess they want to affect foreign radicals. There'll be seminars in dialectics, and so on. I love it. But it's not Trudy's dish."

Steady-handed, Mosby on his patio took ice with tongs, and poured more mescal flavored with *gusano de maguey*—a worm or slug of delicate flavor. These notes on Lustgarten pleased him. It was essential, at this point in his memoirs, to disclose new depths. The preceding chapters had been heavy. Many unconventional things were said about the state of political theory. The weakness of conservative doctrine, the lack, in America, of conservative alternatives, of resistance to the prevailing liberalism. As one who had personally tried to create a more rigorous environment for slovenly intellectuals, to force them to do their homework, to harden the categories of political thought, he was aware that on the Right as on the Left the results were barren. Absurdly, the college-bred dunces of America had longed for a true Left Wing movement on the European model. They still dreamed of it. No less absurd were the Right Wing idiots. You cannot grow a rose in a coal mine. Mosby's own Right Wing graduate students had disappointed him. Just a lot of television actors. Bad guys for the Susskind interview programs. They had transformed the master's manner of acid elegance, logical tightness, factual punctiliousness, and merciless laceration in debate into a sort of shallow Noël Coward style. The real, the original Mosby approach brought Mosby hatred, got Mosby fired. Princeton University had offered Mosby a lump sum to retire seven years early. One hundred and forty thousand dollars. Because his mode of discourse was so upsetting to the academic community. Mosby was invited to no television programs. He was like the Guerrilla Mosby of the Civil War. When he galloped in, all were slaughtered.

Most carefully, Mosby had studied the memoirs of Santayana, Malraux, Sartre, Lord Russell, and others. Unfortunately, no one was reliably or consistently great. Men whose
lives had been devoted to thought, who had tried mightily to
govern the disorder of public life, to put it under some sort of
intellectual authority, to get ideas to save mankind or to offer
it mental aid in saving itself, would suddenly turn into grue-
some idiots. Wanting to kill everyone. For instance, Sartre
calling for the Russians to drop A-bombs on American bases
in the Pacific because America was now presumably monstrous. And exhorting the Blacks to butcher the Whites. This
moral philosopher! Or Russell, the Pacifist of World War I,
urging the West to annihilate Russia after World War II. And
sometimes, in his memoirs—perhaps he was gaga—strangely
illogical. When, over London, a Zeppelin was shot down, the
bodies of Germans were seen to fall, and the brutal men in
the street horribly cheered, Russell wept, and had there not
been a beautiful woman to console him in bed that night, this
heartlessness of mankind would have broken him utterly.
What was omitted was the fact that these same Germans who
fell from the Zeppelin had come to bomb the city. They were
going to blow up the brutes in the street, explode the lovers.
This Mosby saw.

It was earnestly to be hoped—this was the mescal attempting to invade his language—that Mosby would avoid the
common fate of intellectuals. The Lustgarten digression should
help. The correction of pride by laughter.

There were twenty minutes yet before the chaffeur came to
take the party to Mitla, to the ruins. Mosby had time to
continue. To say that in September the Lustgarten who reap-
peared looked frightful. He had lost no less than fifty pounds.
Sun-blackened, creased, in a filthy stained suit, his eyes
infected. He said he had had diarrhea all summer.

"What did they feed their foreign V.I.P.s?"

And Lustgarten shyly bitter—the lean face and inflamed
eyes materializing from a spiritual region very different from
any heretofore associated with Lustgarten by Mosby—said,
"It was just a chain gang. It was hard labor. I didn't understand the deal. I thought we were invited, as I told you. But
we turned out to be foreign volunteers of construction. A

labor brigade. And up in the mountains. Never saw the Dalmatian coast. Hardly even shelter for the night. We slept on the ground and ate shit fried in rancid oil."

"Why didn't you run away?" asked Mosby.

"How? Where?"

"Back to Belgrade. To the American Embassy at least?"

"How could I? I was a guest. Came at their expense. They held the return ticket."

"And no money?"

"Are you kidding? Dead broke. In Macedonia. Near Skoplje. Bug-stung, starved, and running to the latrine all night. La-boring on the roads all day, with pus in my eyes, too."

"No first aid?"

"They may have had the first, but they didn't have the second."

Mosby thought it best to say nothing of Trudy. She had divorced him.

Commiseration, of course.

Mosby shaking his head.

Lustgarten with a certain skinny dignity walking away. He himself seemed amused by his encounters with Capitalism and Socialism.

The end? Not quite. There was a coda: The thing had quite good form.

Lustgarten and Mosby met again. Five years later. Mosby enters an elevator in New York. Express to the forty-seventh floor, the executive dining room of the Rangeley Foundation. There is one other passenger, and it is Lustgarten. Grinning. He is himself again, filled out once more.

"Lustgarten!"

"Willis Mosby!"

"How are you, Lustgarten?"

"I'm great. Things are completely different. I'm happy. Successful. Married. Children."

"In New York?"

"Wouldn't live in the U.S. again. It's godawful. Inhuman. I'm visiting."

Without a blink in its brilliancy, without a hitch in its smooth, regulated power, the elevator containing only the two of us was going up. The same Lustgarten. Strong words, vocal insufficiency, the Zapotec nose, and under it the frog smile, the kindly gills.

"Where are you going now?"

"Up to *Fortune*," said Lustgarten. "I want to sell them a story."

He was on the wrong elevator. This one was not going to *Fortune*. I told him so. Perhaps I had not changed either. A voice which for many years had informed people of their errors said, "You'll have to go down again. The other bank of elevators."

At the forty-seventh floor we emerged together.

"Where are you settled now?"

"In Algiers," said Lustgarten. "We have a Laundromat there."

"We?"

"Klonsky and I. You remember Klonsky?"

They had gone legitimate. They were washing burnooses. He was married to Klonsky's sister. I saw her picture. The image of Klonsky, a cat-faced woman, head ferociously encased in kinky hair, Picasso eyes at different levels, sharp teeth. If fish, dozing in the reefs, had nightmares, they would be of such teeth. The children also were young Klonskys. Lustgarten had the snapshots in his wallet of North African leather. As he beamed, Mosby recognized that pride in his success was Lustgarten's opiate, his artificial paradise.

"I thought," said Lustgarten, "that *Fortune* might like a piece on how we made it in North Africa."

We then shook hands again. Mine the hand that had shaken Franco's hand—his that had slept on the wheel of the Cadillac. The lighted case opened for him. He entered in. It shut.

Thereafter, of course, the Algerians threw out the French, expelled the Jews. And Jewish-Daddy-Lustgarten must have moved on. Passionate fatherhood. He loved those children. For Plato this childbreeding is the lowest level of creativity.

Still, Mosby thought, under the influence of mescal, my parents begot me like a committee of two.

From a feeling of remotion, though he realized that the car for Mitla had arrived, a shining conveyance waited, he noted the following as he gazed at the afternoon mountains:

Until he was some years old
People took care of him
Cooled his soup, sang, chirked,
Drew on his long stockings,
Carried him upstairs sleeping.
He recalls at the green lakeside
His father's solemn navel,
Nipples like dog's eyes in the hair
Mother's thigh with wisteria of blue veins.

After they retired to death,
He conducted his own business
Not too modestly, not too well.
But here he is, smoking in Mexico
Considering the brown mountains
Whose fat laps are rolling
On the skulls of whole families.

Two Welsh women were his companions. One was very ancient, lank. The Wellington of lady travelers. Or like C. Aubrey Smith, the actor who used to command Gurkha regiments in movies about India. A great nose, a gaunt jaw, a pleated lip, a considerable mustache. The other was younger. She had a small dewlap, but her cheeks were round and dark eyes witty. A very satisfactory pair. Decent was the word. English traits. Like many Americans, Mosby desired such traits for himself. Yes, he was pleased with the Welsh ladies. Though the guide was unsuitable. Overweening. His fat cheeks a red pottery color. And he drove too fast.

The first stop was at Tule. They got out to inspect the celebrated Tule tree in the churchyard. This monument of vegetation, intricately and densely convolved, a green cypress, more than two thousand years old, roots in a vanished lake bottom, older than the religion of this little heap of white and gloom, this charming peasant church. In the comfortable dust, a dog slept. Disrespectful. But unconscious. The old lady, quietly dauntless, tied on a scarf and entered the church. Her stiff genuflection had real quality. She must be Christian. Mosby looked into the depths of the Tule. A world in itself! It could contain communities. In fact, if he recalled his Gerald Heard, there was supposed to be a primal tree occupied by early ancestors, the human horde housed in such appealing, dappled, commodious, altogether beautiful organisms. The facts seemed not to support this golden myth of an encompassing paradise. Earliest man probably ran about on the ground, horribly violent, killing everything. Still, this dream of gentleness, this aspiration for arboreal peace was no small achievement for the descendants of so many killers. For his religion, this tree would do, thought Mosby. No church for him.

He was sorry to go. *He* could have lived up there. On top, of course. The excrements would drop on you below. But the Welsh ladies were already in the car, and the bossy guide began to toot the horn. Waiting was hot.

The road to Mitla was empty. The heat made the landscape beautifully crooked. The driver knew geology, archaeology. He was quite ugly with his information. The Water Table, the Caverns, the Triassic Period. Inform me no further! Vex not my soul with more detail. I cannot use what I have! And now Mitla appeared. The right fork continued to Tehuantepec. The left brought you to the Town of Souls. Old Mrs. Parsons (Elsie Clews Parsons, as Mosby's mental retrieval system told him) had done ethnography here, studied the Indians in these baked streets of adobe and fruit garbage. In the shade, a dark urinous tang. A long-legged pig struggling on a tether. A sow. From behind, observant Mosby identified its pink small female opening. The dungy earth feeding beast as man.

But here were the fascinating temples, almost intact. This place the Spanish priests had not destroyed. All others they had razed, building churches on the same sites, using the same stones.

A tourist market. Coarse cotton dresses, Indian embroidery, hung under flour-white tarpaulins, the dust settling on the pottery of the region, black saxophones, black trays of glazed clay.

Following the British travelers and the guide, Mosby was going once more through an odd and complex fantasy. It was that he was dead. He had died. He continued, however, to live. His doom was to live life to the end as Mosby. In the fantasy, he considered this his purgatory. And when had death occurred? In a collision years ago. He had thought it a

near thing then. The cars were demolished. The actual Mosby
was killed. But another Mosby was pulled from the car. A
trooper asked, "You okay?"

Yes, he was okay. Walked away from the wreck. But he
still had the whole thing to do, step by step, moment by
moment. And now he heard a parrot blabbing, and children
panhandled him and women made their pitch, and he was
getting his shoes covered with dust. He had been working at
his memoirs and had provided a diverting recollection of a
funny man—Lustgarten. In the manner of Sir Harold Nicolson. Much less polished, admittedly, but in accordance with a
certain protocol, the language of diplomacy, of mandarin
irony. However certain facts had been omitted. Mosby had
arranged, for instance, that Trudy should be seen with Alfred
Ruskin. For when Lustgarten was crossing the Rhine, Mosby
was embracing Trudy in bed. Unlike Lord Russell's beautiful
friend, she did not comfort Mosby for the disasters he had (by
intellectual commitment) to confront. But Mosby had not
advised her about leaving Lustgarten. He did not mean to
interfere. However, his vision of Lustgarten as a funny man
was transmitted to Trudy. She could not be the wife of such a
funny man. But he *was*, he *was* a funny man! He was, like
Napoleon in the eyes of Comte, an anachronism. Inept, he
wished to be a colossus, something of a Napoleon himself,
make millions, conquer Europe, retrieve from Hitler's fall a
colossal fortune. Poorly imagined, unoriginal, the rerun of
old ideas, and so inefficient. Lustgarten didn't have to happen. And so he *was* funny. Trudy too was funny, however.
What a large belly she had. Since individuals are sometimes
born from a twin impregnation, the organism carrying the
undeveloped brother or sister in vestigial form—at times no
more than an extra organ, a rudimentary eye buried in the
leg, or a kidney or the beginnings of an ear somewhere in the
back—Mosby often thought that Trudy had a little sister
inside her. And to him she was a clown. This need not mean
contempt. No, he liked her. The eye seemed to wander in one
hemisphere. She did not know how to use perfume. Her
atonal compositions were foolish.

At this time, Mosby had been making fun of people.
"Why?"

"Because he had needed to."

"Why?"

"Because!"

The guide explained that the buildings were raised without mortar. The mathematical calculations of the priests had been perfect. The precision of the cut stone was absolute. After centuries you could not find a chink, you could not insert a razor blade anywhere. These geometrical masses were balanced by their own weight. Here the priests lived. The walls had been dyed. The cochineal or cactus louse provided the dye. Here were the altars. Spectators sat where you are standing. The priests used obsidian knives. The beautiful youths played on flutes. Then the flutes were broken. The bloody knife was wiped on the head of the executioner. Hair must have been clotted. And here, the tombs of the nobles. Stairs leading down. The Zapotecs, late in the day, had practiced this form of sacrifice, under Aztec influence.

How game this Welsh crone was. She was beautiful. Getting in and out of these pits, she required no assistance.

Of course you cannot make yourself an agreeable, desirable person. You can't will yourself into it without regard to the things to be done. Imperative tasks. Imperative comprehensions, monstrous compulsions of duty which deform. Men will grow ugly under such necessities. This one a director of espionage. That one a killer.

Mosby had evoked, to lighten the dense texture of his memoirs, a Lustgarten whose doom was this gaping comedy. A Lustgarten who didn't have to happen. But himself, Mosby, also a separate creation, a finished product, standing under the sun on large blocks of stone, on the stairs descending into this pit, he was complete. He had completed himself in this cogitating, unlaughing, stone, iron, nonsensical form.

Having disposed of all things human, he should have encountered God.

Would this occur?

But having so disposed, what God was there to encounter?

But they had now been led below, into the tomb. There was a heavy grille, the gate. The stones were huge. The vault was close. He was oppressed. He was afraid. It was very damp. On the elaborately zigzag-carved walls were thin, thin pipings of fluorescent light. Flat boxes of ground lime were here to absorb moisture. His heart was paralyzed. His lungs would not draw. Jesus! I cannot catch my breath! To be shut in here! To be dead here! Suppose one were! Not as in accidents which ended, but did not quite end, existence. *Dead*-dead. Stooping, he looked for daylight. Yes, it was there. The light was there. The grace of life still there. Or, if not grace, air. Go while you can.

"I must get out," he told the guide. "Ladies, I find it very hard to breathe."

(1951)

Walter Miller, Jr.

Walter Miller, Jr., was born in 1923, in Florida. He was educated at the University of Tennessee (1940–42) and at the University of Texas (1947–49), with some years of service in the U.S. Air Force in between. He was present at the destruction of Monte Cassino, in 1944. His first story appeared in 1951. From 1951 through 1955 he published stories in leading science fiction magazines; they were collected, in 1962 and 1965, as Conditionally Human *and* The View From the Stars, *and again in 1980 as* The Best of Walter M. Miller, Jr. *In 1959 he published perhaps the most powerful science fiction novel of the century,* A Canticle for Leibowitz, *portions of which had begun to appear in magazines as early as 1955. Since then he seems to have published nothing.*

A Canticle for Leibowitz, *like the shorter fiction which preceded it, is apocalyptic, terrifying, grimly funny at times, astonishingly complex and disturbing. (Miller's novel makes even such masterful books as Frank Herbert's* Dune *seem just a bit glib, even at times amateurish.) It is also a profoundly religious novel. Like James Joyce, whom he in many ways resembles, Miller is apparently of Catholic background. He can sometimes paint his grim scenes in overbright hues. At his best he is unequaled in the entire literature of science fiction.*

DUMB WAITER

He came riding a battered bicycle down the bullet-scarred
highway that wound among the hills, and he whistled a
tortuous flight of the blues. Hot August sunlight glistened on
his forehead and sparkled in the droplets that collected in his
week's growth of blond beard. He wore faded khaki trousers
and a ragged shirt, but his clothing was no shabbier than that
of the other occasional travelers on the road. His eyes were
half-closed against the glare of the road, and his head swayed
listlessly to the rhythm of the melancholy song. Distant artil-
lery was rumbling gloomily, and there were black flecks of
smoke in the northern sky. The young cyclist watched with
only casual interest.

The bombers came out of the east. The ram-jet fighters
thundered upward from the outskirts of the city. They charged,
spitting steel teeth and coughing rockets at the bombers. The
sky snarled and slashed at itself. The bombers came on in
waves, occasionally loosing an earthward trail of black smoke.
The bombers leveled and opened their bays. The bays yawned
down at the city. The bombers aimed. Releases clicked. No
bombs fell. The bombers closed their bays and turned away
to go home. The fighters followed them for a time, then
returned to land. The big guns fell silent. And the sky began
cleaning away the dusky smoke.

The young cyclist rode on toward the city, still whistling
the blues. An occasional pedestrian had stopped to watch the
battle.

"You'd think they'd learn someday," growled a chubby
man at the side of the road. "You'd think they'd know they
didn't drop anything. Don't they realize they're out of bombs?"

"They're only machines, Edward," said a plump lady who
stood beside him. "How can they know?"

"Well, they're supposed to *think*. They're supposed to be
able to learn."

The voices faded as he left them behind. Some of the

wanderers who had been walking toward the city now turned around and walked the other way. Urbanophiles looked at the city and became urbanophobes. Occasionally a wanderer who had gone all the way to the outskirts came trudging back. Occasionally a phobe stopped a phile and they talked. Usually the phile became a phobe and they both walked away together. As the young man moved on, the traffic became almost non-existent. Several travelers warned him back, but he continued stubbornly. He had come a long way. He meant to return to the city. Permanently.

He met an old lady on top of a hill. She sat in an antique chair in the center of the highway, staring north. The chair was light and fragile, of handcarved cherrywood. A knitting bag lay in the road beside her. She was muttering softly to herself: "Crazy machines! War's over. Crazy machines! Can't quit fightin'. Somebody oughta—"

He cleared his throat softly as he pushed his bicycle up beside her. She looked at him sharply with haggard eyes, set in a seamy mask.

"Hi!" he called, grinning at her.

She studied him irritably for a moment. "Who're you, boy?"

"Name's Mitch Laskell, Grandmaw. Hop on behind. I'll give you a ride."

"Hm-m! I'm going t'other way. You will too, if y'got any sense."

Mitch shook his head firmly. "I've been going the other way too long. I'm going back, to stay."

"To the city? Haw! You're crazier than them machines."

His face fell thoughtful. He kicked at the bike pedal and stared at the ground. "You're right, Grandmaw."

"Right?"

"Machines—they aren't crazy. It's just people."

"Go on!" she snorted. She popped her false teeth back in her mouth and chomped them in place. She hooked withered hands on her knees and pulled herself wearily erect. She hoisted the antique chair lightly to her shoulder and shuffled slowly away toward the south.

* * *

Mitch watched her, and marveled on the tenacity of life. Then he resumed his northward journey along the trash-littered road where motor vehicles no longer moved. But the gusts of wind brought faint traffic noises from the direction of the city, and he smiled. The sound was like music, a deep-throated whisper of the city's song.

There was a man watching his approach from the next hill. He sat on an apple crate by the side of the road, and a shotgun lay casually across his knees. He was a big, red-faced man, wearing a sweat-soaked undershirt, and his eyes were narrowed to slits in the sun. He peered fixedly at the approaching cyclist, then came slowly to his feet and stood as if blocking the way.

"Hi, fellow," he grunted.

Mitch stopped and gave him a friendly nod while he mopped his face with a kerchief. But he eyed the shotgun suspiciously.

"If this is a stick-up—"

The big man laughed. "Naw, no heist. Just want to talk to you a minute. I'm Frank Ferris." He offered a burly paw.

"Mitch Laskell."

They shook hands gingerly and studied each other.

"Why you heading north, Laskell?"

"Going to the city."

"The planes are still fighting. You know that?"

"Yeah. I know they've run out of bombs, too."

"You know the city's still making the Geigers click?"

Mitch frowned irritably. "What *is* this? There can't be much radioactivity left. It's been three years since they scattered the dust. I'm not corn-fed, Ferris. The half-life of that dust is five months. It should be less than one per cent—"

The big man chuckled. "O.K., you win. But the city's not safe anyhow. The central computer's still at work."

"So what?"

"Ever think what would happen to a city if every ordinance was kept in force after the people cleared out?"

Mitch hesitated, then nodded. "I see. Thanks for the warning." He started away.

Frank Ferris caught the handle bars in a big hand. "Hold on!" he snapped. "I ain't finished talking."

The smaller man glanced at the shotgun and swallowed his

anger. "Maybe your audience isn't interested, Buster," he said with quiet contempt.

"You will be. Just simmer down and listen!"

"I don't hear anything."

Ferris glowered at him. "I'm recruitin' for the Sugarton crowd, Laskell. We need good men."

"Count me out. I'm a wreck."

"Cut the cute stuff boy! This is serious. We've got two dozen men now. We need twice that many. When we get them, we'll go into the city and dynamite the computer installations. Then we can start cleaning it up."

"Dynamite? *Why?*" Mitch Laskell's face slowly gathered angry color.

"So people can live in it, of course! So we can search for food without having a dozen mechanical cops jump us when we break into a store."

"How much did Central cost?" Mitch asked stiffly. It was a rhetorical question.

Ferris shook his head irritably. "What does that matter now? Money's no good anyway. You can't sell Central for junk. Heh heh! Wake up, boy!"

The cyclist swallowed hard. A jaw muscle tightened in his cheek, but his voice came calmly.

"You help build Central, Ferris? You help design her?"

"Wh-why, no! What kind of a question is that?"

"You know anything about her? What makes her work? How she's rigged to control all the subunits? You know that?"

"No, I—"

"You got any idea about how much sweat dripped on the drafting boards before they got her plans drawn? How many engineers slaved over her, and cussed her, and got drunk when their piece of the job was done?"

Ferris was sneering faintly. "You *know*, huh?"

"Yeah."

"Well that's all too bad, boy. But she's no good to anybody now. She's a hazard to life and limb. Why you can't go inside the city without—"

"She's a machine, Ferris. An intricate machine. You don't

destroy a tool just because you're finished with it for a while.''

They glared at each other in the hot sunlight.

"Listen, boy—people built Central. People got the right to wreck her, too."

"I don't care about rights," Mitch snapped. "I'm talking about what's sensible, sane. But nobody's got the right to be stupid."

Ferris stiffened. "Watch your tongue, smart boy."

"I didn't ask for this conversation."

Ferris released the handle bars. "Get off the bicycle," he grunted ominously.

"Why? You want to settle it the hard way?"

"No. We're requisitioning your bicycle. You can walk from here on. The Sugarton crowd needs transportation. We need good men, but I guess you ain't one. Start walking."

Mitch hesitated briefly. Then he shrugged and dismounted on the side away from Ferris. The big man held the shotgun cradled lazily across one forearm. He watched Mitch with a mocking grin.

Mitch grasped the handle bars tightly and suddenly rammed the front wheel between Ferris' legs. The fender made a tearing sound. The shotgun exploded skyward as the big man fell back. He sat down screaming and doubling over. The gun clattered in the road. He groped for it with a frenzied hand. Mitch kicked him in the face, and a tooth slashed at his toe through the boot leather. Ferris fell aside, his mouth spitting blood and white fragments.

Mitch retrieved the shotgun and helped himself to a dozen shells from the other's pockets then mounted the bicycle and pedaled away. When he had gone half a mile, a rifle slug spanged off the pavement beside him. Looking back, he saw three tiny figures standing beside Ferris in the distance. The "Sugarton crowd" had come to take care of their own, no doubt. He pedaled hard to get out of range, but they wasted no more ammunition.

He realized uneasily that he might meet them again, if they came to the city intending to sabotage Central. And Ferris wouldn't miss a chance to kill him, if the chance came. Mitch didn't believe he was really hurt, but he was badly humiliated. And for some time to come, he would dream of pleasant ways to murder Mitch Laskell.

Mitch no longer whistled as he rode along the deserted highway toward the sun-drenched skyline in the distance. To a man born and bred to the tune of mechanical thunder, amid vistas of concrete and steel, the skyline looked good—looked good even with several of the buildings twisted into ugly wreckage. It had been dusted in the radiological attack, but not badly bombed. Its defenses had been more than adequately provided for—which was understandable, since it was the capital, and the legislators had appropriated freely.

It seemed unreasonable to him that Central was still working. Why hadn't some group of engineers made their way into the main power vaults to kill the circuits temporarily? Then he remembered that the vaults were self-defending, and that there were probably very few technicians left who knew how to handle the job. Technicians had a way of inhabiting industrial regions, and wars had a way of destroying these regions. Dirt farmers usually had the best survival value.

Mitch had been working with aircraft computers before he became displaced, but a city's Central Service Co-ordinator was a far cry from a robot pilot. Centrals weren't built all at once; they grew over a period of years. At first, small units were set up in power plants and water works to automatically regulate voltages and flows and circuit conditions. Small units replaced switchboards in telephone exchanges. Small computers measured traffic-flow and regulated lights and speed-limits accordingly. Small computers handled bookkeeping where large amounts of money were exchanged. A computer checked books in and out at the library, also assessing the fines. Computers operated the city buses, and eventually drove most of the routine traffic.

That was the way the city's Central Service grew. As more computers were assigned to various tasks, engineers were hired to coordinate them, to link them with special circuits and to set up central "data tanks," so that a traffic regulator in the north end would be aware of traffic conditions in the main thoroughfares to the south. Then, when the micro-learner relay was invented, the engineers built a central unit to be used in conjunction with the central "data tanks." With the learning units in operations, Central was able to perform most of the city's routine tasks without attention from human supervisors.

The system had worked well. Apparently, it was still working well three years after the inhabitants had fled before the chatter of the Geiger counters. In one sense, Ferris had been right: a city whose machines carried on as if nothing had happened—that city might be a dangerous place for a lone wanderer.

But dynamite certainly wasn't the answer, Mitch thought. Most of Man's machinery was already wrecked or lying idle. Humanity had waited a hundred thousand years before deciding to build a technological civilization. If he wrecked this one completely, he might never decide to build another.

Some men thought that a return to the soil was desirable. Some men tried to pin their guilt on the machines, to lay their own stupidity on the head of a mechanical scapegoat and absolve themselves with dynamite. But Mitch Laskell was a man who liked the feel of a wrench and a soldering iron— liked it better than the feel of even the most well-balanced stone ax or wooden plow. And he liked the purr of a pint-sized nuclear engine much better than the braying of a harnessed jackass.

He was willing to kill Frank Ferris or any other man who sought to wreck what little remained. But gloom settled over him as he thought, "If everybody decides to tear it down, what can *I* do to stop it?" For that matter, would he then be right in trying to stop it?

At sundown he came to the limits of the city, and he stopped just short of the outskirts. Three blocks away a robot cop rolled about in the center of the intersection, rolled on tricycle wheels while he directed the thin trickle of traffic with candy-striped arms and with "eyes" that changed color like a stop-light. His body was like an oil drum, painted fire-engine red. The head, however, had been cast in a human mold, with a remarkably Irish face and a perpetual predatory smile. A short radar antenna grew from the center of his head, and the radar was his link with Central.

Mitch sat watching him with a nostalgic smile, even though

he knew such cops might give him considerable trouble, once he entered the city. The "Skaters" were incapable of winking at petty violations of ordinance.

As the daylight faded, photronic cells notified Central, and the streetlights winked promptly on. A moment later, a car without a tail light whisked by the policeman's corner. A siren wailed in the policeman's belly. He skated away in hot pursuit, charging like a mechanical bull. The car screeched to a stop. "O'Reilley" wrote out a ticket and offered it to an empty back seat. When no one took it, the cop fed it into a slot in his belly, memorized the car's license number, and came clattering back to his intersection where the traffic had automatically begun obeying the ordinances governing non-policed intersections.

The cars were empty, computer-piloted. Their destinations were the same as when they had driven regular daily routes for human passengers: salesmen calling on regular customers, inspectors making their rounds, taxis prowling their assigned service-areas.

Mitch Laskell stood shivering. The city sounded sleepy but alive. The city moved and grumbled. But as far as he could see down the wide boulevard, no human figure was visible. The city was depopulated. There was a Geiger on a nearby lamp post. It clucked idly through a loud-speaker. But it indicated no danger. The city should be radiologically safe.

But after staring for a long time at the weirdly active streets, Mitch muttered, "It'll wait for tomorrow."

He turned onto a side road that led through a residential district just outside the city limits. Central's jurisdiction did not extend here, except for providing water and lights. He meant to spend the night in a deserted house, then enter the city at dawn.

Here and there, a light burned in one of the houses, indicating that he was not alone in his desire to return. But the pavement was scattered with rusty shrapnel, with fragments fallen from the sky battles that still continued. Even by streetlight, he could see that some of the roofs were damaged. Even though the bombers came without bombs, there was still danger from falling debris and from fire. Most former city-dwellers who were still alive preferred to remain in the country.

Once he passed a house from which music floated softly into the street, and he paused to listen. The music was scratchy—a worn record. When the piece was finished, there was a moment of silence, and the player played it again—the last record on the stack, repeating itself. Otherwise, the house was still.

Mitch frowned, sensing some kind of trouble. He wheeled the bicycle toward the curb, meaning to investigate.

"I live there," said a woman's voice from the shadows.

She had been standing under a tree that overhung the sidewalk, and she came slowly out into the streetlight. She was a dark, slender girl with haunted eyes, and she was holding a baby in her arms.

"Why don't you turn off your record player?" he asked. "Or change to the other side?"

"My husband's in there," she told him. "He's listening to it. He's been listening to it for a long time. His name is George. Why don't you go say hello to him?"

Mitch felt vaguely disturbed. There was a peculiar note in the girl's quiet Spanish accent. Still, he wanted to talk to someone who had ventured into the city. He nodded and smiled at the girl.

"I'd like to."

"You just go on in. I'll stay out here. The baby needs fresh air."

He thanked her and strolled up on the porch. The record player stopped, tried to change, and played the same piece again. Mitch knocked once. Hearing no answer, he entered and moved along the hallway toward the light in the kitchen. But suddenly he stopped.

The house smelled musty. And it smelled of something else. Many times he had smelled the syrup-and-stale-fish odor of death. He advanced another step toward the kitchen.

He saw a porcelain-topped table. He saw a hand lying across the table. The hand was bloated, and lying amid brown stains that also covered the forearm and sleeve. The hand had dropped a butcher knife.

Dead several days, he thought—and backed away.

He turned the record player off as he left the house. The girl was standing at the curb gazing down at his bicycle. She glanced at him amiably and spoke.

"I'm glad you turned that record off, George. A man just came by and wanted to know why you played it so often. You must have been asleep."

Mitch started. He moistened his lips and stared at her wonderingly. "I'm not—" He fell silent for a moment, then stuttered, "You haven't been in the house?"

"Yes, but you were asleep in the kitchen. Did the man come talk to you?"

"Look, I'm not—" He choked and said nothing. The dark-eyed baby was eying him suspiciously. He lifted the bicycle and swung a long leg across the saddle.

"George, where are you going?"

"Just for a little ride," he managed to gasp.

"On the man's bicycle?"

Something was twisting cruelly at his insides. He stared at the girl's wide brown eyes for a moment. And then he said it.

"Sure, it's all right. He's asleep—at the kitchen table."

Her mouth flickered open, and for an instant sanity threatened to return. She rocked dizzily. Then after a deep breath, she straightened.

"Don't be gone too long, George."

"I won't! Take good care of the baby."

He pedaled away on wings of fright. For a time he cursed himself, and then he fell to cursing the husband who had taken an easy road, leaving his wife to stumble along. Mitch wondered if he should have stayed to help her. But there was nothing to be done for her, nothing at least that was in his power to do. Any gesture of help might become an irreparable blunder. At least she still had the child.

A few blocks away he found another house with an intact roof, and he prepared to spend the night. He wheeled the bicycle into the parlor and fumbled for the lights. They came on, revealing a dusty room and furniture with frayed upholstery. He made a brief tour of the house. It had been recently occupied, but there were still unopened cans in the kitchen, and still crumpled sheets on the bed. He ate a cold supper,

shaved, and prepared to retire. Tomorrow would be a dangerous day.

Sleep came slowly. Sleep was full of charging ram-jets in
flak-scarred skies, full of tormented masses of people that
swarmed in exodus from death-sickened cities. Sleep was full
of babies wailing, and women crying in choking sobs. Sleep
became white arms and soft caresses.

The wailing and sobbing had stopped. It was later. Was he
awake? Or still asleep? He was warm, basking in a golden
glow, steeped in quiet pleasure. Something—something was
there, something that breathed.

"What—!"

"*Sshhh!*" purred a quiet voice. "Don't say anything."

Some of the warmth fled before a sudden shiver. He
opened his eyes. The room was full of blackness. He shook
his head dizzily and stuttered.

"*Sshhh!*" she whispered again.

"What is this?" he gasped. "How did you get—?"

"Be quiet, George. You'll wake the baby."

He sank back in utter bewilderment, with winter frosts
gathering along his spine.

Night was dreamlike. And dawn came, washing the shadows with grayness. He opened his eyes briefly and went back
to sleep. When he opened them again, sunlight was flooding
the room.

He sat up. *He was alone*. Of course! It had only been a
dream.

He muttered irritably as he dressed. Then he wandered to
the kitchen for breakfast.

Warm biscuits waiting in the oven! The table was set!
There was a note on his plate. He read it, and slowly flushed.

There's jam in the cupboard, and I hope you like the
biscuits. I know he's dead. Now I think I can go on alone.
Thanks for the shotgun and the bicycle. Marta.

He bellowed a curse and charged into the parlor. The bike
was gone. He darted to the bedroom. The shotgun was gone.
He ran shouting to the porch, but the street was empty.

Sparrows fluttered about the eaves. The skyline of the

business district lay lonesome in the morning sun. Squirrels were rustling in the branches of the trees. He looked at the weedy lawns where no children played, at the doors askew on their hinges, at a bit of aircraft wreckage jutting from the roof of a fire-gutted home—the rotting porches—the emptiness.

He rubbed his cheek ruefully. It was no world for a young mother and her baby. The baby would fit nicely in the bicycle's basket. The shotgun would offer some protection against the human wolf-packs that prowled everywhere these days.

"Little thief!" he growled half-heartedly.

But when the human animal would no longer steal to protect its offspring, then its prospects for survival would be bleak indeed. He shrugged gloomily and wandered back to the kitchen. He sat down and ate the expensive biscuits—and decided that George couldn't have cut his throat for culinary reasons. Marta was a good cook.

He entered the city on foot and unarmed, later in the morning.

He chose the alleyways, avoiding the thoroughfares, where traffic purred, and where the robot cops enforced the letter of the law. At each corner, he paused to glance in both directions against possible mechanical observers before darting across the open street to the next alley. The Geigers on the lamp posts were clicking faster as he progressed deeper into the city, and twice he paused to inspect the readings of their integrating dials. The radioactivity was not yet dangerous, but it was higher than he had anticipated. Perhaps it had been dusted again after the exodus.

He stopped to prowl through an empty house and an empty garage. He came out with a flashlight, a box of tools, and a crowbar. He had no certain plan, but tools would be needed if he meant to call a temporary halt to Central's activities. It was dangerous to enter any building however; Central would call it burglary, unless the prowler could show legitimate reason for entering. He needed some kind of identification.

After an hour's search through several houses in the residential district, he found a billfold containing a union card and a pass to several restricted buildings in the downtown area. The billfold belonged to a Willie Jesser, an air-conditioning and refrigeration mechanic for the Howard Cooler Company. He pocketed it after a moment's hesitation. It might not be enough to satisfy Central, but for the time being, it would have to do.

By early afternoon he had reached the beginning of the commercial area. Still he had seen no signs of human life. The thinly scattered traffic moved smoothly along the streets, carrying no passengers. Once he saw a group of robot climbers working high on a telephone pole. Some of the telephone cables carried the coordinating circuits for the city's network of computers. He detoured several blocks to avoid them, and wandered glumly on. He began to realize that he was wandering aimlessly.

The siren came suddenly from half a block away. Mitch stopped in the center of the street and glanced fearfully toward it. A robot cop was rolling toward him at twenty miles an hour! He broke into a run.

"You will halt, please!" croaked the cop's mechanical voice. "The pedestrian with the toolbox will please halt!"

Mitch stopped at the curb. Flight was impossible. The skater could whisk along at forty miles an hour if he chose.

The cop's steel wheels screeched to a stop a yard away. The head nodded a polite but jerky greeting. Mitch stared at the creature's eyes, even though he knew the eyes were duds; the cop was seeing him by the heat waves from his bodily warmth, and touching him with a delicate aura of radar.

"You are charged with jay-walking, sir. I must present you with a summons. Your identification, please."

Mitch nervously produced the billfold and extracted the cards. The cop accepted them in a pair of tweezerlike fingers and instantly memorized the information.

"This is insufficient identification. Have you nothing else?"

"That's all I have with me. What's wrong with it?"

"The pass and the union card expired in 1987."

Mitch swallowed hard and said nothing. He had been afraid of this. Now he might be picked up for vagrancy.

"I shall consult Central Co-ordinator for instructions," croaked the cop. "One moment, please."

A dynamotor purred softly in the policeman's cylindrical

body. Then Mitch heard the faint twittering of computer code as the cop's radio spoke to Central. There was a silence lasting several seconds. Then an answer twittered back. Still the cop said nothing. But he extracted a summons form from a pad, inserted it in a slot in his chassis, and made chomping sounds like a small typesetter. When he pulled the ticket out again, it was neatly printed with a summons for Willie Jesser to appear before Traffic Court on July 29, 1989. The charge was jay-walking.

Mitch accepted it with bewilderment. "I believe I have a right to ask for an explanation," he muttered.

The cop nodded crisply. "Central Service units are required to furnish explanations of decisions when such explanations are demanded."

"Then why did Central regard my identification as sufficient?"

"Pause for translation of Central's message," said the cop. He stood for a moment, making burring and clicking sounds. Then: "Referring to arrest of Willie Jesser by unit Six-Baker. Do not book for investigation. Previous investigations have revealed no identification papers dated later than May 1987 in the possession of any human pedestrian. Data based on one hundred sample cases. Tentative generalization by Central Service: it has become impossible for humans to produce satisfactory identification. Therefore, 'satisfactory identification' is temporarily redefined, pending instruction from authorized human legislative agency."

Mitch nodded thoughtfully. The decision indicated that Central was still capable of "learning," of gathering data and making generalizations about it. But the difficulty was still apparent. She was allowed to act on such generalizations only in certain very minor matters. Although she might very well realize the situation in the city, she could do nothing about it without authority from an authorized agency. That agency was a department of the city government, currently nonexistent.

The cop croaked a courteous "Good day, sir!" and skated smoothly back to his intersection.

Mitch stared at his summons for a moment. The date was

still four days away. If he weren't out of the city by then, he
might find himself in the lockup, since he had no money to
pay a fine.

Reassured now that his borrowed identity gave him a certain amount of safety, he began walking along the sidewalks
instead of using the alleys. Still he knew that Central was
observing him through a thousand eyes. Counters on every
corner were set to record the passage of pedestrian traffic,
and to relay the information to Central, thus helping to avoid
congestion. But Mitch *was* the pedestrian traffic. And the
counters clocked his passage. Since the data was available to
the logic units, Central might make some unpleasant deduc-
tions about his presence in the city.

Brazenness, he decided, was probably the safest course to
steer. He stopped at the next intersection and called to another mechanical cop, requesting directions to City Hall.

But the cop paused before answering, paused to speak with
Central, and Mitch suddenly regretted his question. The cop
came skating slowly to the curb.

"Six blocks west and four blocks north, sir," croaked the
cop. "Central requests the following information which you
may refuse to furnish if you so desire: As a resident of the
city; how is it that you do not know the way to City Hall, Mr.
Jesser?"

Mitch whitened and stuttered nervously. "Why, I've been
gone three years. I . . . I had forgotten."

The cop relayed the information, then nodded. "Central
thanks you. Data has been recorded."

"Wait," Mitch muttered, "is there a direct contact with
Central in City Hall?"

"Affirmative."

"I want to speak to Central. May I use it?"

The computer code twittered briefly. "Negative. You are
not listed among the city's authorized computer personnel.
Central suggests you use the Public Information Unit, also in
City Hall, ground floor rotunda."

Grumbling to himself, Mitch wandered away. The P.I.U.
was better than nothing, but if he had access to the direct
service contact, perhaps to some extent, he could have altered

Central's rigid behavior pattern. The P.I.U. however would be well guarded.

A few minutes later he was standing in the center of the main lobby of the city hall. The great building had suffered some damage during an air raid, and one wing was charred by fire. But the rest of it was still alive with the rattle of machinery. A headless servo-secretary came rolling past him, carrying a trayful of pink envelopes. Delinquent utility bills, he guessed. Central would keep sending them out, but of course human authority would be needed to suspend service to the delinquent customers. The servo-secretary deposited the envelopes in a mailbox by the door, then rolled quickly back to its office.

Mitch looked around the gloomy rotunda. There was a desk at the far wall. Recessed in a panel behind the desk were a microphone, a loud-speaker, and the lens of a television camera. A sign hung over the desk, indicating that here was the place to complain about utility bills, garbage disposal service, taxes, and inaccurate weather forecasts. A citizen could also request any information contained in Central Data except information relating to defense or to police records.

Mitch crossed the rotunda and sat at the desk facing the panel. A light came on overhead. The speaker crackled for a moment.

"Your name, please?" it asked.

"Willie Jesser."

"What do you wish from Information Service, please?"

"A direct contact with Central Data."

"You have a screened contact with Central Data. Unauthorized personnel are not permitted an unrestricted contact, for security reasons. Your contact must be monitored by this unit."

Mitch shrugged. It was as he had expected. Central Data was listening, and speaking, but the automatics of the P.I.U. would be censoring the exchange.

"All right," he grumbled. "Tell me this: Is Central aware that the city has been abandoned? That its population is gone?"

"Screening, screening, screening," said the unit. "Question relates to civil defense."

"Is Central aware that her services are now interfering with human interests?"

There was a brief pause. "Is this question in the nature of a complaint?"

"Yes," he grated acidly. "It's a complaint."

"About your utility services, Mr. Jesser?"

Mitch spat an angry curse. "About all services!" he bellowed. "Central has got to suspend all operations until new ordinances are fed into Data."

"That will be impossible, sir."

"Why?"

"There is no authorization from Department of City Services."

He slapped the desk and groaned. "There *is* no such department now! There is no city government! The city is abandoned!"

The speaker was silent.

"Well?" he snapped.

"Screening," said the machine.

"Listen," he hissed. "Are you screening what I say, or are you just blocking Central's reply?"

There was a pause. "Your statements are being recorded in Central Data. Replies to certain questions must be blocked for security reasons."

"The war is over!"

"Screening."

"You're trying to maintain a civil status quo that went out of existence three years ago. Can't you use your logic units to correct for present conditions?"

"The degree of self-adjustment permitted to Central Service is limited by ordinance number—"

"Never mind!"

"Is there anything else?"

"Yes! What will you do when fifty men come marching in to dynamite the vaults and destroy Central Data?"

"Destroying city property is punishable by a fine of—"

Mitch cursed softly and listened to the voice reading the applicable ordinance.

"Well, they're planning to do it anyway," he snapped. "Conspiracy to destroy city property is punishable by—"

Mitch stood up and walked away in disgust. But he had taken perhaps ten steps when a pair of robot guards came skating out from their wall niches to intercept him.

"One moment, sir," they croaked in unison.

"Well?"

"Central wishes to question you in connection with the alleged conspiracy to destroy city property. You are free to refuse. However, if you refuse, and if such a conspiracy is shown to exist, you may be charged with complicity. Will you accompany us to Interrogation?"

A step closer to jail, he thought gloomily. But what was there to lose? He grunted assent and accompanied the skaters out the entrance, down an inclined ramp, and past a group of heavily barred windows. They entered the police court, where a booking computer clicked behind its desk. Several servosecretaries and robot cops were waiting quietly for task assignments.

Mitch stopped suddenly. His escorts waited politely.

"Will you come with us, please?"

He stood staring around at the big room—at the various doorways, one leading to traffic court, and at the iron gate to the cell block.

"I hear a woman crying," he muttered.

The guards offered no comment.

"Is someone locked in a cell?"

"We are not permitted to answer."

"Suppose I wanted to go bail," he snapped. "I have a right to know."

"You may ask the booking desk whether a specific individual is being held. But generalized information cannot be released."

Mitch strode to the booking computer. "Are you holding a woman in jail?"

"Screening."

It was only a vague suspicion, but he said, "A woman named Marta."

"Full name, please."

"I don't know it. Can't you tell me?"

"Screening."

"Listen! I loaned my bicycle to a woman named Marta. If you have the bicycle, I want it!"

"License number, please."

"A 1987 license—number Six Zebra Five Zero."

"Check with Lost and Found, please."

Mitch controlled himself slowly. "Look—*you* check. I'll wait."

The computer paused. "A bicycle with that license number has been impounded. Can you produce proof of ownership?"

"On a bicycle? I knew the number. Isn't that enough?"

"Describe it please?"

Mitch described it wearily. He began to understand Ferris' desire to retire Central permanently and forcibly. At the moment, he longed to convert several sub-computers to scrap metal.

"Then," said the speaker, "if vehicle is yours, you may have it by applying for a new license and paying the required fee."

"Refer that to Central Data," Mitch groaned.

The booking computer paused to confer with the Co-ordinator. "Decision stands, sir."

"But there aren't any new licenses!" he growled. "A while ago, Central said—Oh, never mind!"

"That decision applied to identification, sir. This applies to licensing of vehicles. Insufficient data has been gathered to permit generalization."

"Sure, sure. All right, what do I do to get the girl out of jail?"

There was another conference with the Co-ordinator, then: "She is being held for investigation. She may not be released for seventy-two hours."

Mitch dropped the toolbox that he had been carrying since morning. With a savage curse, he rammed the crowbar through a vent in the device's front panel, and slashed it about in the opening. There was a crash of shattering glass and a shower of sparks. Mitch yelped at the electric jolt and lurched away. Steel fingers clutched his wrists.

Five minutes later he was being led through the gate to the

cell blocks, charged with maliciously destroying city property; and he cursed himself for a hot-tempered fool. They would hold him until a grand jury convened, which would probably be forever.

The girl's sobbing grew louder as he was led along the iron corridors toward a cell. He passed three cells and glanced inside. The cells were occupied by dead men's bones. *Why?* The rear wall was badly cracked, and bits of loose masonry were scattered on the floor. Had they died of concussion during an attack? Or been gassed to death?

They led him to the fifth cell and unlocked the door. Mitch stared inside and grinned. The rear wall had been partially wrecked by a bomb blast, and there was room to crawl through the opening to the street. The partition that separated the adjoining cell was also damaged, and he caught a glimpse of a white, frightened face peering through the hole. Marta.

He glanced at his captors. They were pushing him gently through the door. Evidently Central's talents did not extend to bricklaying, and she could not judge that the cell was less than escapeproof.

The door clanged shut behind him.

"Marta," he called.

Her face had disappeared from the opening. There was no answer.

"Marta."

"Let me alone," grumbled a muffled voice.

"I'm not angry about the bicycle."

He walked to the hole and peered through the partition into the next cell. She crouched in a corner, peering at him with frightened, tear-reddened eyes. He glanced at the opening in the rear wall.

"Why haven't you gone outside?" he asked.

She giggled hysterically. "Why don't you go look down?"

He stepped to the opening and glanced twenty feet down to a concrete sidewalk. He went back to stare at the girl.

"Where's your baby?"

"They took him away," she whimpered.

Mitch frowned and thought about it for a moment. "To the city nursery, probably—while you're in jail."

"They won't take care of him! They'll let him die!"

"Don't scream like that. He'll be all right."

"Robots don't give milk!"

"No but there are such things as bottles, you know," he chuckled.

"Are there?" Her eyes were wide with horror. "And what will they put in the bottles?"

"Why—" He paused. Central certainly wasn't running any dairy farms.

"Wait'll they bring you a meal," she said. "You'll see."

"Meal?"

"Empty tray," she hissed. "Empty tray, empty paper cup, paper fork, clean paper napkin. No food."

Mitch swallowed hard. Central's logic was sometimes hard to see. The servo-attendants probably went through the motions of ladling stew from an empty pot and drawing coffee from an empty urn. Of course, there weren't any truck farmers to keep the city supplied with produce.

"So that's why . . . the bones . . . in the other cells," he muttered.

"They'll starve us to death!"

"Don't scream so. We'll get out. All we need is something to climb down on."

"There isn't any bedding."

"There's our clothing. We can plait a rope. And if necessary, we can risk a jump."

She shook her head dully and stared at her hands. "It's no use. They'd catch us again."

Mitch sat down to think. There was bound to be a police arsenal somewhere in the building, probably in the basement. The robot cops were always unarmed. But, of course, there had been a human organization for investigation purposes and to assume command in the event of violence. When one of the traffic units faced a threat, it could do nothing but try to handcuff the offender and call for human help. There were arms in the building somewhere, and a well-placed rifle shot could penetrate the thin sheet-steel bodies.

He deplored the thought of destroying any of the city's service machinery, but if it became necessary to wreck a few subunits, it would have to be done. He must somehow get access to the vaults where the central data tanks and the co-ordinators were located—get to them before Ferris' gang came to wreck them completely so that they might be free to pick the city clean.

An hour later, he heard the cell block gate groan open, and he arose quickly. Interrogation, he thought. They were coming to question him about the plot to wreck Central. He paused to make a hasty decision, then scrambled for the narrow opening and clambered through it into the adjoining cell while the skater came rolling down the corridor.

The girl's eyes widened. "Wh-what are you—"

"*Shhh!*" he hissed. "This might work."

The skater halted before his cell while he crouched against the wall beyond the opening.

"Willie Jesser, please," the robot croaked.

There was a silence. He heard the door swing open. The robot rolled around inside his cell for a few seconds, repeating his name and brushing rubble aside to make way. If only he failed to look through the opening!

Suddenly a siren growled, and the robot went tearing down the corridor again. Mitch stole a quick glance. The robot had left the door ajar. He dragged the girl to her feet and snapped, "Let's go."

They squeezed through the hole and raced out into the corridor. The cell-block gate was closed. The girl moaned weakly. There was no place to hide.

The door bolts were operated from remote boxes, placed in the corridor so as to be beyond the reach of the inmates. Mitch dragged the girl quickly toward another cell, opened the control panel, and threw the bolt. He closed the panel, leaving the bolt open. They slipped quickly inside the new cell, and he pulled the door quietly closed. The girl made a choking sound as she stumbled over the remains of a former inmate.

"Lie down in the corner," he hissed, "and keep still. They're coming back in force."

"What if they notice the bolt is open?"

"Then we're sunk. But they'll be busy down at our end of the hall. Now shut up."

They rolled under the steel cot and lay scarcely breathing.

The robot was returning with others. The faint twitter of
computer code echoed through the cell blocks. Then the
skaters rushed past, and screeched to a stop before the escap-
ee's cell. He heard them enter. He crawled to the door for a
look, then pushed it open and stole outside.

He beckoned the girl to his side and whispered briefly.
Then they darted down the corridor on tiptoe toward the
investigators. They turned as he raced into view. He seized
the bars and jerked the door shut. The bolt snapped in place
as Marta tugged at the remote.

Three metal bodies crashed simultaneously against the door,
and rebounded. One of them spun around three times before
recovering.

"Release the lock, please."

Mitch grinned through the bars. "Why don't you try the
hole in the wall?"

The robot who had spun crazily away from the door now
turned. He went charging across the cell floor at full
acceleration—and sailed out wildly into space.

An ear-splitting crash came from the street. Shattered metal
skidded across pavement. A siren wailed, and brakes shrieked.
The others went to look—and began twittering.

Then they turned. "You will surrender, please. We have
summoned armed guards to seize you if you resist."

Mitch laughed and tugged at the whimpering girl.

"Wh-where—?"

"To the gate. Come on."

They raced swiftly along the corridor. And the gate was
opening to admit the "armed guards." But, of course, no
human bluecoats charged through. The girl muttered frightened bewilderment, and he explained on the run.

"Enforced habit pattern. Central has to do it, even when
no guards are available."

Two repair units were at work on the damaged booking
computer as the escapees raced past. The repair units paused,
twittered a notation to Central, then continued with their
work.

Minutes later they found the arsenal, and the mechanical
attendant had set out a pair of .45s for the "armed guards."
Mitch caught one of them up and fired at the attendant's

sheet-metal belly. The robot careened crazily against the wall, emitted a shower of blue sparks, and stood humming while the metal around the hole grew cherry red. There was a dull cough. The machine smoked and fell silent.

Mitch vaulted across the counter and caught a pair of submachine guns from the rack. But the girl backed away, shaking her head.

"I couldn't even use your shotgun," she panted.

He shrugged and laid it aside. "Carry as much ammunition as you can, then," he barked.

Alarm bells were clanging continuously as they raced out of the arsenal, and a loud-speaker was thundering a request for all human personnel to be alert and assist in their capture. Marta was staggering against him as they burst out of the building into the street. He pushed her back against the wall and fired a burst at two skaters who raced toward them down the sidewalk. One crashed into a fire plug; the other went over the curb and fell in the street.

"To the parking lot!" he called over his shoulder.

But the girl had slumped in a heap on the sidewalk. He grumbled a curse and hurried to her side. She was semiconscious, but her face was white and drawn. She shivered uncontrollably.

"What's wrong?" he snapped.

There was no answer. Fright had dazed her. Her lips moved, seemed to frame a soundless word: "George."

Muttering angrily, Mitch stuffed a fifty-round drum of ammunition in his belt, took another between his teeth, and lifted the girl over one shoulder. He turned in time to fire a one-handed burst at another skater. The burst went wide. But the skater stopped. Then the skater ran away.

He gasped, and stared after it. The blare of the loud-speaker was furnishing the answer.

". . . All human personnel. Central patrol service has reached the limit of permissible subunit expenditure. Responsibility for capture no longer applied without further orders to expend subunits. Please instruct. Commissioner of Police, please instruct. Waiting. Waiting."

Mitch grinned. Carrying the girl, he stumbled toward a car

on the parking lot. He dumped her in the back seat and started in behind her, but a loud-speaker in the front protested.

"Unauthorized personnel. This is Mayor Sarquist's car. Unauthorized personnel. Please use an extra."

Mitch looked around. There were no extras on the lot. And if there had been one, it would refuse to carry him unless he could identify himself as authorized to use it.

Mayor Sarquist's car began twittering a radio protest to Central. Mitch climbed inside and wrenched loose the cable that fed the antenna. The loud-speaker began barking complaints about sabotage. Mitch found a toolbox under the back seat and removed several of the pilot-computer's panels. He tugged a wire loose, and the speaker ceased complaining. He ripped at another, and a bank of tubes went dead.

He drove away, using a set of dial controls for steering. The girl in the back seat began to recover her wits. She sat up and stared out the window at the thin traffic. The sun was sinking, and the great city was immersing itself in gloom.

"You're worthless!" he growled at Marta. "The world takes a poke at you, and you jump in your mental coffin and nail the lid shut. How do you expect to take care of your baby?"

She continued to stare gloomily out the window. She said nothing. The car screeched around a corner, narrowly missing a mechanical cop. The cop skated after them for three blocks, siren wailing; then it abandoned the chase.

"You're one of the machine-age's spoiled children," he fumed. "Technologists gave you everything you could possibly want. Push a button, and you get it. Instead of taking part in the machine age, you let it wait on you. You spoiled yourself. When the machine age cracks up, you crack up, too. Because you never made yourself its master; you just let yourself be mechanically pampered."

She seemed not to hear him. He swung around another corner and pulled to the curb. They were in front of a three-story brick building set in the center of a green-lawned block and surrounded by a high iron fence. The girl stared at it for a moment, and raised her chin slowly from her fist.

"The city orphanage!" she cried suddenly, and bounded

outside. She raced across the sidewalk and beat at the iron gate with her fists.

Mitch climbed out calmly and opened it for her. She darted up toward the porch, but a servo-attendant came rolling out to intercept her. Its handcuff-hand was open to grasp her wrist.

"Drop low!" he bellowed at her.

She crouched on the walkway, then rolled quickly aside on the lawn. A burst of machine-gun fire brightened the twilight. The robot spun crazily and stopped, hissing and sputtering. Wrecking a robot could be dangerous. If a bullet struck the tiny nuclear reactor just right, there would be an explosion.

They skirted wide around it and hurried into the building. Somewhere upstairs, a baby was crying. A servo-nurse sat behind a desk in the hall, and she greeted them as if they were guests.

"Good evening, sir and madam. You wish to see one of the children?"

Marta started toward the stairs, but Mitch seized her arm. "No! Let *me* go up. It won't be pretty."

But she tore herself free with a snarl and bounded up the steps toward the cry of her child. Mitch shrugged to himself and waited. The robot nurse protested the illegal entry, but did nothing about it.

"Noooo—!"

A horrified shriek from the girl. He glanced up the staircase, knowing what was wrong, but unable to help her. A moment later, he heard her vomiting. He waited.

A few minutes later, she came staggering down the stairway, sobbing and clutching her baby tightly against her. She stared at Mitch with tear-drenched eyes, gave him a wild shake of her head, and babbled hysterically.

"Those cribs! They're full of little bones. Little bones—all over the floor. Little bones—"

"Shut up!" he snapped. "Be thankful yours is all right. Now let's get out of here."

After disposing of another robotic interferer, they reached the car, and Mitch drove rapidly toward the outskirts. The girl's sobbing ceased, and she purred a little unsung lullaby to her child, cuddling it as if it had just returned from the dead.

Remorse picked dully at Mitch's heart, for having growled at her. Motherwise, she was still a good animal, despite her lack of success in adjusting to the reality of a ruptured world.

"Marta—?"

"What?"

"You're not fit to take care of yourself."

He said it gently. She only stared at him as he piloted the car.

"You ought to find a big husky gal who wants a baby, and let her take care of it for you."

"No."

"It's just a suggestion. None of my business. You want your baby to live, don't you?"

"George promised he'd take care of us. George always took care of us."

"George killed himself."

She uttered a little whimper. "Why did he do it? Why? I went to look for food. I came back, and there he was. Why, *why?*"

"Possibly because he was just like you. What did he do—before the war?"

"Interior decorator. He was good, a real artist."

"Yeah."

"Why do you say it *that* way? He *was.*"

"Was he qualified to live in a mechanical culture?"

"I don't know what you mean."

"I mean—could he control his slice of mechanical civilization, or did it control him?"

"I don't see—"

"Was he a button-pusher and a switch-puller? Or did he care what made the buttons and switches work? Men misuse their tools because they don't understand the principles of the tools. A man who doesn't know how a watch works might try to fix it with a hammer. If the watch is communal property, he's got no right to fool with it. A nontechnologist has no right to take part in a technological civilization. He's a bull in a china shop. That's what happened to our era. Politicians were given powerful tools. They failed to understand the tools. They wrecked our culture with them."

"You'd have a scientist in the White House?"

"If all men were given a broad technical education, there could be nothing else there, could there?"

"Technocracy—"

"No. Simply a matter of education."

"People aren't smart enough."

"You mean they don't *care* enough. Any man above the level of a dullard has enough sense to grasp the principles of physics and basic engineering and mechanics. They just aren't motivated to grasp them. The brain is a tool, not a garbage can for oddments of information! Your baby there—he should learn the principles of logic and semantics before he's ten. He should be taught *how to use* the tool, the brain. We've just begun to learn how to think. If the common man were trained in scientific reasoning methods, we'd solve our problems in a hurry."

"What has this got to do with us?"

"Everything. Your George folded up because he couldn't control his slice of civilization, and he couldn't live without it. He couldn't fix the broken toy, but he suffered from its loss. And you're in the same fix. I haven't decided yet whether you're crazy or just neurotic."

She gave him an icy stare. "Let me know when you figure it out."

They were leaving the city, driving out through the suburbs again into the night-shrouded residential areas. He drove by streetlight, for the car—accustomed to piloting itself by radar—had no headlights. Mitch thought gloomily that he had stalked into the city without a plan, and had accomplished nothing. He had alerted Central, and had managed to get himself classified as a criminal in the central data tanks. Instead of simplifying his task, he had made things harder for himself.

Whenever they passed a cop at an intersection, the cop retreated to the curb and called Central to inform the Coordinator of their position. But no attempt was made to arrest the fugitives. Having reached her limit of subunit expenditures, Central was relying on the nonexistent human police force.

"Mayor Sarquist's house," the girl muttered suddenly.

"Huh? Where?"

"Just ahead. The big cut-stone house on the right—with part of the roof caved in."

Mitch twisted a dial in the heart of the pilot-computer, and the car screeched to a stop at the curb. The girl lurched forward.

"You woke the baby," she complained. "Why stop here? We're still in the city limits."

"I don't know," he murmured, staring thoughtfully at the dark hulk of the two-story mansion set in a nest of oaks. "Just sort of a hunch."

There was a long silence while Mitch chewed his lip and frowned at the house.

"I hear a telephone ringing," she said.

"Central calling Mayor Sarquist. You can't tell. It might have been ringing for three years."

She was looking out the rear window. "Mitch—?"

"Huh?"

"There's a cop at the intersection."

He seemed not to hear her. He opened the door. "Let's go inside. I want to look around. Bring the gun."

They strolled slowly up the walkway toward the damaged and deserted house. The wind was breathing in the oaks, and the porch creaked loudly beneath their feet. The door was still locked. Mitch kicked the glass out of a window, and they slipped into an immense living room. He found the light.

"The cop'll hear that noise," she muttered, glancing at the broken glass.

The noisy clatter of the steelwheeled skater answered her. The cop was coming to investigate. Mitch ignored the sound and began prowling through the house. The phone was still ringing, but he could not answer it without knowing Sarquist's personal identifying code.

The girl called suddenly from the library. "What's this thing, Mitch?"

"What thing?" he yelled.

"Typewriter keyboard, but no type. Just a bunch of wires and a screen."

His jaw fell agape. He trotted quickly toward the library.

"A direct channel to the data tanks!" he gasped, staring at the metal wall-panel with its encoders and the keyboard.

"What's it doing here?"

He thought about it briefly. "Must be . . . I remember: just before the exodus, they gave Sarquist emergency powers in the defense setup. He could requisition whatever was needed for civil defense—draft workers for first aid, traffic direction, and so on. He had the power to draft anybody or anything during an air raid."

Mitch approached the keyboard slowly. He closed the main power switch, and the tubes came alive. He sat down and typed: *Central from Sarquist; You will completely clear the ordinance section of your data tanks and await revised ordinances. The entire city code is hereby repealed.*

He waited. Nothing happened. There was no acknowledgement. The typed letters had not even appeared on the screen.

"Broken?" asked the girl.

"Maybe," Mitch grunted. "Maybe not. I think I know."

The mechanical cop had lowered his retractable sprockets, climbed the porch steps, and was hammering at the door. "Mayor Sarquist, please!" he was calling. "Mayor Sarquist, please!"

"Let him rave," Mitch grunted, and looked around the library.

There was a mahogany desk, several easy-chairs, a solid wall of books, and a large safe in another wall. The safe—

"Sarquist should have some rather vital papers in there," he murmured.

"What do you want with papers?" the girl snapped. "Why don't we get out of the city while we can?"

He glanced at her coldly. "Like to go the rest of the way alone?"

She opened her mouth, closed it, and frowned. She was holding the tommy gun, and he saw it twitch slightly in her hand, as if reminding him that she didn't *have* to go alone.

He walked to the safe and idly spun the dial. "Locked," he muttered. "It'd take a good charge of T.N.T. . . . . or—"

"Or what?"

"Central." He chuckled dryly. "Maybe she'll do it for us."

"Are you crazy?"

"Sure. Go unlock the door. Let the policeman in."

"No!" she barked.

Mitch snorted impatiently. "All right then, I'll do it. Pitch me the gun."

"No!" She pointed it at him and backed away.

"Give me the gun!"

"No!"

She had laid the baby on the sofa where it was now sleeping peacefully. Mitch sat down beside it.

"Trust your aim?"

She caught her breath. Mitch lifted the child gently into his lap.

"Give me the gun."

"You wouldn't!"

"I'll give the kid back to the cops."

She whitened, and handed the weapon to him quickly. Mitch saw that the safety was on, laid the baby aside, and stood up.

"Don't look at me like that!" she said nervously.

He walked slowly toward her.

"Don't you dare *touch me!*"

He picked up a ruler from Sarquist's desk, then dived for her. A moment later she was stretched out across his lap, clawing at his legs and shrieking while he applied the ruler resoundingly. Then he dumped her on the rug, caught up the gun, and went to admit the insistent cop.

Man and machine stared at each other across the threshold. The cop radioed a visual image of Mitch to Central, and got an immediate answer.

"Request you surrender immediately, sir."

"Am I now charged with breaking and entering?" he asked acidly.

"Affirmative."

"You planning to arrest me?"

Again the cop consulted Central. "If you will leave the city at once, you will be granted safe passage."

Mitch lifted his brows. Here was a new twist. Central was doing some interpretation, some slight modification of ordinance. He grinned at the cop and shook his head.

"I locked Mayor Sarquist in the safe," he stated evenly.

The robot consulted Central. There was a long twittering of computer code. Then it said, "This is false information."

"Suit yourself, tin-boy. I don't care whether you believe it or not."

Again there was a twittering of code. Then: "Stand aside, please."

Mitch stepped out of the doorway. The subunit bounced over the threshold with the aid of the four-footed sprockets and clattered hurriedly toward the library. Mitch followed, grinning to himself. Despite Central's limitless "intelligence," she was as naive as a child.

He lounged in the doorway to watch the subunit fiddling with the dials of the safe. He motioned the girl down, and she crouched low in a corner. The tumblers clicked. There was a dull snap. The door started to swing.

"Just a minute!" Mitch barked.

The subunit paused and turned. The machine gun exploded, and the brief hail of bullets tore off the robot's antenna. Mitch lowered the gun and grinned. The cop just stood there, unable to contact Central, unable to decide. Mitch crossed the room through the drifting plaster dust and rolled the robot aside. The girl whimpered her relief, and came out of the corner.

The cop was twittering continually as it tried without success to contact the Co-ordinator. Mitch stared at it for a moment, then barked at the girl.

"Go find some tools. Search the garage, attic, basement. I want a screw driver, pliers, soldering iron, solder, whatever you can find."

She departed silently.

Mitch cleaned out the safe and dumped the heaps of papers, money, and securities on the desk. He began sorting them out. Among the various stacks of irrelevant records, he found a copy of the original specifications for the Central Co-ordinator vaults, dating from the time of installation. He found blue-prints of the city's network of computer circuits, linking the subunits into one. His hands became excited as he shuffled through the stacks. Here was data. Here was substance for reasonable planning.

Heretofore, he had gone off half-cocked, and quite naturally had met with immediate failure. No one ever won a battle by being good, pure, or ethically right, despite Galahad's claims to the contrary. Victories were won by intelligent planning, and Mitch felt ashamed for his previous impulsiveness. To work out a scheme for redirecting Central's efforts would require time.

The girl brought a boxful of assorted small tools. She set them on the floor and sat down to glower at him.

"More cops outside now," she said. "Standing and waiting. The place is surrounded."

He ignored her. Sarquist's identifying code—it had to be here somewhere.

"I tell you, we should get out of here!" she whined.

"Shut up."

Mitch occasionally plucked a paper from the stack and laid it aside while the girl watched.

"What are those?" she asked.

"Messages he typed into the unit at various times."

"What good are *they*?"

He showed her one of the slips of yellowed paper. It said: *Unit 67-BJ is retired for repairs.* A number was scrawled in one corner: 5.00326.

"So?"

"That number. It was his identifying code at the time."

"You mean it's different every day?"

"More likely, it's different every minute. The code is probably based on an equation whose independent variable is *time*, and whose dependent variable is the code number."

"How silly!"

"Not at all. It's just sort of a combination lock whose combination is continuously changing. All I've got to do is find the equation that describes the change. Then I can get to the Central Coordinator."

She paced restlessly while he continued the search. Half an hour later, he put his head in his hands and gazed despondently at the desk top. The key to the code was not there.

"What's the matter?" she asked.

"Sarquist. I figured he'd have to write it down somewhere. Evidently he memorized it. Or else his secretary did. I didn't figure a politician even had sense enough to substitute numbers in a simple equation."

The girl walked to the bookshelf and picked out a volume. She brought it to him silently. The title was *Higher Mathematics for Engineers and Physicists*.

"So I was wrong," he grunted.

"Now what?"

He shuffled the slips of paper idly while he thought about it. "I've got eleven code numbers here, and the corresponding times when they were good. I might be able to find it empirically."

"I don't understand."

"Find an equation that gives the same eleven answers for the same eleven times and use it to predict the code number for now."

"Will it work?"

He grinned. "There are an infinite number of equations that would give the same eleven answers for the same eleven substitutions. But it might work, if I assume that the code equation was of a simple form."

She paced restlessly while he worked at making a graph with time as the abscissa and the code numbers for ordinates. But the points were scattered across the page, and there was no connecting them with any simple sort of curve. "It almost has to be some kind of repeating function," he muttered, "something that Central could check by means of an irregular cam. The normal way for setting a code into a machine is to turn a cam by clock motor, and the height of the cam's rider is the code number for that instant."

He tried it on polar co-ordinates, hoping to get the shape of such a cam, but the resulting shape was too irregular to be possible, and he had no way of knowing the period of the repeating function.

"That's the craziest clock I ever saw," the girl murmured.

"What?" He looked up quickly.

"That electric wall clock. Five minutes ahead of the electric clock in the living room. But when we first came, it was twenty minutes ahead."

"It's stopped, maybe."

"Look at the second hand."

The red sweep was running. Mitch stared at it for a moment, then came slowly to his feet and walked to her side. He took the small clock down from its hook and turned it over in his hands. Then he traced the cord to the wall outlet. The plug was held in place by a bracket so that it could not be removed.

The sweep hand moved slowly, it seemed. Silently he removed the screws from the case and stared inside at the works. Then he grunted surprise. "First clock I ever saw with elliptical gears!"

"What?"

"Look at these two gears in the train. Ellipses, mounted at the foci. That's the story. For a while the clock will run faster than the other one. Then it'll run slower." He handled it with growing excitement. "That's *it*, Marta—the key. Central must have another clock just like this one. The amount of lead or lag—in minutes, is probably the code!"

He moved quickly to the direct contact unit. "Tell me the time on the other clock!"

She hurried into the living room and called back, "Ten seventeen and forty seconds . . . forty-five . . . fifty—"

The other clock was leading by five minutes and fifteen seconds. He typed 5.250 on the keyboard. Nothing happened.

"You sure that's right?" he called.

"It's now 10:10 . . . fifteen . . . twenty."

The clock was still slowing down. He tried 5.230, but again nothing happened. The unit refused to respond. He arose with an angry grunt and began prowling around the library. "There's something else," he muttered. "There must be a modifying factor. That clock's too obvious anyway. But what else could they be measuring together except time?"

"Is that another clock on his desk?"

"No, it's a barometer. It doesn't—"

He paused to grin. "Could be! The barometric pressure-difference from the mean could easily be mechanically added or subtracted from the reading of that wacky clock. Visualize this, inside of Central: The two clock motors mounted on the same shaft, with the distance between their indicator needles as the code number. Except that the distance is modified by having a barometer rigged up to shift one of the clocks one way or the other on its axis when the pressure varies. It's simple enough.''

She shook her head. Mitch took the barometer with him to the unit. The dial was caibrated in atmospheres, and the pressure was now 1.03. Surely, he thought, for simplicity's sake, there would be no other factor involved in the code. This way, Sarquist could have glanced at his watch and the wall clock and the barometer, and could have known the code number with only a little mental arithmetic. The wall time minus the wrist time plus the barometer's reading.

He called to the girl again, and the lag was now a little over four minutes. He typed again. There was a sharp click as the relays worked. The screen came alive, fluttered with momentary phosphorescence, then revealed the numbers in glowing type.

"We've got it!" he yelled at Marta.

She came to sit down on the rug. "I still don't see what we've got."

"Watch!" He began typing hurriedly, and the message flashed neatly upon the screen.

CENTRAL FROM SARQUIST. CLEAR YOUR TANKS OF ALL ORDINANCE DATA, EXCEPT ORDINANCES PERTAINING TO RECORDING OF INFORMATION IN YOUR TANKS. PREPARE TO RECORD NEW DATA.

He pressed the answer button, and the screen went blank, but the reply was slow to come.

"It won't work!" Marta snorted. "It knows you aren't Sarquist. The subunits in the street have seen us."

"What do you mean by 'know,' and what do you mean by 'see'? Central isn't human."

"It *knows* and it *sees*."

He nodded. "Provided you mean those words in a mechanical sense. Provided you don't imply that she *cares* what she knows and sees, except where she's required to 'care' by enforced behavior-patterns—ordinances.''

Then the reply began crawling across the screen. SARQUIST FROM CENTRAL. INCONSISTENT INSTRUCTIONS. ORDINANCE 36-J, PERTAINING TO THE RECORDING OF INFORMATION, STATES THAT ORDINANCE-DATA MAY NOT BE TOTALLY VOIDED BY YOU, EXCEPT DURING RED ALERT AIR WARNING.

"See?" the girl hissed.

DEFINE THE LIMITS OF MY AUTHORITY IN PRESENT CONDITIONS, he typed. MAY I TEMPORARILY SUSPEND SPECIFIC ORDINANCES?

YOU MAY SUSPEND SPECIFIC ORDINANCES FOR CAUSE, BUT THE CAUSE MUST BE RECORDED WITH THE ORDER OF SUSPENSION.

Mitch put on a gloating grin. READ ME THE SERIES NUMBERS OF ALL LAWS IN CRIMINAL AND TRAFFIC CODES.

The reaction was immediate. Numbers began flashing on the screen in rapid sequence. "Write these down!" he called to the girl.

A few moments later, the flashing numbers paused. WAIT, EMERGENCY INTERRUPTION, said the screen.

Mitch frowned. The girl glanced up from her notes. "What's—"

Then it came. A dull booming roar that rattled the windows and shook the house.

"Not another raid!" she whimpered.

"It doesn't sound like—"

Letters began splashing across the screen. EMERGENCY ADVICE TO SARQUIST. MY CIVILIAN DEFENSE CO-ORDINATOR HAS BEEN DESTROYED. MY ANTI-AIR-CRAFT CO-ORDINATOR HAS BEEN DESTROYED. ADVISE, PLEASE.

"What happened?"

"Frank Ferris!" he barked suddenly. "The Sugarton crowd—with their dynamite! They got into the city."

CENTRAL FROM SARQUIST, he typed. WHERE ARE THE DAMAGED CO-ORDINATORS LOCATED?

UNDERGROUND VAULT AT MAP CO-ORDINATES K-81.

"Outside the city," he breathed. "They haven't got to the main tanks yet. We've got a little time."

PROCEED WITH THE ORDINANCE LISTING, he commanded.

Half-an-hour later, they were finished. Then he began the long task of relisting each ordinance number and typing after it: REPEALED, CITY EVACUATED.

"I hear gunshots," Marta interrupted. She went to the window to peer up and down the dimly lighted streets.

Mitch worked grimly. It would take them a couple of hours to get into the heart of the city, unless they knew how to capture a robot vehicle and make it serve them. But with enough men and enough guns, they would wreck subunits until Central withdrew. Then they could walk freely into the heart of the city and wreck the main co-ordinators, with a consequent cessation of all city services. Then they would be free to pillage, to make a mechanical graveyard of the city that awaited the return of Man.

"They're coming down this street, I think," she called.

"Then turn out all the lights!" he snapped, "and keep quiet."

"They'll see all the cops out in the street. They'll wonder why."

He worked frantically to get all the codes out of the machine before the Sugarton crowd came past. He was destroying its duties, its habit-patterns, its normal functions. When he was finished, it would stand helplessly by and let Ferris' gang wreak their havoc unless he could replace the voided ordinances with new, more practical ones.

"Aren't you finished yet?" she called. "They're a couple of blocks away. The cops have quit fighting, but the men are still shooting them."

"I'm finished now!" He began rattling the keyboard frantically.

SUPPLEMENTAL ORDINANCES: #1, THERE IS NO LIMIT OF SUBUNIT EXPENDITURE.

#2, YOU WILL NOT PHYSICALLY INJURE ANY HU-

MAN BEING, EXCEPT IN DEFENSE OF CENTRAL CO-
ORDINATOR UNITS.

#3, ALL MECHANICAL TRAFFIC WILL BE CLEARED
FROM THE STREETS IMMEDIATELY.

#4, YOU WILL DEFEND CENTRAL CO-ORDINATOR
AT ALL COSTS.

#5, THE HUMAN LISTED IN YOUR MEMORY UNITS
UNDER THE NAME "WILLIE JESSER" WILL BE AL-
LOWED ACCESS TO CENTRAL DATA WITHOUT CHAL-
LENGE.

#6, TO THE LIMIT OF YOUR ABILITY, YOU WILL
SET YOUR OWN TASKS IN PURSUANCE OF THIS GOAL:
TO KEEP THE CITY'S SERVICE INTACT AND IN GOOD
REPAIR, READY FOR HUMAN USAGE.

#7, YOU WILL APPREHEND HUMANS ENGAGED IN
ARSON, GRAND THEFT, OR PHYSICAL VIOLENCE,
AND EJECT THEM SUMMARILY FROM THE CITY.

#8, YOU WILL OFFER YOUR SERVICE TO PROTECT
THE PERSON OF WILLIE JESSER—

"They're here!" shouted the girl. "They're coming up the
walk!"

. . . AND WILL ASSIST HIM IN THE TASK OF RENO-
VATING THE CITY, TOGETHER WITH SUCH PERSONS
WILLING TO HELP REBUILD.

The girl was shaking him. "They're here, I tell you!"

Mitch punched a button labeled "commit to data," and the
screen went blank. He leaned back and grinned at her. There
was a sound of shouting in the street, and someone was
beating at the door.

Then the skaters came rolling in a tide of sound two blocks
away. The shouting died, and there were several bursts of
gunfire. But the skaters came on, and the shouting grew
frantic.

She muttered: "Now we're in for it."

But Mitch just grinned at her and lit a cigarette. Fifty men
couldn't stand for long against a couple of thousand subunits
who now had no expenditure limit.

He typed one last instruction into the unit. WHEN THE
PLUNDERERS ARE TAKEN PRISONER, OFFER THEM

THIS CHOICE: STAY AND HELP REBUILD, OR KEEP AWAY FROM THE CITY.

From now on, there weren't going to be any nonparticipators.

Mitch closed down the unit and went out to watch the waning fight.

A bigger job was ahead.

(1952)

Flannery O'Connor

Flannery O'Connor was born in Georgia, in 1925. Although she left her native state to take an M.A. at the University of Iowa, and made many trips to Yaddo and to the home of Robert and Sally Fitzgerald, in Connecticut, she remained a deeply, almost totally Southern writer in style and theme. But she was also a Southern writer on her own terms—Catholic, Gothic, and scrupulously, sometimes painfully honest and direct. "The fact is," she wrote, "that the materials of the fiction writer are the humblest. Fiction is about everything human and we are made out of dust, and if you scorn getting yourself dusty, then you shouldn't try to write fiction." As she also declared, emphatically, "Fiction operates through the senses."

Hers was not an easy or a long life. She had inherited a fatal disease, which killed her in 1964. Editors were often troubled by her fiction, especially at the start of her career. The trustees of the Guggenheim Foundation were troubled too, for they turned down her 1949 fellowship application, though among her sponsors were Robert Lowell, Philip Rahv, and one of her teachers at Iowa, Robert Penn Warren.

Her first novel, Wise Blood *(1952), received favorable but somewhat puzzled reviews. Her first collection of stories, however,* A Good Man Is Hard to Find *(1953), the title story from which is here reprinted, converted the critics, and her second novel,* The Violent Bear It Away *(1960), and the posthumous collection of stories,* Everything That Rises Must

Converge (1965), were showered with well-deserved critical praise.

For there is no one quite like her in American literature. Elizabeth Bishop summed up O'Connor's stature in beautifully accurate terms: "Her few books will live on and on . . . They are narrow, possibly, but they are clear, hard, vivid, and full of bits of description, phrases, and an odd insight that contains more real poetry than a dozen books of poems."

The Complete Stories *was published in 1971.*

A GOOD MAN IS HARD TO FIND

The grandmother didn't want to go to Florida. She wanted to visit some of her connections in east Tennessee and she was seizing at every chance to change Bailey's mind. Bailey was the son she lived with, her only boy. He was sitting on the edge of his chair at the table, bent over the orange sports section of the *Journal*. "Now look here, Bailey," she said, "see here, read this," and she stood with one hand on her thin hip and the other rattling the newspaper at his bald head. "Here this fellow that calls himself The Misfit is aloose from the Federal Pen and headed toward Florida and you read here what it says he did to these people. Just you read it. I wouldn't take my children in any direction with a criminal like that aloose in it. I couldn't answer to my conscience if I did."

Bailey didn't look up from his reading so she wheeled around then and faced the children's mother, a young woman in slacks, whose face was as broad and innocent as a cabbage and was tied around with a green head-kerchief that had two points on the top like a rabbit's ears. She was sitting on the sofa, feeding the baby his apricots out of a jar. "The children have been to Florida before," the old lady said. "You all ought to take them somewhere else for a change so they would see different parts of the world and be broad. They never have been to east Tennessee.''

The children's mother didn't seem to hear her but the eight-year-old boy, John Wesley, a stocky child with glasses, said, "If you don't want to go to Florida, why dontcha stay at home?" He and the little girl, June Star, were reading the funny papers on the floor.

"She wouldn't stay at home to be queen for a day," June Star said without raising her yellow head.

"Yes and what would you do if this fellow, The Misfit, caught you?" the grandmother asked.

"I'd smack his face," John Wesley said.

"She wouldn't stay at home for a million bucks," June Star said. "Afraid she'd miss something. She has to go everywhere we go."

"All right, Miss," the grandmother said. "Just remember that the next time you want me to curl your hair."

June Star said her hair was naturally curly.

The next morning the grandmother was the first one in the car, ready to go. She had her big black valise that looked like the head of a hippopotamus in one corner, and underneath it she was hiding a basket with Pitty Sing, the cat, in it. She didn't intend for the cat to be left alone in the house for three days because he would miss her too much and she was afraid he might brush against one of the gas burners and accidentally asphyxiate himself. Her son, Bailey, didn't like to arrive at a motel with a cat.

She sat in the middle of the back seat with John Wesley and June Star on either side of her. Bailey and the children's mother and the baby sat in front and they left Atlanta at eight forty-five with the mileage on the car at 55890. The grandmother wrote this down because she thought it would be interesting to say how many miles they had been when they got back. It took them twenty minutes to reach the outskirts of the city.

The old lady settled herself comfortably, removing her white cotton gloves and putting them up with her purse on the shelf in front of the back window. The children's mother still had on slacks and still had her head tied up in a green kerchief, but the grandmother had on a navy blue straw sailor hat with a bunch of white violets on the brim and a navy blue dress with a small white dot in the print. Her collars and cuffs were white organdy trimmed with lace and at her neckline she had pinned a purple spray of cloth violets containing a sachet. In case of an accident, anyone seeing her dead on the highway would know at once that she was a lady.

She said she thought it was going to be a good day for driving, neither too hot nor too cold, and she cautioned Bailey that the speed limit was fifty-five miles an hour and that the patrolmen hid themselves behind billboards and small clumps of trees and sped out after you before you had a chance to slow down. She pointed out interesting details of the scenery: Stone Mountain; the blue granite that in some places came up to both sides of the highway; the brilliant red clay banks slightly streaked with purple; and the various crops that made rows of green lace-work on the ground. The trees were full of silver-white sunlight and the meanest of them sparkled. The children were reading comic magazines and their mother had gone back to sleep.

"Let's go through Georgia fast so we won't have to look at it much," John Wesley said.

"If I were a little boy," said the grandmother, "I wouldn't talk about my native state that way. Tennessee has the mountains and Georgia has the hills."

"Tennessee is just a hillbilly dumping ground," John Wesley said, "and Georgia is a lousy state too."

"You said it," June Star said.

"In my time," said the grandmother, folding her thin veined fingers, "children were more respectful of their native states and their parents and everything else. People did right then. Oh look at the cute little pickaninny!" she said and pointed to a Negro child standing in the door of a shack. "Wouldn't that make a picture, now?" she asked and they all turned and looked at the little Negro out of the back window. He waved.

"He didn't have any britches on," June Star said.

"He probably didn't have any," the grandmother explained. "Little niggers in the country don't have things like we do. If I could paint, I'd paint that picture," she said.

The children exchanged comic books.

The grandmother offered to hold the baby and the children's mother passed him over the front seat to her. She set him on her knee and bounced him and told him about the things they were passing. She rolled her eyes and screwed up her mouth and stuck her leathery thin face into his smooth bland one. Occasionally he gave her a faraway smile. They passed a large cotton field with five or six graves fenced in the middle of it, like a small island. "Look at the graveyard!" the grandmother said, pointing it out. "That was the old family burying ground. That belonged to the plantation."

"Where's the plantation?" John Wesley asked.

"Gone With the Wind," said the grandmother. "Ha. Ha."

When the children finished all the comic books they had brought, they opened the lunch and ate it. The grandmother ate a peanut butter sandwich and an olive and would not let the children throw the box and the paper napkins out the window. When there was nothing else to do they played a game by choosing a cloud and making the other two guess what shape it suggested. John Wesley took one the shape of a cow and June Star guessed a cow and John Wesley said, no, an automobile, and June Star said he didn't play fair, and they began to slap each other over the grandmother.

The grandmother said she would tell them a story if they would keep quiet. When she told a story, she rolled her eyes and waved her head and was very dramatic. She said once when she was a maiden lady she had been courted by a Mr. Edgar Atkins Teagarden from Jasper, Georgia. She said he was a very good-looking man and a gentleman and that he brought her a watermelon every Saturday afternoon with his initials cut in it, E. A. T. Well, one Saturday, she said, Mr. Teagarden brought the watermelon and there was nobody at home and he left it on the front porch and returned in his buggy to Jasper, but she never got the watermelon, she said, because a nigger boy ate it when he saw the initials, E. A. T.! This story tickled John Wesley's funny bone and he giggled and giggled but June Star didn't think it was any good. She said she wouldn't marry a man that just brought her a watermelon on Saturday. The grandmother said she would have done well to marry Mr. Teagarden because he was a gentleman and had bought Coca-Cola stock when it first came out and that he had died only a few years ago, a very wealthy man.

They stopped at The Tower for barbecued sandwiches. The Tower was a part stucco and part wood filling station and dance hall set in a clearing outside of Timothy. A fat man named Red Sammy Butts ran it and there were signs stuck here and there on the building and for miles up and down the highway saying, TRY RED SAMMY'S FAMOUS BARBE-CUE. NONE LIKE FAMOUS RED SAMMY'S! RED SAM! THE FAT BOY WITH THE HAPPY LAUGH! A VET-ERAN! RED SAMMY'S YOUR MAN!

Red Sammy was lying on the bare ground outside The Tower with his head under a truck while a gray monkey about a foot high, chained to a small chinaberry tree, chattered nearby. The monkey sprang back into the tree and got on the highest limb as soon as he saw the children jump out of the car and run toward him.

Inside, The Tower was a long dark room with a counter at one end and tables at the other and dancing space in the middle. They all sat down at a board table next to the nickelodeon and Red Sam's wife, a tall burnt-brown woman with hair and eyes lighter than her skin, came and took their order. The children's mother put a dime in the machine and played "The Tennessee Waltz," and the grandmother said that tune always made her want to dance. She asked Bailey if he would like to dance but he only glared at her. He didn't have a naturally sunny disposition like she did and trips made him nervous. The grandmother's brown eyes were very bright. She swayed her head from side to side and pretended she was dancing in her chair. June Star said play something she could tap to so the children's mother put in another dime and played a fast number and June Star stepped out onto the dance floor and did her tap routine.

"Ain't she cute?" Red Sam's wife said, leaning over the counter. "Would you like to come be my little girl?"

"No, I certainly wouldn't," June Star said. "I wouldn't live in a broken-down place like this for a million bucks!" and she ran back to the table.

"Ain't she cute?" the woman repeated, stretching her mouth politely.

"Aren't you ashamed?" hissed the grandmother.

Red Sam came in and told his wife to quit lounging on the counter and hurry up with those people's order. His khaki trousers reached just to his hip bones and his stomach hung over them like a sack of meal swaying under his shirt. He came over and sat down at a table nearby and let out a combination sigh and yodel. "You can't win," he said. "You can't win," and he wiped his sweating red face off with a gray handkerchief. "These days you don't know who to trust," he said. "Ain't that the truth?"

"People are certainly not nice like they used to be," said the grandmother.

"Two fellers come in here last week," Red Sammy said, "driving a Chrysler. It was a old beat-up car but it was a good one and these boys looked all right to me. Said they worked at the mill and you know I let them fellers charge the gas they bought? Now why did I do that?"

"Because you're a good man!" the grandmother said at once.

"Yes'm, I suppose so," Red Sam said as if he were struck with this answer.

His wife brought the orders, carrying the five plates all at once without a tray, two in each hand and one balanced on her arm. "It isn't a soul in this green world of God's that you can trust," she said. "And I don't count nobody out of that, not nobody," she repeated, looking at Red Sammy.

"Did you read about that criminal, The Misfit, that's escaped?" asked the grandmother.

"I wouldn't be a bit surprised if he didn't attact this place right here," said the woman. "If he hears about it being here, I wouldn't be none surprised to see him. If he hears it's two cent in the cash register, I wouldn't be a tall surprised if he . . ."

"That'll do," Red Sam said. "Go bring these people their Co'-Colas," and the woman went off to get the rest of the order.

"A good man is hard to find," Red Sammy said. "Everything is getting terrible. I remember the day you could go off and leave your screen door unlatched. Not no more."

He and the grandmother discussed better times. The old

lady said that in her opinion Europe was entirely to blame for the way things were now. She said the way Europe acted you would think we were made of money and Red Sam said it was no use talking about it, she was exactly right. The children ran outside into the white sunlight and looked at the monkey in the lacy chinaberry tree. He was busy catching fleas on himself and biting each one carefully between his teeth as if it were a delicacy.

They drove off again into the hot afternoon. The grandmother took cat naps and woke up every few minutes with her own snoring. Outside of Toombsboro she woke up and recalled an old plantation that she had visited in this neighborhood once when she was a young lady. She said the house had six white columns across the front and that there was an avenue of oaks leading up to it and two little wooden trellis arbors on either side in front where you sat down with your suitor after a stroll in the garden. She recalled exactly which road to turn off to get to it. She knew that Bailey would not be willing to lose any time looking at an old house, but the more she talked about it, the more she wanted to see it once again and find out if the little twin arbors were still standing. "There was a secret panel in this house," she said craftily, not telling the truth but wishing that she were, "and the story went that all the family silver was hidden in it when Sherman came through but it was never found . . ."

"Hey!" John Wesley said. "Let's go see it! We'll find it! We'll poke all the woodwork and find it! Who lives there? Where do you turn off at? Hey Pop, can't we turn off there?"

"We never have seen a house with a secret panel!" June Star shrieked. "Let's go to the house with the secret panel! Hey Pop, can't we go see the house with the secret panel!"

"It's not far from here, I know," the grandmother said. "It wouldn't take over twenty minutes."

Bailey was looking straight ahead. His jaw was as rigid as a horseshoe. "No," he said.

The children began to yell and scream that they wanted to see the house with the secret panel. John Wesley kicked the back of the front seat and June Star hung over her mother's shoulder and whined desperately into her ear that they never had any fun even on their vacation, that they could never do what THEY wanted to do. The baby began to scream and John Wesley kicked the back of the seat so hard that his father could feel the blows in his kidney.

"All right!" he shouted and drew the car to a stop at the side of the road. "Will you all shut up? Will you all just shut up for one second? If you don't shut up, we won't go anywhere."

"It would be very educational for them," the grandmother murmured.

"All right," Bailey said, "but get this: this is the only time we're going to stop for anything like this. This is the one and only time."

"The dirt road that you have to turn down is about a mile back," the grandmother directed. "I marked it when we passed."

"A dirt road," Bailey groaned.

After they had turned around and were headed toward the dirt road, the grandmother recalled other points about the house, the beautiful glass over the front doorway and the candle-lamp in the hall. John Wesley said that the secret panel was probably in the fireplace.

"You can't go inside this house," Bailey said. "You don't know who lives there."

"While you all talk to the people in front, I'll run around behind and get in a window," John Wesley suggested.

"We'll all stay in the car," his mother said.

They turned onto the dirt road and the car raced roughly along in a swirl of pink dust. The grandmother recalled the times when there were no paved roads and thirty miles was a day's journey. The dirt road was hilly and there were sudden washes in it and sharp curves on dangerous embankments. All at once they would be on a hill, looking down over the blue tops of trees for miles around, then the next minute, they would be in a red depression with the dust-coated trees looking down on them.

"This place had better turn up in a minute," Bailey said, "or I'm going to turn around."

The road looked as if no one had traveled on it in months.

"It's not much farther," the grandmother said and just as she said it, a horrible thought came to her. The thought was so embarrassing that she turned red in the face and her eyes dilated and her feet jumped up, upsetting her valise in the corner. The instant the valise moved, the newspaper top she had over the basket under it rose with a snarl and Pitty Sing, the cat, sprang onto Bailey's shoulder.

The children were thrown to the floor and their mother, clutching the baby, was thrown out the door onto the ground; the old lady was thrown into the front seat. The car turned over once and landed right-side-up in a gulch off the side of the road. Bailey remained in the driver's seat with the cat—gray-striped with a broad white face and an orange nose—clinging to his neck like a caterpillar.

As soon as the children saw they could move their arms and legs, they scrambled out of the car, shouting, "We've had an ACCIDENT!" The grandmother was curled up under the dashboard, hoping she was injured so that Bailey's wrath would not come down on her all at once. The horrible thought she had had before the accident was that the house she had remembered so vividly was not in Georgia but in Tennessee.

Bailey removed the cat from his neck with both hands and flung it out the window against the side of a pine tree. Then he got out of the car and started looking for the children's mother. She was sitting against the side of the red gutted ditch, holding the screaming baby, but she only had a cut down her face and a broken shoulder. "We've had an ACCI-DENT!" the children screamed in a frenzy of delight.

"But nobody's killed," June Star said with disappointment as the grandmother limped out of the car, her hat still pinned to her head but the broken front brim standing up at a jaunty angle and the violet spray hanging off the side. They all sat down in the ditch, except the children, to recover from the shock. They were all shaking.

"Maybe a car will come along," said the children's mother hoarsely.

"I believe I have injured an organ," said the grandmother, pressing her side, but no one answered her. Bailey's teeth were clattering. He had on a yellow sport shirt with bright blue parrots designed in it and his face was as yellow as the shirt. The grandmother decided that she would not mention that the house was in Tennessee.

The road was about ten feet above and they could see only the tops of the trees on the other side of it. Behind the ditch they were sitting in there were more woods, tall and dark and deep. In a few minutes they saw a car some distance away on top of a hill, coming slowly as if the occupants were watching them. The grandmother stood up and waved both arms dramatically to attract their attention. The car continued to come on slowly, disappeared around a bend and appeared again, moving even slower, on top of the hill they had gone over. It was a big black battered hearse-like automobile. There were three men in it.

It came to a stop just over them and for some minutes, the driver looked down with a steady expressionless gaze to where they were sitting, and didn't speak. Then he turned his head and muttered something to the other two and they got out. One was a fat boy in black trousers and a red sweat shirt with a silver stallion embossed on the front of it. He moved around on the right side of them and stood staring, his mouth partly open in a kind of loose grin. The other had on khaki pants and a blue striped coat and a gray hat pulled down very low, hiding most of his face. He came around slowly on the left side. Neither spoke.

The driver got out of the car and stood by the side of it, looking down at them. He was an older man than the other two. His hair was just beginning to gray and he wore silver-rimmed spectacles that gave him a scholarly look. He had a long creased face and didn't have on any shirt or undershirt. He had on blue jeans that were too tight for him and was holding a black hat and a gun. The two boys also had guns.

"We've had an ACCIDENT!" the children screamed.

The grandmother had the peculiar feeling that the bespectacled man was someone she knew. His face was as familiar to her as if she had known him all her life but she could not recall who he was. He moved away from the car and began to come down the embankment, placing his feet carefully so that he wouldn't slip. He had on tan and white shoes and no socks, and his ankles were red and thin. "Good afternoon," he said. "I see you all had you a little spill."

"We turned over twice!" said the grandmother.

"Oncet," he corrected. "We seen it happen. Try their car and see will it run, Hiram," he said quietly to the boy with the gray hat.

"What you got that gun for?" John Wesley asked. "Whatcha gonna do with that gun?"

"Lady," the man said to the children's mother, "would you mind calling them children to sit down by you? Children make me nervous. I want all you all to sit down right together there where you're at."

"What are you telling US what to do for?" June Star asked.

Behind them the line of woods gaped like a dark open mouth. "Come here," said their mother.

"Look here now," Bailey began suddenly, "we're in a predicament! We're in . . ."

The grandmother shrieked. She scrambled to her feet and stood staring. "You're The Misfit!" she said. "I recognized you at once!"

"Yes'm," the man said, smiling slightly as if he were pleased in spite of himself to be known, "but it would have been better for all of you, lady, if you hadn't of reckernized me."

Bailey turned his head sharply and said something to his mother that shocked even the children. The old lady began to cry and The Misfit reddened.

"Lady," he said, "don't you get upset. Sometimes a man says things he don't mean. I don't reckon he meant to talk to you thataway."

"You wouldn't shoot a lady, would you?" the grand-mother said and removed a clean handkerchief from her cuff and began to slap at her eyes with it.

The Misfit pointed the toe of his shoe into the ground and made a little hole and then covered it up again. "I would hate to have to," he said.

"Listen," the grandmother almost screamed, "I know you're a good man. You don't look a bit like you have common blood. I know you must come from nice people!"

"Yes mam," he said, "finest people in the world." When he smiled he showed a row of strong white teeth. "God never made a finer woman than my mother and my daddy's heart was pure gold," he said. The boy with the red sweatshirt had come around behind them and was standing with his gun at his hip. The Misfit squatted down on the ground. "Watch them children, Bobby Lee," he said. "You know they make me nervous." He looked at the six of them huddled together in front of him and he seemed to be embarrassed as if he couldn't think of anything to say. "Ain't a cloud in the sky," he remarked, looking up at it. "Don't see no sun but don't see no cloud neither."

"Yes, it's a beautiful day," said the grandmother. "Listen," she said, "you shouldn't call yourself The Misfit because I know you're a good man at heart. I can just look at you and tell."

"Hush!" Bailey yelled. "Hush! Everybody shut up and let me handle this!" He was squatting in the position of a runner about to sprint forward but he didn't move.

"I pre-chate that, lady," The Misfit said and drew a little circle in the ground with the butt of his gun.

"It'll take a half a hour to fix this here car," Hiram called, looking over the raised hood of it.

"Well, first you and Bobby Lee get him and that little boy to step over yonder with you," The Misfit said, pointing to Bailey and John Wesley. "The boys want to ast you something," he said to Bailey. "Would you mind stepping back in them woods there with them?"

"Listen," Bailey began, "we're in a terrible predicament! Nobody realizes what this is," and his voice cracked. His eyes were as blue and intense as the parrots in his shirt and he remained perfectly still.

The grandmother reached up to adjust her hat brim as if she were going to the woods with him but it came off in her hand. She stood staring at it and after a second she let it fall on the ground. Hiram pulled Bailey up by the arm as if he were assisting an old man. John Wesley caught hold of his father's hand and Bobby Lee followed. They went off toward the woods and just as they reached the dark edge, Bailey turned and supporting himself against a gray naked pine trunk, he shouted, "I'll be back in a minute, Mamma, wait on me!"

"Come back this instant!" his mother shrilled but they all disappeared into the woods.

"Bailey Boy!" the grandmother called in a tragic voice but she found she was looking at The Misfit squatting on the ground in front of her. "I just know you're a good man," she said desperately. "You're not a bit common!"

"Nome, I ain't a good man," The Misfit said after a second as if he had considered her statement carefully, "but I ain't the worst in the world neither. My daddy said I was a different breed of dog from my brothers and sisters. 'You know,' Daddy said, 'it's some that can live their whole life out without asking about it and it's others has to know why it is, and this boy is one of the latters. He's going to be into everything!'" He put on his black hat and looked up suddenly and then away deep into the woods as if he were embarrassed again. "I'm sorry I don't have on a shirt before you ladies," he said, hunching his shoulders slightly. "We buried our clothes that we had on when we escaped and we're just making do until we can get better. We borrowed these from some folks we met," he explained.

"That's perfectly all right," the grandmother said. "Maybe Bailey has an extra shirt in his suitcase."

"I'll look and see terrectly," The Misfit said.

"Where are they taking him?" the children's mother screamed.

"Daddy was a card himself," The Misfit said. "You couldn't put anything over on him. He never got in trouble with the Authorities though. Just had the knack of handling them."

"You could be honest too if you'd only try," said the grandmother. "Think how wonderful it would be to settle down and live a comfortable life and not have to think about somebody chasing you all the time."

The Misfit kept scratching in the ground with the butt of his gun as if he were thinking about it. "Yes'm, somebody is always after you," he murmured.

The grandmother noticed how thin his shoulder blades were just behind his hat because she was standing up looking down on him. "Do you ever pray?" she asked.

He shook his head. All she saw was the black hat wiggle between his shoulder blades. "Nome," he said.

There was a pistol shot from the woods, followed closely by another. Then silence. The old lady's head jerked around. She could hear the wind move through the tree tops like a long satisfied insuck of breath. "Bailey Boy!" she called.

"I was a gospel singer for a while," The Misfit said. "I been most everything. Been in the arm service, both land and sea, at home and abroad, been twict married, been an undertaker, been with the railroads, plowed Mother Earth, been in a tornado, seen a man burnt alive oncet," and looked up at the children's mother and the little girl who were sitting close together, their faces white and their eyes glassy; "I even seen a woman flogged," he said.

"Pray, pray," the grandmother began, "pray, pray . . ."

"I never was a bad boy that I remember of," The Misfit said in an almost dreamy voice, "but somewheres along the line I done something wrong and got sent to the penitentiary. I was buried alive," and he looked up and held her attention to him by a steady stare.

"That's when you should have started to pray," she said. "What did you do to get sent to the penitentiary that first time?"

"Turn to the right, it was a wall," The Misfit said, looking up again at the cloudless sky. "Turn to the left, it was a wall. Look up it was a ceiling, look down it was a floor. I forget what I done, lady. I set there and set there, trying to remember what it was I done and I ain't recalled it to this day. Oncet in a while, I would think it was coming to me, but it never come."

"Maybe they put you in by mistake," the old lady said vaguely.

"Nome," he said. "It wasn't no mistake. They had the papers on me."

"You must have stolen something," she said.

The Misfit sneered slightly. "Nobody had nothing I wanted," he said. "It was a head-doctor at the penitentiary said what I had done was kill my daddy but I known that for a lie. My daddy died in nineteen ought nineteen of the epidemic flu and I never had a thing to do with it. He was buried in the Mount

Hopewell Baptist churchyard and you can go there and see for yourself.''

"If you would pray," the old lady said, "Jesus would help you."

"That's right," The Misfit said.

"Well then, why don't you pray?" she asked trembling with delight suddenly.

"I don't want no hep," he said. "I'm doing all right by myself."

Bobby Lee and Hiram came ambling back from the woods. Bobby Lee was dragging a yellow shirt with bright blue parrots in it.

"Throw me that shirt, Bobby Lee," The Misfit said. The shirt came flying at him and landed on his shoulder and he put it on. The grandmother couldn't name what the shirt reminded her of. "No, lady," The Misfit said while he was buttoning it up, "I found out the crime don't matter. You can do one thing or you can do another, kill a man or take a tire off his car, because sooner or later you're going to forget what it was you done and just be punished for it."

The children's mother had begun to make heaving noises as if she couldn't get her breath. "Lady," he asked, "would you and that little girl like to step off yonder with Bobby Lee and Hiram and join your husband?"

"Yes, thank you," the mother said faintly. Her left arm dangled helplessly and she was holding the baby, who had gone to sleep, in the other. "Hep that lady up, Hiram," The Misfit said as she struggled to climb out of the ditch, "and Bobby Lee, you hold onto that little girl's hand."

"I don't want to hold hands with him," June Star said. "He reminds me of a pig."

The fat boy blushed and laughed and caught her by the arm and pulled her off into the woods after Hiram and her mother.

Alone with The Misfit, the grandmother found that she had lost her voice. There was not a cloud in the sky nor any sun. There was nothing around her but woods. She wanted to tell him that he must pray. She opened and closed her mouth several times before anything came out. Finally she found herself saying, "Jesus, Jesus," meaning, Jesus will help you, but the way she was saying it, it sounded as if she might be cursing.

"Yes'm," The Misfit said as if he agreed. "Jesus thrown everything off balance. It was the same case with Him as with me except He hadn't committed any crime and they could prove I had committed one because they had the papers on me. Of course," he said, "they never shown me my papers. That's why I sign myself now. I said long ago, you get you a signature and sign everything you do and keep a copy of it. Then you'll know what you done and you can hold up the crime to the punishment and see do they match and in the end you'll have something to prove you ain't been treated right. I call myself The Misfit," he said, "because I can't make what all I done wrong fit what all I gone through in punishment."

There was a piercing scream from the woods, followed closely by a pistol report. "Does it seem right to you, lady, that one is punished a heap and another ain't punished at all?"

"Jesus!" the old lady cried. "You've got good blood! I know you wouldn't shoot a lady! I know you come from nice people! Pray! Jesus, you ought not to shoot a lady. I'll give you all the money I've got!"

"Lady," The Misfit said, looking beyond her far into the woods, "there never was a body that give the undertaker a tip."

There were two more pistol reports and the grandmother raised her head like a parched old turkey hen crying for water and called, "Bailey Boy, Bailey Boy!" as if her heart would break.

"Jesus was the only One that ever raised the dead." The Misfit continued, "and He shouldn't have done it. He thrown everything off balance. If He did what He said, then it's nothing for you to do but throw away everything and follow Him, and if He didn't, then it's nothing for you to do but enjoy the few minutes you got left the best way you can—by killing somebody or burning down his house or doing some other meanness to him. No pleasure but meanness," he said and his voice had become almost a snarl.

"Maybe He didn't raise the dead," the old lady mumbled,

not knowing what she was saying and feeling so dizzy that she sank down in the ditch with her legs twisted under her.

"I wasn't there so I can't say He didn't," The Misfit said. "I wisht I had of been there," he said, hitting the ground with his fist. "It ain't right I wasn't there because if I had of been there I would of known. Listen lady," he said in a high voice, "if I had of been there I would of known and I wouldn't be like I am now." His voice seemed about to crack and the grandmother's head cleared for an instant. She saw the man's face twisted close to her own as if he were going to cry and she murmured, "Why you're one of my babies. You're one of my own children!" She reached out and touched him on the shoulder. The Misfit sprang back as if a snake had bitten him and shot her three times through the chest. Then he put his gun down on the ground and took off his glasses and began to clean them.

Hiram and Bobby Lee returned from the woods and stood over the ditch, looking down at the grandmother who half sat and half lay in a puddle of blood with her legs crossed under her like a child's and her face smiling up at the cloudless sky.

Without his glasses, The Misfit's eyes were red-rimmed and pale and defenseless-looking. "Take her off and throw her where you thrown the others," he said, picking up the cat that was rubbing itself against his leg.

"She was a talker, wasn't she?" Bobby Lee said, sliding down the ditch with a yodel.

"She would of been a good woman," The Misfit said, "if it had been somebody there to shoot her every minute of her life."

"Some fun!" Bobby Lee said.

"Shut up, Bobby Lee," The Misfit said. "It's no real pleasure in life."

(1953)

James Purdy

———————◆———————

James Purdy was born in 1923, in Ohio. He studied at the University of Chicago and at the University of Madrid; he has worked as an editor and as an interpreter. Since 1956, when he published Don't Call Me By My Right Name and Other Stories, *he has been a freelance writer. His books include novels and collections of stories, plays, and poems.* Malcolm *(1969), his first novel, was adapted for the stage in 1965, by Edward Albee.* The Nephew *(1960), a novel of smalltown life, received excellent reviews;* Eustace Chisholm and the Works *(1968), a novel of sexual violence, attracted a good deal of attention.*

Purdy's universe is generally a bizarre one, filled with aggressive sexuality, a large and insistent vein of male homosexuality, and a variety of neuroses and irrationalities, some private, some public. His irony, which is sharp and focused, is frequently connected to the larger theme of alienation from ordinary American life. His prose is exemplary, idiosyncratic, and exceedingly carefully controlled. What often seems to be a kind of poetic indulgence usually turns out, on closer examination, to be a deliberately calculated effect. Purdy is a superb craftsman.

YOU MAY SAFELY GAZE

"Do we always have to begin on Milo at these Wednesday lunches," Philip said to Guy. Carrying their trays, they had already picked out their table in the cafeteria, and Philip, at least, was about to sit down.

"Do I *always* begin on Milo?" Guy wondered, surprised.

"You're the one who knows him, remember," Philip said.

"Of course, Milo is one of the serious problems in our office, and it's only a little natural, I suppose, to mention problems even at one of our Wednesday lunches."

"Oh, forget it," Philip said. Seated, he watched half-amused as Guy still stood over the table with his tray raised like a busboy who will soon now move away with it to the back room.

"I don't dislike Milo," Guy began. "It's not that at all."

Philip began to say something but then hesitated, and looked up at the cafeteria clock that showed ten minutes past twelve. He knew, somehow, that it was going to be Milo all over again for lunch.

"It's his attitude not just toward his work, but life," Guy said, and this time he sat down.

"His life," Philip said, taking swift bites of his chicken à la king.

Guy nodded. "You see now he spares himself the real work in the office due to this physical culture philosophy. He won't even let himself get mad anymore or argue with me because that interferes with the development of his muscles and his mental tranquillity, which is so important for muscular development. His whole life now he says is to be strong and calm."

"A muscle ascetic," Philip laughed without amusement.

"But working with him is not so funny," Guy said, and Philip was taken aback to see his friend go suddenly very pale. Guy had not even bothered to take his dishes off his tray but allowed everything to sit there in front of him as though the lunch were an offering he had no intention of tasting.

"Milo hardly seems anybody you and I could know, if you ask me," Guy pronounced, as though the final decision had at last been made.

"You forget one of us *doesn't*," Philip emphasized again, and he waved his fork as though they had finally finished now with Milo, and could go on to the real Wednesday lunch.

But Guy began again, as though the talk for the lunch had been arranged after all, despite Philip's forgetfulness, around Milo.

"I don't think he is even studying law anymore at night, as he was supposed to do."

"Don't tell me that," Philip said, involuntarily affecting concern and half-resigning himself now to the possibility of a completely wasted hour.

"Oh, of course," Guy softened his statement, "I guess he goes to the law library every night and reads a little. Every waking hour is, after all, not for his muscles, but every real thought, you can bet your bottom dollar, *is*."

"I see," Philip said, beginning on his pineapple snow.

"It's the only thing on his mind, I tell you," Guy began again.

"It's interesting if that's the only thing on his mind, then," Philip replied. "I mean," he continued, when he saw the black look he got from Guy, "to know somebody who is obsessed . . ."

"What do you mean by that?" Guy wondered critically, as though only he could tell what it was that Milo might be.

"You said he wanted to devote himself to just this one thing," Philip wearily tried to define what he had meant.

"I tried to talk to Milo once about it," Guy said, now deadly serious, and as though, with all preliminaries past, the real part of his speech had begun. Philip noticed that his friend had still not even picked up his knife or fork, and his food must be getting stone cold by now. " 'Why do you want to look any stronger,' I said to Milo. He just stared at me, and I said, 'Have you ever taken a good look in the mirror the way you are now,' and he just smiled his sour smile again at

me. 'Have you ever looked, Milo?' I said, and even I had to
laugh when I repeated my own question, and he kind of
laughed then too . . . Well, for God's sake, he knows after
all that nobody but a few freaks are going to look like he
looks, or will look, if he keeps this up. You see he works on
a new part of his body every month. One month he will be
working on his pectorals, the next his calf muscles, then he
will go in for a period on his latissimus dorsi.''

Philip stopped chewing a moment as though seeing these
different muscle groups slowly developing there before him.
Finally, he managed to say, ''Well at least he's interested in
something, which is more than . . .''

''Yes, he's interested in *it*, of course,'' Guy interrupted,
''—what he calls being the sculptor of his own body, and you
can find him almost any noon in the gym straining away
while the other men in our office do as they please with their
lunch hour.''

''You mean they eat their lunch then.'' Philip tried humor.

''That's right,'' Guy hurried on. ''But he and this Austrian
friend of his who also works in my office, they go over to
this gym run by a cripple named Vic somebody, and strain
their guts out, lifting barbells and throwing their arms up and
around on benches, with dumbbells in their fists, and come
back an hour later to their work looking as though they had
been in a rock mixer. They actually stink of gym, and several
of the stenographers have complained saying they always
know when it's exercise day all right. But nothing stops those
boys, and they just take all the gaff with as much good humor
as two such egomaniacs can have.''

''Why egomaniacs, for God's sake,'' Philip wondered,
putting his fork down with a bang.

''Well, Philip,'' Guy pleaded now. ''To think of their own
bodies like that. These are not young boys, you know. They
must be twenty-five or so, along in there, and you would
think they would begin to think of other people, other people's bodies, at least.'' Guy laughed as though to correct his
own severity before Philip. ''But no,'' he went on. ''They
have to be Adonises.''

''And their work suffers?'' Philip wondered vaguely, as

though, if the topic had to be continued, they might now examine it from this aspect.

"The kind of work young men like them do—it don't matter, you know, if you're good or not, nobody knows if you're really good. They do their work and get it out on time, and you know their big boss is still that old gal of seventy who is partial to young men. She sometimes goes right up to Milo, who will be sitting at his desk relaxed as a jellyfish, doing nothing, and she says, 'Roll up your sleeves, why don't you, and take off your necktie on a warm day like this,' and it will be thirty degrees outside and cool even in the office. And Milo will smile like a four-year-old at her because he loves admiration more than anything in the world, and he rolls up his sleeves and then all this bulge of muscle comes out, and the old girl looks like she'd seen glory, she's that gone on having a thug like that around."

"But you sound positively bilious over it," Philip laughed.

"Philip, look," Guy said with his heavy masculine patience, "doesn't it sound wrong to you, now seriously?"

"What in hell do you mean by wrong, though?"

"Don't be that way. You know goddamn well what I mean."

"Well, then, no, I can't say it is. Milo or whatever his name."

"You know it's Milo," Guy said positively disgusted.

"Well, he is, I suppose, more typical than you might think from the time, say, when you were young. Maybe there weren't such fellows around then."

"Oh there were, of course."

"Well, now there are more, and Milo is no exception."

"But he looks at himself all the time, and he has got himself tattooed recently and there in front of the one mirror in the office, it's not the girls who stand there, no, it's Milo and this Austrian boy. They're always washing their hands or combing their hair, or just looking at themselves right out, not sneaky-like the way most men do, but like some goddamn chorus girls. And oh, I forgot, this Austrian fellow got tattooed too because Milo kept after him, and then he was sorry. It seems the Austrian's physical culture instructor gave him hell and said he had spoiled the appearance of his deltoids by having the tattoo work done.''

"Don't tell me," Philip said.

Guy stared as he heard Philip's laugh, but then continued: "They talked about the tattoo all morning, in front of all the stenogs, and whether this Austrian had spoiled the appearance of his deltoid muscles or not."

"Well, it *is* funny, of course, but I couldn't get worked up about it the way you are."

"They're a symbol of the new America and I don't like it."

"You're terribly worked up."

"Men on their way to being thirty, what used to be considered middle age, developing their bodies and special muscles and talking about their parts in front of women."

"But they're married men, aren't they?"

"Oh sure," Guy dismissed this. "Married and with kids."

"What more do you want then. Some men are nuts about their bowling scores and talk about that all the time in front of everybody."

"I see you approve of them."

"I didn't say that. But I think you're overreacting, to use the phrase . . .''

"You don't have to work with them," Guy went on. "You don't have to watch them in front of the one and only office mirror."

"Look, I've known a lot of women who griped me because they were always preening themselves, goddamn narcissists too. I don't care for narcissists of either sex."

"Talk about Narciss-uses," said Guy. "The worst was last summer when I went with Mae to the beach, and there *they* were, both of them, right in front of us on the sand."

Philip stiffened slightly at the prospect of more.

"Milo and the Austrian," Guy shook his head. "And as it was Saturday afternoon there didn't seem to be a damn place free on the beach and Mae wanted to be right up where these Adonises or Narciss-uses, or whatever you call them, were. I said, 'We don't want to camp here, Mae,' and she got suddenly furious. I couldn't tell her how those birds affected me, and they hardly even spoke to me either, come to think about it. Milo spit something out the side of his mouth when he saw me, as though to say *that for you*."

"That was goddamn awful for you," Philip nodded.

"Wait till you hear what happened, for crying out loud. I shouldn't tell this during my lunch hour because it still riles me."

"Don't get riled then. Forget them."

"I have to tell you," Guy said. "I've never told anybody before, and you're the only man I know will listen to a thing like this. . . . You know," he went on then, as though this point were now understood at last between them, "Mae started staring at them right away. 'Who on earth are they?' she said, and I couldn't tell whether she was outraged or pleased, maybe she was a bit of both because she just fixed her gaze on them like paralyzed. 'Aren't you going to put on your sun tan lotion and your glasses?' I said to her, and she turned on me as though I had hit her. 'Why don't you let a woman relax when I never get out of the house but twice in one year,' she told me. I just lay back then on the sand and tried to forget they were there and that she was there and that even I was there."

Philip began to light up his cigarette, and Guy said, "Are you all done eating already?" and he looked at his own plate of veal cutlet and peas which was nearly untouched. "My God, you are a fast eater. Why, do you realize how fast you eat," he told Philip, and Philip said he guessed he half-realized it. He said at night he ate slower.

"In the bosom of your family," Guy laughed.

Philip looked at the cafeteria clock and stirred unceremoniously.

"But I wanted to finish telling you about these boys."

"Is there *more?*" Philip pretended surprise.

"Couldn't you tell the way I told it there was," Guy said, an indeterminate emotion in his voice.

"I hope nothing happened to Mae," Philip offered weakly.

"Nothing ever happens to Mae," Guy dismissed this impatiently. "No, it was them, of course. Milo and the Austrian began putting on a real show, you know, for everybody, and as it was Saturday afternoon, as I said, nearly everybody from every office in the world was there, and they were all watching Milo and the Austrian. So, first they just did the standard routlne, warm-ups, you know, etc., but from the first every eye on the beach was on them, they seemed to have the old presence, even the life guards were staring at them as though nobody would ever dare drown while they were carrying on, so first of all then they did handstands and though they did them good, not good enough for that many people to be watching. After all somebody is always doing handstands on the beach, you know. I think it was their hair attracted people, they have very odd hair, they look like brothers that way. Their hair is way too thick, and of course too long for men of our generation. . . .''

"Well, how old do you think I am?" Philip laughed.

"All right, of *my* generation, then," Guy corrected with surliness. He went on, however, immediately: "I think the reason everybody watched was their hair, which is a peculiar kind of chestnut color, natural and all that, but maybe due to the sun and all their exercising had taken on a funny shade, and then their muscles were so enormous in that light, bulging and shining with oil and matching somehow their hair that I think that was really what kept people looking and not what they did. They didn't look quite real, even though in a way they are the style.

"I kept staring, and Mae said, 'I thought you wasn't going to watch,' and I could see she was completely held captive by their performance as was, I guess, everybody by then on the goddamn beach.

" 'I can't help looking at freaks,' I told Mae, and she gave me one of her snorts and just kept looking kind of bitter and satisfied at seeing something like that. She's a great woman for sights like that, she goes to all the stock shows, and almost every nice Sunday she takes the kids to the zoo. . . .''

"Well, what finally did come off?" Philip said, pushing back his chair.

"The thing that happened, nobody in his right mind would ever believe, and probably lots of men and boys who saw it happen never went home and told their families."

"It should have been carried in the papers then," Philip said coolly and he drank all of his as yet untouched glass of water.

"I don't know what word I would use to describe it," Guy said. "Mae has never mentioned it to this day, though she said a little about it on the streetcar on the way home that afternoon, but just a little, like she would have referred to a woman having fainted and been rushed to the hospital, something on that order."

"Well, for Pete's sake now, what did happen?" Philip's ill humor broke forth for a moment, and he bent his head away from Guy's look.

"As I said," Guy continued quietly, "they did all those more fancy exercises then after their warm-ups, like leaping on one another's necks, jumping hard on each other's abdomens to show what iron men they were, and some rough stuff but which they made look fancy, like they threw one another to the sand as though it was a cross between a wrestling match and an apache dance, and then they began to do some things looked like they were out of the ballet, with lots of things like jumping in air and splits, you know. You know what kind of trunks that kind of Narciss-uses wear, well these were tighter than usual, the kind to make a bullfighter's pants look baggy and oversize, and as though they had planned it, while doing one of their big movements, their trunks both split clear in two, at the same time, with a sound, I swear, you could have heard all over that beach.

"Instead of feeling at least some kind of self-consciousness, if not shame, they both busted out laughing and hugged one another as though they'd made a touchdown, and they might as well both been naked by now, they just stood there and looked down at themselves from time to time like they were alone in the shower, and laughed and laughed, and an old woman next to them just laughed and laughed too, and all Mae did was look once and then away with a funny half-smile on her mouth, she didn't show any more concern over it than the next one. Here was a whole beach of mostly women, just laughing their heads off because two men no longer young, were, well, exposing themselves in front of everybody, for that's all it was."

Philip stared at his empty water glass.

"I started to say something to Mae, and she nearly cut my head off, saying something like *why don't you mind your own goddamn business* in a tone unusually mean even for her. *Don't look damn you if you don't like it* was what my own wife said to me.''

Suddenly Philip had relaxed in his chair as though the water he had drunk had contained a narcotic. He made no effort now to show his eagerness to leave, to hurry, or to comment on what was being said, and he sat there staring in the direction of, but not at, Guy.

"But the worst part came then,'' Guy said, and then looking critically and uneasily at Philip, he turned round to look at the cafeteria clock, but it showed only five minutes to one, and their lunch hour was not precisely over.

"This old woman,'' he continued, swallowing hard, "who had been sitting there next to them got out a sewing kit she had, and do you know what?''

"I suppose she sewed them shut,'' Philip said sleepily and still staring at nothing.

"That's exactly correct,'' Guy said, a kind of irritated disappointment in his voice. "This old woman who looked at least eighty went right up to them the way they were and she must have been a real seamstress, and before the whole crowd with them two grown men laughing their heads off she sewed up their tights like some old witch in a story, and Mae sat there as cool as if we was playing bridge in the church basement, and never said boo, and when I began to really let off steam, she said *Will you keep your big old ugly mouth shut or am I going to have to hit you over the mouth with my beach clogs*. That's how they had affected my own wife.''

"So,'' Guy said, after a pause in which Philip contributed nothing, "this country has certainly changed since I grew up in it. I said that to Mae and that was the final thing I had to say on the subject, and those two grown men went right on lying there on the sand, every so often slapping one another on their muscles, and combing their hair with oil, and laughing all the time, though I think even they did have sense enough not to get up and split their trunks again or even they must have known they would have been arrested by the beach patrol.''

"Sure,'' Philip said vacantly.

"So that's the story of Milo and the Austrian,'' Guy said.

"It's typical," Philip said, like a somnambulist.

"Are you sore at me or something," Guy said, picking up his and Philip's checks.

"Let me pay my own, for Christ's sake," Philip said.

"Listen, you *are* sore at me, I believe," Guy said.

"I have a rotten headache is all," Philip replied, and he picked up his own check.

"I hope I didn't bring it on by talking my head off."

"No," Philip replied. "I had it since morning."

(1956)

Grace Paley

Grace Paley was born in New York City in 1922 and educated at Hunter College. She has taught at Syracuse and Columbia Universities, and more recently at Sarah Lawrence College. Writing only short stories, she has written slowly, publishing her first book, The Little Disturbances of Man: Stories of Men and Women at Love, *in 1959; her second collection,* Enormous Changes at the Last Minute, *did not appear until 1975. And her third volume of stories,* Later the Same Day, *was published a decade later, in 1985. All three are relatively slim volumes. Not only has she won a great many awards, and a singularly high and almost universal critical respect, but she has been and continues to be a profound influence on younger writers of both sexes, but particularly younger women writers. Her critical writings, and her writings (and lectures) on feminist topics, have been important and are likely to prove enduring contributions.*

An urban writer, she is also—though not usually discussed in such terms—very much an urban Jewish writer. The closest counterpart to her work, in many ways, is the work of a writer well known in the United States but not possible to include in this volume, Isaac Bashevis Singer (born in Poland and working, still, in Yiddish rather than in English). If anything, Paley is a tougher and harder writer than Singer, though the pathos and the perception of her work match and

*in many ways parallel the pathos and perception of his.
Scrupulously honest, with a superb ear and a compressed,
sometimes brilliantly terse prose style, Paley is one of the
major voices in American short fiction.*

THE PALE PINK ROAST

Pale green greeted him, grubby buds for nut trees. Packed
with lunch, Peter strode into the park. He kicked aside the
disappointed acorns and endowed a grand admiring grin to
two young girls.

Anna saw him straddling the daffodils, a rosy man in about
the third flush of youth. He got into Judy's eye too. Acquisi-
tive and quick, she screamed, "There's Daddy!"

Well, that's who he was, mouth open, addled by visions.
He was unsettled by a collusion of charm, a conspiracy of
curly hairdos and shiny faces. A year ago, in plain view,
Anna had begun to decline into withering years, just as he
swelled to the maximum of manhood, spitting pipe smoke,
patched with tweed, an advertisement of a lover who startled
men and detained the ladies.

Now Judy leaped over the back of a bench and lunged into
his arms. "Oh, Peter dear," she whispered, "I didn't even
know you were going to meet us."

"God, you're getting big, kiddo. Where's your teeth?" he
asked. He hugged her tightly, a fifty-pound sack of his very
own. "Say, Judy, I'm glad you still have a pussy-cat's sniffy
nose and a pussycat's soft white fur."

"I do not," she giggled.

"Oh yes," he said. He dropped her to her springy hind
legs but held onto one smooth front paw. "But you'd better
keep your claws in or I'll drop you right into the Hudson
River."

"Aw, Peter," said Judy, "quit it."

Peter changed the subject and turned to Anna. "You don't look half bad, you know."

"Thank you," she replied politely, "neither do you."

"Look at me, I'm a real outdoorski these days."

She allowed thirty seconds of silence, into which he turned, singing like a summer bird, "We danced around the May-pole, the Maypole, the Maypole . . .

"Well, when'd you get in?" he asked.

"About a week ago."

"You never called."

"Yes, I did, Peter. I called you at least twenty-seven times. You're never home. Petey must be in love somewhere, I said to myself."

"What is this thing," he sang in tune, "called love?"

"Peter, I want you to do me a favor," she started again. "Peter, could you take Judy for the weekend? We've just moved to this new place and I have a lot of work to do. I just don't want her in my hair. Peter?"

"Ah, that's why you called."

"Oh, for godsakes," Anna said. "I really called to ask you to become my lover. That's the real reason."

"O.K., O.K. Don't be bitter, Anna." He stretched forth a benedicting arm. "Come in peace, go in peace. Of course I'll take her. I like her. She's my kid."

"Bitter?" she asked.

Peter sighed. He turned the palms of his hand up as though to guess at rain. Anna knew him, theme and choreography. The sunshiny spring afternoon seeped through his fingers. He looked up at the witnessing heavens to keep what he could. He dropped his arms and let the rest go.

"O.K.," he said. "Let's go. I'd like to see your place. I'm full of ideas. You should see my living room, Anna. I might even go into interior decorating if things don't pick up. Come on. I'll get the ladder out of the basement. I could move a couple of trunks. I'm crazy about heavy work. You get out of life what you put into it. Right? Let's ditch the kid. I'm not your enemy."

"Who is?" she asked.

"Off my back, Anna. I mean it. I'll get someone to keep an eye on Judy. Just shut up." He searched for a familiar face among the Sunday strollers. "Hey, you," he finally called to an old pal on whom two chicks were leaning. "Hey, you glass-eyed louse, c'mere."

"Not just any of your idiot friends," whispered Anna, enraged.

All three soft-shoed it over to Peter. They passed out happy hellos, also a bag of dried apricots. Peter spoke to one of the girls. He patted her little-boy haircut. "Well, well, baby, you have certainly changed. You must have had a very good winter."

"Oh yes, thanks," she admitted.

"Say, be my friend, doll, will you? There's Judy over there. Remember? She was nuts about you when she was little. How about it? Keep an eye on her about an hour or two?"

"Sure, Petey, I'd love to. I'm not busy today. Judy! She was cute. I was nuts about her."

"Anna," said Peter, "this is Louie; she was a real friend that year you worked. She helped me out with Judy. She was great, a lifesaver."

"You're Anna," Louie said hospitably. "Oh, I think Judy's cute. We were nuts about each other. You have one smart kid. She's *really* smart."

"Thank you," said Anna.

Judy had gone off to talk to the ice cream man. She returned licking a double-lime Popsicle. "You have to give him ten cents," she said. "He didn't even remember me to give me trust."

Suddenly she saw Louie. "Oooh!" she shrieked. "It's Louie. Louie, Louie, Louie!" They pinched each other's cheeks, rubbed noses like the Eskimoses, and fluttered lashes like kissing angels do. Louie looked around proudly. "Gee whiz, the kid didn't forget me. How do you like that?"

Peter fished in his pockets for some change. Louie said, "Don't be ridiculous. It's on me." "O.K., girls," Peter said. "You two go on. Live it up. Eat supper out. Enjoy yourselves. Keep in touch."

"I guess they do know each other," said Anna, absolutely dispirited, waving goodbye.

"There!" said Peter. "If you want to do things, do things."

He took her arm. His other elbow cut their way through a gathering clutter of men and boys. "Going, going, gone," he said. "So long, fellows."

Within five minutes Anna unlocked the door of her new apartment, her snappy city leasehold, with a brand-new key.

In the wide foyer, on the parquet path narrowed by rows of cardboard boxes, Peter stood stock-still and whistled a dozen bars of Beethoven's Fifth Symphony. "Mama," he moaned in joy, "let me live!"

A vista of rooms and doors to rooms, double glass doors, single hard-oak doors, narrow closet doors, a homeful of rooms wired with hallways stretched before. "Oh, Anna, it's a far cry . . . Who's paying for it?"

"Not you; don't worry."

"That's not the point, Mary and Joseph!" He waved his arms at a chandelier. "Now, Anna, I like to see my friends set up this way. You think I'm kidding."

"*I'm* kidding," said Anna.

"Come on, what's really cooking? You look so great, you look like a chick on the sincere make. Playing it cool and living it warm, you know . . ."

"Quit dreaming, Petey," she said irritably. But he had stripped his back to his undershirt and had started to move records into record cabinets. He stopped to say, "How about me putting up the Venetian blinds?" Then she softened and offered one kindness: "Peter, you're the one who really looks wonderful. You look just—well—healthy."

"I take care of myself, Anna. That's why. Vegetables, high proteins. I'm not the night owl I was. Grapefruits, sunlight, oh sunlight, that's my dear love now."

"You always did take care of yourself, Peter."

"No, Anna, this is different." He stopped and settled on a box of curtains. "I mean it's not egocentric and selfish, the way I used to be. Now it has a real philosophical basis. Don't mix me up with biology. Look at me, what do you see?"

Anna had read that cannibals, tasting man, saw him thereafter as the great pig, the pale pink roast.

"Peter, Peter, pumpkin eater," Anna said.

"Ah no, that's not what I mean. You know what you see?

A structure of flesh. You know when it hit me? About two years ago, around the time we were breaking up, you and me. I took my grandpa to the bathroom one time when I was over there visiting—you remember him, Anna, that old jerk, the one that was so mad, he didn't want to die. . . . I was leaning on the door; he was sitting on the pot concentrating on his guts. Just to make conversation—I thought it'd help him relax—I said, 'Pop? Pop, if you had it all to do over again, what would you do different? Any real hot tips?'

"He came up with an answer right away. 'Peter,' he said, 'I'd go to a gym every goddamn day of my life; the hell with the job, the hell with the women. Peter, I'd build my body up till God hisself wouldn't know how to tear it apart. Look at me Peter,' he said. 'I been a mean sonofabitch the last fifteen years. Why? I'll tell you why. This structure, this . . . this thing'—he pinched himself across his stomach and his knees—'this me'—he cracked himself sidewise across his jaw—'this is got to be maintained. The reason is, Peter: *It is the dwelling place of the soul.* In the end, long life is the reward, strength, and beauty.'"

"Oh, Peter!" said Anna. "Are you working?"

"Man," said Peter, "you got the same itsy-bitsy motivations. Of course I'm working. How the hell do you think I live? Did you get your eight-fifty a week out in Scroungeville or not?"

"Eight-fifty is right."

"O.K., O.K. Then listen. I have a vitamin compound that costs me twelve-eighty a hundred. Fifty dollars a year for basic maintenance and repair."

"Did the old guy die?"

"Mother! Yes! Of course he died."

"I'm sorry. He wasn't so bad. He liked Judy."

"Bad or good, Anna, he got his time in, he lived long enough to teach the next generation. By the way, I don't think you've put on an ounce."

"Thanks."

"And the kid looks great. You do take good care of her. You were always a good mother. I'll bet you broil her stuff and all."

"Sometimes," she said.

"Let her live in the air," said Peter. "I bet you do. Let her love her body."

"Let her," said Anna sadly.

"To work, to work, where strike committees shirk," sang Peter. "*Is* the ladder in the cellar?"

"No, no, in that kitchen closet. The real tall closet."

Then Peter put up the Venetian blinds, followed by curtains. He distributed books among the available bookcases. He glued the second drawer of Judy's bureau. Although all the furniture had not been installed, there were shelves for Judy's toys. He had no trouble with them at all. He whistled while he worked.

Then he swept the debris into a corner of the kitchen. He put a pot of coffee on the stove. "Coffee?" he called. "In a minute," Anna said. He stabilized the swinging kitchen door and came upon Anna, winding a clock in the living room whose wide windows on the world he had personally draped. "Busy, busy," he said.

Like a good and happy man increasing his virtue, he kissed her. She did not move away from him. She remained in the embrace of his right arm, her face nuzzling his shoulder, her eyes closed. He tipped her chin to look and measure opportunity. She could not open her eyes. Honorably he searched, but on her face he met no quarrel.

She was faint and leaden, a sure sign in Anna, if he remembered correctly, of passion. "Shall we dance?" he asked softly, a family joke. With great care, a patient lover, he undid the sixteen tiny buttons of her pretty dress and in Judy's room on Judy's bed he took her at once without a word. Afterward, having established tenancy, he rewarded her with kisses. But he dressed quickly because he was obligated by the stories of his life to remind her of transience.

"Petey," Anna said, having drawn sheets and blankets to her chin. "Go on into the kitchen. I think the coffee's all boiled out."

He started a new pot. Then he returned to help her with the innumerable little cloth buttons. "Say, Anna, this dress is wild. It must've cost a dime."

"A quarter," she said.

"You know, we could have some pretty good times together every now and then if you weren't so damn resentful."

"Did you have a real good time, Petey?"

"Oh, the best," he said, kissing her lightly. "You know, I
like the way your hair is now," he said.

"I have it done once a week."

"Hey, say it pays, baby. It does wonders. What's up,
what's up? That's what I want to know. Where'd the classy
TV come from? And that fabulous desk . . . Say, somebody's an operator."

"My husband is," said Anna.

Petey sat absolutely still, but frowned, marking his clear
forehead with vertical lines of pain. Consuming the black
fact, gritting his teeth to retain it, he said, "My God, Anna!
That was a terrible thing to do."

"I thought it was so great."

"Oh, Anna, that's not the point. You should have said
something first. Where is he? Where is this stupid sonofabitch
while his wife is getting laid?"

"He's in Rochester. That's where I met him. He's a lovely
person. He's moving his business. It takes time. Peter, please.
He'll be here in a couple of days."

"You're great, Anna. Man, you're great. You wiggle your
ass. You make a donkey out of me and him both. You
could've said no. No—excuse me, Petey—no. I'm not that
hard up. Why'd you do it? Revenge? Meanness? Why?"

He buttoned his jacket and moved among the cardboard
boxes and the new chairs, looking for a newspaper or a
package. He hadn't brought a thing. He stopped before the
hallway mirror to brush his hair. "That's it!" he said, and
walked slowly to the door.

"Where are you going, Peter?" Anna called across the
foyer, a place for noisy children and forgotten umbrellas.
"Wait a minute, Peter. Honest to God, listen to me, I did it
for love."

He stopped to look at her. He looked at her coldly.

Anna was crying. "I really mean it, Peter, I did it for
love."

"Love?" he asked. "Really?" He smiled. He was embarrassed but happy. "Well!" he said. With the fingers of both hands he tossed her a kiss.

"Oh, Anna, then good night," he said. "You're a good kid. Honest, I wish you the best, the best of everything, the very best."

In no time at all his cheerful face appeared at the door of the spring dusk. In the street among peaceable strangers he did a handstand. Then easy and impervious, in full control, he cartwheeled eastward into the source of night.

(1959)

Philip Roth

———————◆———————

Philip Roth, born in New Jersey in 1933, burst on the literary scene with Goodbye, Columbus *(1959), a collection of stories and a novella which won the National Book Award. He has been an immensely popular and seriously considered writer ever since.*

Roth was educated at Rutgers, Bucknell University, and the University of Chicago. He has taught at the University of Chicago, the University of Iowa, Princeton, the University of Pennsylvania, and other institutions. He is the recipient of many prizes, fellowships, and awards.

Perhaps most widely known for Portnoy's Complaint *(1969), a novel of addictive sexuality in an American-Jewish context, Roth has a range that is actually a good deal wider, though American-Jewish themes and characters are generally basic to his work. Widely read, and well-trained, he deals with large philosophical and social issues in a series of beautifully realized, highly particularized settings.* Our Gang *(1971) is political satire, as is* The Great American Novel *(1973), nominally a baseball novel. The novels now bound in one volume as* Zuckerman Bound *(1979–85) show Roth able to bring together many of his central concerns, in clear, often gleamingly sharp prose.*

Sometimes (but not often) Roth overreaches, as in The Breast *(1972), an overblown and rather pale imitation of Kafka. More usually, his clear, flexible prose and a kind of bubbling psychic energy combine with a fine sense of humor and a polished storytelling ability to produce fiction (short and long) of consistent readability and perception. He is also a wryly accurate critic of himself and of other writers. And he is both a dedicated writer and a man and citizen of clear social concerns. Nothing he has ever published could possibly be called "escapist," though almost everything he has published is vastly entertaining.*

THE CONVERSION OF THE JEWS

"You're a real one for opening your mouth in the first place," Itzie said. "What do you open your mouth all the time for?"

"I didn't bring it up, Itz, I didn't," Ozzie said.

"What do you care about Jesus Christ for anyway?"

"I didn't bring up Jesus Christ. He did. I didn't even know what he was talking about. Jesus is historical, he kept saying. Jesus is historical." Ozzie mimicked the monumental voice of Rabbi Binder.

"Jesus was a person that lived like you and me," Ozzie continued. "That's what Binder said—"

"Yeah? . . . So what! What do I give two cents whether he lived or not. And what do you gotta open your mouth!" Itzie Lieberman favored closed-mouthedness, especially when it came to Ozzie Freedman's questions. Mrs. Freedman had to see Rabbi Binder twice before about Ozzie's questions and this Wednesday at four-thirty would be the third time. Itzie preferred to keep *his* mother in the kitchen; he settled for behind-the-back subtleties such as gestures, faces, snarls and other less delicate barnyard noises.

"He was a real person, Jesus, but he wasn't like God, and we don't believe he is God." Slowly, Ozzie was explaining Rabbi Binder's position to Itzie, who had been absent from Hebrew School the previous afternoon.

"The Catholics," Itzie said helpfully, "they believe in Jesus Christ, that he's God." Itzie Lieberman used "the Catholics" in its broadest sense—to include the Protestants.

Ozzie received Itzie's remark with a tiny head bob, as though it were a footnote, and went on. "His mother was Mary, and his father probably was Joseph," Ozzie said. "But the New Testament says his real father was God."

"His *real* father?"

"Yeah," Ozzie said, "that's the big thing, his father's supposed to be God."

"Bull."

"That's what Rabbi Binder says, that it's impossible—"

"Sure it's impossible. That stuff's all bull. To have a baby you gotta get laid," Itzie theologized. "Mary hadda get laid."

"That's what Binder says: 'The only way a woman can have a baby is to have intercourse with a man.' "

'He said *that*, Ozz?' For a moment it appeared that Itzie had put the theological question aside. "He said that, intercourse?" A little curled smile shaped itself in the lower half of Itzie's face like a pink mustache. "What you guys do, Ozz, you laugh or something?"

"I raised my hand."

"Yeah? Whatja say?"

"That's when I asked the question."

Itzie's face lit up. "Whatja ask about—intercourse?"

"No, I asked the question about God, how if He could create the heaven and earth in six days, and make all the animals and the fish and the light in six days—the light especially, that's what always gets me, that He could make the light. Making fish and animals, that's pretty good—"

"That's damn good." Itzie's appreciation was honest but unimaginative: it was as though God had just pitched a one-hitter.

"But making light . . . I mean when you think about it, it's really something," Ozzie said. "Anyway, I asked Binder if He could make all that in six days, and He could *pick* the six days He wanted right out of nowhere, why couldn't He let a woman have a baby without having intercourse."

"You said intercourse, Ozz, to Binder?"

"Yeah."

"Right in class?"

"Yeah."

Itzie smacked the side of his head.

"I mean, no kidding around," Ozzie said, "that'd really be nothing. After all that other stuff, that'd practically be nothing."

Itzie considered a moment. "What'd Binder say?"

"He started all over again explaining how Jesus was historical and how he lived like you and me but he wasn't God. So I said I under*stood* that. What I wanted to know was different."

What Ozzie wanted to know was always different. The first time he had wanted to know how Rabbi Binder could call the Jews "The Chosen People" if the Declaration of Independence claimed all men to be created equal. Rabbi Binder tried to distinguish for him between political equality and spiritual legitimacy, but what Ozzie wanted to know, he insisted vehemently, was different. That was the first time his mother had to come.

Then there was the plane crash. Fifty-eight people had been killed in a plane crash at La Guardia. In studying a casualty list in the newspaper his mother had discovered among the list of those dead eight Jewish names (his grandmother had nine but she counted Miller as a Jewish name); because of the eight she said the plane crash was "a tragedy." During free-discussion time on Wednesday Ozzie had brought to Rabbi Binder's attention this matter of "some of his relations" always picking out the Jewish names. Rabbi Binder had begun to explain cultural unity and some other things when Ozzie stood up at his seat and said that what he wanted to know was different. Rabbi Binder insisted that he sit down and it was then that Ozzie shouted that he wished all fifty-eight were Jews. That was the second time his mother came.

"And he kept explaining about Jesus being historical, and so I kept asking him. No kidding, Itz, he was trying to make me look stupid."

"So what he finally do?"

"Finally he starts screaming that I was deliberately simple-minded and a wise guy, and that my mother had to come, and this was the last time. And that I'd never get bar-mitzvahed if he could help it. Then, Itz, then he starts talking in that voice like a statue, real slow and deep, and he says that I better think over what I said about the Lord. He told me to go to his office and think it over." Ozzie leaned his body towards Itzie. "Itz, I thought it over for a solid hour, and now I'm convinced God could do it."

Ozzie had planned to confess his latest transgression to his mother as soon as she came home from work. But it was a Friday night in November and already dark, and when Mrs. Freedman came through the door she tossed off her coat, kissed Ozzie quickly on the face, and went to the kitchen table to light the three yellow candles, two for the Sabbath and one for Ozzie's father.

When his mother lit the candles she would move her two arms slowly towards her, dragging them through the air, as though persuading people whose minds were half made up. And her eyes would get glassy with tears. Even when his father was alive Ozzie remembered that her eyes had gotten glassy, so it didn't have anything to do with his dying. It had something to do with lighting the candles.

As she touched the flaming match to the unlit wick of a Sabbath candle, the phone rang, and Ozzie, standing only a foot from it, plucked it off the receiver and held it muffled to his chest. When his mother lit candles Ozzie felt there should be no noise; even breathing, if you could manage it, should be softened. Ozzie pressed the phone to his breast and watched his mother dragging whatever she was dragging, and he felt his own eyes get glassy. His mother was a round, tired, gray-haired penguin of a woman whose gray skin had begun to feel the tug of gravity and the weight of her own history. Even when she was dressed up she didn't look like a chosen person. But when she lit candles she looked like something better; like a woman who knew momentarily that God could do anything.

After a few mysterious minutes she was finished. Ozzie hung up the phone and walked to the kitchen table where she was beginning to lay the two places for the four-course Sabbath meal. He told her that she would have to see Rabbi

Binder next Wednesday at four-thirty, and then he told her why. For the first time in their life together she hit Ozzie across the face with her hand.

All through the chopped liver and chicken soup part of the dinner Ozzie cried; he didn't have any appetite for the rest.

On Wednesday, in the largest of the three basement classrooms of the synagogue, Rabbi Marvin Binder, a tall, handsome, broad-shouldered man of thirty with thick strong-fibered black hair, removed his watch from his pocket and saw that it was four o'clock. At the rear of the room Yakov Blotnik, the seventy-one-year-old custodian, slowly polished the large window, mumbling to himself, unaware that it was four o'clock or six o'clock, Monday or Wednesday. To most of the students Yakov Blotnik's mumbling, along with his brown curly beard, scythe nose, and two heel-trailing black cats, made of him an object of wonder, a foreigner, a relic, towards whom they were alternately fearful and disrespectful. To Ozzie the mumbling had always seemed a monotonous, curious prayer; what made it curious was that old Blotnik had been mumbling so steadily for so many years, Ozzie suspected he had memorized the prayers and forgotten all about God.

"It is now free-discussion time," Rabbi Binder said. "Feel free to talk about any Jewish matter at all—religion, family, politics, sports—"

There was silence. It was a gusty, clouded November afternoon and it did not seem as though there ever was or could be a thing called baseball. So nobody this week said a word about that hero from the past, Hank Greenberg—which limited free discussion considerably.

And the soul-battering Ozzie Freedman had just received from Rabbi Binder had imposed its limitation. When it was Ozzie's turn to read aloud from the Hebrew book the rabbi had asked him petulantly why he didn't read more rapidly. He was showing no progress. Ozzie said he could read faster but that if he did he was sure not to understand what he was reading. Nevertheless, at the rabbi's repeated suggestion Ozzie tried, and showed a great talent, but in the midst of a long passage he stopped short and said he didn't understand a

Philip Roth

word he was reading, and started in again at a drag-footed pace. Then came the soul-battering.

Consequently when free-discussion time rolled around none of the students felt too free. The rabbi's invitation was answered only by the mumbling of feeble old Blotnik.

"Isn't there anything at all you would like to discuss?" Rabbi Binder asked again, looking at his watch. "No questions or comments?"

There was a small grumble from the third row. The rabbi requested that Ozzie rise and give the rest of the class the advantage of his thought.

Ozzie rose. "I forget it now," he said, and sat down in his place.

Rabbi Binder advanced a seat towards Ozzie and poised himself on the edge of the desk. It was Itzie's desk and the rabbi's frame only a dagger's-length away from his face snapped him to sitting attention.

"Stand up again, Oscar," Rabbi Binder said calmly, "and try to assemble your thoughts."

Ozzie stood up. All his classmates turned in their seats and watched as he gave an unconvincing scratch to his forehead.

"I can't assemble any," he announced, and plunked himself down.

"Stand up!" Rabbi Binder advanced from Itzie's desk to the one directly in front of Ozzie; when the rabbinical back was turned Itzie gave it five-fingers off the tip of his nose, causing a small titter in the room. Rabbi Binder was too absorbed in squelching Ozzie's nonsense once and for all to bother with titters. "Stand up, Oscar. What's your question about?"

Ozzie pulled a word out of the air. It was the handiest word. "Religion."

"Oh, now you remember?"

"Yes."

"What is it?"

Trapped, Ozzie blurted the first thing that came to him. "Why can't He make anything He wants to make!"

As Rabbi Binder prepared an answer, a final answer, Itzie, ten feet behind him, raised one finger on his left hand, gestured it meaningfully towards the rabbi's back, and brought the house down.

Binder twisted quickly to see what had happened and in the midst of the commotion Ozzie shouted into the rabbi's back what he couldn't have shouted to his face. It was a loud, toneless sound that had the timbre of something stored inside for about six days.

"You don't know! You don't know anything about God!"

The rabbi spun back towards Ozzie. "What?"

"You don't know—you don't—"

"Apologize, Oscar, apologize!" It was a threat.

"You don't—"

Rabbi Binder's hand flicked out at Ozzie's cheek. Perhaps it had only been meant to clamp the boy's mouth shut, but Ozzie ducked and the palm caught him squarely on the nose.

The blood came in a short, red spurt on to Ozzie's shirt front.

The next moment was all confusion. Ozzie screamed, "You bastard, you bastard!" and broke for the classroom door. Rabbi Binder lurched a step backwards, as though his own blood had started flowing violently in the opposite direction, then gave a clumsy lurch forward and bolted out the door after Ozzie. The class followed after the rabbi's huge blue-suited back, and before old Blotnik could turn from his window, the room was empty and everyone was headed full speed up the three flights leading to the roof.

If one should compare the light of day to the life of man: sunrise to birth; sunset—the dropping down over the edge—to death; then as Ozzie Freedman wiggled through the trapdoor of the synagogue roof, his feet kicking backwards bronco-style at Rabbi Binder's outstretched arms—at that moment the day was fifty years old. As a rule, fifty or fifty-five reflects accurately the age of late afternoons in November, for it is in that month, during those hours, that one's awareness of light seems no longer a matter of seeing, but of hearing: light begins clicking away. In fact, as Ozzie locked shut the trapdoor in the rabbi's face, the sharp click of the bolt into the lock might momentarily have been mistaken for the sound of the heavier gray that had just throbbed through the sky.

With all his weight Ozzie kneeled on the locked door; any instant he was certain that Rabbi Binder's shoulder would fling it open, splintering the wood into shrapnel and catapulting his body into the sky. But the door did not move and below him he heard only the rumble of feet, first loud then dim, like thunder rolling away.

A question shot through his brain. "Can this be *me?*" For a thirteen-year-old who had just labeled his religious leader a bastard, twice, it was not an improper question. Louder and louder the question came to him—"Is it me? Is it me?"—until he discovered himself no longer kneeling, but racing crazily towards the edge of the roof, his eyes crying, his throat screaming, and his arms flying everywhichway as though not his own.

"Is it me? Is it me ME ME ME ME! It has to be me—but is it!"

It is the question a thief must ask himself the night he jimmies open his first window, and it is said to be the question with which bridegrooms quiz themselves before the altar.

In the few wild seconds it took Ozzie's body to propel him to the edge of the roof, his self-examination began to grow fuzzy. Gazing down at the street, he became confused as to the problem beneath the question: was it, is-it-me-who-called-Binder-a-bastard? or, is-it-me-prancing-around-on-the-roof? However, the scene below settled all, for there is an instant in any action when whether it is you or somebody else is academic. The thief crams the money in his pockets and scoots out the window. The bridegroom signs the hotel register for two. And the boy on the roof finds a streetful of people gaping at him, necks stretched backwards, faces up, as though he were the ceiling of the Hayden Planetarium. Suddenly you know it's you.

"Oscar! Oscar Freedman!" A voice rose from the center of the crowd, a voice that, could it have been seen, would have looked like the writing on scroll. "Oscar Freedman, get down from there. Immediately!" Rabbi Binder was pointing one arm stiffly up at him; and at the end of that arm, one finger aimed menacingly. It was the attitude of a dictator, but one—the eyes confessed all—whose personal valet had spit neatly in his face.

Ozzie didn't answer. Only for a blink's length did he look towards Rabbi Binder. Instead his eyes began to fit together the world beneath him, to sort out people from places, friends from enemies, participants from spectators. In little jagged starlike clusters his friends stood around Rabbi Binder, who was still pointing. The topmost point on a star compounded not of angels but of five adolescent boys was Itzie. What a world it was, with those stars below, Rabbi Binder below . . . Ozzie, who a moment earlier hadn't been able to control his own body, started to feel the meaning of the word control: he felt Peace and he felt Power.

"Oscar Freedman, I'll give you three to come down."

Few dictators give their subjects three to do anything; but, as always, Rabbi Binder only looked dictatorial.

"Are you ready, Oscar?"

Ozzie nodded his head yes, although he had no intention in the world—the lower one or the celestial one he'd just entered—of coming down even if Rabbi Binder should give him a million.

"All right then," said Rabbi Binder. He ran a hand through his black Samson hair as though it were the gesture prescribed for uttering the first digit. Then, with his other hand cutting a circle out of the small piece of sky around him, he spoke. "One!"

There was no thunder. On the contrary, at that moment, as though "one" was the cue for which he had been waiting, the world's least thunderous person appeared on the synagogue steps. He did not so much come out the synagogue door as lean out, onto the darkening air. He clutched at the doorknob with one hand and looked up at the roof.

"Oy!"

Yakov Blotnik's old mind hobbled slowly, as if on crutches, and though he couldn't decide precisely what the boy was doing on the roof, he knew it wasn't good—that is, it wasn't-good-for-the-Jews. For Yakov Blotnik life had fractionated itself simply: things were either good-for-the-Jews or no-good-for-the-Jews.

He smacked his free hand to his in-sucked cheek, gently.

"Oy, Gut!" And then quickly as he was able, he jacked down his head and surveyed the street. There was Rabbi Binder (like a man at an auction with only three dollars in his pocket, he had just delivered a shaky "Two!"); there were the students, and that was all. So far it-wasn't-so-bad-for-the-Jews. But the boy had to come down immediately, before anybody saw. The problem: how to get the boy off the roof?

Anybody who has ever had a cat on the roof knows how to get him down. You call the fire department. Or first you call the operator and you ask her for the fire department. And the next thing there is great jamming of brakes and clanging of bells and shouting of instructions. And then the cat is off the roof. You do the same thing to get a boy off the roof.

That is, you do the same thing if you are Yakov Blotnik and you once had a cat on the roof.

When the engines, all four of them, arrived, Rabbi Binder had four times given Ozzie the count of three. The big hook-and-ladder swung around the corner and one of the firemen leaped from it, plunging headlong towards the yellow fire hydrant in front of the synagogue. With a huge wrench he began to unscrew the top nozzle. Rabbi Binder raced over to him and pulled at his shoulder.

"There's no fire . . ."

The fireman mumbled back over his shoulder and, heatedly, continued working at the nozzle.

"But there's no fire, there's no fire . . ." Binder shouted. When the fireman mumbled again, the rabbi grasped his face with both his hands and pointed it up at the roof.

To Ozzie it looked as though Rabbi Binder was trying to tug the fireman's head out of his body, like a cork from a bottle. He had to giggle at the picture they made: it was a family portrait—rabbi in black skullcap, fireman in red fire hat, and the little yellow hydrant squatting beside like a kid brother, bareheaded. From the edge of the roof Ozzie waved at the portrait, a one-handed, flapping, mocking wave; in doing it his right foot slipped from under him. Rabbi Binder covered his eyes with his hands.

Firemen work fast. Before Ozzie had even regained his balance, a big, round, yellowed net was being held on the synagogue lawn. The firemen who held it looked up at Ozzie with stern, feelingless faces.

One of the firemen turned his head towards Rabbi Binder. "What, is the kid nuts or something?"

Rabbi Binder unpeeled his hands from his eyes, slowly, painfully, as if they were tape. Then he checked: nothing on the sidewalk, no dents in the net.

"Is he gonna jump, or what?" the fireman shouted.

In a voice not at all like a statue, Rabbi Binder finally answered. "Yes, yes, I think so . . . He's been threatening to . . ."

Threatening to? Why, the reason he was on the roof, Ozzie remembered, was to get away; he hadn't even thought about jumping. He had just run to get away, and the truth was that he hadn't really headed for the roof as much as he'd been chased there.

"What's his name, the kid?"

"Freedman," Rabbi Binder answered. "Oscar Freedman."

The fireman looked up at Ozzie. "What is it with you, Oscar? You gonna jump, or what?"

Ozzie did not answer. Frankly, the question had just arisen.

"Look, Oscar, if you're gonna jump, jump—and if you're not gonna jump, don't jump. But don't waste our time, willya?"

Ozzie looked at the fireman and then at Rabbi Binder. He wanted to see Rabbi Binder cover his eyes one more time.

"I'm going to jump."

And then he scampered around the edge of the roof to the corner, where there was no net below, and he flapped his arms at his sides, swishing the air and smacking his palms to his trousers on the downbeat. He began screaming like some kind of engine, "Wheeeee . . . wheeeeee," and leaning way out over the edge with the upper half of his body. The firemen whipped around to cover the ground with the net. Rabbi Binder mumbled a few words to Somebody and covered his eyes. Everything happened quickly, jerkily, as in a silent movie. The crowd, which had arrived with the fire engines, gave out a long, Fourth-of-July fireworks, oooh-aahhh. In the excitement no one had paid the crowd much heed, except, of course, Yakov Blotnik, who swung from the door knob counting heads. "Fier und tsvansik . . . finf und tsvantsik . . . Oy, Gut!" It wasn't like this with the cat.

Rabbi Binder peeked through his fingers, checked the sidewalk and net. Empty. But there was Ozzie racing to the other corner. The firemen raced with him but were unable to keep up. Whenever Ozzie wanted to he might jump and splatter himself upon the sidewalk and by the time the firemen scooted to the spot all they could do with their net would be to cover the mess.

"Wheeeee . . . wheeeee . . ."

"Hey, Oscar," the winded fireman yelled, "What the hell is this, a game or something?"

"Wheeeee . . . wheeeee . . ."

"Hey, Oscar—"

But he was off now to the other corner, flapping his wings fiercely. Rabbi Binder couldn't take it any longer—the fire engines from nowhere, the screaming suicidal boy, the net. He fell to his knees, exhausted, and with his hands curled together in front of his chest like a little dome, he pleaded, "Oscar, stop it, Oscar. Don't jump, Oscar. Please come down . . . Please don't jump."

And further back in the crowd a single voice, a single young voice, shouted a lone word to the boy on the roof.

"Jump!"

It was Itzie. Ozzie momentarily stopped flapping.

"Go ahead, Ozz—jump!" Itzie broke off his point of the star and courageously, with the inspiration not of a wise-guy but of a disciple, stood alone. "Jump, Ozz, jump!"

Still on his knees, his hands still curled, Rabbi Binder twisted his body back. He looked at Itzie, then, agonizingly, back to Ozzie.

"OSCAR. DON'T JUMP! PLEASE, DON'T JUMP . . . please please . . ."

"Jump!" This time it wasn't Itzie but another point of the star. By the time Mrs. Freedman arrived to keep her four-thirty appointment with Rabbi Binder, the whole little upside down heaven was shouting and pleading for Ozzie to jump, and Rabbi Binder no longer was pleading with him not to jump, but was crying into the dome of his hands.

*   *   *

Understandably Mrs. Freedman couldn't figure out what her son was doing on the roof. So she asked.

"Ozzie, my Ozzie, what are you doing? My Ozzie, what is it?"

Ozzie stopped wheeeeeing and slowed his arms down to a cruising flap, the kind birds use in soft winds, but he did not answer. He stood against the low, clouded, darkening sky—light clicked down swiftly now, as on a small gear—flapping softly and gazing down at the small bundle of a woman who was his mother.

"What are you doing, Ozzie?" She turned towards the kneeling Rabbi Binder and rushed so close that only a paper-thickness of dusk lay between her stomach and his shoulders.

"What is my baby doing?"

Rabbi Binder gaped up at her but he too was mute. All that moved was the dome of his hands; it shook back and forth like a weak pulse.

"Rabbi, get him down! He'll kill himself. Get him down, my only baby . . ."

"I can't," Rabbi Binder said, "I can't . . ." and he turned his handsome head towards the crowd of boys behind him. "It's them. Listen to them."

And for the first time Mrs. Freedman saw the crowd of boys, and she heard what they were yelling.

"He's doing it for them. He won't listen to me. It's them." Rabbi Binder spoke like one in a trance.

"For them?"

"Yes."

"Why for them?"

"They want him to . . ."

Mrs. Freedman raised her two arms upward as though she were conducting the sky. "For them he's doing it!" And then in a gesture older than pyramids, older than prophets and floods, her arms came slapping down to her sides. "A martyr I have. Look!" She tilted her head to the roof. Ozzie was still flapping softly. "My martyr."

"Oscar, come down, *please*," Rabbi Binder groaned.

In a startlingly even voice Mrs. Freedman called to the boy on the roof. "Ozzie, come down, Ozzie. Don't be a martyr, my baby."

As though it were a litany, Rabbi Binder repeated her words. "Don't be a martyr, my baby. Don't be a martyr."

"Gawhead, Ozz—*be* a Martin!" It was Itzie. "Be a Martin, be a Martin," and all the voices joined in singing for Martindom, whatever *it* was. "Be a Martin, be a Martin . . ."

Somehow when you're on a roof the darker it gets the less you can hear. All Ozzie knew was that two groups wanted two new things: his friends were spirited and musical about what they wanted; his mother and the rabbi were even-toned, chanting, about what they didn't want. The rabbi's voice was without tears now and so was his mother's.

The big net stared up at Ozzie like a sightless eye. The big, clouded sky pushed down. From beneath it looked like a gray corrugated board. Suddenly, looking up into that unsympathetic sky, Ozzie realized all the strangeness of what these people, his friends, were asking: they wanted him to jump, to kill himself; they were singing about it now—it made them that happy. And there was an even greater strangeness: Rabbi Binder was on his knees, trembling. If there was a question to be asked now it was not "Is it me?" but rather "Is it us? . . . Is it us?"

Being on the roof, it turned out, was a serious thing. If he jumped would the singing become dancing? Would it? What would jumping stop? Yearningly, Ozzie wished he could rip open the sky, plunge his hands through, and pull out the sun; and on the sun, like a coin, would be stamped JUMP or DON'T JUMP.

Ozzie's knees rocked and sagged a little under him as though they were setting him for a dive. His arms tightened, stiffened, froze, from shoulders to fingernails. He felt as if each part of his body were going to vote as to whether he should kill himself or not—and each part as though it were independent of *him*.

The light took an unexpected click down and the new darkness, like a gag, hushed the friends singing for this and the mother and rabbi chanting for that.

Ozzie stopped counting votes, and in a curiously high voice, like one who wasn't prepared for speech, he spoke.

"Mamma?"

"Yes, Oscar."

"Mamma, get down on your knees, like Rabbi Binder."

"Oscar—"

"Get down on your knees," he said, "or I'll jump."

Ozzie heard a whimper, then a quick rustling, and when he looked down where his mother had stood he saw the top of a head and beneath that a circle of dress. She was kneeling beside Rabbi Binder.

He spoke again. "Everybody kneel." There was the sound of everybody kneeling.

Ozzie looked around. With one hand he pointed towards the synagogue entrance. "Make *him* kneel."

There was a noise, not of kneeling, but of body-and-cloth stretching. Ozzie could hear Rabbi Binder saying in a gruff whisper, ". . . or he'll *kill* himself," and when next he looked there was Yakov Blotnik off the doorknob and for the first time in his life upon his knees in the Gentile posture of prayer.

As for the firemen—it is not as difficult as one might imagine to hold a net taut while you are kneeling.

Ozzie looked around again; and then he called to Rabbi Binder.

"Rabbi?"

"Yes, Oscar."

"Rabbi Binder, do you believe in God?"

"Yes."

"Do you believe God can do Anything?" Ozzie leaned his head out into the darkness. "Anything?"

"Oscar, I think—"

"Tell me you believe God can do Anything."

There was a second's hesitation. Then: "God can do Anything."

"Tell me you believe God can make a child without intercourse."

"He can."

"Tell me!"

"God," Rabbi Binder admitted, "can make a child without intercourse."

"Mamma, you tell me."

"God can make a child without intercourse," his mother said.

"Make *him* tell me." There was no doubt who *him* was.

In a few moments Ozzie heard an old comical voice say something to the increasing darkness about God.

Next, Ozzie made everybody say it. And then he made them all say they believed in Jesus Christ—first one at a time, then all together.

When the catechizing was through it was the beginning of evening. From the street it sounded as if the boy on the roof might have sighed.

"Ozzie?" A woman's voice dared to speak. "You'll come down now?"

There was no answer, but the woman waited, and when a voice finally did speak it was thin and crying, and exhausted as that of an old man who had just finished pulling the bells.

"Mamma, don't you see—you shouldn't hit me. He shouldn't hit me. You shouldn't hit me about God, Mamma. You should never hit anybody about God—"

"Ozzie, please come down now."

"Promise me, promise me you'll never hit anybody about God."

He had asked only his mother, but for some reason everyone kneeling in the street promised he would never hit anybody about God.

Once again there was silence.

"I can come down now, Mamma," the boy on the roof finally said. He turned his head both ways as though checking the traffic lights. "Now I can come down . . ."

And he did, right into the center of the yellow net that glowed in the evening's edge like an overgrown halo.

(ca. 1959)

Stanley Elkin

Stanley Elkin was born in 1930, in St. Louis. He took a B.A., an M.A., and a Ph.D. at the University of Illinois; since 1960 he has been a professor at Washington University, in St. Louis. His earliest books, the novel Boswell *(1964) and the collection of stories,* Criers and Kibitzers, Kibitzers and Criers *(1967), brought him immediate critical respect but very little popular attention. None of his subsequent volumes, whether novels or assemblages of shorter fiction, has done much to change that situation.*

Sometimes described as a black humorist, Elkin plainly takes an ironic and often a comic view of American life. He sometimes experiments with literary forms, and with literary styles, that are perhaps a bit too unformed, a bit too clearly conceptual in their origins. But at his best he exhibits a consistent, driving power, and a perceptive yet compassionate understanding of American existence, which make him a writer of genuine importance. His intelligence shines, in highly sensate form, through the pages of his best work. He can make terribly sad things funny—and he can make almost anything interesting. His flair for dialogue is superb: two Elkin characters conversing are rarely anything but wonderfully entertaining.

IN THE ALLEY

Four months after he was to have died, Mr. Feldman became very bored. He had been living with his impending death for over a year, and when it did not come he grew first impatient, then hopeful that perhaps the doctors had made a mistake, and then—since the pains stayed with him and he realized that he was not, after all, a well man—bored. He was not really sure what to do. When he had first been informed by the worried-looking old man who was his physician that the disquieting thing he felt in his stomach was malignant, he had taken it for granted that some role had been forced upon him. He knew at once, as though he had been expecting the information and had long since decided his course, what shape that role had to assume, what measures his unique position had forced him to. It was as if until then his intuitions had been wisely laid by, and now, thriftlessly, he might spend them in one grand and overwhelming indulgence. As soon as the implications of the word ''malignant'' had settled peaceably in his mind, Feldman decided he must (it reduced to this) become a hero.

Though the circumstances were not those he might have chosen had he been able to determine them, there was this, at least: what he was going to do had about it a nice sense of rounded finality. Heroism depended upon sacrifice, and that which he was being forced to sacrifice carried with it so much weight, was so monumental, that he could not, even if he were yet more critical of himself than he was, distrust his motives. Motives, indeed, had nothing to do with it. He was not motivated to die; he was motivated to live. His heroism was that he *would* die and did not want to.

The doctor, who would know of and wonder at Feldman's generous act, could serve as an emotional check to the whole affair. He could represent, in a way, the world; thus Feldman, by observing the doctor observing him, might be in a better position to determine whether or not he was going too far.

While Feldman had known with certainty the exact dimension of his heroism, it was almost a disappointment to understand that heroism, in his particular situation, demanded nothing, and therefore everything. It demanded, simply, acquiescence. He must, of course, tell no one. But this was not the drawback. It was, indeed, the one advantage he was sure of, since heroism, *real* heroism, like real treachery, was the more potent for being done in the dark. He knew that the hero who performed his services before an audience risked a surrender to pride, chanced a double vision of himself: a view of himself as he must appear before those who would judge him. All that frightened Feldman was his awareness that his peculiar situation allowed him the same opportunity for change that might come to ordinary men during the course of normal lifetimes—permitting it, moreover, to occur in the split second of his essentially unnatural act. His chance for heroism, then, stretched-out as it had to be by the doctor's pronouncement that he had still one year to live, was precariously and unfortunately timed. For a year he must go on as he had gone on, work for what he had worked for, talk to others as he had talked to others. In this way his heroism would be drawn out, but there would be the sustained temptation to awareness, to sweet but inimical self-consciousness. Since the essence of his role was to pretend that he was playing none, he would have to prevent any knowledge of the wonderful change wrought in himself, even at the moment of his death.

Feldman set upon his course and performed conscientiously everything he thought was required of him. That is, he did until the others found him out. They had, seeing signs of his physical discomfort, pressed the doctor for information. Urged from the beginning by his patient to say nothing, the doctor told them some elaborate lie about ulcers. So, on top of his other discomfitures, Feldman's family saw to it that he remained on a strict diet, directed toward dissolving a nonexistent ulcer. When his family saw that his pains continued, and the doctor refused to carry the joke to the uncomfortable extreme of operating on what did not in fact exist, the family realized that far graver things than they had been led to believe were wrong with Feldman.

The doctor, under pressure and understandably unwilling to

invent further (and anyway he himself, though old, though experienced, though made accustomed by years of practice of his art to the melodramatic issue of his trade, had, despite his age, his experience, his familiarity with crises, still maintained a large measure of that sentimental attachment which the witness to tragedy has toward great rolling moments of life and death: an attachment which, indeed, had first attracted him to medicine and had given him that which in his superb flair for the dramatic would have been called in men of lesser talent their "bedside manner," but which, in him, soared beyond the bedside—beyond, in fact, the sickroom itself to the family in the waiting room, the nurses in the corridor, to the whole hospital, in fact), thought it best that others learn of Feldman's sacrifice, and so went back on his promise and told the anxious family everything. They were, of course, astounded, and misread Feldman's composure as a sign of solicitude lest he might hurt them. Feldman's anger at having been found out was badly translated into a magnificent display of unselfishness. They thought, in their innocence, that he had merely meant not to worry them. Had they had any insight, however, they would have realized, at some cost to their pride, that far from the secrecy of his suffering being unendurable to him, contemplation of it had provided him with his only source of comfort (he had gone back that quickly on his resolves), and that what they had mistaken for unselfishness was Feldman's last desperate attempt to exploit the self. But in a game where certain feelings, of necessity, masquerade as certain others, what is so is hardly to be distinguished from what is *not* so. What they, in their blindness, had forced upon Feldman was the one really unendurable feature of his illness. What had come to him gratuitously— his immediate, heroic reaction to the prospect of his own death—had now to be called back, reappraised, withdrawn.

Feldman had now to compose himself and deliberately scheme out what he was to do with the remainder of his life. He was now the prisoner of his freedom of choice. Further heroism (pretending that death meant nothing) would be ludicrous with all of them looking on, their eyes shielded by impossible lace handkerchiefs. It was almost better deliberately to impale himself upon their sympathies, to cry out for water in the middle of the night, to languish visibly before their frightened stares, to call to strangers in the street, "Look, look, I'm dying."

With their discovery of his situation, what he had hoped would be the dignified end of his life threatened in fact to become a stagey, circusy rout, rather like the disorganized, sentimental farewell of baseball fans to a team moving forever to another city. And since he would not soon die (the one year he had been given had already extended itself to sixteen months and there were no visible signs of any acceleration of his decay) he became rather annoyed with his position. He quickly discovered that planning one's death had as many attendant exigencies as planning one's life. Were he a youth, a mistake in planning could be neutralized, even changed perhaps to an unexpected asset; the simple fact was that he had no time. That he was still alive four months after his year of grace indicated only a mistake in calculation, not in diagnosis. Strangely, the additional four months served to make his expected end more imminent for him.

He found himself suddenly an object. On Sundays, distant cousins and their children would make pilgrimages to his home to see him. They meant no harm, he knew, but in a way they had come for a kind of thrill, and when they discovered this they grew uncomfortable in his presence. Ashamed of what they suddenly realized were their motives, they secretly blamed him for having forced their tastes into a debauch. Others, not so sensitive, made him a hero long after he himself had dismissed this as a possibility. A nephew of his, who consistently mistook in himself as legitimate curiosity what was only morbid necrophilism, would force him into ridiculous conversations which the boy considered somehow ennobling. On one occasion he had completely shocked Feldman.

"Do you find yourself believing in an after-life?"

"I think that's in poor taste," Feldman said.

"No, what I mean is that before it happens, lots of people who had never been particularly religious before suddenly find themselves slipping into a kind of wish-fulfillment they call faith."

"Stop that," Feldman told him angrily.

After his conversation with his nephew Feldman realized something he found very disturbing. He knew that he had not, after all, accepted his death as a very real possibility. Though he had made plans and changed them, though he had indulged in protean fantasies in which he had gone alone to the edge of sheer marble precipices, he had been playing merely. It was as if he had been toying with the idea of a "grim reaper," playing intellectual games with chalky skeletons and bogeymen; he had not in fact thought about his death, only about his dying: the preoccupied man of affairs casually scribbling last words on a telephone memorandum pad. His nephew's absolute acceptance of the likelihood that one day Feldman would cease to exist had offended him. He had considered the boy's proposition an indelicacy, the continuance of the familiar world after his own absence from it a gross insult. He knew the enormity of such vanity and he was ashamed. He thought for the first time of other dying men, and though he knew that each man's cancer was or should be a sacred circumstance of that man's existence, he felt a sudden urgency to know such men, to submerge himself in their presence. Because he could think of no other way of doing this, he determined to speak to his doctor about having himself committed to a hospital.

It was evening and the other patients had left the old man's office. They had gone, he knew, to drugstores to obtain prescriptions which would make them well. The doctor stood over the small porcelain sink, rubbing from his hands the world's germs.

"You've been lucky," the doctor said. "The year I gave you has turned out to be much more than a year. Perhaps your luck will continue longer, but it can't continue indefinitely. Get out of your mind that there's any cure for what you have. You've been mortally wounded."

"I didn't say anything about cures."

"Then what good would a hospital be? Surely you don't mean to die in a hospital? I can't operate. There's no chance." The doctor spoke slowly, his voice soft. Obviously, Feldman thought, he was enjoying the conversation.

"What I have, this imperfection in my side, is too private

to remove,'' Feldman said, rising to the occasion of the
other's rhetoric, engaging the old man's sense of drama, his
conspicuous taste for the heavy-fated wheelings of the Great
Moment. Looking at the doctor, Feldman was reminded of
his nephew. He felt, not unpleasantly, like an actor feeding
cues. ''I thought that with the others . . .''

''You're wrong. Have you ever been in a hospital room
with three old men who are dying, or who think they are?
Each is jealous of the others' pain. Nothing's so selfish.
People die hard. The death rattle, when it comes, is a terrored
whine, the scream of sirens wailing their emergency.''

''You're healthy,'' Feldman told him. ''You don't understand them.''

The doctor did not answer immediately. He remained by
the porcelain bowl and turned on the hot-water tap. When it
was so hot that Feldman could see steam film the mirror
above the sink, the doctor plunged his hands into the water.
''I'm old,'' he finally said.

Oh no, Feldman thought; really, this was too much. Even
this ridiculous old man could not contemplate another's death
without insisting on his own. ''But you're not dying,'' Feldman
said. ''There is nothing imminent.'' He noted with unreasonable sadness that he had soiled the tissue paper which covered
the examination table. He stood up self-consciously. ''I want
to be with the others. Please arrange it.''

''What could you gain from it? I'm tired of this talk. It
smells of voices from the other side. Disease has taught you
nothing, Feldman. When you first knew, you behaved like a
man. You continued to go to business. You weren't frightened. I thought, 'This is wonderful. Here's a man who knows
how to die.' ''

''I didn't know I would be stared at. The others watch me,
as though by rubbing against it now they can get used to it.''

''I had a patient,'' the doctor said, ''who had more or less
what you have. When I told him he was to die, his doom
lifted from him all the restraints he had ever felt. He determined to have the most fun he could in the time he had left.
He left here a dangerous, but a reasonably contented, man.''

''Of course,'' Feldman said. ''I've thought about this too.
It's always the first thing that occurs to you after the earth-

quakes and the air raids, after the ice cream truck overturns. It's a strong argument. To make off with all you can before the militia comes. I feel no real compulsion to appease myself, to reward myself for dying. Had I been forced to this, I would have been forced to it long before I learned I must die. For your other patient, nothing mattered. To me, things matter very much. We're both selfish. Will you send me to the hospital?''

The ring of steam had thickened on the mirror. Feldman could see no reflection, only a hazy riot of light. The doctor told him he would make the arrangements.

At first the rituals of the hospital room strangely excited Feldman. He watched the nurses eagerly as they came into the four-bed ward to take temperatures and pulses. He studied their professional neutrality as they noted the results of blood pressure readings on the charts. When he could he read them. When they brought medication to the men in the other beds, Feldman asked what each thing was, what it could be expected to do. By casually observing the activity in the room, Feldman discovered that he could keep tabs on the health of the others, despite what even the men themselves might tell him when he asked how they were feeling.

He soon knew, though, that his was an outsider's view, a casualness that was the result of a life's isolation from disease, the residual prejudice of the healthy that somehow the sick are themselves to blame for what is wrong with them. Realizing this, he deliberately tried to negate those techniques which had come naturally to him while he was still the stranger in the room. He would have to acknowledge himself their diseased ally. If his stay in the hospital were to help him at all, he knew he had willfully to overcome all reluctance. Thus, he began to watch everything with the demanding curiosity of a child, as though only through a constant exercise of what once he might have considered bad taste could he gain important insight into the processes of life and death. He began, then, non-judiciously to observe everything. It was a palpable disappointment to him when a doctor or a nurse had occasion to place a screen around the bed of one of the other patients, and often he would ask the man after the nurse had gone what had been done for him.

Even the meals they ate together were a new experience for him. There was something elemental in the group feedings. Everything about the eating process became familiar to him. He examined their trays. He studied the impressions their teeth made on unfinished pieces of bread. He stared at bones, bits of chewed meat; he looked for saliva left in spoons. Everything was pertinent. Processes he had before considered inviolate now all had a place in the design. When a nurse brought a bedpan for one of the men and he sat straight up in his bed and pulled the sheet high up over his chest, Feldman would not look away.

He asked them to describe their pain.

The others in the room with Feldman were not, as the doctor had predicted they would be, old men. Only one, the man in the bed next to his own, was clearly older than Feldman. But if they were not as aged as he had expected, they *were* as sick. The chronic stages of their illnesses—even the fetid patterns of the most coarse inroads of their decay— were somehow agreeable to Feldman and seemed to support his decision to come to the hospital. These men shared with him, if not his own unconditional surrender of the future, then certainly a partial disavowal of it; and if they counted on getting better, at least they did not make the claims on that future which Feldman had found (it came to this) so disagreeable in others. It had been suggested to them that they might not get well. They considered this seriously and acknowledged, once they understood the nature of their conditions, the unpleasant priority of doom. Only then did they hire their doctors, call in their specialists, retire from their businesses, and set themselves resolutely to the task of getting well. This much Feldman could accept as long as—and here he drew an arbitrary line—they behaved like gentlemen. He found in the sick what he had wanted to find: a group of people who knew their rights, but would not insist on them. Their calm was his own assurance that his instincts had been right, and so what little he said to them was to encourage them in that calm.

One morning the youngest of the four, a college boy who had been stricken with a severe heart attack, showed signs of rapid weakening. He had vomited several times and was in great pain. Someone called the nurse. Seeing the serious pallor of the suffering man, she called the intern. The intern, a nervous young doctor who gave the air of being at once supremely interested in the patient's convulsions and supremely incapable of rising to their occasion, immediately dispatched a call for the boy's doctor.

"It seems," the boy said, smiling weakly, "that I won't be able to die until all of them have examined me."

It was for Feldman precisely the right note. "Hang on," he said to him. "If you feel yourself going, ask for a specialist from Prague."

The boy laughed and did not die at all. Feldman attributed this to some superior element in this patient's character which fell halfway between resolutely dignified determination and good sportsmanship.

He had come, he knew, to a sort of clearing house for disease, and sometimes at night (he did not sleep much) he could visualize what seemed to him to be the tremendous forces of destruction at work in the room. His own cancer he saw as some horribly lethal worm that inched its way through his body, spraying on everything it touched small death. He saw it work its way up through the channels of his body and watched as pieces of it fell from his mouth when he spit into his handkerchief. He knew that inside the other men something like the same dark ugliness worked with a steady, persevering ubiquity, and supposed that the worm was pridefully aware that its must be the triumph.

One night as Feldman lay between sleep and wakefulness, there came a terrible groan from the next bed. He looked up quickly, not sure he had not made the sound himself. It came again, as if pushed out by unbearable pain. Feldman buried his head in the pillow to smother the sound, but the groan continued. It was a noise that started deep in the man's chest and became at last a gasping yell for breath. Feldman lay very still. He did not want the man to know he was awake. Such pain could not continue long. He would lie quietly and wait it out. When the noise did not stop, Feldman held his breath and bit his lips. There was such urgency in the screams, nothing of gentlemanly relinquishment. He was about to give in to the overbearing insistence of the man's pain, but before he could force himself to do something he heard the sick man push himself nearer. Feldman turned his face to watch, and in the glow from the red night lamp above the door he could see that the man lay half out of the bed. He was trying, with a desperate strength that came from somewhere deep inside, to reach Feldman. He watched as the man's hand clawed the air as though it were some substance by which he could sustain himself. He called to him, but Feldman could not answer.

"Mister, mister. You up?"

The hand continued to reach toward Feldman until the wild strength in it pulled the man off balance and the upper half of his body was thrust suddenly toward the floor. He was almost completely out of the bed.

"Mister. Mister. Please, are you up?"

Feldman forced himself to say yes.

The man groaned again.

"Do you want me to get the nurse?" Feldman asked him.

"Help me. Help me in the bed."

Feldman got out of bed and put his arms around the man's body. The other worked his arms around Feldman's neck and they remained for a moment in a crazy embrace. Suddenly all his weight fell heavily in Feldman's arms. Feldman feared the man was dead and half lifted, half pushed him back onto the bed. He listened carefully and heard at last, gratefully, spasms of breath. They sounded like sobs.

He was an old man. Whatever he had been like before, his contact and exchange with what Feldman had come to think of as a kind of poisoned, weathering rain, had left his skin limp, flaccid. (He had discovered that people die from the outside in.) After a minute the man opened his eyes. He looked at Feldman, who still held him, leaning over his bed with his arms around his shoulders as though to steady them.

"It's gone now," the man said. His breath was sweetly sick, like garbage fouled by flies and birds. "I'm better."

The man closed his eyes and lowered his head on his chest. "I needed," he said after a while, "someone's arms to hold me. At the house my daughter would come when I cried. My wife couldn't take it. She's not so well herself, and my daughter would come to hold me when I cried from the pain. She's just a teenager.'' The man sobbed.

Feldman took his hands from the man's shoulders and sat on the edge of the bed.

"It's all right," the man said. "Nothing will happen now. I'm sorry I made a nuisance."

"You'll be all right?"

"Sure. Yes. I'm good now."

Feldman watched the man's hand draw the blanket up over him. He held the blanket as one would hold the reins of a horse. The man turned his face away, and Feldman got up and started to go back to his own bed. "Mister," the man called. Feldman turned quickly around. "Mister, would you ring the nurse? I think . . . I think I wet myself."

After that, in the last stages of the man's last illness, the disease multiplied itself; it possessed him, occupied him like an angry invader made to wait too long in siege beyond the gates. For Feldman it represented a stage in the process of decay he knew he might some day reach himself. When he spoke to the man he found that what he really wanted to say circled somewhere above them both like an unsure bird. It became increasingly difficult for him to speak to him at all. Instead, he lay quietly at night when in the urgency of his remarkable pain the man screamed, and pretended he was asleep. He could stand it only a week. Like the man's wife, Feldman thought, I am not so well myself. No, I am not so very damned well myself. And one more thing, dissolution and death are not as inscrutable as they're cracked up to be. They're scrutable as hell. I'm tired, Feldman thought, of all this dying.

Once he had determined to leave he was impatient. He had wasted too much time already. He had been, he realized, so in awe of death that he had cut his own to his notions of it as a tailor cuts cloth to his model.

He moved quickly. That morning, while the old man slept and the two others were in private sections of the hospital for treatment, Feldman dressed. He hoped that the nurse would not come in. "Don't you groan. Be still," he silently addressed the sleeping body in the next bed. In the closet he found his clothes where the nurse had hung them. When he put them on he discovered that though he had worn them into the hospital only a few weeks before, they were now too big for him. They hung, almost without shape, over a body he did not remember until he began to clothe it. He dressed quickly, but could not resist tying his tie before the mirror in the bathroom. Knotting and reknotting it, adjusting the ends, gave him pleasure, imposed a kind of happiness.

He started to leave the room, but something held him. It was a vase of flowers set carefully on the window sill. The flowers had been a gift for the old man. They had been there for several days and now were fading. He walked to the window, lifted the vase and took it with him into the hospital corridor.

He waited until a student nurse came by. "Miss," Feldman called after her softly. "Miss." The nurse did not recognize him. "I want you to give these flowers to Feldman in Room 420." She looked at the decayed blossoms. Feldman shrugged and said, "Alas, poor man, he's dying. I did not want to offend him with anything too bright." The nurse, bewildered, took the flowers he pushed into her hands. Feldman walked to the elevator and jabbed at the button. When the elevator did not come at once, he decided he couldn't wait and took the four flights of steps down.

At the main desk in the lobby he had an inspiration. "How is Feldman, Room 420?" he asked the receptionist.

The girl thumbed through the card file in front of her. When she found his card she said, "Feldman, sir? He's satisfactory."

"I understood he was very sick. Condemned."

The girl looked again at the card. "My card says 'Satisfactory.' "

"Oh," Feldman said.

"That only means he's comfortable. In these terminal cases that's all they ever say."

"Satisfactory? Comfortable? Why doesn't the hospital tell him? He'd be pleased."

"I beg your pardon?"

"Sure," Feldman said.

Outside, it occurred to him that since he had been partner

to him in everything else, he would call his doctor. He went into a drugstore and dialed.

"It's me. It's Feldman. I'm out."

"Where are you, Feldman?" the doctor asked.

"In a phone booth. You've cured me. You've made me well. I wanted to thank you."

"What are you talking about? Where are you?"

"I told you. I've left the hospital. That idea of mine about a fraternity among the sick? It wasn't any good. I just blackballed myself. A man almost died in my room a few days ago and it paralyzed me. I couldn't help him. I held him away from me as though he were soiled linen."

"Get back to the hospital."

"What for?"

"What am I going to say, that you're cured? The charts still exist."

"So do I. I'm not going back. I'm going to business."

"You're in no condition to go to business. Do you want to aggravate an already untenable position?"

"You are maybe the world's all-time lousy doctor. You promised death. Now you threaten it. You said a year, and I sat down to wait. Well, I'm not waiting any more, that's all." He wondered if the old doctor's passion for rhetoric were still strong in him. He decided to try him. "On every occasion I am going to hit for the solar plexus of the solar system," Feldman said.

There was silence. Then the doctor, calmer, said, "I'll call your wife."

Outside the drugstore the sun was shining brightly and everything looked clean and new. Feldman was aware of the keenness of his impressions, but astonished more by the world itself than by his perception of it, he wondered at the absolute luminescence of the things about him. Objects seemed bathed in their own light. Things looked not new, he decided, so much as extraordinarily well kept up.

Across the street was a park, but between the park and Feldman was a boulevard where traffic raced by swiftly. He had to dodge the cars. It was an exciting game, having to dodge cars for one's life as though death were, after all, something that could be held off by an effort of the will. The idea that he could control death made him giddy, and once, in his excitement, he almost slipped and fell. He thought, even in the act of regaining his lost balance, how strange that the death that might have resulted from his misstep would have been an accident unrelated to his disease. I've cured cancer, he thought happily.

In the park he sat down on a bench to rest. His activity had made him tired. "Slowly, slowly," he cautioned himself. He had been aware of pain in his stomach since he left the hospital. Though it was not great, it was becoming gradually more severe, and he was afraid that it would become too much for him. He found that by holding his breath and remaining very still he could control the pain. Does it hurt? he asked himself. Only when I breathe, he answered. Nevertheless, he waited until he thought he could move without reawakening what he still thought of as the slothful parasite within himself, and then he looked around.

The world he had thought he was never to see again when he entered the hospital lay now around and before him in adjacent strata, disparate but continuous planes in space. Because of his heightened awareness it seemed compartmentalized. He had the impression that he could distinguish where each section had been sewn onto the next. He saw the wide-arced slope of grass and trees—the park. Interrupting it—the busy boulevard like an uncalm sea. Beyond the angry roll and toss of traffic and black frozen asphalt like queer, dark ice in perpetual lap against the gutters of a foreign shore—an avenue. A commercial country of bank and shop where the billboards and marquees hung appended and unfurled, annexed like gaudily partisan consulate flags—almost, it seemed to Feldman in its smugly high-tariffed insularity, like a young and enterprising foreign power. Tall apartment buildings backstopped the planet, mountain ranges stacked against the world's last margins, precarious and unbalanced. He knew that over these and beyond the curve of his world there were many leftover worlds. And the sun shone on them all. It was remarkable to him that people and worlds should be dying beneath such a sun.

A young Negro girl came by, pushing a baby carriage. She sat down on Feldman's bench.

Feldman smiled at her. "Is your baby a boy or a girl?" he asked her.

The girl laughed brightly. "My baby an elevator operator downtown. This one here is a white child, mister."

"Oh," Feldman said.

"It's okay," she said.

Feldman wondered whether she would get up now, whether she had taken him for one of the old men who sit in parks and tamper with the healthy they meet there.

He got up to go. " 'Bye, mister," the girl said.

He looked to see if she was mocking him.

He started toward the corner. He could catch a bus there. With a panic that startled the worm sleeping in his stomach and made it lurch forward, bringing him pain, he realized that in leaving the hospital he had given no thought to where he would go. He understood for the first time that when he had gone into the hospital not to be cured but to die, he had relinquished a sort of citizenship. Now he had no rights in a place given over to life. People did not come back from the grave. Others wouldn't stand for it. He could not even stay in the park, unless he was to stay as one of the old men he had for a moment feared he had become.

He could go home, of course. He could kiss his wife and explain patiently to her what had happened to him. He could tell her that his disease had been a joke between the doctor and himself—not a joke in the sense that it didn't really exist, but merely a sort of pale irony in that while it *did* exist, it did not behave as it had in others; that he was going to die, all right, but that they must both be patient.

He saw a large green and yellow bus halted at the stop light. He did not recognize its markings, but when it came abreast of him he got on. He sat up front, near the driver. When the bus had made its circuit two times, the driver turned toward Feldman.

"Okay, mister, end of the line."

"What?"

"You should have slept it off by this time. End of the line. Far as we go."

"But there are still people on the bus."

"Sorry. Company rule."

"If I pay another fare?"

"Sorry."

"Look," he started to say, but he was at a loss as to how to complete his thought. "All right," he said. "Thank you."

He got off and saw that he had come to a part of the city with which he was unfamiliar. He could not remember ever having been there before. It was a factory district, and the smoke from many furnaces forced on the day, still in its early afternoon, a twilight haze. He walked down a block to where the bare, unpainted shacks of the workers led into a half-commercial, half-residential section. He saw that secured between the slate-colored homes was more than the usual number of taverns. The windows in all the houses were smudged with the opaque soot from the chimneys. The brown shades behind them had been uniformly pulled down almost to the sills. Feldman sensed that the neighborhood had a peculiar unity. Even the deserted aspect of the streets seemed to suggest that the people who lived there acted always in concert.

The porches, their peeling paint like dead, flaking skin, were wide and empty except for an occasional piece of soiled furniture. One porch Feldman passed, old like the rest, had on it a new card table and four brightly chromed, red plastic-upholstered chairs, probably the prize in a church bingo party. The self-conscious newness of the set, out of place in the context of the neighborhood, had been quickly canceled by the universal soot which had already begun to settle over it, and which, Feldman imagined, through that same silent consent to all conditions here, had not been wiped away.

Behind the window of each tavern Feldman passed was the sign of some brewery. They hung, suspended neon signatures, red against the dark interiors. He went into one of the bars. Inside it was almost dark, but the room glowed with weird, subdued colors, as though it were lighted by a juke box which was burning out. The place smelled of urine and beer. The floor was cement, the color of an overcast sky.

There were no other men in the tavern. Two women, one the barmaid, a coarse, thick-set woman whose dirty linen apron hung loosely from her big body, stood beside an electric bowling machine. She held the hands of a small boy who was trying to intercept the heavy silver disk that the other woman, probably his mother, aimed down the sanded wooden alley of the machine.

"Let me. Let me," the boy said.

The mother, a thin girl in a man's blue jacket, was wearing a red babushka. Under it, her blond hair, pulled tightly back on her head, almost looked wet. The child continued to squirm in the older woman's grasp. The mother, looking toward a glass of beer set on the edge of the machine, spoke to the woman in the apron. "Don't let him, Rose. He'll knock over the beer."

"He wants to play."

"I'll break his hands he wants to play. Where's his dime?"

Feldman sat down on a stool at the bar. The barmaid, seeing him, let go of the child and stepped behind the bar. "What'll you have?" she said.

"Have you sandwiches?"

"Yeah. Cheese. Salami. Ham and cheese."

"Ham and cheese."

She took a sandwich wrapped in wax paper from a dusty plastic pie bell and brought it to him. "You must be new around here. Usually I say 'What'll you have?' the guy answers 'Pabst Blue Ribbon.' It's a joke."

Feldman, who had not often drunk beer even before his illness, suddenly felt a desire to have some. "I'll have some 'Pabst Blue Ribbon.' "

The woman drew it for him and put it next to his sandwich. "You a social worker?" she asked.

"No," Feldman said, surprised.

"Rose thinks every guy wears a suit he's a social worker," the blond girl said, sitting down next to him. "Especially the suit don't fit too good." The child had run to the machine and was throwing the silver disk against its back wall. The machine, still activated, bounced the disk back to him.

"Don't scratch the surface," the woman behind the bar yelled at him. "Look, he scratches the surface, the company says I'm responsible. They won't give me a machine."

"Petey, come away from the machine. Rose is gonna

break your hands." Looking again at Rose, she said, "He don't even carry a case."

"Could be he's a parole officer," Rose said.

"No," Feldman said.

"We ain't used up the old one yet," the blond woman said, grinning.

Feldman felt the uncomfortable justice of these speculations, made almost as though he were no longer in the room with them. He finished his beer and held up his glass to be refilled.

"You got people in this neighborhood, mister?"

"Yes," he said. "My old grandmother lives here."

"Yeah?" the woman behind the bar said.

"What's her name?" the blond girl asked suspiciously.

Feldman looked at the thin blonde. "Sterchik," he said. "Dubja Sterchik."

"Dubja *Finklestein*," the girl said. She took off her blue jacket. Feldman saw that her arms, though thin, were very muscular. She raised her hand to push some hair that had come loose back under the tight caress of the red babushka. He saw that the inside of her white wrist was tattooed. In thin blue handwriting, the letters not much thicker than ink on an ordinary envelope, was the name "Annie." He looked away quickly, as though inadvertently he had seen something he shouldn't have, as though the girl had leaned forward and he had looked down her blouse and seen her breasts.

"I don't know nobody named Dubja Sterchik," Rose said to him. "Maybe she drinks across the street with Stanley," she added.

He finished the second glass of beer and, getting used to the taste, asked for another. He wondered whether, had they known he was a dying man, they would have been alarmed at his outlandish casualness in strolling into a strange bar in a neighborhood where he had never been. He wondered whether they would be startled to realize that he had brought to them, strangers, the last pieces of his life, giving no thought now to reclamation, since one could not reclaim, ever, what one still had, no matter how fragile or even broken it might be. He held the beer in his mouth until it burned the soft skin behind his lips. It felt good to feel pain in an area where, for once, it was not scheduled. He felt peculiarly light-hearted.

He turned to the girl beside him. "Your husband work around here?"

"Al?"

"Yes, Al. Does Al work around here?"

She nodded. "When Al works, he works around here."

Feldman smiled. He felt stirrings which were now so unfamiliar to him he had to remember deliberately what they were. The death rattle is starting in my pants, he thought, dismissing what he could not take seriously. It would not be dismissed. Instead, the warmth he felt began to crowd him, to push him into unaccustomed corners. You've got the wrong man, he thought. He was not sure, however, which instincts he encouraged, which side he was on.

Feldman was surprised to discover that he really wanted to talk to her, to tell her that he had come with his disease into their small tavern to die for them. He thought jealously of the blond girl's husband, the man Al, with lunch pail and silk team bowling jacket. She rubs him with her wounded wrist, he thought, excited.

"Would you like another drink?" he asked the girl haltingly. "Would you?" he asked again. He looked at her shabby clothes. "I just got paid today," he added.

"Why not?" she said lightly. The little boy came over to her, drew her down and whispered something in her ear. The woman looked up at Feldman. "Excuse me," she said, "he needs to pee."

"Of course," Feldman said stiffly. She took the child through a little door at the back of the tavern. When the door swung open Feldman could see cases of beer stacked on both sides of the lidless toilet. He turned to the woman behind the bar. "I want to buy a bottle of whiskey," he said to her. "We'll sit in that booth over there."

"I don't sell by the bottle. This ain't no package store."

"I'll pay you," he said.

"What are you, a jerk, mister? I run a nice place. I don't want to have to throw you out."

"It's all right. I just want to talk."

"She's got a kid."

"I just want to talk to her," he said. "Here, here," he said quietly. He reached into his pocket and pulled out two loose bills and flung them on the counter. The woman laughed at him.

"I'll be damned," she said. She handed him a bottle.

Feldman took it and walked unsteadily to the booth. When the woman brought two glasses, he poured a drink and swallowed it quickly. He felt as though a time limit had been imposed upon him, that it was all right to do anything in the world he wanted so long as he did it quickly. He saw the door at the rear of the tavern open and the girl step out. She leaned over her son, buttoning his pants. Feldman bit his lips. She straightened and, seeing Feldman sitting in the booth, glanced quickly at the woman behind the bar. The woman shrugged and held up the two five-dollar bills. The girl took the boy to the bowling machine and put a dime into its slot for him. He watched her as she came slowly toward his table. He was sure she wore no underclothing. He motioned for her to sit down. "There's more room," he said apologetically, indicating the booth.

She sat down and Feldman nodded toward her drink. "That's yours," he said. "That's for you."

"Thanks," she said absently, but made no effort to drink it. Feldman raised his own glass and touched hers encouragingly in some mute toast. She continued to stare at him blankly.

"Look," he said, "I'm bad at this. I don't know what to say to you."

She smiled, but said nothing.

"I want you to understand," he went on stiffly, "I'm not trying to be funny with you."

"Better not," she said.

"I know," Feldman said. "That girl behind the bar said she'd throw me out of here."

"Rose could do it," the girl said. "I could do it."

"Anyone can do it," Feldman said glumly. "Look, do you want me to go? Do you want to forget about it?"

"No," she said, "Just be nice is all. What's the matter with you, Jack?"

"I'm dying." He had not meant to say it. It was out of his

mouth before he could do anything about it. He thought of
telling her a lie, of expanding his statement to something not
so preposterously silly: that he was dying of boredom, of love
for her, of fear for his job. Anything with more reason behind
it than simply death. It occurred to him that dying was
essentially ludicrous. In any real context it was out of place.
It was not merely unwelcome; it was unthinkable. Then he
realized that this was what he had meant to say all along. He
had no interest in the girl; his body had played tricks on him,
had made him believe for a moment that it was still strong.
What he wanted now was to expose it. It was his enemy. Its
sexlessness was a good joke on it. He could tell her that.

"I'm dying," he said again. "I don't know what to do."
He could no longer hear himself speaking. The words tumbled out of his mouth in an impotent rage. He wondered
absently if he was crying. "The doctor told me I'm supposed
to die, only I don't do it, do you see?"

"Go to a different doctor," the girl said.

She joked with him. It was impossible that she didn't
understand. He held the worm in his jaws. It was in his
stomach, in the hollows of his armpits. Pieces of it stoppered
his ears. "No, no. I'm really dying. There have been tests.
Everything."

"Yeah?"

"Yes. You don't know what it's like."

"You married?"

"Yes."

"Got kids, I suppose, and a family?"

"Yes."

"They know about this?"

He nodded.

"Don't care, probably, right? Hey," she said, "look at me
sitting and talking to you like this. You ain't got something
contagious, have you?"

"No," he said. "Where are you going?" The girl was
standing. "No, don't go. Please sit down."

"I'm sorry for your trouble, mister. Thanks for the drink."

"Have another. There's a whole bottle."

She was looking down at him. He wondered if she really
meant to go, whether her standing up was merely a form, a

confused deference to death. She leaned toward him unex-
pectedly. "What is it, mister?" she said. She came to his
side of the booth and sat down. "What is it, mister? Do you
want to kiss me?" He was sure he had not heard her correctly. She repeated her question. She was smiling. He saw
now that she had made a decision, had determined to cheat
him. He didn't care.

"Yes," he answered weakly. "Would you kiss me?"

"Sure," she said, her voice level, flat. Her eyes were
nowhere. She sat closer. He put his hand on her warm thighs.
They were hard and thin. She put one arm around Feldman
and ground her lips against his. Her kid was staring at them.
Feldman could taste the girl's breath. It was foul. He put his
hand inside the girl's skirt and touched her thighs. He felt
nothing inside himself. There was no urgency. The girl,
incorrectly gauging Feldman's responses, took his hand in
one of hers and began to squeeze it. She held his wrist. Her
hands, as Feldman had known they would be, were powerful.
She dug her nails into his wrist. He could not get free. He
tried to pull his wrist away. "Stop it," he said. "Stop it,
you're hurting me."

"See?" she said. "I'll break your wrist."

Under the table he kicked at her. She let go of him.

"You son of a bitch, I'll break your face for that." She
started to scratch him. He struck her wildly and she began to
cry. The little boy had rushed over and was pulling at Feldman's
suit jacket. The woman behind the bar came over with a billy
club she had taken from some hiding place, and began to hit
Feldman on his neck and chest. The girl recovered and pulled
him from the booth. She sat on his chest, her legs straddling
his body as a jockey rides a horse, thighs spread wide, knees
up. Her body was exposed to him. He smelled her cunt. He
saw it. They beat him until he was unconscious.

The men from the factories lifted him from the floor where
he lay and carried him into the street. It was dark now. Under
the lamplight they marched with him. Children ran behind
and chanted strange songs. He heard the voices even in his
sleep, and dreamed that he was an Egyptian king awaking in
the underworld. About him were the treasures, the artifacts

with which his people mocked his death. He was betrayed, forsaken. He screamed he was not dead and for answer heard their laughter as they retreated through the dark passage.

Before he died Feldman awoke in an alley. The pains in his stomach were more severe than ever. He knew he was dying. On his torn jacket was a note, scribbled in an angry hand: STAY AWAY FROM WHITE WOMEN, it said.

He thought of the doctor's somber face telling him more than a year ago that he was going to die. He thought of his family and the way they looked at him, delicately anticipating in his every sudden move something breaking inside himself, and of the admiration in all their eyes, and the unmasked hope that it would never come to this for them, but that if it should, if it ever should, it would come with grace. But nothing came gracefully—not to heroes.

In the alley, before the dawn, by the waiting garbage, by the coffee grounds in their cups of wasted orange hemispheres, by the torn packages of frozen fish, by the greased, ripped labels of hollow cans, by the cold and hardened fat, by the jagged scraps of flesh around the nibbled bones, and the coagulated blood of cow and lamb, Feldman saw the cunt one last time and raised himself and crawled in the darkness toward a fence to sit upright against it. He tugged at his jacket to straighten it, tugged at the note appended to him like a price tag: STAY AWAY FROM WHITE WOMEN. He did not have the strength to pull the tag from his jacket. Smiling, he thought sadly of the dying hero.

(1965)

Bernard Malamud

———◆———

Bernard Malamud was born in Brooklyn, in 1914, and educated at City College and Columbia University. After teaching in New York City high schools from 1940 to 1949, he taught at Oregon State University from 1949 to 1961 and thereafter for many years at Bennington College. His work attracted critical attention from the start, but was not initially appreciated as the large and important accomplishment it in fact was. And popular acclaim took still longer to occur. The Magic Barrel (1958), a collection of stories, won the National Book award. The Fixer (1967), a long and rather artificial novel of Russian Jewish life (and perhaps his weakest book), won him both the Pulitzer Prize and the National Book Award, as well as a great deal of popular interest and respect.

The Natural (1952), one of the most powerful fictional treatments of baseball ever put on paper, and The Assistant (1957), a grimly taut story of lower-class Jewish life in an American city, both reveal the range and the high moral purpose behind all of Malamud's writing. His stories and novels are proverbial page-turners: no one who starts them is likely to stop. He has a droll and sometimes a wickedly pointed sense of humor. His prose, too, is extremely flexible, always clear and intelligent, and able to take on virtually any color Malamud wants to achieve. The opening pages of his novel, Dubin's Lives (1979), seem to re-create the tone and the sweep of the great Russian novelists of the nineteenth

century. His more recent (and riskier) novel, God's Grace
(1982), *takes on something like the voice of Daniel Defoe,
crossed with that of Evelyn Waugh.* A New Life (1961) *a
novel of academia, shows too that Malamud can be as American as anyone. It is wrong to classify him as an exclusively
American-Jewish writer, though many of his best books, and
most of his stories, have American-Jewish themes.*

THE JEWBIRD

The window was open so the skinny bird flew in. Flappity-
flap with its frazzled black wings. That's how it goes. It's
open, you're in. Closed, you're out and that's your fate. The
bird wearily flapped through the open kitchen window of
Harry Cohen's top-floor apartment on First Avenue near the
lower East River. On a rod on the wall hung an escaped
canary cage, its door wide open, but this black-type long-
beaked bird—its ruffled head and small dull eyes, crossed a
little, making it look like a dissipated crow—landed if not
smack on Cohen's thick lamb chop, at least on the table,
close by. The frozen foods salesman was sitting at supper
with his wife and young son on a hot August evening a year
ago. Cohen, a heavy man with hairy chest and beefy shorts;
Edie, in skinny yellow shorts and red halter; and their ten-
year-old Morris (after her father)—Maurie, they called him, a
nice kid though not overly bright—were all in the city after
two weeks out, because Cohen's mother was dying. They had
been enjoying Kingston, New York, but drove back when
Mama got sick in her flat in the Bronx.

"Right on the table," said Cohen, putting down his beer
glass and swatting at the bird. "son of a bitch."

"Harry, take care with your language," Edie said, looking
at Maurie, who watched every move.

The bird cawed hoarsely and with a flap of its bedraggled

wings—feathers tufted this way and that—rose heavily to the top of the open kitchen door, where it perched staring down.

"Gevalt, a pogrom!"

"It's a talking bird," said Edie in astonishment.

"In Jewish," said Maurie.

"Wise guy," muttered Cohen. He gnawed on his chop, then put down the bone. "So if you can talk, say what's your business. What do you want here?"

"If you can't spare a lamb chop," said the bird, "I'll settle for a piece of herring with a crust of bread. You can't live on your nerve forever."

"This ain't a restaurant," Cohen replied. "All I'm asking is what brings you to this address?"

"The window was open," the bird sighed; adding after a moment, "I'm running. I'm flying but I'm also running."

"From whom?" asked Edie with interest.

"Anti-Semeets."

"Anti-Semites?" they all said.

"That's from who."

"What kind of anti-Semites bother a bird?" Edie asked.

"Any kind," said the bird, "also including eagles, vultures, and hawks. And once in a while some crows will take your eyes out."

"But aren't you a crow?"

"Me? I'm a Jewbird."

Cohen laughed heartily. "What do you mean by that?"

The bird began dovening. He prayed without Book or tallith, but with passion. Edie bowed her head though not Cohen. And Maurie rocked back and forth with the prayer, looking up with one wide-open eye.

When the prayer was done Cohen remarked, "No hat, no phylacteries?"

"I'm an old radical."

"You're sure you're not some kind of a ghost or dybbuk?"

"Not a dybbuk," answered the bird, "though one of my relatives had such an experience once. It's all over now, thanks God. They freed her from a former lover, a crazy jealous man. She's now the mother of two wonderful children."

"Birds?" Cohen asked slyly.

"Why not?"

"What kind of birds?"

"Like me. Jewbirds."

Cohen tipped back in his chair and guffawed. "That's a big laugh. I've heard of a Jewfish but not a Jewbird."

"We're once removed." The bird rested on one skinny leg, then on the other. "Please, could you spare maybe a piece of herring with a small crust of bread?"

Edie got up from the table.

"What are you doing?" Cohen asked her.

"I'll clear the dishes."

Cohen turned to the bird. "So what's your name, if you don't mind saying?"

"Call me Schwartz."

"He might be an old Jew changed into a bird by somebody," said Edie, removing a plate.

"Are you?" asked Harry, lighting a cigar.

"Who knows?" answered Schwartz. "Does God tell us everything?"

Maurie got up on his chair. "What kind of herring?" he asked the bird in excitement.

"Get down, Maurie, or you'll fall," ordered Cohen.

"If you haven't got matjes, I'll take schmaltz," said Schwartz.

"All we have is marinated, with slices of onion—in a jar," said Edie.

"If you'll open for me the jar I'll eat marinated. Do you have also, if you don't mind, a piece of rye bread—the spitz?"

Edie thought she had.

"Feed him out on the balcony," Cohen said. He spoke to the bird. "After that take off."

Schwartz closed both bird eyes. "I'm tired and it's a long way."

"Which direction are you headed, north or south?"

Schwartz, barely lifting his wings, shrugged.

"You don't know where you're going?"

"Where there's charity I'll go."

"Let him stay, papa," said Maurie. "He's only a bird."

"So stay the night," Cohen said, "but no longer."

In the morning Cohen ordered the bird out of the house but

Maurie cried, so Schwartz stayed for a while. Maurie was still on vacation from school and his friends were away. He was lonely and Edie enjoyed the fun he had, playing with the bird.

"He's no trouble at all," she told Cohen, "and besides his appetite is very small."

"What'll you do when he makes dirty?"

"He flies across the street in a tree when he makes dirty, and if nobody passes below, who notices?"

"So all right," said Cohen, "but I'm dead set against it. I warn you he ain't gonna stay here long."

"What have you got against the poor bird?"

"Poor bird, my ass. He's a foxy bastard. He thinks he's a Jew."

"What difference does it make what he thinks?"

"A Jewbird, what chuzpah. One false move and he's out on his drumsticks."

At Cohen's insistence Schwartz lived out on the balcony in a new wooden birdhouse Edie had bought him.

"With many thanks," said Schwartz, "though I would rather have a human roof over my head. You know how it is at my age. I like the warm, the windows, the smell of cooking. I would also be glad to see once in a while the *Jewish Morning Journal* and have now and then a schnapps because it helps my breathing, thanks God. But whatever you give me, you won't hear complaints."

However, when Cohen brought home a bird feeder full of dried corn, Schwartz said, "Impossible."

Cohen was annoyed. "What's the matter, crosseyes, is your life getting too good for you? Are you forgetting what it means to be migratory? I'll bet a helluva lot of crows you happen to be acquainted with, Jews or otherwise, would give their eyeteeth to eat this corn."

Schwartz did not answer. What can you say to a grubber yung?

"Not for my digestion," he later explained to Edie. "Cramps. Herring is better even if it makes you thirsty. At least rainwater don't cost anything." He laughed sadly in breathy caws.

And herring, thanks to Edie, who knew where to shop, was

what Schwartz got, with an occasional piece of potato pancake, and even a bit of soupmeat when Cohen wasn't looking.

When school began in September, before Cohen would once again suggest giving the bird the boot, Edie prevailed on him to wait a little while until Maurie adjusted.

"To deprive him right now might hurt his school work, and you know what trouble we had last year."

"So okay, but sooner or later the bird goes. That I promise you."

Schwartz, though nobody had asked him, took on full responsibility for Maurice's performance in school. In return for favors granted, when he was let in for an hour or two at night, he spent most of his time overseeing the boy's lessons. He sat on top of the dresser near Maurie's desk as he laboriously wrote out his homework. Maurie was a restless type and Schwartz gently kept him to his studies. He also listened to him practice his screechy violin, taking a few minutes off now and then to rest his ears in the bathroom. And they afterwards played dominoes. The boy was an indifferent checker player and it was impossible to teach him chess. When he was sick, Schwartz read him comic books though he personally disliked them. But Maurie's work improved in school and even his violin teacher admitted his playing was better. Edie gave Schwartz credit for these improvements though the bird pooh-poohed them.

Yet he was proud there was nothing lower than C minuses on Maurie's report card, and on Edie's insistence celebrated with a little schnapps.

"If he keeps up like this," Cohen said, "I'll get him in an Ivy League college for sure."

"Oh I hope so," sighed Edie.

But Schwartz shook his head. "He's a good boy—you don't have to worry. He won't be a shicker or a wifebeater, God forbid, but a scholar he'll never be, if you know what I mean, although maybe a good mechanic. It's no disgrace in these times."

"If I were you," Cohen said, angered, "I'd keep my big snoot out of other people's private business."

"Harry, please," said Edie.

"My goddamn patience is wearing out. That crosseyes butts into everything."

Though he wasn't exactly a welcome guest in the house, Schwartz gained a few ounces although he did not improve in appearance. He looked bedraggled as ever, his feathers unkempt, as though he had just flown out of a snowstorm. He spent, he admitted, little time taking care of himself. Too much to think about. "Also outside plumbing," he told Edie. Still there was more glow to his eyes so that though Cohen went on calling him crosseyes he said it less emphatically.

Liking his situation, Schwartz tried tactfully to stay out of Cohen's way, but one night when Edie was at the movies and Maurie was taking a hot shower, the frozen foods salesman began a quarrel with the bird.

"For Christ sake, why don't you wash yourself sometimes? Why must you always stink like a dead fish?"

"Mr. Cohen, if you'll pardon me, if somebody eats garlic he will smell from garlic. I eat herring three times a day. Feed me flowers and I will smell like flowers."

"Who's obligated to feed you anything at all? You're lucky to get herring."

"Excuse me, I'm not complaining," said the bird. "You're complaining."

"What's more," said Cohen, "even from out on the balcony I can hear you snoring away like a pig. It keeps me awake at night."

"Snoring," said Schwartz, "isn't a crime, thanks God."

"All in all you are a goddamn pest and freeloader. Next thing you'll want to sleep in bed next to my wife."

"Mr. Cohen," said Schwartz, "on this rest assured. A bird is a bird."   .

"So you say, but how do I know you're a bird and not some kind of a goddamn devil?"

"If I was a devil you would know already. And I don't mean because your son's good marks."

"Shut up, you bastard bird," shouted Cohen.

"Grubber yung," cawed Schwartz, rising to the tips of his talons, his long wings outstretched.

Cohen was about to lunge for the bird's scrawny neck but Maurie came out of the bathroom, and for the rest of the evening until Schwartz's bedtime on the balcony, there was pretended peace.

But the quarrel had deeply disturbed Schwartz and he slept badly. His snoring woke him, and awake, he was fearful of what would become of him. Wanting to stay out of Cohen's way, he kept to the birdhouse as much as possible. Cramped by it, he paced back and forth on the balcony ledge, or sat on the birdhouse roof, staring into space. In the evenings, while overseeing Maurie's lessons, he often fell asleep. Awakening, he nervously hopped around exploring the four corners of the room. He spent much time in Maurie's closet, and carefully examined his bureau drawers when they were left open. And once when he found a large paper bag on the floor, Schwartz poked his way into it to investigate what the possibilities were. The boy was amused to see the bird in the paper bag.

"He wants to build a nest," he said to his mother.

Edie, sensing Schwartz's unhappiness, spoke to him quietly.

"Maybe if you did some of the things my husband wants, you would get along better with him."

"Give me a for instance," Schwartz said.

"Like take a bath, for instance."

"I'm too old for baths," said the bird. "My feathers fall out without baths."

"He says you have a bad smell."

"Everybody smells. Some people smell because of their thoughts or because who they are. My bad smell comes from the food I eat. What does his come from?"

"I better not ask him or it might make him mad," said Edie.

In late November Schwartz froze on the balcony in the fog and cold, and especially on rainy days he woke with stiff joints and could barely move his wings. Already he felt twinges of rheumatism. He would have liked to spend more time in the warm house, particularly when Maurie was in school and Cohen at work. But though Edie was good-hearted and might have sneaked him in in the morning, just to thaw out, he was afraid to ask her. In the meantime Cohen, who had been reading articles about the migration of birds, came out on the balcony one night after work when Edie was in the kitchen preparing pot roast, and peeking into the birdhouse, warned Schwartz to be on his way soon if he knew what was good for him. "Time to hit the flyways."

"Mr. Cohen, why do you hate me so much?" asked the bird. "What did I do to you?"

"Because you're an A-number-one troublemaker, that's why. What's more, whoever heard of a Jewbird? Now scat or it's open war."

But Schwartz stubbornly refused to depart so Cohen embarked on a campaign of harassing him, meanwhile hiding it from Edie and Maurie. Maurie hated violence and Cohen didn't want to leave a bad impression. He thought maybe if he played dirty tricks on the bird he would fly off without being physically kicked out. The vacation was over, let him make his easy living off the fat of somebody else's land. Cohen worried about the effect of the bird's departure on Maurie's schooling but decided to take the chance, first because the boy now seemed to have the knack of studying— give the black bird-bastard credit—and second, because Schwartz was driving him bats by being there always, even in his dreams.

The frozen foods salesman began his campaign against the bird by mixing watery cat food with the herring slices in Schwartz's dish. He also blew up and popped numerous paper bags outside the birdhouse as the bird slept, and when he had got Schwartz good and nervous, though not enough to leave, he brought a full-grown cat into the house, supposedly a gift for little Maurie, who had always wanted a pussy. The cat never stopped springing up at Schwartz whenever he saw him, one day managing to claw out several of his tailfeathers. And even at lesson time, when the cat was usually excluded from Maurie's room, though somehow or other he quickly found his way in at the end of the lesson, Schwartz was desperately fearful of his life and flew from pinnacle to pinnacle—light fixture to clothes-tree to door-top—in order to elude the beast's wet jaws.

Once when the bird complained to Edie how hazardous his existence was, she said, "Be patient, Mr. Schwartz. When the cat gets to know you better he won't try to catch you any more."

"When he stops trying we will both be in Paradise," Schwartz answered. "Do me a favor and get rid of him. He makes my whole life worry. I'm losing feathers like a tree loses leaves."

"I'm awfully sorry but Maurie likes the pussy and sleeps with it."

What could Schwartz do? He worried but came to no decision, being afraid to leave. So he ate the herring garnished with cat food, tried hard not to hear the paper bags bursting like firecrackers outside the birdhouse at night, and lived terror-stricken closer to the ceiling than the floor, as the cat, his tail flicking, endlessly watched him.

Weeks went by. Then on the day after Cohen's mother had died in her flat in the Bronx, when Maurie came home with a zero on an arithmetic test, Cohen, enraged, waited until Edie had taken the boy to his violin lesson, then openly attacked the bird. He chased him with a broom on the balcony and Schwartz frantically flew back and forth, finally escaping into his birdhouse. Cohen triumphantly reached in, and grabbing both skinny legs, dragged the bird out, cawing loudly, his wings wildly beating. He whirled the bird around and around his head. But Schwartz, as he moved in circles, managed to swoop down and catch Cohen's nose in his beak, and hung on for dear life. Cohen cried out in great pain, punched the bird with his fist, and tugging at its legs with all his might, pulled his nose free. Again he swung the yawking Schwartz around until the bird grew dizzy, then with a furious heave, flung him into the night. Schwartz sank like stone into the street. Cohen then tossed the birdhouse and feeder after him, listening at the ledge until they crashed on the sidewalk below. For a full hour, broom in hand, his heart palpitating and nose throbbing with pain, Cohen waited for Schwartz to return but the brokenhearted bird didn't.

That's the end of that dirty bastard, the salesman thought and went in. Edie and Maurie had come home.

"Look," said Cohen, pointing to his bloody nose swollen three times its normal size, "what that sonofabitchy bird did. It's a permanent scar."

"Where is he now?" Edie asked, frightened.

"I threw him out and he flew away. Good riddance."

Nobody said no, though Edie touched a handkerchief to her eyes and Maurie rapidly tried the nine times table and found he knew approximately half.

In the spring when the winter's snow had melted, the boy, moved by a memory, wandered in the neighborhood, looking for Schwartz. He found a dead black bird in a small lot near the river, his two wings broken, neck twisted, and both bird-eyes plucked clean.

"Who did it to you, Mr. Schwartz?" Maurie wept.

"Anti-Semeets," Edie said later.

(1963)

Joyce Carol Oates

Joyce Carol Oates was born in upstate New York in 1938. She attended Syracuse University, took an M.A. at the University of Wisconsin, and became a full-time college teacher of English, first at the University of Detroit, for many years at the University of Windsor (in Ontario, Canada), and most recently at Princeton.

Hers has been one of the most meteoric (and prolific) writing careers in modern American letters. Her first novel, With Shuddering Fall (1964) was received with immense critical respect, and the ensuing torrent of novels, story collections, books of poetry, books of essays, and even plays, has in the last two decades elevated her to the status of a major writer. Her 1970 novel, them, won the National Book Award, and she has over the years won virtually all the awards and honors available to any American artist. She has also begun to enjoy a considerable degree of popular acclaim: her books sell a great deal better today than ever before, and many of them remain in print.

No writer writes too much: that is a silly canard. But there are writers who write prolifically but, so far as one can see, without a corresponding depth of insight or substantive information to communicate. Oates is plainly one such writer. At her best, which is usually her shorter work—the story form seems to restrict and confine her in useful ways, while the novel encourages her prolixity and semi-vacuity—she is a sensitive creator of complex characters, and an expert han-

dler of plots and denouements. Her story collections include By the North Gate *(1963)*, Upon the Sweeping Flood *(1966)*, The Wheel of love *(1970)*, *from which volume "In the Region of Ice" is taken*, Marriages and Infidelties *(1972)*, The Hungry Ghosts *(1974)*, The Goddess and Other Women *(1974)*, Where Are You Going, Where Have You Been? *(1974)*, The Poisoned Kiss *(1975)*, The Seduction *(1975)*, Crossing the Border *(1976)*, *and* Night-side *(1977)*.

IN THE REGION OF ICE

Sister Irene was a tall, deft woman in her early thirties. What one could see of her face made a striking impression—serious, hard gray eyes, a long slender nose, a face waxen with thought. Seen at the right time, from the right angle, she was almost handsome. In her past teaching positions she had drawn a little upon the fact of her being young and brilliant and also a nun, but she was beginning to grow out of that.

This was a new university and an entirely new world. She had heard—of course it was true—that the Jesuit administration of this school had hired her at the last moment to save money and to head off the appointment of a man of dubious religious commitment. She had prayed for the necessary energy to get her through this first semester. She had no trouble with teaching itself; once she stood before a classroom she felt herself capable of anything. It was the world immediately outside the classroom that confused and alarmed her, though she let none of this show—the cynicism of her colleagues, the indifference of many of the students, and, above all, the looks she got that told her nothing much would be expected of her because she was a nun. This took energy, strength. At times she had the idea that she was on trial and that the excuses she made to herself about her discomfort were only the common excuses made by guilty people. But in front of a class she had no time to worry about herself or the conflicts in her mind. She became, once and for all, a figure existing only for the benefit of others, an instrument by which facts were communicated.

About two weeks after the semester began, Sister Irene noticed a new student in her class. He was slight and fair-haired, and his face was blank, but not blank by accident, blank on purpose, suppressed and restricted into a dumbness that looked hysterical. She was prepared for him before he raised his hand, and when she saw his arm jerk, as if he had at last lost control of it, she nodded to him without hesitation.

"Sister, how can this be reconciled with Shakespeare's vision in *Hamlet?* How can these opposing views be in the same mind?"

Students glanced at him, mildly surprised. He did not belong in the class, and this was mysterious, but his manner was urgent and blind.

"There is no need to reconcile opposing views," Sister Irene said, leaning forward against the podium. "In one play Shakespeare suggests one vision, in another play another; the plays are not simultaneous creations, and even if they were, we never demand a logical—"

"We must demand a logical consistency," the young man said. "The idea of education is itself predicated upon consistency, order, sanity—"

He had interrupted her, and she hardened her face against him—for his sake, not her own, since she did not really care. But he noticed nothing, "Please see me after class," she said.

After class the young man hurried up to her.

"Sister Irene, I hope you didn't mind my visiting today. I'd heard some things, interesting things," he said. He stared at her, and something in her face allowed him to smile. "I . . . could we talk in your office? Do you have time?"

They walked down to her office. Sister Irene sat at her desk, and the young man sat facing her; for a moment they were self-conscious and silent.

"Well, I suppose you know—I'm a Jew," he said.

Sister Irene stared at him. "Yes?" she said.

"What am I doing at a Catholic university, huh?" He grinned. "That's what you want to know."

She made a vague movement of her hand to show that she had no thoughts on this, nothing at all, but he seemed not to catch it. He was sitting on the edge of the straight-backed chair. She saw that he was young but did not really look young. There were harsh lines on either side of his mouth, as if he had misused that youthful mouth somehow. His skin was almost as pale as hers, his eyes were dark and not quite in focus. He looked at her and through her and around her, as his voice surrounded them both. His voice was a little shrill at times.

"Listen, I did the right thing today—visiting your class! God, what a lucky accident it was; some jerk mentioned you, said you were a good teacher—I thought, what a laugh! These people know about good teachers here? But yes, listen, yes, I'm not kidding—you are good. I mean that."

Sister Irene frowned. "I don't quite understand what all this means."

He smiled and waved aside her formality, as if he knew better. "Listen, I got my B.A. at Columbia, then I came back here to this crappy city. I mean, I did it on purpose, I wanted to come back. I wanted to. I have my reasons for doing things. I'm on a three-thousand-dollar fellowship," he said, and waited for that to impress her. "You know, I could have gone almost anywhere with that fellowship, and I came back home here—my home's in the city—and enrolled here. This was last year. This is my second year. I'm working on a thesis, I mean I was, my master's thesis—but the hell with that. What I want to ask you is this: Can I enroll in your class, is it too late? We have to get special permission if we're late."

Sister Irene felt something nudging her, some uneasiness in him that was pleading with her not to be offended by this abrupt, familiar manner. He seemed to be promising another self, a better self, as if his fair, childish, almost cherubic face were doing tricks to distract her from what his words said.

"Are you in English studies?" she asked.

"I was in history. Listen," he said, and his mouth did something odd, drawing itself down into a smile that made the lines about it deepen like knives, "listen, they kicked me out."

He sat back, watching her. He crossed his legs. He took out a package of cigarettes and offered her one. Sister Irene shook her head, staring at his hands. They were small and stubby and might have belonged to a ten-year-old, and the nails were a strange near-violet color. It took him awhile to extract a cigarette.

"Yeah, kicked me out. What do you think of that?"

"I don't understand."

"My master's thesis was coming along beautifully, and then this bastard—I mean, excuse me, this professor, I won't pollute your office with his name—he started making criticisms, he said some things were unacceptable, he—" The boy leaned forward and hunched his narrow shoulders in a parody of secrecy. "We had an argument. I told him some frank things, things only a broad-minded person could hear about himself. This takes courage, right? He didn't have it! He kicked me out of the master's program, so now I'm coming into English. Literature is greater than history; European history is one big pile of garbage. Sky-high. Filth and rotting corpses, right? Aristotle says that poetry is higher than history; he's right; in your class today I suddenly realized that this is my field, Shakespeare, only Shakespeare is—"

Sister Irene guessed that he was going to say that only Shakespeare was equal to him, and she caught the moment of recognition and hesitation, the half-raised arm, the keen, frowning forehead, the narrowed eyes; then he thought better of it and did not end the sentence. "The students in your class are mainly negligible, I can tell you that. You're new here, and I've been here a year—I would have finished my studies last year but my father got sick, he was hospitalized, I couldn't take exams and it was a mess—but I'll make it through English in one year or drop dead. I can do it, I can do anything. I'll take six courses at once—" He broke off, breathless. Sister Irene tried to smile. "All right then, it's settled? You'll let me in? Have I missed anything so far?"

He had no idea of the rudeness of his question. Sister Irene, feeling suddenly exhausted, said, "I'll give you a syllabus of the course."

"Fine! Wonderful!"

He got to his feet eagerly. He looked through the schedule,

muttering to himself, making favorable noises. It struck Sister Irene that she was making a mistake to let him in. There were these moments when one had to make an intelligent decision. . . . But she was sympathetic with him, yes. She was sympathetic with something about him.

She found out his name the next day: Allen Weinstein.

After this she came to her Shakespeare class with a sense of excitement. It became clear to her at once that Weinstein was the most intelligent student in the class. Until he had enrolled, she had not understood what was lacking, a mind that could appreciate her own. Within a week his jagged, protean mind had alienated the other students, and though he sat in the center of the class, he seemed totally alone, encased by a miniature world of his own. When he spoke of the "frenetic humanism of the High Renaissance," Sister Irene dreaded the raised eyebrows and mocking smiles of the other students, who no longer bothered to look at Weinstein. She wanted to defend him, but she never did, because there was something rude and dismal about his knowledge; he used it like a weapon, talking passionately of Nietzsche and Goethe and Freud until Sister Irene would be forced to close discussion.

In meditation, alone, she often thought of him. When she tried to talk about him to a young nun, Sister Carlotta, everything sounded gross. "But no, he's an excellent student," she insisted. "I'm very grateful to have him in class. It's just that . . . he thinks ideas are real." Sister Carlotta, who loved literature also, had been forced to teach grade-school arithmetic for the last four years. That might have been why she said, a little sharply, "You don't think ideas are real?"

Sister Irene acquiesced with a smile, but of course she did not think so: only reality is real.

When Weinstein did not show up for class on the day the first paper was due, Sister Irene's heart sank, and the sensation was somehow a familiar one. She began her lecture and kept waiting for the door to open and for him to hurry noisily back to his seat, grinning an apology toward her—but nothing happened.

If she had been deceived by him, she made herself think

angrily, it was as a teacher and not as a woman. He had promised her nothing.

Weinstein appeared the next day near the steps of the liberal arts building. She heard someone running behind her, a breathless exclamation: "Sister Irene!" She turned and saw him, panting and grinning in embarrassment. He wore a dark-blue suit with a necktie, and he looked, despite his childish face, like a little old man; there was something oddly precarious and fragile about him. "Sister Irene, I owe you an apology, right?" He raised his eyebrows and smiled a sad, forlorn, yet irritatingly conspiratorial smile. "The first paper—not in on time, and I know what your rules are. . . . You won't accept late papers, I know—that's good discipline, I'll do that when I teach too. But, unavoidably, I was unable to come to school yesterday. There are many—many—" He gulped for breath, and Sister Irene had the startling sense of seeing the real Weinstein stare out at her, a terrified prisoner behind the confident voice. "There are many complications in family life. Perhaps you are unaware—I mean—"

She did not like him, but she felt this sympathy, something tugging and nagging at her the way her parents had competed for her love so many years before. They had been whining, weak people, and out of their wet need for affection, the girl she had been (her name was Yvonne) had emerged stronger than either of them, contemptuous of tears because she had seen so many. But Weinstein was different; he was not simply weak—perhaps he was not weak at all—but his strength was confused and hysterical. She felt her customary rigidity as a teacher begin to falter. "You may turn your paper in today if you have it," she said, frowning.

Weinstein's mouth jerked into an incredulous grin. "Wonderful! Marvelous!" he said. "You are very understanding, Sister Irene, I must say. I must say . . . I didn't expect, really . . ." He was fumbling in a shabby old briefcase for the paper. Sister Irene waited. She was prepared for another of his excuses, certain that he did not have the paper, when he suddenly straightened up and handed her something. "Here! I took the liberty of writing thirty pages instead of just fifteen," he said. He was obviously quite excited; his cheeks were mottled pink and white. "You may disagree violently with my interpretation—I expect you to, in fact I'm counting on it—but let me warn you, I have the exact proof, right here in the play itself!'' He was thumping at a book, his voice growing louder and shriller. Sister Irene, startled, wanted to put her hand over his mouth and soothe him.

"Look," he said breathlessly, "may I talk with you? I have a class now I hate, I loathe, I can't bear to sit through! Can I talk with you instead?"

Because she was nervous, she stared at the title page of the paper: '' 'Erotic Melodies in *Romeo and Juliet*' by Allen Weinstein, Jr.''

"All right?" he said. "Can we walk around here? Is it all right? I've been anxious to talk with you about some things you said in class."

She was reluctant, but he seemed not to notice. They walked slowly along the shaded campus paths. Weinstein did all the talking, of course, and Sister Irene recognized nothing in his cascade of words that she had mentioned in class. "The humanist must be committed to the totality of life," he said passionately. "This is the failing one finds everywhere in the academic world! I found it in New York and I found it here and I'm no ingénu, I don't go around with my mouth hanging open—I'm experienced, look, I've been to Europe, I've lived in Rome! I went everywhere in Europe except Germany, I don't talk about Germany . . . Sister Irene, think of the significant men in the last century, the men who've changed the world! Jews, right? Marx, Freud, Einstein! Not that I believe Marx, Marx is a madman . . . and Freud, no, my sympathies are with spiritual humanism. I believe that the Jewish race is the exclusive . . . the exclusive, what's the word, the exclusive means by which humanism will be extended. . . . Humanism begins by excluding the Jew, and now," he said with a high, surprised laugh, "the Jew will perfect it. After the Nazis, only the Jew is authorized to understand humanism, its limitations and its possibilities. So, I say that the humanist is committed to life in its totality and not just to his profession! The religious person is totally religious, he is his religion! What else? I recognize in you a humanist and a religious person—"

But he did not seem to be talking to her or even looking at her.

"Here, read this," he said. "I wrote it last night." It was a long free-verse poem, typed on a typewriter whose ribbon was worn out.

"There's this trouble with my father, a wonderful man, a lovely man, but his health—his strength is fading, do you see? What must it be to him to see his son growing up? I mean, I'm a man now, he's getting old, weak, his health is bad—it's hell, right? I sympathize with him. I'd do anything for him, I'd cut open my veins, anything for a father—right? That's why I wasn't in school yesterday," he said, and his voice dropped for the last sentence, as if he had been dragged back to earth by a fact.

Sister Irene tried to read the poem, then pretended to read it. A jumble of words dealing with "life" and "death" and "darkness" and "love." "What do you think?" Weinstein said nervously, trying to read it over her shoulder and crowding against her.

"It's very . . . passionate," Sister Irene said.

This was the right comment; he took the poem back from her in silence, his face flushed with excitement. "Here, at this school, I have few people to talk with. I haven't shown anyone else that poem." He looked at her with his dark, intense eyes, and Sister Irene felt them focus upon her. She was terrified at what he was trying to do—he was trying to force her into a human relationship.

"Thank you for your paper," she said, turning away.

When he came the next day, ten minutes late, he was haughty and disdainful. He had nothing to say and sat with his arms folded. Sister Irene took back with her to the convent a feeling of betrayal and confusion. She had been hurt. It was absurd, and yet— She spent too much time thinking about him, as if he were somehow a kind of crystallization of her own loneliness; but she had no right to think so much of him. She did not want to think of him or of her loneliness. But Weinstein did so much more than think of his predicament: he embodied it, he acted it out, and that was perhaps why he fascinated her. It was as if he were doing a dance for her, a dance of shame and agony and delight, and so long as he did it, she was safe. She felt embarrassment for him, but also anxiety; she wanted to protect him. When the dean of the graduate school questioned her about Weinstein's work, she insisted that he was an "excellent" student, though she knew the dean had not wanted to hear that.

She prayed for guidance, she spent hours on her devotions, she was closer to her vocation than she had been for some years. Life at the convent became tinged with unreality, a misty distortion that took its tone from the glowering skies of the city at night, identical smokestacks ranged against the clouds and giving to the sky the excrement of the populated and successful earth. This city was not her city, this world was not her world. She felt no pride in knowing this, it was a fact. The little convent was not like an island in the center of this noisy world, but rather a kind of hole or crevice the world did not bother with, something of no interest. The convent's rhythm of life had nothing to do with the world's rhythm, it did not violate or alarm it in any way. Sister Irene tried to draw together the fragments of her life and synthesize them somehow in her vocation as a nun: she was a nun, she was recognized as a nun and had given herself happily to that life, she had a name, a place, she had dedicated her superior intelligence to the Church, she worked without pay and without expecting gratitude, she had given up pride, she did not think of herself but only of her work and her vocation, she did not think of anything external to these, she saturated herself daily in the knowledge that she was involved in the mystery of Christianity.

A daily terror attended this knowledge, however, for she sensed herself being drawn by that student, that Jewish boy, into a relationship she was not ready for. She wanted to cry out in fear that she was being forced into the role of a Christian, and what did that mean? What could her studies tell her? What could the other nuns tell her? She was alone, no one could help; he was making her into a Christian, and to her that was a mystery, a thing of terror, something others slipped on the way they slipped on their clothes, casually and thoughtlessly, but to her a magnificent and terrifying wonder.

For days she carried Weinstein's paper, marked A, around with her; he did not come to class. One day she checked with the graduate office and was told that Weinstein had called in to say his father was ill and that he would not be able to attend classes for a while. "He's strange, I remember him," the secretary said. "He missed all his exams last spring and made a lot of trouble. He was in and out of here every day."

So there was no more of Weinstein for a while, and Sister Irene stopped expecting him to hurry into class. Then, one morning, she found a letter from him in her mailbox.

He had printed it in black ink, very carefully, as if he had not trusted handwriting. The return address was in bold letters that, like his voice, tried to grab onto her: Birchcrest Manor. Somewhere north of the city. "Dear Sister Irene," the block letters said, "I am doing well here and have time for reading and relaxing. The Manor is delightful. My doctor here is an excellent, intelligent man who has time for me, unlike my former doctor. If you have time, you might drop in on my father, who worries about me too much, I think, and explain to him what my condition is. He doesn't seem to understand. I feel about this new life the way that boy, what's his name, in *Measure for Measure,* feels about the prospects of a different life; you remember what he says to his sister when she visits him in prison, how he is looking forward to an escape into another world. Perhaps you could *explain* this to my father and he would stop worrying." The letter ended with the father's name and address, in letters that were just a little too big. Sister Irene, walking slowly down the corridor as she read the letter, felt her eyes cloud over with tears. She was cold with fear, it was something she had never experienced before. She knew what Weinstein was trying to tell her, and the desperation of his attempt made it all the more pathetic; he did not deserve this, why did God allow him to suffer so?

She read through Claudio's speech to his sister, in *Measure for Measure:*

> *Ay, but to die, and go we know not where;*
> *To lie in cold obstruction and to rot;*
> *This sensible warm motion to become*
> *A kneaded clod; and the delighted spirit*
> *To bathe in fiery floods, or to reside*
> *In thrilling region of thick-ribbed ice,*

To be imprison'd in the viewless winds
And blown with restless violence round about
The pendent world; or to be worse than
    worst
Of those that lawless and incertain thought
Imagines howling! 'Tis too horrible!
The weariest and most loathed worldly life
That age, ache, penury, and imprisonment
Can lay on nature is a paradise
To what we fear of death.

Sister Irene called the father's number that day. "Allen Weinstein residence, who may I say is calling?" a woman said, bored. "May I speak to Mr. Weinstein? It's urgent—about his son," Sister Irene said. There was a pause at the other end. "You want to talk to his mother, maybe?" the woman said. "His mother? Yes, his mother, then. Please. It's very important."

She talked with this strange, unsuspected woman, a disembodied voice that suggested absolutely no face, and insisted upon going over that afternoon. The woman was nervous, but Sister Irene, who was a university professor, after all, knew enough to hide her own nervousness. She kept waiting for the woman to say, "Yes, Allen has mentioned you . . ." but nothing happened.

She persuaded Sister Carlotta to ride over with her. This urgency of hers was something they were all amazed by. They hadn't suspected that the set of her gray eyes could change to this blurred, distracted alarm, this sense of mission that seemed to have come to her from nowhere. Sister Irene drove across the city in the late afternoon traffic, with the high whining noises from residential streets where trees were being sawed down in pieces. She understood now the secret, sweet wildness that Christ must have felt, giving himself for man, dying for the billions of men who would never know of him and never understand the sacrifice. For the first time she approached the realization of that great act. In her troubled mind the city traffic was jumbled and yet oddly coherent, an image of the world that was always out of joint with what was happening in it, its inner history struggling with its external spectacle. This sacrifice of Christ's, so mysterious and legendary now, almost lost in time—it was that by which Christ transcended both God and man at one moment, more than man because of his fate to do what no other man could do, and more than God because no god could suffer as he did. She felt a flicker of something close to madness.

She drove nervously, uncertainly, afraid of missing the street and afraid of finding it too, for while one part of her rushed forward to confront these people who had betrayed their son, another part of her would have liked nothing so much as to be waiting as usual for the summons to dinner, safe in her room. . . . When she found the street and turned onto it, she was in a state of breathless excitement. Here lawns were bright green and marred with only a few leaves, magically clean, and the houses were enormous and pompous, a mixture of styles: ranch houses, colonial houses, French country houses, white-bricked wonders with curving glass and clumps of birch trees somehow encircled by white concrete. Sister Irene stared as if she had blundered into another world. This was a kind of heaven, and she was too shabby for it.

The Weinsteins' house was the strangest one of all: it looked like a small Alpine lodge, with an inverted-V-shaped front entrance. Sister Irene drove up the black-topped driveway and let the car slow to a stop; she told Sister Carlotta she would not be long.

At the door she was met by Weinstein's mother, a small, nervous woman with hands like her son's. "Come in, come in," the woman said. She had once been beautiful, that was clear, but now in missing beauty she was not handsome or even attractive but looked ruined and perplexed, the misshapen swelling of her white-blond professionally set hair like a cap lifting up from her surprised face. "He'll be right in. Allen?" she called, "our visitor is here." They went into the living room. There was a grand piano at one end and an organ at the other. In between were scatterings of brilliant modern furniture in conversational groups, and several puffed-up white rugs on the polished floor. Sister Irene could not stop shivering.

"Professor, it's so strange, but let me say when the phone

rang I had a feeling—I had a feeling," the woman said, with damp eyes. Sister Irene sat, and the woman hovered about her. "Should I call you Professor? We don't . . . you know . . . we don't understand the technicalities that go with— Allen, my son, wanted to go here to the Catholic school; I told my husband why not? Why fight? It's the thing these days, they do anything they want for knowledge. And he had to come home, you know. He couldn't take care of himself in New York, that was the beginning of the trouble. . . . Should I call you Professor?"

"You can call me Sister Irene."

"Sister Irene?" the woman said, touching her throat in awe, as if something intimate and unexpected had happened.

Then Weinstein's father appeared, hurrying. He took long, impatient strides. Sister Irene stared at him and in that instant doubted everything—he was in his fifties, a tall, sharply handsome man, heavy but not fat, holding his shoulders back with what looked like an effort, but holding them back just the same. He wore a dark suit and his face was flushed, as if he had run a long distance.

"Now," he said, coming to Sister Irene and with a precise wave of his hand motioning his wife off, "now, let's straighten this out. A lot of confusion over that kid, eh?" He pulled a chair over, scraping it across a rug and pulling one corner over, so that its brown underside was exposed. "I came home early just for this, Libby phoned me. Sister, you got a letter from him, right?"

The wife looked at Sister Irene over her husband's head as if trying somehow to coach her, knowing that this man was so loud and impatient that no one could remember anything in his presence.

"A letter—yes—today—"

"He says what in it? You got the letter, eh? Can I see it?"

She gave it to him and wanted to explain, but he silenced her with a flick of his hand. He read through the letter so quickly that Sister Irene thought perhaps he was trying to impress her with his skill at reading. "So?" he said, raising his eyes, smiling, "so what is this? He's happy out there, he says. He doesn't communicate with us any more, but he writes to you and says he's happy—what's that? I mean, what the hell is that?''

"But he isn't happy. He wants to come home," Sister Irene said. It was so important that she make him understand that she could not trust her voice; goaded by this man, it might suddenly turn shrill, as his son's did. "Someone must read their letters before they're mailed, so he tried to tell me something by making an allusion to—"

"What?"

"—an allusion to a play, so that I would know. He may be thinking suicide, he must be very unhappy—"

She ran out of breath. Weinstein's mother had begun to cry, but the father was shaking his head jerkily back and forth. "Forgive me, Sister, but it's a lot of crap, he needs the hospital, he needs help—right? It costs me fifty a day out there, and they've got the best place in the state, I figure it's worth it. He needs help, that kid, what do I care if he's unhappy? He's unbalanced!" he said angrily. "You want us to get him out again? We argued with the judge for two hours to get him in, an acquaintance of mine. Look, he can't control himself—he was smashing things here, he was hysterical. They need help, lady, and you do something about it fast! You do something! We made up our minds to do something and we did it! This letter—what the hell is this letter? He never talked like that to us!"

"But he means the opposite of what he says—"

"Then he's crazy! I'm the first to admit it." He was perspiring, and his face had darkened. "I've got no pride left this late. He's a little bastard, you want to know? He calls me names, he's filthy, got a filthy mouth—that's being smart, huh? They give him a big scholarship for his filthy mouth? I went to college too, and I got out and knew something, and I for Christ's sake did something with it; my wife is an intelligent woman, a learned woman, would you guess she does book reviews for the little newspaper out here? Intelligent isn't crazy—crazy isn't intelligent. Maybe for you at the school he writes nice papers and gets an A, but out here, around the house, he can't control himself, and we got him committed!"

"But—"

"We're fixing him up, don't worry about it!" He turned to his wife. "Libby, get out of here, I mean it. I'm sorry, but get out of here, you're making a fool of yourself, go stand in the kitchen or something, you and the goddamn maid can cry on each other's shoulders. That one in the kitchen is nuts too, they're all nuts. Sister," he said, his voice lowering, "I thank you immensely for coming out here. This is wonderful, your interest in my son. And I see he admires you—that letter there. But what about that letter? If he did want to get out, which I don't admit—he was willing to be committed, in the end he said okay himself—if he wanted out I wouldn't do it. Why? So what if he wants to come back? The next day he wants something else, what then? He's a sick kid, and I'm the first to admit it."

Sister Irene felt that sickness spread to her. She stood. The room was so big it seemed it must be a public place; there had been nothing personal or private about their conversation. Weinstein's mother was standing by the fireplace, sobbing. The father jumped to his feet and wiped his forehead in a gesture that was meant to help Sister Irene on her way out. "God, what a day," he said, his eyes snatching at hers for understanding, "you know—one of those days all day long? Sister, I thank you a lot. There should be more people in the world who care about others, like you. I mean that."

On the way back to the convent, the man's words returned to her, and she could not get control of them; she could not even feel anger. She had been pressed down, forced back, what could she do? Weinstein might have been watching her somehow from a barred window, and he surely would have understood. The strange idea she had had on the way over, something about understanding Christ, came back to her now and sickened her. But the sickness was small. It could be contained.

About a month after her visit to his father, Weinstein himself showed up. He was dressed in a suit as before, even the necktie was the same. He came right into her office as if he had been pushed and could not stop.

"Sister," he said, and shook her hand. He must have seen fear in her because he smiled ironically. "Look, I'm released. I'm let out of the nut house. Can I sit down?"

He sat. Sister Irene was breathing quickly, as if in the presence of an enemy who does not know he is an enemy.

"So, they finally let me out. I heard what you did. You talked with him, that was all I wanted. You're the only one who gave a damn. Because you're a humanist and a religious person, you respect . . . the individual. Listen," he said, whispering, "it was hell out there! Hell Birchcrest Manor! All fixed up with fancy chairs and *Life* magazines lying around—and what do they do to you? They locked me up, they gave me shock treatments! Shock treatments, how do you like that, it's discredited by everybody now—they're crazy out there themselves, sadists. They locked me up, they gave me hypodermic shots, they didn't treat me like a human being! Do you know what that is," Weinstein demanded savagely, "not to be treated like a human being? They made me an animal—for fifty dollars a day! Dirty filthy swine! Now I'm an outpatient because I stopped swearing at them. I found somebody's bobby pin, and when I wanted to scream I pressed it under my fingernail and it stopped me—the screaming went inside and not out—so they gave me good reports, those sick bastards. Now I'm an outpatient and I can walk along the street and breathe in the same filthy exhaust from the buses like all you normal people! Christ," he said, and threw himself back against the chair.

Sister Irene stared at him. She wanted to take his hand, to make some gesture that would close the aching distance between them. "Mr. Weinstein—"

"Call me Allen!" he said sharply.

"I'm very sorry—I'm terribly sorry—"

"My own parents committed me, but of course they didn't know what it was like. It was hell," he said thickly, "and there isn't any hell except what other people do to you. The psychiatrist out there, the main shrink, he hates Jews too, some of us were positive of that, and he's got a bigger nose than I do, a real beak." He made a noise of disgust. "A dirty bastard, a sick, dirty, pathetic bastard—all of them. Anyway, I'm getting out of here, and I came to ask you a favor."

"What do you mean?"

"I'm getting out. I'm leaving. I'm going up to Canada and lose myself. I'll get a job, I'll forget everything, I'll kill myself maybe—what's the difference? Look, can you lend me some money?''

"Money?"

"Just a little! I have to get to the border, I'm going to take a bus.''

"But I don't have any money—"

"No money?" He stared at her. "You mean—you don't have any? Sure you have some!''

She stared at him as if he had asked her to do something obscene. Everything was splotched and uncertain before her eyes.

"You must . . . you must go back," she said, "you're making a—"

"I'll pay it back. Look, I'll pay it back, can you go to where you live or something and get it? I'm in a hurry. My friends are sons of bitches: one of them pretended he didn't see me yesterday—I stood right in the middle of the sidewalk and yelled at him, I called him some appropriate names! So he didn't see me, huh? You're the only one who understands me, you understand me like a poet, you—"

"I can't help you, I'm sorry—I . . .''

He looked to one side of her and flashed his gaze back, as if he could control it. He seemed to be trying to clear his vision.

"You have the soul of a poet," he whispered, "you're the only one. Everybody else is rotten! Can't you lend me some money, ten dollars maybe? I have three thousand in the bank, and I can't touch it! They take everything away from me, they make me into an animal. . . . You know I'm not an animal, don't you? Don't you?''

"Of course," Sister Irene whispered.

"You could get money. Help me. Give me your hand or something, touch me, help me—please. . . .'' He reached for her hand and she drew back. He stared at her and his face seemed about to crumble, like a child's. "I want something from you, but I don't know what—I want something!'' he cried. "Something real! I want you to look at me like I was a human being, is that too much to ask? I have a brain, I'm alive, I'm suffering—what does that mean? Does that mean nothing? I want something real and not this phony Christian love garbage—it's all in the books, it isn't personal—I want something real—look. . . ."

He tried to take her hand again, and this time she jerked away. She got to her feet. "Mr. Weinstein," she said, "please—"

"You! You nun!" he said scornfully, his mouth twisted into a mock grin. "You nun! There's nothing under that ugly outfit, right? And you're not particularly smart even though you think you are; my father has more brains in his foot than you—"

He got to his feet and kicked the chair.

"You bitch!" he cried.

She shrank back against her desk as if she thought he might hit her, but he only ran out of the office.

Weinstein: the name was to become disembodied from the figure, as time went on. The semester passed, the autumn drizzle turned into snow, Sister Irene rode to school in the morning and left in the afternoon, four days a week, anonymous in her black winter cloak, quiet and stunned. University teaching was an anonymous task, each day dissociated from the rest, with no necessary sense of unity among the teachers: they came and went separately and might for a year just miss a colleague who left his office five minutes before they arrived, and it did not matter.

She heard of Weinstein's death, his suicide by drowning, from the English Department secretary, a handsome white-haired woman who kept a transistor radio on her desk. Sister Irene was not surprised; she had been thinking of him as dead for months. "They identified him by some special television way they have now," the secretary said. "They're shipping the body back. It was up in Quebec. . . ."

Sister Irene could feel a part of herself drifting off, lured by the plains of white snow to the north, the quiet, the emptiness, the sweep of the Great Lakes up to the silence of Canada. But she called that part of herself back. She could only be one person in her lifetime. That was the ugly truth, she thought, that she could not really regret Weinstein's suffering and death; she had only one life and had already given it to someone else. He had come too late to her. Fifteen years ago, perhaps, but not now.

She was only one person, she thought, walking down the corridor in a dream. Was she safe in this single person, or was she trapped? She had only one identity. She could make only one choice. What she had done or hadn't done was the result of that choice, and how was she guilty? If she could have felt guilt, she thought, she might at least have been able to feel something.

(1965)

John Updike

John Updike was born in Pennsylvania, in 1932. He was educated at Harvard University and the Ruskin School of Drawing and Fine Art at Oxford University. After working for The New Yorker from 1955 to 1957, and beginning to publish both stories and poems in that magazine, he became a free-lance writer. His first novel, the short and poignant The Poorhouse Fair (1959), was both a critical and a popular success. Rabbit, Run (1960) was an even more successful novel; it has been followed by a steady succession of novels and collections of stories, poems, and plays, and more recently by Hugging the Shore (1983), a volume of over 900 pages, collecting essays and critical writing.

Updike is prolific, precise, and blessed with a carefully modulated, compulsively readable way with words. At his best, in his less obviously ambitious stories and novels, he writes modestly but persuasively about the lives of smalltown Americans, suburban Americans, and Americans trying, not always successfully, to cope with the stresses and strains of modern life. At his worst, in his more ambitious fiction and in his usually vacuous poetry, he often seems to be writing for the sake of writing—or in order to keep his deft pen busily at work. Neither deeply perceptive nor richly comic, he never writes down to his audience or pretends to learning and insights he does not in fact have. When he writes about people he truly knows, and whose lives engage him, his fiction is among the most polished and quietly effective of the postwar years.

THE TASTE OF METAL

Metal, strictly, has no taste; its presence in the mouth is felt as disciplinary, as a *No* spoken to other tastes. When Richard Maple, after thirty years of twinges, jagged edges, and occasional extractions, had all his remaining molars capped and bridges shaped across the gaps, the gold felt chilly to his cheeks and its regularity masked holes and roughnesses that had been a kind of mirror wherein his tongue had known itself. The Friday of the final cementing, he went to a small party. As he drank a variety of liquids that tasted much the same, he moved from feeling slightly less than himself (his native teeth had been ground to stumps of dentine) to feeling slightly more. The shift in tonality that permeated his skull whenever his jaws closed corresponded, perhaps, to the heightened clarity that fills the mind after a religious conversion. He saw his companions at the party with a new brilliance—a sharpness of vision that, like a camera's, was specific and restricted in focus. He could see only one person at a time, and found himself focusing less on his wife Joan than on Eleanor Dennis, the long-legged wife of a municipal-bond salesman.

Eleanor's distinctness in part had to do with the legal fact that she and her husband were "separated." It had happened recently; his absence from the party was noticeable. Eleanor, in the course of a life that she described as a series of harrowing survivals, had developed the brassy social manner that converts private catastrophe into public humorousness; but tonight her agitation was imperfectly converted. She listened as if for an echo that wasn't there, and twitchily crossed and recrossed her legs. Her legs were handsome and vivid and so long that, after midnight, when parlor games began, she hitched up her brief skirt and kicked the lintel of a doorframe. The host balanced a glass of water on his forehead. Richard, demonstrating a headstand, mistakenly tumbled forward, delighted at his own softness, which he felt to be an ironical comment upon flesh that his new metal teeth were making. He was all mortality, all porous erosion save for these stars in his head, an impervious polar cluster at the zenith of his slow whirling.

His wife came to him with a face as neat and unscarred as the face of a clock. It was time to go home. And Eleanor needed a ride. The three of them, plus the hostess in her bangle earrings and coffee-stained culottes, went to the door, and discovered a snowstorm. As far as the eye could probe, flakes were falling in a jostling crowd through the whispering lavender night. "God bless us, every one," Richard said.

The hostess suggested that Joan should drive.

Richard kissed her on the cheek and tasted the metal of her bitter earring and got in behind the wheel. His car was a brand-new Corvair; he wouldn't dream of trusting anyone else to drive it. Joan crawled into the back seat, grunting to emphasize the physical awkwardness, and Eleanor serenely arranged her coat and pocketbook and legs in the space beside him. The motor sprang alive. Richard felt resiliently cushioned: Eleanor was beside him, Joan behind him, God above him, the road beneath him. The fast-falling snow dipped brilliant—explosive, chrysanthemumesque—into the car headlights. On a small hill the tires spun—a loose, reassuring noise, like the slither of a raincoat.

In the knobbed darkness lit by the green speed gauge, Eleanor, showing a wealth of knee, talked at length of her separated husband. "You have no *idea*," she said, "you two are so sheltered you have no idea what men are capable of. I didn't know myself. I don't mean to sound ungracious, he gave me nine reasonable years and I wouldn't *dream* of punishing him with the children's visiting hours the way some women would, but that *man!* You know what he had the crust to tell me? He actually told me that when he was with another woman he'd sometimes close his eyes and pretend it was *me*."

"Sometimes," Richard said.

His wife behind him said, "Darley, are you aware that the road is slippery?"

"That's the shine of the headlights," he told her.

Eleanor crossed and recrossed her legs. Half the length of a thigh flared in the intimate green glow. She went on, "And his *trips*. I wondered why the same city was always putting out bond issues. I began to feel sorry for the mayor, I thought they were going bankrupt. Looking back at myself, I was so *good,* so wrapped up in the children and the house, always on the phone to the contractor or the plumber or the gas company trying to get the new kitchen done in time for Thanksgiving when his silly, *silly* mother was coming to visit. About once a day I'd sharpen the carving knife. Thank God that phase of my life is over. I went to his mother for sympathy I suppose and very indignantly she asked me, What had I done to her boy? The children and I had tuna-fish sandwiches by ourselves and it was the first Thanksgiving I've ever enjoyed, frankly."

"I always have trouble," Richard told her, "finding the second joint."

Joan said, "Darley, you know you're coming to that terrible curve?"

"You should see my father-in-law carve. Snick, snap, snap, snick. Your blood runs cold."

"On my birthday, my *birth*day," Eleanor said, accidentally kicking the heater, "the bastard was with his little dolly in a restaurant, and he told me, he solemnly told me—men are incredible—he told me he ordered cake for dessert. That was his tribute to me. That night he confessed all this, it was the end of the world, but I had to laugh. I asked him if he'd had the restaurant put a candle on the cake. He told me he'd thought of it but hadn't had the guts."

Richard's responsive laugh was held in suspense as the car skidded on the curve. A dark upright shape had appeared in the center of the windshield, and he tried to remove it, but the automobile proved impervious to the steering wheel and instead drew closer, as if magnetized, to a telephone pole that rigidly insisted on its position in the center of the windshield. The pole enlarged. The little splinters pricked by the linemen's cleats leaped forward in the headlights, and there was a flat whack surprisingly unambiguous, considering how casually it had happened. Richard felt the sudden refusal of motion, the *No,* and knew, though his mind was deeply cushioned in a cottony indifference, that an event had occurred which in another incarnation he would regret.

"You jerk," Joan said. Her voice was against his ear. "Your pretty new car." She asked, "Eleanor, are you all right?" With a rising inflection she repeated, "Are you all right?" It sounded like scolding.

Eleanor giggled softly, embarrassed. "I'm fine," she said, "except that I can't seem to move my legs." The windshield near her head had become a web of light, an exploded star.

Either the radio had been on or had turned itself on, for mellow, meditating music flowed from a realm behind time. Richard identified it as one of Handel's oboe sonatas. He noticed that his knees distantly hurt. Eleanor had slid forward and seemed unable to uncross her legs. Shockingly, she whimpered. Joan asked, "Sweetheart, didn't you know you were going too fast?"

"I am very stupid," he said. Music and snow poured down upon them, and he imagined that, if only the oboe sonata were played backwards, they would leap backwards from the telephone pole and be on their way home again. The little distances to their houses, once measured in minutes, had frozen and become immense.

Using her hands, Eleanor uncrossed her legs and brought herself upright in her seat. She lit a cigarette. Richard, his knees creaking, got out of the car and tried to push it free. He told Joan to come out of the back seat and get behind the wheel. Their motions were clumsy, wriggling in and out of darkness. The headlights still burned, but the beams were bent inward, toward each other. The Corvair had a hollow head, its engine being in the rear. Its face, an unimpassioned insect's face, was inextricably curved around the pole; the bumper had become locked mandibles. When Richard pushed and Joan fed gas, the wheels whined in a vacuum. The smooth encircling night extended around them, above and beyond the snow. No window light had acknowledged their accident.

Joan, who had a social conscience, asked, "Why doesn't anybody come out and help us?"

Eleanor, the voice of bitter experience, answered, "This pole is hit so often it's just a nuisance to the neighborhood."

Richard announced, "I'm too drunk to face the police." The remark hung with a neon clarity in the night.

A car came by, slowed, stopped. A window rolled down and revealed a frightened male voice. "Everything O.K.?"

"Not entirely," Richard said. He was pleased by his powers, under stress, of exact expression.

"I can take somebody to a telephone. I'm on my way back from a poker game."

A lie, Richard reasoned—otherwise, why advance it? The boy's face had the blurred pallor of the sexually drained. Taking care to give each word weight, Richard told him, "One of us can't move and I better say with her. If you could take my wife to a phone, we'd all be most grateful."

"Who do I call?" Joan asked.

Richard hesitated between the party they had left, the babysitter at home, and Eleanor's husband, who was living in a motel on Route 128.

The boy answered for him: "The police."

As Iphigenia redeemed the becalmed fleet at Aulis, so Joan got into the stranger's car, a rusty red Mercury. The car faded through the snow, which was slackening. The storm had been just a flurry, an illusion conjured to administer this one rebuke. It wouldn't even make tomorrow's newspapers.

Richard's knees felt as if icicles were being pressed against the soft spot beneath the caps, where the doctor's hammer searches for a reflex. He got in behind the wheel again, and switched off the lights. He switched off the ignition. Eleanor's cigarette glowed. Though his system was still adrift in liquor, he could not quite forget the taste of metal in his teeth. That utterly flat *No:* through several dreamlike thicknesses something very hard had touched him. Once, swimming in surf, he had been sucked under by a large wave. Tons of sudden surge had enclosed him and, with an implacable downward shrug, thrust him deep into dense green bitterness and stripped him of weight; his struggling became nothing, he was nothing within the wave. There had been no hatred. The wave simply hadn't *cared*.

He tried to apologize to the woman beside him in the darkness.

She said, "Oh, please. I'm sure nothing's broken. At the worst I'll be on crutches for a few days." She laughed and added, "This just isn't my year."

"Does it hurt?"

"No, not at all."

"You're probably in shock. You'll be cold. I'll get the heat back." Richard was sobering, and an infinite drabness was dawning for him. Never again, never ever, would his car be new, would he chew on his own enamel, would she kick so high with her vivid long legs. He turned the ignition back on and started up the motor, for warmth. The radio softly returned, still Handel.

Moving from the hips up with surprising strength, Eleanor turned and embraced him. Her cheeks were wet; her lipstick tasted manufactured. Searching for her waist, for the smallness of her breasts, he fumbled through thicknesses of cloth. They were still in each other's arms when the whirling blue light of the police car broke upon them.

(ca. 1965)

George P. Elliott

George P. Elliott was born in Indiana, in 1918, and raised in California. He was educated at the University of California at Berkeley, taking a B.A. in 1939 and an M.A. in 1941. He spent most of his life as an active teacher, first at St. Mary's College, in California, and then at Cornell, Barnard, the University of Iowa and, from 1963 to his death in 1980, at Syracuse University. Author of four novels and two collections of stories, he also published two collections of poems, two collections of essays, and in addition to a teaching text, Types of Prose Fiction (1964), edited Fifteen Modern American Poets (1956). He won a good many prizes and awards, though no major ones.

Elliott's work as a whole suffers from a degree of sameness, and a degree of thinness. His best-known story, "Among the Dangs" (1958), would be a good deal better, and more readable, had its insistently episodic structure been modified— and had the story as a whole been cut by perhaps a third, to avoid unnecessary and wearying repetitions. But at his best, as in the story here reprinted, Elliott is a ripe, mature craftsman who not only knows exactly what he wants to do but has the craft and the patience to do it.

He died in 1980.

WORDS WORDS WORDS

The words were ready: "Our marriage will be a contract of equals freely joined." He had decided upon them two weeks after leaving port, in a rolling sea. Everything else he'd thought about for the past four months, everything of importance to him, had been adornment, explanation, preparation for the delivery of those words. He had not written them to her, for he felt never so stiff as with a pen in his hand; written, that sentence said everything he meant; yet he knew that, uncircumstanced, it would be impotent upon her. And he intended it to bind; he meant her never to forget it so long as they should be married.

Words, as he believed, bind only when delivered with ceremony, and here was his problem. Their love being free from authority, Jane and he were deprived of ceremony; indeed, once when they had talked about two of her friends who were living together, they had agreed that marriage itself was a social convention to be deferred to only for convenience's sake and the sentiments of relatives; they had therefore never talked about getting married. But off the coast of Venezuela outward bound, he had decided to propose to her. He needed, atavistically, a profounder tie than New York lovers were bound by. They would be bound to freedom, that must be absolutely clear, but bound. He had had to invent his own ceremony.

His plan was this. He would phone her at her office as soon as his ship docked; he would have air-mailed her a letter from the last port so that she would know which day to expect him; she would be sure to have kept that evening free for him. He would go to her apartment a little after six; they would talk for a while, till the flush of reunion should have subsided; he would take her to the Captain's Table, where they would have shrimp cocktail and broiled lobster; then, over coffee and, he hoped, at the same table from which she had first accepted him for her lover, he would say what he had to say. It was a ceremony of sentiment, he knew that, wholly private, devoid of sacrament; but he knew no other way to freight the words of his proposal with the gravity he wanted them to bear. No words repeated to a justice of the peace in a courthouse office could bind them more than legally, and an altar would make liars of them. The Captain's Table; shrimp, lobster, and white burgundy; her left hand in his right at the edge of the table, as it had been when she had said, "Come make love to me"—he would ask her to wear the same green dress and her Toledo earrings.

The ship arrived on a Tuesday; good, the restaurant would not be crowded. It was berthed in Brooklyn by nine thirty in the morning; he was second only to the first mate in getting to the pay booth. Jane's "Darling, you're here at last" greeted him in the accents of every sailor's dream of welcome; she had been waiting for him; she adored him.

He got to his hotel-rooming house in Greenwich Village by five. His room was made up and his clothes were hanging pressed in the closet. There was his father's invariable card waiting for him: the old man's leg was bothering him again, they'd had the coldest March fifth in thirty years and the gas north of Syracuse had failed for eight hours, thank God nobody died of it, business was about as usual but every year the new cars got harder to work on, come home for a good long stay. And there was another envelope from Syracuse too, in a hand and with a return address he did not recognize, postmarked more than three months earlier.

The letter was a short paragraph, signed, "Very sincerely yours, Rosannah," and the salutation read, "Dear Mark." Well, good. She'd never called him Mark during the time they'd known one another. He'd sent her a picture postcard from Beirut, where her father had gone to medical school, a neutral greeting which he'd signed Mark and sent in care of her father at his hospital. The May before, waiting for his mate's papers, he'd substituted at The Drumlins for the golf pro, who'd sprained his ankle; Rosannah had taken lessons three afternoons a week; in the midst of the last lesson they'd had a spring half hour at the sixth hole; she was engaged; he got the impression that she wished she weren't; he did not even kiss her; she said, "Good-bye, Mr. Birch," and ran off with her head bent; he'd cried before going to sleep; and thence to sea. "Dear Mark, It was so nice of you to send me that card. It made Daddy quite homesick. I am living away from home now, as you can see by my address. I'm teaching first grade in the poorer section of town and loving it. At least I love my children, every one of them. Our acquaintance (I guess that's what it was) came to an end so fast, I didn't have an opportunity to thank you for everything. I hope we meet again." Well, well. Such girlish handwriting. He was at least six years older than she and felt six more than that. She'd shown promise of becoming a good golfer. "I hope we meet again." No more engagement. Well. Too late now, kid, you had your chance. He wondered whether she'd let her hair grow as he'd told her she should.

Jane's door opened as he came down the hall, but she was not in sight. The room was dimly lit. "Jane?" He stepped inside. In the fireplace two logs were flickering softly. "Darling," she whispered behind him and pushed the door closed. She held her arms out to him. She was wearing the silk dragon coat he'd sent her from Saigon on his first trip, held by a gold cord at the waist; her feet were bare; she wore no make-up. He tossed the yellow roses he'd brought onto a table and took her in his arms. She had perfumed herself heavily, as she did only when they were about to make love. Even so, he might have had fortitude to resist her, for the moment, as he had planned, were it not for the Scotch and ice already poured and waiting. "Not yet," he said as she reached one to him.

"I thought you wouldn't want to," she answered, "but it wouldn't be loverly to make me drink alone, now would it?"

"But I wanted to talk."

"Of course, darling, we'll talk till dawn if we want to. I don't *have* to go to work tomorrow."

What could he do? Good whiskey, four months' abstinence, her perfume, her white shoulder bare where he'd pushed the coat askew, her lips after kissing tumescent between pain and invitation till gradually they closed back to the little smile which meant she was content, her voice of dreamlike welcome—what could he want to do? The words would wait. He lost the wish to say them.

"How brown you are, darling. Look how wintry pale I am beside you. Aren't I revolting? Take off your shirt." Well, she was exactly as she had been, as nearly perfect as she could be. The room and the rug, her straight hair helmeted to her head, her somewhat stubby legs, the just audible chamber music from the record player, all the same. "I have been faithful to you, you third mate you. You'd better make it up to me, good good good." So he was not able to delight her first off with Madagascar as he had planned, nor to learn whether she had been made head of the domestic workers section of the agency as she had hoped; he was not able to do it and could not will it; her dreamy perfection, which had won him in the first place and which at sea he had wanted to crack, englobed him now again belly, brain, and members. The ceremonies they performed were those of sailors' dreams.

The *I love you*'s with which he bejeweled her lost their luster as the fire burned down.

Also, by nine he was hungry beyond crackers and blue cheese. "Let's go out for dinner."

"How thoughtful, darling. I didn't want to cook, even for you, not tonight. Where shall we go?"

"The Captain's Table."

"Marvelous. You know everything I want. I was there a couple of weeks ago for lunch and had the best oyster stew in the world. It was the best."

Instead of entering her game, he said rather gruffly, remembering his plan, "I want shrimp cocktail and lobster. A two-pound lobster. Don't you?"

She looked at him with an expression of worry about the eyes, an expression that had always annoyed him; for the concern, which seemed to be for him, turned out to be for herself, anxiety for fear he should attack her, apology for having displeased him, displeasure at his ill temper. "You have something on your mind, Markie."

"Love."

"Love on your mind? Now?" She laughed with relief. She had never said she loved him. "You got to wait, sailor boy. Which dress do you want me to wear?"

"The green one with the full skirt."

"Oh, you remember! You're my favorite lover ever."

"And those earrings Mike gave you." Mike had been the friend from whom he'd taken Jane.

They sat at the same table all right; she obviously did not remember it; perhaps she did not remember the event either. Perhaps she did not remember that two weeks after they had first become lovers, just before he had sailed on his first voyage, she had told him, in this same room, that she would not go around with other men while he was gone. He must remind her. For so sentimental a ceremony to have any force at all, each step in it must be recognized and savored. He decided to wait till they had finished their lobster before speaking; they were hungry; there was plenty of time; he was not in the right frame of mind. It was so comfortable inside her globe of perfection that only the memory of his resolution and the knowledge that his dissatisfaction was sure to resurrect itself had power to move him on.

Yet even as he began to speak of love he felt the weakness of his words. She was able to treat what he said as mere tenderness, and to preen. He said, intensely because he was angry, "But I mean it," and knew that to say *I mean it* at such a moment meant *I want to mean it.* "I want to marry you," he said, of momentum.

"Oh darling, so fast?"

"We've known each other since last June. You gave up other men for me. You were faithful while I was gone. I think of you all the time. I love you."

"Grim grim grim." He had the impulse to smile with her because he loved her mouth, but he repressed it.

"Our marriage would be a contract of equals freely joined." And they were even holding hands in the same way too.

But *will be* had become *would be*; he had forgotten to remind her of what had happened here before; the ceremony lacked even sentiment. He felt hermetically sealed. "No," she said, "you know I am not sure. Marriage must be all thought out. No, darling, not now. Don't you like what we have?"

"You know I do."

"Then let's don't spoil it by rushing things. It's so wonderful that you're a sailor. I don't think I'll ever get tired of you. The perfect solution!" Solution to love? Very well. He would play her rational, esthetic game of solving love problems. She had defeated him. Or else, not really wanting to be bound even by free and equal marriage, he had capitulated to her.

"Okay, Jane. I just wanted you to know where I stand."

"I do, darling, I know so well and I adore you. So. And if you don't keep scaring me like that maybe I'll let myself love you. Huh?"

"Okay. Say, who did you come here with anyway a couple of weeks ago?"

"Oh, I was afraid you weren't ever going to ask me that. Good boy." She settled down to curry him sleek with jealousy; he relaxed and enjoyed it.

For five days they were, perfectly, lovers. Only when he was alone and quiet—not often—was he discontent. Ceremony in a restaurant—what had he expected? He was disgusted with himself. Yet he could not help reflecting sometimes that even when they were sharing her pillow with the breath of her repose warm against his neck, he said nothing to her that he might not have said in a Village restaurant in the same tone of voice, nor she to him.

On Sunday he left for Syracuse to visit his father, his Baptist father. Jane cried a little when he was about to leave and laughed at herself for crying, and just before he put his hand on the door handle she brusquely ordered him, "Goodbye."

Two weeks became two hours; the coast of Venezuela became the shores of the Hudson, and the rolling sea a landscape bleared by the sleet and the train window; words of a marriage proposal became a nostalgia. He supposed their love affair would dream along, artificially stimulated by his absences, without rupture for a long time; he should think of it, as Jane did, as a sort of refuge or nocturne, an experience of its own genre, signifying nothing. That is, insignificant. He damned his father for having polluted his childhood with religion; religion's lies he had worked to cleanse his mind of, but its residual sentimentality was harder to purge. He wished he felt emotionally, as well as he admitted intellectually, that Jane was right about their love affair.

The sidewalk and path of his father's house were swept clean. There was smoke from the chimney. When he opened the unlocked front door, the odor of baking ham welcomed him. At his call, his father, beaming and hand outstretched, came from the kitchen in an apron. "Well, son, I'm so glad to see you. It's been lonely without you here." They embraced; Mark's hand avoided with the practice of years the hump on his father's shoulder. "Come in and warm yourself by the fire. I saved some apple logs for this occasion, son. I hope you're good and cold. And hungry. Your letter came yesterday and the first thing I did was go down to the A&P and get a ham, the best that money could buy." Mark said he was grateful, and he was; but also he wished that just once his father would celebrate with something besides ham. The moment this thought irritated him, he was ashamed of it, for he knew that his father worked nine hours a day in the shop and knew how much labor it was for him to cook a big meal. "I called up Calvin and Mona to tell them I wouldn't be out to dinner today. This will make three Sundays in a row I haven't seen them."

"I'm sorry, Dad."

"It's all right, son, Mona's been feeling sort of drug down recently. The winter's been hard on her, no sun for so long. She's not as young as she used to be." The cheeriness which expressed itself on Mr. Birch's face opposed his tendency to look on the worst side of things; the result was neither cheery nor dour, but dry. Mark got the fidgets—the Sunday-afternoon fidgets in his first fifteen minutes at home.

He had not had to stay on the ship the night before but had lied to his father about it—lied so that he could arrive on a Sunday afternoon when there could be no question of his father's suggesting, however despondently, that he go to church. "Dad," he said, "what was the sermon about today?"

Mr. Birch had been Sunday school teacher, deacon, and elder in the same church for twenty-five years, but he would never call a minister by his first name. "Dr. Walker spoke on the text from John, 'And the Word was made flesh and dwelt among us.' He threw light in a dark place." Mark could not imagine what Walker, who leaned toward homely stories and bad metaphors, could say about the Word; but Mark cared enough to ask his father to go on; he knew that an evening of watching TV giveaways, gags, and ads yawned before him; he would rather have the Word.

In the beginning was the Word. How did God create the world? He *said* Let there be light and there was light. He *said* Let us make man in our image. When God said Let there be a man who shall redeem all men, that man existed. His name was Jesus. He was the Word of God. Mark sank into a sermon-listening apathy under this; I don't care what you're talking about, I don't understand it, I don't think you do either. But suddenly, in a burst of irritation no doubt at his apathy, his father said, "Jesus said, 'Why do ye not understand my speech? Even because ye cannot hear my word.' " And Mark appreciated abruptly that Jesus' feeling and his father's were the same as his own had been with Jane; each had been cut off by the very words which were meant to bind. For a moment he and his father cast a look of recognition across to one another. But he knew that his father would not rest content with that look.

"I'm getting hungry, Dad."

It occurred to him at ten next morning, staring out the window at the patches of snow in the shade, that the only person in town he would actively enjoy seeing was Rosannah; she would be teaching till three thirty or so. Strange, he'd seen her at nine lessons, then once downtown in Grant's, and for the eleventh and last time at the tenth golf lesson; he had touched her only in the ways a golf teacher must touch his pupil, for the grip's sake, for the swing's sake, and embracing her thus formally had not excited him at all; yet he remembered the intensity with which they had talked on the sixth green, just beside it near a bush, not even holding hands. He had seen her, three days before that, at the stationery counter in Grant's intently choosing among address books; on impulse he had stepped up immediately behind her, bent over so that his lips were at her ear, and said, "Keep your eye on that ball, Rosannah." Her head toddled in a way that unmistakably meant emotion; he stood straight, and her head for a moment touched his shoulder as she looked up at him; in her eyes there was no questioning about whose voice that had been, nor surprise exactly, but only for that surprised moment an unveiled warmth. He responded instantly. Then they dropped their eyes to the address book in her hand. They talked inanities about address books. When she'd paid for the one she picked, she said that his would be the first address to go into her book; it was supposed to be a little joke, but when he did not smile at it her mouth fell; he gave her his address and told her that he would be gone to sea in less than a month, and her mouth ohed in a dismay as pleasing to him as the pressure of her head on his shoulder had been. Then they'd gone to Schrafft's for ice cream and coffee, and he'd told her how dull civil engineers were and how he'd be coming to Syracuse hereafter only to visit. Thinking of this encounter now ten months later, he wondered why he had stolen up behind her in the department store and why, three days later toward the end of her last lesson, he had told her he loved her; for he had not even tried to kiss her, though he knew she returned his feeling in some kind. It occurred to him now that it would be interesting to find out what so tenuous an infatuation could have left behind it, and to compare it to his relationship with Jane, anchored substantially in sex.

He telephoned the Board of Education to find out what school Rosannah was teaching at, and discovered instead that schools were closed for spring vacation. Splendid, he'd have lunch with her. Her name was not in the phone book. Well, he had her address. The unexpected chance excited him to action: he would surprise her. He put on his dark red sports shirt, light gray slacks, and tweed jacket, and walked the couple of miles to her place, swinging his arms in the sunshine.

But the look he surprised onto her face was not of the sort he had had in mind. Her hair was in a bandanna, her jeans were rolled up to her knees, she was wearing a half-buttoned man's shirt with the tails hanging out, her bare feet were grimy. Her wide eyes of astonishment became raised eyebrows of disapproval. "You should have phoned me."

"Your name isn't listed in the book."

"Anybody who can find out where I live should be clever enough to find my phone number."

"But," he was aggrieved, "you put your return address on the letter you wrote me."

"Hmph," she said with a flourish of the nose. She had not admitted him into her apartment. "I'm cleaning."

"*I* don't care. It's nearly time for lunch."

"Lunch? Very well. Come back in one hour. Okay?"

"But I don't have anywhere to go!"

"Oh yes, you do, sir. Syracuse is full of places for you to go to. Good-bye." And she closed the door. He was offended and left with the intention of not returning. Why, she'd given him her address herself and then said he'd cleverly found it! But the voice of her good-bye, slightly angry and yet warm, lingered in his ears; he had forgotten how sensual her voice was and how bright her eyes; she had been inviting him to return even as she was punishing him good-bye. Well, he would go back and see what came of it.

Jane's "Good-bye," her parting word, was resurrected in his memory—abrupt, timed so as to mean, "I'm glad to see you go," with a sort of drill sergeant's emphasis, in a voice devoid of affection. He flushed with postponed anger. To be sure, she had warned him that she would hate him every time he left on a trip, that each time he went from her he would be deserting her though she knew better; but that gave her no right to spoil his leavetaking. On the other hand, Rosannah, having scolded and punished him, had forgiven him in the very inflections of her reproof.

And having forgiven, she forgot: she greeted him upon his return as though they'd had this date for a week, stood aside as she opened the door for him, shook hands, and excused herself to put on the finishing touches. Her living room was conventionally feminine; there were doilies on the stand, and the pillows on the couch had ruffles; he smiled indulgently. She came out in the same sort of clothes she had worn at the golf course, blue pullover sweater, brown skirt, the same dirty white tennis shoes; but her eyelashes were blackened, her lips and cheeks rouged, and her bangs in front and pony tail behind were flawless. (And she had let her hair grow.) He had, without thinking about it, rather expected her to have fixed lunch for them in her apartment, but she went directly to the coat closet and pulled out a trench coat. She made a small, imperious gesture with her head, and he held her coat for her, delighted by her arrogance. They walked to Meltzer's and ate hot pastrami sandwiches and cole slaw. She told him about her first-graders, and he told her about Madagascar. She did not seem very keen to play golf next day, when he suggested it, but she let him persuade her—"if the weather held." At a slushy crossing he offered her his arm but she did not take it. Nor did she invite him in when they returned to her apartment.

Yet as he walked along the streets home from her place, he understood why he had said to her that he loved her: she was at once desirable and chaste. He was opposed to chastity on principle, but in her he respected it; still it was clear that the yearning he had built up for her he had translated into infatuation; a simple case of frustration and wish-fulfillment. So he laughed her out of his mind for the rest of the afternoon. The phone rang at dinner: a wrong number. "I forgot to mention it to you, son, but a young lady telephoned me one evening some time ago. Maybe it was around Thanksgiving. Anyway it was after the first snow, which was toward the middle of November this winter. What she wanted was your address."

"Thanks, Dad, she wrote me."

"The same one? She had a funny name."

"Tavolga? Rosannah Tavolga?"

"That sounds right. What is she, a Jewess?"

"It's a Russian name. I don't think she's Jewish. I never asked her." So, for the tedious hours till his father went off to bed, she was back in his mind most of the time, her name especially. It occurred to him that he had always remembered her name from the time he'd first met her, whereas he'd had the devil's own time remembering Jane's name. Jane Mercer— an ordinary name. Nevertheless, he found it odd that he had taken so long to get the Mercer stuck in his head; well into his second voyage he had been able to write her address on the envelope far more readily than her last name. But Rosannah Tavolga—the words fell together as though they were meant to, like Eleanor of Aquitaine, or Kubla Khan.

"Oh, my Lord, you're not the girl I was teaching."

"Why do you say that?"

"Your drive. You've got it down beautifully."

"Thank you, Mr. Birch."

"Oh, come off it."

"I had to use all my courage to put Mark down when I wrote to you. You had signed your card Mark, so I thought I should. But here on the golf course again, I feel like calling you Mr. Birch."

"Is that why you didn't much want to come out with me today?" She nodded. "Are names that important to you, Rosannah?" She nodded again and walked aside while he teed off; then she started ahead of him down the fairway. He caught up with her. "I was thinking last night how I had liked your name the very first time I heard it."

"I'm glad somebody likes it."

"Don't you?"

"Not particularly."

"Do you like my name?"

She gave him a complicated look. "Fishing, Mark?" She made the second hole in par.

"Did you take lessons after I left?" he asked her.

"No, I'm just lucky today."

"You must have played a lot last summer."

"I did. Nearly every day. Hollis liked golf."

"Hollis was the fellow you were engaged to?" She nodded. "Hollis," he repeated. "Now there's a name I could do without."

He decided that at the sixth hole he would remind her of their parting here. He would make a little burlesque of gallantry so that they could laugh together over it, so that she would not feel threatened again. They were both silent at the sixth tee waiting for a party of four middle-aged women to divot their progress up the fairway; the women insisted they play through, so that when they got to the green they were conscious of an admiring audience. The occasion was spoiled; Mark's anger cost him two strokes on the green, but Rosannah sank a twenty-foot putt slantwise up a slope. As they were walking to the seventh tee they passed the bush beside which he had spoken to her of love. "We've been here before," she said without stopping, in a low voice. "Do you remember?" There was no joke in her voice, but intimacy and shyness.

"I remember," he said.

"You were so silly."

"I meant it."

"No, no," she said, "you meant something but not that. You were sweet. You kept banging the toe of your shoe with your putter."

"Your eyes sort of crossed, or wandered around, one of them."

"You noticed that?"

"Sure," he said, "I was watching you so hard I still remember everything you did."

"It's so humiliating; sometimes when I get all excited my eyes won't stay focused."

"You're not engaged any longer?"

"Oh no! You don't think I'd be— Say, are we playing golf, or aren't we?"

As they walked from the clubhouse to the car he held her hand, and she sat close to him on the way home. But she would not let him see her to the door. She had a date that evening, dinner and dancing; "a new doctor in town, an acquaintance of Daddy's, an internist, a dreamy dancer."

"I thought," said Mr. Birch during the first commercial of the evening, "that we'd drive out and see Calvin and Mona tomorrow night, right after supper."

"Sorry, Dad, I've got a date."

"A woman?" said his father heavily and scratched his hump.

"The girl we spoke of last evening, Rosannah Tavolga."

"You never used to mention her."

"No."

"You don't go see your old friends any more. You'd rather spend an evening alone with your old man than go see your oldest school friends, but here a new girl jumps up out of nowhere and off you go."

"Her father's a doctor, a skin specialist."

"And a Jew for all you know. You're a sailor all right, my boy. A sailor, God help me." Mark could think of nothing but where Rosannah and the internist might have gone on a Tuesday evening and whether they would neck. He was thankful that being with Jane had relieved him of any simply physical impulse to make a pass at Rosannah; as it was, he could play at having a love affair with her, hurting nothing, serious about nothing, just hold hands and talk, kid stuff.

Next day by noon he had the jitters bad. He felt imprisoned in his father's house, yet there was absolutely no place in Syracuse he wanted to go to, no one he wanted to see except Rosannah. Their date was for five thirty. He felt encapsulated within himself; he thought of breaking the date and flying down to New York so that Jane might tease him out of it, or tease him at least out of thinking about it; Jane was a fellow captive whose art it was to make him not mind his captivity, and sometimes even to enjoy it. He telephoned Rosannah. He knew that his own voice was more intense than was required to ask a girl whether she wanted to play golf; nevertheless, he was quite put off by the brisk, arrangement-making roughness in her telephone manner; she said she would play, not that she would like to play or looked forward to it, just that she would; he wondered if his manner had affected her.

She chattered with him brightly, as though he were a friend's cousin who had to be entertained for the afternoon. The pro caught them in the clubhouse and jawed for half an hour. As they were approaching the fourth hole, a one-armed fellow shouted, "Coming through," at them, and came through without so much as a nod. She sliced her next drive off into a gully. And he blew up. "I've told you a hundred times not to do that," he scolded, and holding her head rigid made her swing correctly three or four times.

"Is that all right, Mark?" she said, mocking his fierceness a little but at least he was Mark again.

"Yes," he answered in a remote voice, "it's all right." He was thinking that he must get to her at this moment or he might not have another chance like it. He decided to risk a high trump. "I'm going back to New York tomorrow morning."

"Why?"

"My ship is sailing before long."

"You won't come back before you sail?" Her voice was gentle and sensual again, and a little alarmed.

"No, I won't."

"I'm sorry."

"I'll miss you, darling."

She turned to put her driver in the bag. "Don't call me darling."

"Why not?"

"Oh, it's sort of a New York word, the way you pronounce it. I'm not going to be anybody's New York darling."

"All right, Rosannah. Anyway, I *will* miss you." She strode angrily.

"Then why," she said without looking at him, "did you come look me up? Just to get everything all churned up again?"

"Why, I don't know what to say. I like you."

"Hmph."

He wanted to pull her back into shallow water. "How was your doctor last night?"

"Sick," she said miserably. "He got drunk and told me that he hates God. Very sick, very sick." Mark suddenly thought of Jane's light way of saying three monosyllables quickly together, especially sick sick sick, and he realized that Rosannah, who could not take another person's sickness lightly, would not toy with her own emotions; nor should he do so.

"I'm sorry."

"Sure." In a few minutes he saw her blow her nose on the other side of the fairway, with her head averted from him; his vanity was tickled that he had made her cry a little, but he did not want to do it again. And apparently she believed in God. But maybe she didn't go to church.

Until they got to the sixth green they spoke only of the game. There were no players in sight behind them. They both shot the hole in par, and laughing, arm in arm, did a victorious little schottische around the pole.

"Why did you go to sea?"

"Hey," he answered, pretending to stagger, "it's not fair to hit a fellow when he's off-balance."

"Couldn't you get a job as an engineer?"

"Sure. I just thought it would be fun to go to sea."

"Was it?"

"Yes."

"Were you ever married?"

"No, but what on earth does that have to do with anything?"

"Nothing." She was looking off at the trees in a preoccupied way. She glanced at him for a moment, and a secret smile appeared on her lips. "So you're going back to your New York darling tomorrow."

"What? I said no such thing."

"Oh yes, you did, Mark Birch."

"I did not."

"Is she prettier than I am?" He trembled inside; he did not know where she was leading him. He gave her her bag and they started strolling toward the seventh tee.

"No, about the same as you, in prettiness, that is."

"Do you know why I think you went to sea?"

"No, why?"

"Women. You're afraid to get too much involved with a woman."

"Oh, I am, am I."

"I think."

"What am I doing here with you right this minute?"

"Playing golf. Sort of flirting. Do you have to go back to New York tomorrow?"

"No. I'm not due back on the ship till Sunday morning."

"I want you to stay."

"Well." Everything she'd said seemed to him true.

"I dare you," she said.

"I won't rise to that bait," he answered. She dropped her clubs by the bush and pulled a budding branch down so that she might caress a downy bud with her lips. "That is," he said, "I could stay if we had a chance, you know, if you liked me so that . . ."

"Oh, don't be stupid. You know perfectly well I like you. You're even afraid to say the word, aren't you? Listen, Mark." She put her hand to the side of his throat. "The question is whether you will let yourself find out if you love me. And let me find out too. I had hoped we would."

"I'll stay till Saturday," he said, and even as he spoke he argued that at least he would have Saturday night to spend with Jane. He did not touch Rosannah. Her hand caressed his hair a moment. She had not paid much attention to his words.

She said, "I still hope we will."

He was sure she had not planned this; yet it seemed to him ceremonial of her to say this by the same bush, the two of them alone after he had scolded her again like a teacher. And the words: of course the words were unprepared, just the words which the occasion brought forth from her, not, as his words to Jane had been, rigidly memorized; they were as nearly exact as words could be about such a matter; they were true. Yet, he thought, their power was not just in their truth nor in their spontaneity nor in the unconscious ceremony of the time and place, but in all these together and in his assent to all these. She was smiling a little, in innocent triumph, he supposed, at having got him to stay for three more days, but her eyes, meeting his, were unwavering and affectionate. It was time to kiss, his lips were ready to kiss; but his mind, the IBM machine in his mind, was ticking away at a great rate sorting out the ways by which he could tell her how well she had handled him. What his ears and thence his reaching hands heard his lips say was this:

"Rosannah, you have opened my heart."

(1968)

Wright Morris

—————————◆—————————

*Wright Morris was born in Nebraska in 1910. Educated at
Pomona College, and resident in California since 1961, he
has however continued to use material drawn primarily from
his Midwestern background. In 1962 he became professor of
English at San Francisco State College.*

*Essayist, critic, and memoirist as well as novelist and
writer of short stories, Morris has written a great deal and
always written well.* Real Losses, Imaginary Gains *(1976)
collects his stories.* The Field of Vision *(1956) is perhaps his
best-known novel, though* Ceremony in Lone Tree *(1960)
attracted much critical attention.* Will's Boy *(1981), a mem-
oir, was also very well received. Nevertheless, his critical
reputation is somewhat uneven. Many take him as a truly
important writer; many take him as a fine but somewhat
limited craftsman, more interesting as a stylist than as a
handler of people or of narrative. His novels, though beautifully written, lack the clear focus and the energy of more
successful writers. He excels in the essay (and in collections
of essays) and the short story form, where structure is not as
serious an issue and where his frequently piercing percep-
tions and dry sense of humor can work to best effect.*

SINCE WHEN DO THEY
CHARGE ADMISSION

On the morning they left Kansas, May had tuned in for the weather and heard of the earthquake in San Francisco, where her daughter, Janice, was seven months pregnant. So she had called her. Her husband, Vernon Dickey, answered the phone. He was a native Californian so accustomed to earthquakes he thought nothing of them. It was the wind he feared.

"When I read about those twisters," he said to May, "I don't know how you people stand it." He wouldn't believe that May had never seen a twister till she saw one on TV, and that one in Missouri.

"Ask him about the riots," Cliff had asked her.

"What riots, Mrs. Chalmers?"

It was no trouble for May to see that Janice could use someone around the house to talk to. She was like her father, Cliff, in that it took children to draw her out. Her sister, Charlene, would talk the leg off a stranger but the girls had never talked much to each other. But now they would, once the men got out of the house. It had been Cliff's idea to bring Charlene along since she had never been out of Kansas. She had never seen an ocean. She had never been higher than Estes Park.

On their way to the beach, Charlene cried, "Look! Look!" She pointed into the sunlight; May could see the light shimmering on the water.

"That's the beach," said Janice.

"Just *look*," Charlene replied.

"You folks come over here often?" asked Cliff.

"On Vernon's day off," replied Janice.

"If it's a weekday," said May, "you wouldn't find ten people on a beach in Merrick County."

"You wouldn't because there's no beach for them to go to," said Janice.

Cliff liked the way Janice spoke up for California, since that was what she was stuck with. He didn't like it, himself. Nothing had its own place. Hardly any of the corners were square. All through the Sunday morning service he could hear the plastic propellers spinning at the corner gas station, and the loud bang when they checked the oil and slammed down the hood. Vernon Dickey took it all in his stride, the way he did the riots.

Janice said, "Vernon's mother can't understand anybody who lives where they have dust storms."

"I'd rather see it blow than feel it shake," said Cliff.

"Ho-ho!" said Vernon.

"I suppose it's one thing or another," said May. "When I read about India I'm always thankful."

Cliff honked his horn at the sharp turns in the road. The fog stood offshore just far enough to let the sun shine yellow on the beach sand. At the foot of the slope the beach road turned left through a grove of trees. Up ahead of them a chain, stretched between two posts, blocked the road. On the left side a portable contractor's toilet was brightly painted with green and yellow flowers. A cardboard sign attached to the chain read: *Admission 50¢.*

"Since when do they charge admission?" Janice asked. She looked at her husband, a policeman on his day off. As Cliff stopped the car a young man in the booth put out his head.

"In heaven's name," May said. She had never seen a man with such a head of hair outside of *The National Geographic*. He had a beard that seemed to grow from the hair on his chest. A brass padlock joined the ends of a chain around his neck.

"How come the fifty-cent fee?" said Vernon. "It's a public beach."

"It's a racket," said the youth. "You can pay it or not pay it." He didn't seem to care. At his back stood a girl with brown hair to her waist, framing a smiling, vacant, pimpled face. She was eating popcorn; the butter and salt greased her lips.

"I don't know why anyone should pay it," said May. "Cliff, drive ahead."

Cliff said, "You like to lower the chain?"

When the boy stepped from the booth he had nothing on but a jockstrap. The way his plump buttocks were tanned it was plain that was all he was accustomed to wear. He stooped with his backside toward the car, but the hood was between him and the ladies. As the chain slacked Cliff drove over it, slowly, into the parking lot.

"What in the world do you make of *that?*" asked May.

"He's a hippie," said Janice. "They're hippies."

"Now I've finally seen one," said May. She twisted in the seat to take a look back.

"Maybe they're having a love-in down here," said Vernon, and guffawed. Cliff had never met a man with a sense of humor that stayed within bounds.

"Park anywhere," said Janice.

"You come down here alone?" asked May.

Vernon said, "Mrs. Chalmers, you don't need to worry. They're crazy but they're not violent."

Cliff maneuvered between the trucks and cars to where the front wheels thumped against a driftwood log. The sand began there, some of it blowing in the offshore breeze. The tide had washed up a sandbar, just ahead, that concealed the beach and most of the people on it. Way over, maybe five or ten miles, was the coastline just west of the Golden Gate, with the tier on tier of houses that Cliff knew to be Daly City. From the bridge, on the way over, Vernon had pointed it out. Vernon and Janice had a home there, but they wanted something more out in the open, nearer the beach. As a matter of fact, Cliff had come up with the idea of building them something. He was a builder. He and May lived in a house that he had built. If Vernon would come up with the piece of land, Cliff would more or less promise to put a house on it. Vernon would help him on the weekends, and his days off.

"What about a little place over there?" said Cliff, and wagged his finger at the slope near the beach. Right below it were the huge rocks black as the water, but light on their tops. That was gull dung. One day some fellow smarter than the rest would make roof tiles or fertilizer out of it.

"Most of the year it's cold and foggy," said Vernon, "too cold for the kids."

"What good is a cold, windy beach?" said May. She had turned to take the whip of the wind on her back. No one answered her question. It didn't seem the right time to give it much thought. Cliff got the picnic basket out of the rear and tossed the beach blanket to Vernon. There was enough sand in it, when they shook it, to blow back in his face.

"Just like at home," Cliff said to Vernon, who guffawed.

Vernon had been born and raised in California, but he had got his army training near Lubbock, Texas, where the dust still blew. Now he led off toward the beach, walking along the basin left where the tide had receded. Charlene trailed along behind him wearing the flowered pajama suit she had worn since they left Colby, on the fourth of June. They had covered twenty-one hundred and forty-eight miles in five days and half of one night, Cliff at the wheel. Charlene could drive, but May didn't feel she could be trusted on the interstate freeways, where they drove so fast. There was a time, every day, about an hour after lunch, when nothing Cliff could think or do would keep him from dozing off. He'd jerk up when he'd hear the sound of gravel or feel the pull of the wheel on the road's shoulder. Then he'd be good for a few more miles till it happened again. The score of times that happened Cliff might have killed them all but he couldn't bring himself to pull over and stop. It scared him to think of the long drive back.

"Except where it was green, in Utah," said May, "it's looked the same to me since we left home."

"Mrs. Chalmers," said Vernon, "you should've sat on the other side of the car."

It was enlightening to Cliff, after all he'd heard about the population explosion, to see how wide open and empty most of the country was. In the morning he might feel he was all alone in it. The best time of day was the forty miles or so he got in before breakfast. They slipped by so easy he sometimes felt he would just like to drive forever, the women in the car quiet until he stopped for food. Anything May saw before she had her coffee was lost on her. After breakfast Cliff didn't know what seemed longer: the day he put in waiting for the dark, or the long night he put in waiting for

the light. He had forgotten about trains until they had to stop
for the night.

Vernon said, "I understand that when they take the salt out
of the water there'll be no more water problems. Is that right,
Mr. Chalmers?"

Like her mother, Charlene said, "There'll just be others."
Was there anything Cliff had given these girls besides a poor
start? He turned to see how Janice, who was seven months
pregnant, was making out. The way her feet had sunk into the
sand she was no taller than her mother. With their backsides
to the wind both women looked broad as a barn. One day
Janice was a girl—the next day you couldn't tell her from her
mother. That part of her life that she looked old would prove
to be the longest, but seem the shortest. Her mother hardly
knew a thing, or cared, about what had happened since the
war. The sight of anything aging, or anything just beginning,
like that unborn child she was lugging, affected Cliff so
strongly he could wet his lips and taste it. Where did people
get the strength to do it all over again? He turned back to face
the beach and the clumps of people who were sitting around,
or lying. One played a guitar. A wood fire smoked in the
shelter of a few smooth rocks. Vernon said, "It's like the
coast of Spain." Cliff could believe it might well be true: it
looked old and bleak enough. Where the sand was wet about
half-a-dozen dogs ran up and down, yapping like kids.

"Dogs are fun! They just seem to know almost everything." This side of Charlene made her good with her kids,
but Cliff sometimes wondered about her husband.

"How's this?" said Vernon, taking Cliff by the arm, and
indicated where he thought they should spread the blanket.
On one side were two boys, stretched out on their bellies, and
nearer at hand was this blanket-covered figure, his back
humped up. His problem seemed to be that he couldn't find a
spot in the sand to his liking. He squirmed a good deal. Now
and then his backside rose and fell. Cliff took one end of the
blanket and Vernon the other, and they managed to hold it
against the wind, flatten it to the sand. Charlene plopped
down on it to keep it from blowing. It seemed only yesterday
that Cliff and his father would put her in a blanket and toss
her like a pillow, scaring her mother to death. Charlene was

one of those girls who was more like a boy in the way nothing fazed her. Out of the water, toward Vernon, a girl came running so wet and glistening she looked naked.

"Look at that!" said Cliff, and then stood there, his mouth open, looking. She was actually naked. She ran right up and passed him, her feet kicking wet sand on him, then she dropped to lie for a moment on her face, then roll on her back. Only the gold-flecked sand clung to her white belly and breasts. Grains of sand, cinnamon colored, clung to her prominent, erectile nipples. Her eyes were closed, her head tipped to the left to avoid the wind. For a long moment Cliff gazed at her body as if in thought. When he blinked his eyes the peculiar thing was that he was the one who felt in the fishbowl. Surrounded by them. What did they think of a man down at the beach with all his clothes on? He was distracted by a tug on the blanket and turned to see Vernon pointing at the women. They waddled along like turtles. All he could wonder was what had ever led them to come to a beach. Buttoned at the collar, Janice's coat draped about her like a tent she was dragging. Cliff just stood there till they came along beside him, and May put out a hand to lean on him. Sand powdered her face.

"It's always so windy?" she asked Vernon.

"You folks call this windy?" May looked closely at him to see if he meant to be taken seriously. He surely knew, if he knew anything, that she knew more about wind than he did.

"Get Cliff to tell you how it blows around Chadron," she said. "It blows the words right out of your mouth, if you'd let it." Cliff was silent, so she added, "Don't it, Cliff?"

"Don't it what?" he answered. He allowed himself to turn so that his eyes went to the humped, squirming figure, under the blanket. The humping had pulled it up so the feet were uncovered. Four of them. Two of them were toes down, with tar spots on the bottoms: two of them were toes up, the heels dipped into the sand. In a story Cliff had heard but never fully understood, the point had hinged on the four-footed monster. Now he got the point.

"Blow the words right out of your mouth if you'd let it," said May. At a loss for words, Cliff moved to stand so he blocked her view. He took a grip on her hands and let her sag, puffing sour air at him, down to the blanket. "It's hard enough work just to get here," she said, and raised her eyes to squint at the water. "Charlene, you wanted to see the ocean: well, there it is."

Cliff was thinking that Charlene looked no older than the summer she was married. It was hard to understand her. She had had three children without ever growing up.

"If I'd known the sand was going to blow," said May, "we'd have stayed home to eat, then come over later. I hate sand in my food. Charlene, you going to sit down?"

Charlene stood there staring at a girl up to her ankles in the shallow water. She stooped to hold a child pressed to her front, the knees buckled up as if she squeezed it. A stream of water arched from the slit between the child's legs. The way she held it, pressed to her front, it was like squeezing juice from a bladder. There was nothing Cliff could do but wait for it to stop. Charlene's handbag dangled to where it almost dragged in the sand.

"That's Farrallon Island," said Vernon, pointing. Without his glasses Cliff couldn't see it. Janice tipped forward, as far as she could, to cup handfuls of sand over her ankles: she couldn't reach her feet. "We hear and read so much about their being so dirty," said May.

"It's the hippies," said Vernon. "They've taken it over."

Why was he such a fool as to say so? Even Cliff, who knew what he would see, twisted his head on his neck and looked all around him. The stark-naked girl had dried a lighter color: she didn't look so good. The sand sprinkled her like brown sugar, but the mole-colored nipples were flat on her breasts, like they'd been snipped off. At her feet, using her legs as a backrest, a lank-haired boy, chewing bubble gum, sunned his pimpled face. On his hairless chest someone had painted his nipples to look like staring eyes. Now that Cliff was seated it was plainer than ever what was going on under the blanket: the heels of two of the feet thrust deep into the sand, piling it up. Cliff felt the eyes of Janice on the back of his head, but he missed those of her mother. Where were they?

"Cliff," she said.

He did not turn to look.

"Cliff," she repeated.

At the edge of the water a dappled horse galloped with two long-haired, naked riders. If one was a boy, Cliff couldn't tell which was which.

"Who's ready for a beer?" asked Vernon, and peeled the towel off the basket. When no one replied he said, "Mr. Dickey, have yourself a beer," and took one. He moved the basket of food to where both Cliff and the women could reach it. Along with the bowl of potato salad there were two broiled chickens from the supermarket. The chickens were still warm.

"All I've done since we left home is eat," Cliff said.

"We just ate," said Janice.

"We didn't drag all this stuff here," said Cliff, "just to turn around and drag it back." He took out the bowl of salad. He fished around in the basket for the paper cups and plates. He didn't look up at May until he knew for certain she had got her head and eyes around to the front. The sun glinted on her glasses. Absent-mindedly she raked her fingers across her forehead for loose strands of hair. "We eat the salad first or along with the chicken?"

None of the women made any comment. One of the maverick beach dogs, his coat heavy with sand, stood off a few yards and sniffed at the chicken. "They shouldn't allow dogs on a beach," said Cliff. "They run around and get hot and can't drink the water. In the heat they go mad."

"There's salt in there somewhere," said Janice. "I don't put all the salt I could on the salad."

Cliff took out one of the chickens, and using his fingers pried the legs off the body. He then broke the drumsticks off at the thighs, and placed the pieces on one of the plates.

"You still like the dark meat?" he said to Charlene. She nodded her head. He peeled the plastic cover off the potato salad and forked it out on the paper plates. "Eat it before the sand gets at it," he said, and passed a plate to May. Janice reached to take one, and placed it on the slope of her lap. Vernon took the body of one of the birds, tore off the wings, and tossed one to the dog.

"I can't stand to see a dog watch me eat," he said.

"Vernon was in Korea for a year," said Janice.

*　　*　　*

Cliff began to eat. After the first few swallows it tasted all right. He hadn't been hungry at all when he started, but now he ate like he was famished. When he traveled all he seemed to do was sit and eat. He glanced up to see that they were all eating except for May, who just sat there. She had her head cocked sidewise as if straining to hear something. Not twenty yards away a boy plucked a guitar but Cliff didn't hear a sound with the wind against him. Two other boys, with shorts on, one with a top on, lay out on their bellies with their chins on their hands. One used a small rock to drive a short piece of wood into the sand. It was the idle sort of play Cliff would expect from a kid about six, not one about twenty. On the sand before them a shadow flashed and eight or ten feet away a bird landed, flapping its wings. Cliff had never set eyes on a bigger crow. He was shorter in the leg but as big as the gulls that strutted on the firm sand near the water. A little shabby at the tail, big glassy hatpin eyes. Cliff watched him dip his beak into the sand like one of these glass birds that go on drinking water, rocking on the perch. One of the boys said, "Hey, you, bird, come here!" and wiggled a finger at him. When the bird did just that Cliff couldn't believe his eyes. He had a stiff sort of strut, pumping his head, and favored one leg more than the other. No more than two feet away from the heads of those boys he stopped and gave them a look. Either one of them might have reached out and touched him. Cliff had never seen a big, live bird as tame as that. The crows around Chadron were smarter than most people and had their own meetings and cawed crow language. They had discussions. You could hear them decide what to do next. The boy with the rock held it out toward him and damn if the crow didn't peck at it. Cliff could hear the click of his beak tapping the rock. He turned to see if May had caught that, but her eyes were on the plate in her lap.

"May, look—" he said.

Her eyes down she said, "I've seen all I want to see the rest of my life."

"The crow—" said Cliff, and took another look at him. He had his head cocked to one side, like a parrot, and his beak clamped down on one of the sticks driven into the sand. He tried to wiggle it loose as he tugged at it. He braced his legs and strained back like a robin pulling a worm from a hole. So Vernon wouldn't miss it, Cliff put out his hand to nudge him. "Well, I'll be damned," Vernon said.

Two little kids, one with a plastic pail, ran up to within about a yard of the bird, stopped and stared. He stared right back at them. Who was to say which of the two looked the strangest. The kids were naked as the day they were born. One was a boy. Whatever they had seen before they had never seen a crow that close up.

"Come on, bird," said the boy with the rock, and waved it. Nobody would ever believe it, but that bird took a tug at the stick, then rocked back and cawed. He made such a honk the kids were frightened. The little girl backed off and giggled. The crow clamped his beak on the stick again and had another try. A lanky-haired hippie girl, just out of the water, ran up and said, "Sam—are they teasing you, Sam?" She had on no top at all but a pair of blue-jean shorts on her bottom. "Come on, bird!" yelled the boy with the rock, and pounded his fists on the sand. That crow had figured out a way to loosen up the stick by clamping down on it, hard, then moving in a circle, like he was drilling a well. He did that twice, then he pulled it free, clamped one claw on it, and cawed. "Good bird!" said the boy, and tried to take it from him, but the crow wouldn't let him. He backed off, flapped his wings, and soared off with his legs dangling. Cliff could see what it took a big bird like that to fly.

"What does he do with it?" said the girl. She looked off toward the cliffs where the bird had flown. Somewhere up there he had a lot of sticks: no doubt about that.

"Buries it," said the boy. "He thinks it's a bone."

The little girl with the plastic pail said, "Why don't you give him a real bone, then?" The boy and girl laughed. The hippie girl said, "Can I borrow a comb?" and the boy replied, "If you don't get sand in it." He moved so he could reach the comb in his pocket, and stroked it on his sleeve as he passed it to her. Combing her hair, her head tipped back, Cliff might have mistaken her for a boy. The little girl asked, "When will he do it again?"

"Soon as he's buried it," said the boy.

Cliff didn't believe that. He had watched crows all his life, but he had never seen a crow behave like that. He wanted to bring the point up, but how could he discuss it with a girl without her clothes on?

"Here he comes," said the boy, and there he was, his shadow flashing on the sand before them. He made a circle and came in for a landing on the firm sand. What if he did bury those sticks? His beak·was shiny, yellow as a banana. "Come here, bird!" said the boy, and held out the rock, but the girl leaned forward and grabbed it from him.

"You want to hurt him?" she cried. "Why don't you give him a real bone?" She looked around as if she might see one, raking the sand with her hands.

"Here's one, miss!" said Cliff, and held the chicken leg out toward her. He could no more help himself than duck when someone took a swing at him. On her hands and knees the girl crawled toward him to where she could reach it. Her lank hair framed her face.

"There's meat on it," she said.

"Don't you worry," said Cliff, "crows like meat. They're really good meat-eaters."

She looked at him closely to see how he meant that. About her neck a fine gold-colored chain dangled an ornament. Cliff saw it plainly. Two brass nails were twisted to make some sort of puzzle. She looked at the bone Cliff had given her, the strip of meat on it, and turned to hold it out to the bird. He limped forward like he was trained and took it in his beak. Cliff caught his eye, and what worried him was that he might want to crow over it and drop it. He didn't want him to drop it and have to gulp down sandy meat. But that bird actually knew he had something unusual since he didn't put it down to clamp his claws on it. Instead he strutted. Up and down he went, like a sailor with a limp. Vernon laughed so hard he gave Cliff a slap on the knee. "Don't laugh at him," said the girl, and when she put out her hand he limped toward her to where she could touch him, stroking with her fingers the flat top of his head. The little boy suddenly yelled and ran around them in a circle, kicking up sand, and hooting. The crow took off. The heavy flap of his wings actually stirred the hair of the boy who was lying there, nearest to him; he raised one of his hands to wave as the bird soared away.

"I never seen anything like it!" said Vernon.

"Maybe you'd like to come oftener." Janice picked at the bread crumbs in her lap.

"Did you see him?" asked Cliff. "You get to see him?"

"We can go now if the men have eaten." May made a wad of the napkin and scraps in her lap, put them under the towel and plates in the basket.

Vernon said, "Honey, you see that crazy bird?"

Janice shaded her eyes with one hand, peered at the sky. Up there, high, a bird was wheeling. Cliff took it for a gull. The wind had caked the color she had put on her lips, and sand powdered the wrinkles around her eyes. Cliff remembered they were called crow's feet, which was how they looked. Now she lowered her hand and held it out to Vernon to pull her up. The sand caught up in the folds of her dress blew over May and the girl lying behind her, one arm across her face.

"People must be crazy to come and eat on a beach," said May.

Cliff pushed himself to his feet, sand clinging to his chicken-sticky fingers. He helped Vernon with the blanket, walking toward the water where they could shake it and not disturb people. A bearded youth without pants, but with a striped T-shirt, sat with crossed legs at the edge of the water. The horse that had galloped off to the south came galloping back with just one rider on it. Cliff could see it was a girl. Janice and her mother had begun the long walk back toward the car. Along the way they passed the naked girl, still sprawled on her back.

"She's going to get herself a sunburn," said Vernon.

To Charlene Cliff said, "You see that bird?" Charlene nodded. "Just remember you did, when I ask you. Nobody back in Chadron is going to believe me if you don't."

"What bird was it?" asked May.

"A crow," said Cliff.

"I would think you'd seen enough of crows," said May.

At the car Cliff turned for a last look at the beach. The tide had washed up a sort of reef so that he could no longer see the water. The girl and the dogs that ran along it were like black paper cutouts. Nobody would know if she had her clothes on or off. He had forgotten to check on the two of them who had been squirming under the blanket. One still lay there. The other one crouched with lowered head, as if reading something. From the back Cliff wouldn't know which one was the girl.

May said, "I've never before really believed it when I said that I can't believe my eyes, but now I believe it."

"You wouldn't believe them if you'd seen that crow," said Cliff.

"I didn't come all this way to look at a crow," she replied.

They all got into the car, and Cliff put the picnic basket into the rear. He took a moment, squinting, to see if the crazy bird had come back for more bones. If he had just thought, he would have given the girl the other two legs to feed him.

"I'd like a cup of coffee," said May, "but I'm willing to wait till we get home for it."

Vernon said, "Mr. Chalmers, you like me to drive?" Cliff agreed that he would. They went out through the gate where they had entered but the boy and the girl had left the booth. The chain was already half-covered with drifting sand.

"It's typical of your father," said May, "to drive all the way out here and look at a crow."

Charlene said, "Wait until I tell Leonard!" They looked to see what she would tell him. On the dry slope below them a small herd of cattle were being fed from a hovering helicopter. Bundles of straw were dropped to spread on the slope.

"If I were you," said May, "I'd tell him about *that* and nothing else."

Cliff felt his head wagging. He stopped it and said, "Charlene, now you tell him about that crow. What's a few crazy people to one crow in a million?"

There was no comment.

"We're going up now," said Vernon. "You feel that poppin' in your ears?"

(1969)

Leonard Michaels

Leonard Michaels was born in New York City, in 1933. He took his B.A. at New York University, and then his Ph.D. at the University of Michigan. After teaching at Paterson State College in New Jersey and the University of California at Davis, in 1969 he became professor of English at the University of California in Berkeley.

Michaels' first two books, Going Places (1969) and I Would Have Saved Them If I Could (1975), were collections of stories. Both were extremely well received by critics and won an unusual degree of public acclaim; Going Places was nominated for the National Book Award. Michaels received a number of grants and other honors. In 1981 he published a short novel, The Men's Club, which was well but not uncritically received.

Like many of the younger writers in this book, Michaels writes on a number of planes at the same time. Time slows down, speeds up, collapses, in his stories. Past and present and future jumble together. And the fictive vehicle, his dense, rich prose, works overtime, much as it does in good poetry, carrying evocations and allusions, as well as narrative transitions and resolutions. His dialogue, on the other hand, is—again, like many of the younger American writers— pungently direct, totally realistic. It is as if there is one sort of time for people speaking, another for the author's exposition. The stories are in almost every way non-synchronous—as, indeed, modern life is desperately non-synchronous. In his *fiction, the line between prose and poetry is obscured, as in much of modern writing the line between reality and fantasy has been obscured, as the line between life and death is becoming obscured. Michaels' stories are thus fully, powerfully representative of basic movements in our culture, and in the culture of the world as a whole. Part poetry, part essay, part real, part surreal: this is how many of our younger writers see us and the life we lead.*

MURDERERS

When my uncle Moe dropped dead of a heart attack I became expert in the subway system. With a nickel I'd get to Queens, twist and zoom to Coney Island, twist again toward the George Washington Bridge—beyond which was darkness. I wanted proximity to darkness, strangeness. Who doesn't? The poor in spirit, the ignorant and frightened. My family came from Poland, then never went any place until they had heart attacks. The consummation of years in one neighborhood: a black Cadillac, corpse inside. We should have buried Uncle Moe where he shuffled away his life, in the kitchen or toilet, under the linoleum, near the coffee pot. Anyhow, they were dropping on Henry Street and Cherry Street. Blue lips. The previous winter it was cousin Charlie, forty-five years old. Moe, Charlie, Sam, Adele—family meant a punch in the chest, fire in the arm. I didn't want to wait for it. I went to Harlem, the Polo Grounds, Far Rockaway, thousands of miles on nickels, mainly underground. Tenements watched me go, day after day, fingering nickels. One afternoon I stopped to grind my heel against the curb. Melvin and Arnold Bloom appeared, then Harold Cohen. Melvin said, "You step in dog shit?" Grinding was my answer. Harold Cohen said, "The rabbi is home. I saw him on Market Street. He was walking fast." Oily Arnold, eleven years old, began to urge: "Let's go up to our roof." The decision waited for me. I considered the roof, the view of industrial Brooklyn, the Battery, ships in the river, bridges, towers, and the rabbi's apartment. "All right," I said. We didn't giggle or look to one another for moral signals. We were running.

The blinds were up and curtains pulled, giving sunlight, wind, birds to the rabbi's apartment—a magnificent metropolitan view. The rabbi and his wife never took it, but in the light and air of summer afternoons, in the eye of gull and pigeon, they were joyous. A bearded young man, and his young pink wife, sacramentally bald. Beard and Baldy, with everything to see, looked at each other. From a water tank on the opposite roof, higher than their windows, we looked at them. In psycho-analysis this is "The Primal Scene." To achieve the primal scene we crossed a ledge six inches wide. A half-inch indentation in the brick gave us fingerholds. We dragged bellies and groins against the brick face to a steel ladder. It went up the side of the building, bolted into brick, and up the side of the water tank to a slanted tin roof which caught the afternoon sun. We sat on that roof like angels, shot through with light, derealized in brilliance. Our sneakers sucked hot slanted metal. Palms and fingers pressed to bone on nailheads.

The Brooklyn Navy Yard with destroyers and aircraft carriers, the Statue of Liberty putting the sky to the torch, the dull remote skyscrapers of Wall Street, and the Empire State Building were among the wonders we dominated. Our view of the holy man and his wife, on their living-room couch and floor, on the bed in their bedroom, could not be improved. Unless we got closer. But fifty feet across the air was right. We heard their phonograph and watched them dancing. We couldn't hear the gratifications or see pimples. We smelled nothing. We didn't want to touch.

For a while I watched them. Then I gazed beyond into shimmering nullity, gray, blue, and green murmuring over rooftops and towers. I had watched them before. I could tantalize myself with this brief ocular perversion, the general cleansing nihil of a view. This was the beginning of philosophy. I indulged in ambience, in space like eons. So what if my uncle Moe was dead? I was philosophical and luxurious. I didn't even have to look at the rabbi and his wife. After all,

how many times had we dissolved stickball games when the
rabbi came home? How many times had we risked shameful
discovery, scrambling up the ladder, exposed to their windows—
if they looked. We risked life itself to achieve this eminence.
I looked at the rabbi and his wife.

Today she was a blonde. Bald didn't mean no wigs. She
had ten wigs, ten colors, fifty styles. She looked different,
the same, and very good. A human theme in which nothing
begat anything and was gorgeous. To me she was the world's
lesson. Aryan yellow slipped through pins about her ears. An
olive complexion mediated yellow hair and Arabic black
eyes. Could one care what she really looked like? What was
really? The minute you wondered, she looked like something
else, in another wig, another style. Without the wigs she was
a baldy-bean lady. Today she was a blonde. Not blonde. *A*
blonde. The phonograph blared and her deep loops flowed
Tommy Dorsey, Benny Goodman, and then the thing itself,
Choo-Choo Lopez. Rumba! One, two-three. One, two-three.
The rabbi stepped away to delight in blonde imagination.
Twirling and individual, he stepped away snapping fingers,
going high and light on his toes. A short bearded man, balls
afling, cock shuddering like a springboard. Rumba! One,
two-three. *Ole! Vaya,* Choo-Choo!

> I was on my way to spend some time in Cuba.
> Stopped off at Miami Beach, la-la.
> Oh, what a rumba they teach, la-la.
> Way down in Miami Beach,
> Oh, what a chroombah they teach, la-la.
> Way-down-in-Miami-Beach.

She, on the other hand, was somewhat reserved. A shift in
one lush hip was total rumba. He was Mr. Life. She was
dancing. He was a naked man. She was what she was in the
garment of her soft, essential self. He was snapping, clap-
ping, hopping to the beat. The beat lived in her visible music,
her lovely self. Except for the wig. Also a watchband that
desecrated her wrist. But it gave her a bit of the whorish. She
never took it off.

Harold Cohen began a cocktail-mixer motion, masturbating
with two fists. Seeing him at such hard futile work, braced

only by sneakers, was terrifying. But I grinned. Out of terror,
I twisted an encouraging face. Melvin Bloom kept one hand
on the tin. The other knuckled the rumba numbers into the
back of my head. Nodding like a defective, little Arnold
Bloom chewed his lip and squealed as the rabbi and his wife
smacked together. The rabbi clapped her buttocks, fingers
buried in the cleft. They stood only on his legs. His back
arched, knees bent, thighs thick with thrust, up, up, up. Her
legs wrapped his hips, ankles crossed, hooked for constric-
tion. "Oi, oi, oi," she cried, wig flashing left, right, tossing
the Brooklyn Navy Yard, the Statue of Liberty, and the
Empire State Building to hell. Arnold squealed oi, squealing
rubber. His sneaker heels stabbed tin to stop his slide. Melvin
said, "Idiot." Arnold's ring hooked a nailhead and the ring
and ring finger remained. The hand, the arm, the rest of him,
were gone.

We rumbled down the ladder. "Oi, oi, oi," she yelled. In
a freak of ecstasy her eyes had rolled and caught us. The
rabbi drilled to her quick and she had us. "OI, OI," she
yelled above congas going clop, doom-doom, clop, doom-
doom on the way to Cuba. The rabbi flew to the window, a
red mouth opening in his beard: "Murderers." He couldn't
know what he said. Melvin Bloom was crying. My fingers
were tearing, bleeding into brick. Harold Cohen, like an
adding machine, gibbered the name of God. We moved down
the ledge quickly as we dared. Bongos went tocka-ti-tocka,
tocka-ti-tocka. The rabbi screamed. "MELVIN BLOOM,
PHILLIP LIEBOWITZ, HAROLD COHEN, MELVIN
BLOOM," as if our names, screamed this way, naming us
where we hung, smashed us into brick.

Nothing was discussed.

The rabbi used his connections, arrangements were made.
We were sent to a camp in New Jersey. We hiked and played
volleyball. One day, apropos of nothing, Melvin came to me
and said little Arnold had been made of gold and he, Melvin,
of shit. I appreciated the sentiment, but to my mind they were
both made of shit. Harold Cohen never again spoke to either
of us. The counselors in the camp were World War II veterans, introspective men. Some carried shrapnel in their bodies.
One had a metal plate in his head. Whatever you said to them

they seemed to be thinking of something else, even when they answered. But step out of line and a plastic lanyard whistled burning notice across your ass.

At night, lying in the bunkhouse, I listened to owls. I'd never before heard that sound, the sound of darkness, blooming, opening inside you like a mouth.

(1970)

Alice Walker

Alice Walker was born in 1944, in Georgia. Educated at Sarah Lawrence, she taught at Wellesley and at Yale, and worked as an editor at Ms. magazine. Her first two novels, The Third Life of Grange Copeland (1970) and Meridian (1976), attracted little attention. But with her third novel, The Color Purple (1982), Walker was hailed, in Tillie Olsen's words, as "a major American writer."

Poet, critic, and memoirist as well as a writer of fiction, Walker has bluntly and sensitively dealt with the dual and difficult experience of being both black and female in twentieth-century America. The first paragraph of her story "Everyday Use," taken from the same 1970 collection, In Love & Trouble, as "Her Sweet Jerome," shows how carefully, even delicately she handles her material:

I will wait for her in the yard that Maggie and I made so clean and wavy yesterday afternoon. A yard like this is more comfortable than most people know. It is not just a yard. It is like an extended living room. When the hard clay is swept clean as a floor and the fine sand around the edges lined with tiny, irregular grooves, anyone can come and sit and look up into the elm tree and wait for the breezes that never come inside the house.

Walker writes with a fine, clear awareness of geographical and personal context. Her fiction is sometimes violent; it is never loud. And her voice, though often sorrowful, is never despairing.

HER SWEET JEROME

Ties she had bought him hung on the closet door, which now swung open as she hurled herself again and again into the closet. Glorious ties, some with birds and dancing women in grass skirts painted on by hand, some with little polka dots with bigger dots dispersed among them. Some red, lots red and green, and one purple, with a golden star, through the center of which went his gold mustang stickpin, which she had also given him. She looked in the pockets of the black leather jacket he had reluctantly worn the night before. Three of his suits, a pair of blue twill work pants, an old gray sweater with a hood and pockets lay thrown across the bed. The jacket leather was sleazy and damply clinging to her hands. She had bought it for him, as well as the three suits: one light blue with side vents, one gold with green specks, and one reddish that had a silver imitation-silk vest. The pockets of the jacket came softly outward from the lining like skinny milktoast rats. Empty. Slowly she sank down on the bed and began to knead, with blunt anxious fingers, all the pockets in all the clothes piled around her. First the blue suit, then the gold with green, then the reddish one that he said he didn't like most of all, but which he would sometimes wear if she agreed to stay home, or if she promised not to touch him anywhere at all while he was getting dressed.

She was a big awkward woman, with big bones and hard rubbery flesh. Her short arms ended in ham hands, and her neck was a squat roll of fat that protruded behind her head as a big bump. Her skin was rough and puffy, with plump molelike freckles down her cheeks. Her eyes glowered from under the mountain of her brow and were circled with expensive mauve shadow. They were nervous and quick when she was flustered and darted about at nothing in particular while she was dressing hair or talking to people.

Her troubles started noticeably when she fell in love with a studiously quiet schoolteacher, Mr. Jerome Franklin Washington III, who was ten years younger than her. She told herself that she shouldn't want him, he was so little and cute and young, but when she took into account that he was a schoolteacher, well, she just couldn't seem to get any rest until, as she put it, "I were Mr. and Mrs. Jerome Franklin Washington the third, *and that's the truth!*"

She owned a small beauty shop at the back of her father's funeral home, and they were known as "colored folks with money." She made pretty good herself, though she didn't like standing on her feet so much, and her father let anybody know she wasn't getting any of his money while he was alive. She was proud to say she had never asked him for any. He started relenting kind of fast when he heard she planned to add a schoolteacher to the family, which consisted of funeral directors and bootleggers, but she cut him off quick and said she didn't want anybody to take care of her man but her. She had learned how to do hair from an old woman who ran a shop on the other side of town and was proud to say that she could make her own way. And much better than some. She was fond of telling schoolteachers (women schoolteachers) that she didn't miss her "eddicashion" as much as some did who had no learning and no money both together. She had a low opinion of women schoolteachers, because before and after her marriage to Jerome Franklin Washington III, they were the only females to whom he cared to talk.

The first time she saw him he was walking past the window of her shop with an armful of books and his coat thrown casually over his arm. Looking so neat and *cute*. What popped into her mind was that if he was hers the first thing she would get him was a sweet little red car to drive. And she worked and went into debt and got it for him, too—after she got him—but then she could tell he didn't like it much because it was only a Chevy. She had started right away to save up so she could make a down payment on a brand-new white Buick deluxe, with automatic drive and whitewall tires.

Jerome was dapper, every inch a gentleman, as anybody with half an eye could see. That's what she told everybody before they were married. He was beating her black and blue even then, so that every time you saw her she was sporting her "shades." She could not open her mouth without him wincing and pretending he couldn't stand it, so he would knock her out of the room to keep her from talking to him. She tried to be sexy and stylish, and was, in her fashion, with a predominant taste for pastel taffetas and orange shoes. In the summertime she paid twenty dollars for big umbrella hats with bows and flowers on them and when she wore black and white together she would liven it up with elbow-length gloves of red satin. She was genuinely undecided when she woke up in the morning whether she really outstripped the other girls in town for beauty, but could convince herself that she was equally good-looking by the time she had breakfast on the table. She was always talking with a lot of extra movement to her thick coarse mouth, with its hair tufts at the corners, and when she drank coffee she held the cup over the saucer with her little finger sticking out, while she crossed her short hairy legs at the knees.

If her husband laughed at her high heels as she teetered and minced off to church on Sunday mornings, with her hair greased and curled and her new dress bunching up at the top of her girdle, she pretended his eyes were approving. Other times, when he didn't bother to look up from his books and only muttered curses if she tried to kiss him good-bye, she did not know whether to laugh or cry. However, her public manner was serene.

"I just don't know how some womens can stand it, honey," she would say slowly, twisting her head to the side and upward in an elegant manner. "One thing my husband does not do," she would enunciate grandly, "he don't beat me!" And she would sit back and smile in her pleased oily fat way. Usually her listeners, captive women with wet hair, would simply smile and nod in sympathy and say, looking at one another or at her black eye, "You say he don't? Hummmm, well, hush your mouf.'' And she would continue curling or massaging or straightening their hair, fixing her face in a steamy dignified mask that encouraged snickers.

2

It was in her shop that she first heard the giggling and saw the smirks. It was at her job that gossip gave her to understand, as one woman told her, ''Your cute little man is sticking his finger into somebody else's pie.'' And she was not and could not be surprised, as she looked into the amused and self-contented face, for she had long been aware that her own pie was going—and for the longest time had been going—strictly untouched.

From that first day of slyly whispered hints, ''Your old man's puttin' something *over* on you, sweets,'' she started trying to find out who he was fooling around with. Her sources of gossip were malicious and mean, but she could think of nothing else to do but believe them. She searched high and she searched low. She looked in taverns and she looked in churches. She looked in the school where he worked.

She went to whorehouses and to prayer meetings, through parks and outside the city limits, all the while buying axes and pistols and knives of all descriptions. Of course she said nothing to her sweet Jerome, who watched her maneuverings from behind the covers of his vast supply of paperback books. This hobby of his she heartily encouraged, relegating reading to the importance of scanning the funnies; and besides, it was something he could do at home, if she could convince him she would be completely silent for an evening, and, of course, if he would stay.

She turned the whole town upside down, looking at white girls, black women, black beauties, ugly hags of all shades. She found nothing. And Jerome went on reading, smiling smugly as he shushed her with a carefully cleaned and lustred finger. ''Don't interrupt me,'' he was always saying, and he would read some more while she stood glowering darkly behind him, muttering swears in her throaty voice, and then tramping flatfooted out of the house with her collection of weapons.

Some days she would get out of bed at four in the morning

after not sleeping a wink all night, throw an old sweater around her shoulders, and begin the search. Her firm bulk became flabby. Her eyes were bloodshot and wild, her hair full of lint, nappy at the roots and greasy on the ends. She smelled bad from mouth and underarms and elsewhere. She could not sit still for a minute without jumping up in bitter vexation to run and search a house or street she thought she might have missed before.

"You been messin' with my Jerome?" she would ask whomever she caught in her quivering feverish grip. And before they had time to answer she would have them by the chin in a headlock with a long knife pressed against their necks below the ear. Such bloodchilling questioning of its residents terrified the town, especially since her madness was soon readily perceivable from her appearance. She had taken to grinding her teeth and tearing at her hair as she walked along. The townspeople, none of whom knew where she lived—or anything about her save the name of her man, "Jerome"—were waiting for her to attempt another attack on a woman openly, or, better for them because it implied less danger to a resident, they hoped she would complete her crack-up within the confines of her own home, preferably while alone; in that event anyone seeing or hearing her would be obliged to call the authorities.

She knew this in her deranged but cunning way. But she did not let it interfere with her search. The police would never catch her, she thought; she was too clever. She had a few disguises and a thousand places to hide. A final crack-up in her own home was impossible, she reasoned contemptuously, for she did not think her husband's lover bold enough to show herself on his wife's own turf.

Meanwhile, she stopped operating the beauty shop, and her patrons were glad, for before she left for good she had had the unnerving habit of questioning a woman sitting underneath her hot comb—"You the one ain't you?!"—and would end up burning her no matter what she said. When her father died he proudly left his money to "the schoolteacher" to share or not with his wife, as he had "learnin' enough to see fit." Jerome had "learnin' enough" not to give his wife one cent. The legacy pleased Jerome, though he never bought anything with the money that his wife could see. As long as the money lasted Jerome spoke of it as "insurance." If she asked insurance against what, he would say fire and theft. Or burglary and cyclones. When the money was gone, and it seemed to her it vanished overnight, she asked Jerome what he had bought. He said, Something very big. She said, Like what? He said, Like a tank. She did not ask any more questions after that. By that time she didn't care about the money anyhow, as long as he hadn't spent it on some woman.

As steadily as she careened downhill, Jerome advanced in the opposite direction. He was well known around town as a "shrewd joker" and a scholar. An "intellectual," some people called him, a word that meant nothing whatever to her. Everyone described Jerome in a different way. He had friends among the educated, whose talk she found unusually trying, not that she was ever invited to listen to any of it. His closest friend was the head of the school he taught in and had migrated south from some famous university in the North. He was a small slender man with a ferociously unruly beard and large mournful eyes. He called Jerome "brother." The women in Jerome's group wore short kinky hair and large hoop earrings. They stuck together, calling themselves by what they termed their "African" names, and never went to church. Along with the men, the women sometimes held "workshops" for the young toughs of the town. She had no idea what went on in these; however, she had long since stopped believing they had anything to do with cabinetmaking or any other kind of woodwork.

Among Jerome's group of friends, or "comrades," as he sometimes called them jokingly (or not jokingly, for all she knew), were two or three whites from the community's white college and university. Jerome didn't ordinarily like white people, and she could not understand where they fit into the group. The principal's house was the meeting place, and the whites arrived looking backward over their shoulders after nightfall. She knew, because she had watched this house night after anxious night, trying to rouse enough courage to go inside. One hot night, when a drink helped stiffen her backbone, she burst into the living room in the middle of the evening. The women, whom she had grimly "suspected," sat together in debative conversation in one corner of the room. Every once in a while a phrase she could understand touched her ear. She heard "slave trade" and "violent overthrow" and "off de pig," an expression she'd never heard before. One of the women, the only one of this group to acknowledge her, laughingly asked if she had come to "join the revolution." She had stood shaking by the door, trying so hard to understand she felt she was going to faint. Jerome rose from among the group of men, who sat in a circle on the other side of the room, and, without paying any attention to her, began reciting some of the nastiest-sounding poetry she'd ever heard. She left the room in shame and confusion, and no one bothered to ask why she'd stood so long staring at them, or whether she needed anyone to show her out. She trudged home heavily, with her head down, bewildered, astonished, and perplexed.

3

And now she hunted through her husband's clothes looking for a clue. Her hands were shaking as she emptied and shook, pawed and sometimes even lifted to her nose to smell. Each time she emptied a pocket, she felt there was something, *something*, some little thing that was escaping her.

Her heart pounding, she got down on her knees and looked under the bed. It was dusty and cobwebby, the way the inside of her head felt. The house was filthy, for she had neglected it totally since she began her search. Now it seemed that all the dust in the world had come to rest under her bed. She saw his shoes; she lifted them to her perspiring cheeks and kissed them. She ran her fingers inside them. Nothing.

Then, before she got up from her knees, she thought about the intense blackness underneath the headboard of the bed. She had not looked there. On her side of the bed on the floor beneath the pillow there was nothing. She hurried around to the other side. Kneeling, she struck something with her hand on the floor under his side of the bed. Quickly, down on her stomach, she raked it out. Then she raked and raked. She was panting and sweating, her ashen face slowly coloring with the belated rush of doomed comprehension. In a rush it came to her: "It ain't no woman." Just like that. It had never occurred to her there could be anything more serious. She stifled the cry that rose in her throat.

Coated with grit, with dust sticking to the pages, she held in her crude, indelicate hands, trembling now, a sizable pile of paperback books. Books that had fallen from his hands behind the bed over the months of their marriage. She dusted them carefully one by one and looked with frowning concentration at their covers. Fists and guns appeared everywhere. "Black" was the one word that appeared consistently on each cover. *Black Rage, Black Fire, Black Anger, Black Revenge, Black Vengeance, Black Hatred, Black Beauty, Black Revolution*. Then the word "revolution" took over. *Revolution in the Streets, Revolution from the Rooftops, Revolution in the Hills, Revolution and Rebellion, Revolution and Black People in the United States, Revolution and Death*. She looked with wonder at the books that were her husband's preoccupation, enraged that the obvious was what she had never guessed before.

How many times had she encouraged his light reading? How many times been ignorantly amused? How many times had he laughed at her when she went out looking for "his" women? With a sob she realized she didn't even know what the word "revolution" meant, unless it meant to go round and round, the way her head was going.

With quiet care she stacked the books neatly on his pillow. With the largest of her knives she ripped and stabbed them through. When the brazen and difficult words did not disappear with the books, she hastened with kerosene to set the marriage bed afire. Thirstily, in hopeless jubilation, she watched the room begin to burn. The bits of words transformed themselves into luscious figures of smoke, lazily arching toward the ceiling. "Trash!" she cried over and over, reaching through the flames to strike out the words, now raised from the dead in glorious colors. "I kill you! I kill you!" she screamed against the roaring fire, backing enraged and trembling into a darkened corner of the room, not near the open door. But the fire and the words rumbled against her together, overwhelming her with pain and enlightenment. And she hid her big wet face in her singed then sizzling arms and screamed and screamed.

(1970)

Richard Elman

Richard Elman was born in Brooklyn, New York, in 1934. He took a B.A. at Syracuse University in 1955, and an M.A. at Stanford in 1957. Thereafter he worked for the Pacifica Foundation, as public affairs director at WBAI-FM in New York (one of the earliest of the listener-supported radio stations), and as a researcher at the Columbia University School of Social Work. He has taught at Hunter and Bennington Colleges and at Columbia University.

Elman's novels have had good critical receptions but very little popular success. Critics have said that his fiction was "unequivocally honest" and that he exhibited an "ironic, stinging intelligence," but the books have not sold well. Virtually his only popular book has been the nonfictional The Poorhouse State: The American Way of Life on Public Assistance (1966), which inspired reviewers to say, among other things, that it was "an exciting treatise on a very unpopular subject" and that Elman had displayed "much compassion, objectivity and insight. . . ." A poet and critic as well as novelist and writer of stories, Elman has continued to work in radio as a reviewer and commentator.

Elman is often an experimentalist, and a remarkably fine one, for behind his experiments lies not simply a desire to play with form and style, not simply a concern with technique, but a consistent vision of social justice and moral living. His irony too is focused, and never used for its own sake.

CROSSING OVER

An ordinary life can be a disaster. You don't despise people any less for not being very much at all. They are people, and we all make errors, some of us, of course, more than others. If only they knew there were others making errors just like themselves they would be no less ordinary. But they are not our peers, or friends, just our brothers.

When my own particular long lost brother Joseph Perkell was born he was not considered ordinary by the ordinary people who populated our household. They considered him extraordinary. Could anybody say they were wrong? He was certainly bigger than they were in some respects, and they were certainly not midgets at all. As older brother, I was a bit of a gnome, though certainly not a midget either.

At the time I was seven, five years my brother's senior, and we had very little in common to begin with. It was not surprising this should be so but it was upsetting to him, for I thought I should love him, and he always said he loved me. Those, in fact, were his very first words at birth.

"I love you, Joseph." The red-faced boy, my brother.

I did not immediately return the feeling. I was not in love with anybody, certainly not a red-faced boy of two who went around claiming to be my brother.

The family was naturally quite upset. He was said to be bigger than me already and growing like a weed. What did I have to show to them for all their pains? I must try to love my brother.

Loving Joseph was never very easy. He was the sort of infant who was always getting in the way of things. Like myself, for example. Joseph always made me feel as if I owed him something. For what? Being so much smaller than he was nothing to feel that badly about. I was just so much older that it couldn't be helped.

Nor could it be helped that we sometimes felt together as if there was something approaching liking between us. It is many years since it last happened and what it felt like I do not remember, though it was nice.

None of our many parents, of course, approved. They wanted us to be nice to each other, but not to like each other. At least not openly. It got everybody in the house so nervous when we were that upset.

The really difficult period came between us when it was time to assign roles, and careers. As older brother I was certain to be an engineer. My function would be to design those bridges that my late brother Joseph was so determined to cross over. He wished simply to get to the other side, wherever that was, but as I was pretty anxious to get there too, this made for difficult complications in design and stress.

Of course, my brother Joseph said he would go first. Of course, I agreed, since he was the youngest, but first, would you let me, I added, design it.

Not at all, he said, crossing over into nowhere, quickly, by himself. Needless to say he was very very lonely there but he did not fall all the way down and when he did there was always somebody around to catch him. Joseph called what we had just done together our span together. He then asked me if I would help design another for him to be all alone.

Our parents were, to be very sure, upset with the idea that one so old as myself could dare to contrive for one so young, all alone, and they, of course, suggested that we try next time to work in concert, too, as sibling to sibling. The problem might also be solved with pontoons.

Joseph said I had come up with none worth standing on and I said Joseph you are a damn fool. The question isn't floating here or there but flying over the water to the moon and stars.

Never in my life, said my ornery little brother who was doomed to live forever.

We went back to work at being brothers again.

By now I was nearly forty-eight and Joseph who had once been my younger brother was at least fifty-six. Together we had meant so much to each other, but we were not now, for different reasons.

I can remember the time Joseph said it could be very different with us if we would only design another bridge, with a definite blueprint in advance, and lots of supplies of iron beams, rivets, nuts, spanners, bolts, stanchions, and what-have-yous to get across.

I wasn't what you might call in disagreement. However, I also thought I was pretty brilliant, and also pretty busy.

Joseph couldn't seem to understand any of this at all.

We parted then and went our separate ways, myself going off to Italy to study the works of the great masters, while Joseph remained at home turning somersaults into the air until such time as I could return and we could relate face to face, as one brother to another.

That it never happened is as much a function of my careless indolence as of Joseph's spectacular turnabouts on the various rigmaroles of his profession. We were such brothers it could not possibly be any other way.

It was as if the moon wanted to come down out of the clouds but did not know how. It could be said equally, I suppose, that the clouds had blotted out the moon for a spell, though that did not seem to matter.

My first thought was to give up entirely. I thought of that again and again in the intervals between trying to bring Joseph around to my way of thinking. Meanwhile, as I say, our parents fumed.

Then it occurred to me to stop lying altogether, but how would that help Joseph, and our parents, and all our other friends? Surely they needed to lie with me as much as myself, and with whom and about whom did not seem to matter so long as the lie was good enough, which I had insisted all along it was. They sometimes said, for example, it's our misfortune and none of your own, but I always insisted it was a common misfortune, particularly so with Joseph.

It seemed as if a dramatic gesture was called for that would not scare people half to death. On the brightest day of all I would announce to the world that my brother Joseph was *the* most accomplished crosser over I had ever known to exist. In fact I could become his press agent. In the world of our parents that was still considered important. The question was would Joseph.

Another important question was about myself. Did I have the right to exist side by side with such a brother when I was always being asked to kiss his ass in public which, of course, I should have done gladly, if no other role for me had been available.

We had come to a parting of our ways. Joseph and his various friends were going off somewhere. In time I would join them with our parents, if only I knew how. Meantime, there were all the other little gnomes and midgets to think about, including myself.

I decided to take an advertisement on the front page of the *New York Times:* MY BROTHER JOSEPH IS THE WORLD'S GREATEST BRIDGE CROSSER I HAVE EVER KNOWN AND ALL I EVER DID WAS SIT AND WATCH.

As if everybody hadn't known that all along.

When this didn't work I decided to hold a press conference to announce that I was scared to death of Joseph and his stunts and wouldn't somebody please help us to get along with each other.

A child offered herself in public but I was much too afraid of getting her into trouble with her mother for being out so late.

A black crow flew in through my open window, then, one bright sunny day and said, HELP ME, I'M A BLACKBIRD, AND I'LL HAVE ONE FOR THE ROAD WITH YOU.

That seemed like taking such advantage of the misfortunes of others that I said: GET OUT OF MY LIFE UNLESS I CAN FLY YOU ACROSS ON MY WINGS, OR YOUR WINGS, OR BOTH.

The crowd of midgets and gnomes congregating every day outside my window was truly getting fierce.

Their leader was a certain Julia Pierce.

I pleaded with her not to make me do a thing like that, but when I did it again she said it's too late already, now you'll have to do it like this.

Or else, she said, just come down out of that house and I'll show you a thing or two.

I could show you a thing or two myself, I said, but she said frankly, I doubt that, and there we were again, and again, and again, like brothers, and sisters, now and forever.

I guess that's how I got to be such a student of human nature, though if you ask me I prefer building bridges any day of the week, especially next Tuesday, when I'm scheduled to be five years old again.

As for my brother Joseph he's been gone a long long time ago when he was my friend and there's not much I can do about that except cry out occasionally, I LOVE YOU, JOSEPH, WHEREVER YOU ARE.

And maybe hope for a postcard back now and then.

(1973)

Ann Beattie

———————————◆———————————

Ann Beattie was born in Washington, D.C., in 1947. Her first novel, Chilly Scenes of Winter *(1976), was a Book-of-the-Month Club selection and was subsequently made into a movie. Her settings and her characters are somewhat like those in John Updike's books. But Beattie has a tougher approach, and a firmer style, and is in most respects a more powerful, more interesting, and is probably destined to be a more enduring writer. Her two collections of stories,* Distortions *(1976) and* Secrets and Surprises *(1978) have earned her a very high degree of critical acclaim—and it is not hard to understand why. Here, for example, is the first sentence of "Dwarf House," which is the first story in* Distortions *("Snakes' Shoes" is the second):*

> "Are you happy?" MacDonald says. "Because if you're happy I'll leave you alone."

There is an easy, compelling strength in virtually all her work. If she develops as she has begun, she will be without much doubt a major literary figure.

SNAKES' SHOES

The little girl sat between her Uncle Sam's legs. Alice and Richard, her parents, sat next to them. They were divorced, and Alice had remarried. She was holding a ten-month-old baby. It had been Sam's idea that they all get together again, and now they were sitting on a big flat rock not far out into the pond.

"Look," the little girl said.

They turned and saw a very small snake coming out of a crack between two rocks on the shore.

"It's nothing," Richard said.

"It's a snake," Alice said. "You have to be careful of them. Never touch them."

"Excuse me," Richard said. "Always be careful of everything."

That was what the little girl wanted to hear, because she didn't like the way the snake looked.

"You know what snakes do?" Sam asked her.

"What?" she said.

"They can tuck their tail into their mouth and turn into a hoop."

"Why do they do that?" she asked.

"So they can roll down hills easily."

"Why don't they just walk?"

"They don't have feet. See?" Sam said.

The snake was still; it must have sensed their presence.

"Tell her the truth now," Alice said to Sam.

The little girl looked at her uncle.

"They have feet, but they shed them in the summer," Sam said. "If you ever see tiny shoes in the woods, they belong to the snakes."

"Tell her the truth," Alice said again.

"Imagination is better than reality," Sam said to the little girl.

The little girl patted the baby. She loved all the people who were sitting on the rock. Everybody was happy, except that in the back of their minds the grownups thought that their being together again was bizarre. Alice's husband had gone to Germany to look after his father, who was ill. When Sam learned about this, he called Richard, who was his brother. Richard did not think that it was a good idea for the three of them to get together again. Sam called the next day, and Richard told him to stop asking about it. But when Sam called again that night, Richard said sure, what the hell.

They sat on the rock looking at the pond. Earlier in the afternoon a game warden had come by and he let the little girl look at the crows in the trees through his binoculars. She was impressed. Now she said that she wanted a crow.

"I've got a good story about crows," Sam said to her. "I know how they got their name. You see, they all used to be sparrows, and they annoyed the king, so he ordered one of his servants to kill them. The servant didn't want to kill all the sparrows, so he went outside and looked at them and prayed, 'Grow. Grow.' And miraculously they did. The king could never kill anything as big and as grand as a crow, so the king and the birds and the servant were all happy."

"But why are they called crows?" the little girl said.

"Well," Sam said, "long, long ago, a historical linguist heard the story, but he misunderstood what he was told and thought that the servant had said 'crow,' instead of 'grow.' "

"Tell her the truth," Alice said.

"That's the truth," Sam said. "A lot of our vocabulary is twisted around."

"Is that true?" the little girl asked her father.

"Don't ask me," he said.

Back when Richard and Alice were engaged, Sam had tried to talk Richard out of it. He told him that he would be tied down; he said that if Richard hadn't got used to regimentation in the Air Force he wouldn't even consider marriage at twenty-four. He was so convinced that it was a bad idea that he cornered Alice at the engagement party (there were heart-shaped boxes of heart-shaped mints wrapped in paper printed with hearts for everybody to take home) and asked her to back down. At first Alice thought this was amusing. "You make me sound like a vicious dog,'' she said to Sam. ''It's not going to work out,'' Sam said. ''Don't do it.'' He showed her the little heart he was holding. ''Look at these God-damned things,'' he said.

''They weren't my idea. They were your mother's,'' Alice said. She walked away. Sam watched her go. She had on a lacy beige dress. Her shoes sparkled. She was very pretty. He wished she would not marry his brother, who had been kicked around all his life—first by their mother, then by the Air Force (''Think of me as you fly into the blue,'' their mother had written Richard once. Christ!)—and now would be watched over by a wife.

The summer Richard and Alice married, they invited Sam to spend his vacation with them. It was nice that Alice didn't hold grudges. She also didn't hold a grudge against her husband, who burned a hole in an armchair and who tore the mainsail on their sailboat beyond repair by going out on the lake in a storm. She was a very patient woman. Sam found that he liked her. He liked the way she worried about Richard out in a boat in the middle of the storm. After that, Sam spent part of every summer vacation with them, and went to their house every Thanksgiving. Two years ago, just when Sam was convinced that everything was perfect, Richard told him that they were getting divorced. The next day, when Sam was alone with Alice after breakfast, he asked why.

''He burns up all the furniture,'' she said. ''He acts like a madman with that boat. He's swamped her three times this year. I've been seeing someone else.''

''Who have you been seeing?''

''No one you know.''

''I'm curious, Alice. I just want to know his name.''

''Hans.''

''Hans. Is he a German?''

''Yes.''

''Are you in love with this German?''

''I'm not going to talk about it. Why are you talking to me? Why don't you go sympathize with your brother?''

''He knows about this German?''

''His name is Hans.''

"That's a German name," Sam said, and he went outside to find Richard and sympathize with him.

Richard was crouching beside his daughter's flower garden. His daughter was sitting on the grass across from him, talking to her flowers.

"You haven't been bothering Alice, have you?" Richard said.

"Richard, she's seeing a God-damned German," Sam said.

"What does that have to do with anything?"

"What are you talking about?" the little girl asked.

That silenced both of them. They stared at the bright-orange flowers.

"Do you still love her?" Sam asked after his second drink.

They were in a bar, off a boardwalk. After their conversation about the German, Richard had asked Sam to go for a drive. They had driven thirty or forty miles to this bar, which neither of them had seen before and neither of them liked, although Sam was fascinated by a conversation now taking place between two blond transvestites on the bar stools to his right. He wondered if Richard knew that they weren't really women, but he hadn't been able to think of a way to work it into the conversation, and he started talking about Alice instead.

"I don't know," Richard said. "I think you were right. The Air Force, Mother, marriage—"

"They're not real women," Sam said.

"What?"

Sam thought that Richard had been staring at the two people he had been watching. A mistake on his part; Richard had just been glancing around the bar.

"Those two blondes on the bar stools. They're men."

Richard studied them. "Are you sure?" he said.

"Of course I'm sure. I live in N.Y.C., you know."

"Maybe I'll come live with you. Can I do that?"

"You always said you'd rather die than live in New York."

"Well, are you telling me to kill myself, or is it O.K. if I move in with you?"

"If you want to," Sam said. He shrugged. "There's only one bedroom, you know."

"I've been to your apartment, Sam."

"I just wanted to remind you. You don't seem to be thinking too clearly."

"You're right," Richard said. "A God-damned German."

The barmaid picked up their empty glasses and looked at them.

"This gentleman's wife is in love with another man," Sam said to her.

"I overheard," she said.

"What do you think of that?" Sam asked her.

"Maybe German men aren't as creepy as American men," she said. "Do you want refills?"

After Richard moved in with Sam he began bringing animals into the apartment. He brought back a dog, a cat that stayed through the winter, and a blue parakeet that had been in a very small cage that Richard could not persuade the pet-store owner to replace. The bird flew around the apartment. The cat was wild for it, and Sam was relieved when the cat eventually disappeared. Once, Sam saw a mouse in the kitchen and assumed that it was another of Richard's pets, until he realized that there was no cage for it in the apartment. When Richard came home he said that the mouse was not his. Sam called the exterminator, who refused to come in and spray the apartment because the dog had growled at him. Sam told this to his brother, to make him feel guilty for his irresponsibility. Instead, Richard brought another cat in. He said that it would get the mouse, but not for a while yet—it was only a kitten. Richard fed it cat food off the tip of a spoon.

Richard's daughter came to visit. She loved all the animals—the big mutt that let her brush him, the cat that slept in her lap, the bird that she followed from room to room, talking to it, trying to get it to land on the back of her hand. For Christmas, she gave her father a rabbit. It was a fat white rabbit with one brown ear, and it was kept in a cage on the night table when neither Sam nor Richard was in the apartment to watch it and keep it away from the cat and the dog. Sam said that the only vicious thing Alice ever did was giving her daughter the rabbit to give Richard for Christmas. Eventually the rabbit died of a fever. It cost Sam one hundred and sixty dollars to treat the rabbit's illness; Richard did not have a job, and could not pay anything. Sam kept a book of I.O.U.s. In it he wrote, "Death of rabbit—$160 to vet." When Richard did get a job, he looked over the debt book. "Why couldn't you just have written down the sum?" he asked Sam. "Why did you want to remind me about the rabbit?" He was so upset that he missed the second morning of his new job. "That was inhuman," he said to Sam. " 'Death of rabbit—$160'—that was horrible. The poor rabbit. God damn you." He couldn't get control of himself.

A few weeks later, Sam and Richard's mother died. Alice wrote to Sam, saying that she was sorry. Alice had never liked their mother, but she was fascinated by the woman. She never got over her spending a hundred and twenty-five dollars on paper lanterns for the engagement party. After all these years, she was still thinking about it. "What do you think became of the lanterns after the party?" she wrote in her letter of condolence. It was an odd letter, and it didn't seem that Alice was very happy. Sam even forgave her for the rabbit. He wrote her a long letter, saying that they should all get together. He knew a motel out in the country where they could stay, perhaps for a whole weekend. She wrote back, saying that it sounded like a good idea. The only thing that upset her about it was that his secretary had typed his letter. In her letter to Sam, she pointed out several times that he could have written in longhand. Sam noticed that both Alice and Richard seemed to be raving. Maybe they would get back together.

Now they were all staying at the same motel, in different rooms. Alice and her daughter and the baby were in one room, and Richard and Sam had rooms down the hall. The little girl spent the nights with different people. When Sam bought two pounds of fudge, she said she was going to spend the night with him. The next night, Alice's son had colic, and when Sam looked out his window he saw Richard holding the baby, walking around and around the swimming pool. Alice was asleep. Sam knew this because the little girl left her mother's room when she fell asleep and came looking for him.

"Do you want to take me to the carnival?" she asked.

She was wearing a nightgown with blue bears upside down on it, headed for a crash at the hem.

"The carnival's closed," Sam said. "It's late, you know."

"Isn't anything open?"

"Maybe the doughnut shop. That's open all night. I suppose you want to go there?"

"I love doughnuts," she said.

She rode to the doughnut shop on Sam's shoulders, wrapped in his raincoat. He kept thinking, Ten years ago I would never have believed this. But he believed it now; there was a definite weight on his shoulders, and there were two legs hanging down his chest.

The next afternoon, they sat on the rock again, wrapped in towels after a swim. In the distance, two hippies and an Irish setter, all in bandannas, rowed toward shore from an island.

"I wish I had a dog," the little girl said.

"It just makes you sad when you have to go away from them," her father said.

"I wouldn't leave it."

"You're just a kid. You get dragged all over," her father said. "Did you ever think you'd be here today?"

"It's strange," Alice said.

"It was a good idea," Sam said. "I'm always right."

"You're not always right," the little girl said.

"When have I ever been wrong?"

"You tell stories," she said.

"Your uncle is *imaginative*," Sam corrected.

"Tell me another one," she said to him.

"I can't think of one right now."

"Tell the one about the snakes' shoes."

"Your uncle was kidding about the snakes, you know," Alice said.

"I know," she said. Then she said to Sam, "Are you going to tell another one?"

"I'm not telling stories to people who don't believe them," Sam said.

"Come on," she said.

Sam looked at her. She had bony knees, and her hair was brownish-blond. It didn't lighten in the sunshine like her mother's. She was not going to be as pretty as her mother. He rested his hand on the top of her head.

The clouds were rolling quickly across the sky, and when they moved a certain way it was possible for them to see the moon, full and faint in the sky. The crows were still in the treetops. A fish jumped near the rock, and someone said, "Look," and everyone did—late, but in time to see the circles widening where it had landed.

"What did you marry Hans for?" Richard asked.

"I don't know why I married either of you," Alice said.

"Where did you tell him you were going while he was away?" Richard asked.

"To see my sister."

"How is your sister?" he asked.

She laughed. "Fine, I guess."

"What's funny?" Richard asked.

"Our conversation," she said.

Sam was helping his niece off the rock. "We'll take a walk," he said to her. "I have a long story for you, but it will bore the rest of them."

The little girl's knees stuck out. Sam felt sorry for her. He lifted her on his shoulders and cupped his hands over her knees so he wouldn't have to look at them.

"What's the story?" she said.

"One time," Sam said, "I wrote a book about your mother."

"What was it about?" the little girl asked.

"It was about a little girl who met all sorts of interesting animals—a rabbit who kept showing her his pocket watch, who was very upset because he was late—"

"I know that book," she said. "You didn't write that."

"I did write it. But at the time I was very shy, and I didn't want to admit that I'd written it, so I signed another name to it.''

"You're not shy," the little girl said.

Sam continued walking, ducking whenever a branch hung low.

"Do you think there are more snakes?" she asked.

"If there are, they're harmless. They won't hurt you."

"Do they ever hide in trees?"

"No snakes are going to get you," Sam said. "Where was I?"

"You were talking about *Alice in Wonderland*."

"Don't you think I did a good job with that book?" Sam asked.

"You're silly," she said.

It was evening—cool enough for them to wish they had more than two towels to wrap around themselves. The little girl was sitting between her father's legs. A minute before, he had said that she was cold and they should go, but she said that she wasn't and even managed to stop shivering. Alice's son was asleep, squinting. Small black insects clustered on the water in front of the rock. It was their last night there.

"Where will we go?" Richard said.

"How about a seafood restaurant? The motel owner said he could get a babysitter."

Richard shook his head.

"No?" Alice said, disappointed.

"Yes, that would be fine," Richard said. "I was thinking more existentially."

"What does that mean?" the little girl asked.

"It's a word your father made up," Sam said.

"Don't tease her," Alice said.

"I wish I could look through that man's glasses again," the little girl said.

"Here," Sam said, making two circles with the thumb and first finger of each hand. "Look through these."

She leaned over and looked up at the trees through Sam's fingers.

"Much clearer, huh?" Sam said.

"Yes," she said. She liked this game.

"Let me see," Richard said, leaning to look through his brother's fingers.

"Don't forget me," Alice said, and she leaned across Richard to peer through the circles. As she leaned across him, Richard kissed the back of her neck.

(ca. 1975)

Donald Barthelme

Donald Barthelme was born in 1931, in Philadelphia, and raised in Texas. Many of his extremely short, extremely clever, sometimes witty, sometimes darkly romantic stories made their first appearance in The New Yorker. *He published his first collection,* Come Back, Dr. Caligari, *in 1964,* Unspeakable Practices, Unnatural Acts *in 1968,* City Life *in 1971, and* Sadness, *which won the National Book Award, in 1972. His novels include* Snow White *(1964) and* The Dead Father *(1975).*

Surreal fragmentation and Barthelme's particular form of black humor have been discussed in the introduction to this book, in which it is noted that he is in many ways the epitome of certain major trends in the modern short story. At his best quixotically fascinating, he is also, at his worst, obscure, pretentious, and even mawkishly sentimental. Perhaps most important about his work, however, is the plain fact that it is not in any way meretricious. Barthelme is not being cute for the sake of being cute, when he falls into the error of cuteness: he is an immensely serious, deeply concerned man and writer, struggling to deal with exceedingly difficult subjects. What is important for the reader, accordingly, is to try to understand what Barthelme is reacting to, and how he is reacting, and in what directions (if any) he seems to be trying to point. Barthelme is massively influential in modern American fiction, and it is no accident.

REBECCA

Rebecca Lizard was trying to change her ugly, reptilian, thoroughly unacceptable last name.

"Lizard," said the judge. "Lizard, Lizard, Lizard. Lizard. There's nothing wrong with it if you say it enough times. You can't clutter up the court's calendar with trivial little minor irritations. And there have been far too many people changing their names lately. Changing your name countervails the best interests of the telephone company, the electric company, and the United States government. Motion denied."

Lizard in tears.

Lizard led from the courtroom. A chrysanthemum of Kleenex held under her nose.

"Shaky lady," said a man, "are you a schoolteacher?"

Of course she's a schoolteacher, you idiot. Can't you see the poor woman's all upset? Why don't you leave her alone?

"Are you a homosexual lesbian? Is that why you never married?"

Christ, yes, she's a homosexual lesbian, as you put it. *Would you please shut your face?*

Rebecca went to the damned dermatologist (a new damned dermatologist), but he said the same thing the others had said. "Greenish," he said, "slight greenishness, genetic anomaly, nothing to be done, I'm afraid, Mrs. Lizard."

"Miss Lizard."

"Nothing to be done, Miss Lizard."

"Thank you, Doctor. Can I give you a little something for your trouble?"

"Fifty dollars."

When Rebecca got home the retroactive rent increase was waiting for her, coiled in her mailbox like a pupil about to strike.

Must get some more Kleenex. Or a Ph.D. No other way.

She thought about sticking her head in the oven. But it was an electric oven.

Rebecca's lover, Hilda, came home late.

"How'd it go?" Hilda asked, referring to the day.

"Lousy."

"Hmmm," Hilda said, and quietly mixed strong drinks of busthead for the two of them.

Hilda is a very good-looking woman. So is Rebecca. They love each other—an incredibly dangerous and delicate business, as we know. Hilda has long blond hair and is perhaps a shade the more beautiful. Of course Rebecca has a classic and sexual figure which attracts huge admiration from every beholder.

"You're late," Rebecca said. "Where were you?"

"I had a drink with Stephanie."

"Why did you have a drink with Stephanie?"

"She stopped by my office and said let's have a drink."

"Where did you go?"

"The Barclay."

"How is Stephanie?"

"She's fine."

"Why did you have to have a drink with Stephanie?"

"I was ready for a drink."

"Stephanie doesn't have a slight greenishness, is that it? Nice, pink Stephanie."

Hilda rose and put an excellent C & W album on the record player. It was David Rogers's "Farewell to the Ryman," Atlantic SD 7283. It contains such favorites as "Blue Moon of Kentucky," "Great Speckled Bird," "I'm Movin' On," and "Walking the Floor Over You." Many great Nashville personnel appear on this record.

"Pinkness is not everything," Hilda said. "And Stephanie is a little bit boring. You know that."

"Not so boring that you don't go out for drinks with her."

"I am not interested in Stephanie."

"As I was leaving the courthouse," Rebecca said, "a man unzipped my zipper."

David Rogers was singing "Oh please release me, let me go."

"What were you wearing?"

"What I'm wearing now."

"So he had good taste," Hilda said, "for a creep." She hugged Rebecca, on the sofa. "I love you," she said.

"Screw that," Rebecca said plainly, and pushed Hilda away. "Go hang out with Stephanie Sasser."

"I am not interested in Stephanie Sasser," Hilda said for the second time.

Very often one "pushes away" the very thing that one most wants to grab, like a lover. This is a common, although distressing, psychological mechanism, having to do (in my opinion) with the fact that what is presented is not presented "purely," that there is a tiny little canker or grim place in it somewhere. However, worse things can happen.

"Rebecca," said Hilda, "I really don't like your slight greenishness."

The term "lizard" also includes geckos, iguanas, chameleons, slowworms, and monitors. Twenty existing families make up the order, according to the *Larousse Encyclopedia of Animal Life,* and four others are known only from fossils. There are about twenty-five hundred species, and they display adaptations for walking, running, climbing, creeping, or burrowing. Many have interesting names, such as the Bearded Lizard, the Collared Lizard, the Flap-Footed Lizard, the Frilled Lizard, the Girdle-Tailed Lizard, and the Wall Lizard.

"I have been overlooking it for these several years, because I love you, but I really don't like it so much," Hilda said. "It's slightly—"

"Knew it," said Rebecca.

Rebecca went into the bedroom. The color television set was turned on, for some reason. In a greenish glow, a film called *Green Hell* was unfolding.

I'm ill, I'm ill.

I will become a farmer.

Our love, our sexual love, our ordinary love!

Hilda entered the bedroom and said, "Supper is ready."

"What is it?"

"Pork with red cabbage."

"I'm drunk," Rebecca said.

Too many of our citizens are drunk at times when they should be sober—suppertime, for example. Drunkenness leads to forgetting where you have put your watch, keys, or money clip, and to a decreased sensitivity to the needs and desires and calm good health of others. The causes of overuse of alcohol are not as clear as the results. Psychiatrists feel in general that alcoholism is a serious problem but treatable, in some cases. AA is said to be both popular and effective. At base, the question is one of willpower.

"Get up," Hilda said. "I'm sorry I said that."

"You told the truth," said Rebecca.

"Yes, it was the truth," Hilda admitted.

"You didn't tell me the truth in the beginning. In the beginning, you said it was beautiful."

"I was telling you the truth, in the beginning. I did think it was beautiful. Then."

This "then," the ultimate word in Hilda's series of three brief sentences, is one of the most pain-inducing words in the human vocabulary, when used in this sense. Departed time! And the former conditions that went with it! How is human pain to be measured? But remember that Hilda, too . . . It is correct to feel for Rebecca in this situation, but, reader, neither can Hilda's position be considered an enviable one, for truth, as Bergson knew, is a hard apple, whether one is throwing it or catching it.

"What remains?" Rebecca said stonily.

"I can love you *in spite of*—"

Do *I* want to be loved *in spite of?* Do you? Does anyone? But aren't we all, to some degree? Aren't there important parts of all of us which must be, so to say, gazed past? I turn a blind eye to that aspect of you, and you turn a blind eye to that aspect of me, and with these blind eyes eyeball-to-eyeball, to use an expression from the early 1960s, we continue our starched and fragrant lives. Of course it's also called "making the best of things," which I have always considered a rather soggy idea for an American ideal. But my criticisms of this idea must be tested against those of others— the late President McKinley, for example, who maintained that maintaining a good, if not necessarily sunny, disposition was the one valuable and proper course.

Hilda placed her hands on Rebecca's head.

"The snow is coming," she said. "Soon it will be snow time. Together then as in other snow times. Drinking busthead 'round the fire. Truth is a locked room that we knock the lock off from time to time, and then board up again. Tomorrow you will hurt me, and I will inform you that you have done so, and so on and so on. To hell with it. Come, viridian friend, come and sup with me."

They sit down together. The pork with red cabbage steams before them. They speak quietly about the McKinley Administration, which is being revised by revisionist historians. The story ends. It was written for several reasons. Nine of them are secrets. The tenth is that one should never cease considering human love, which remains as grisly and golden as ever, no matter what is tattooed upon the warm tympanic page.

(1975)

Robert Greenwood

———————————

Robert Greenwood studied with Allan Swallow at the University of Denver, taking his M.A. in 1953. After serving as an associate editor of Swallow's periodical, Twentieth Century Literature, *he became first co-publisher and, more recently, Director of Talisman Research (formerly Talisman Press), in California. Talisman publishes fiction, poetry, and western American history.*

Greenwood's own fiction has appeared widely in such journals as Paris Review, Yale Review, Antioch Review, *and* The Denver Quarterly, *from the Winter 1976 issue of which I have taken the story here reprinted. In 1985 Talisman brought out his first collection of stories,* Arcadia & Other Stories.

Just as Walter Miller, Jr., writes in what has often been thought of as a sub-literary genre, science fiction, so too Greenwood's tale is in another sometimes scorned genre, the detective story. It seems to me one of the most gripping, and also one of the most perceptive stories of its kind in the entire genre—and the genre does not deserve the scorn in which it is sometimes held. Read the first page or so, and just see if you can stop. And if that sort of narrative excitement, that sort of insight into character, and that sort of character portrayal is not first-class fiction, I don't know what is.

ARCHETYPES

Through a ten-power glass I was looking upon the face of Alexander the Great. When I saw that distinctive cut on Alexander's cheek, I'd first thought it was an old banker's mark, left there by some harpagon of antiquity. But then I realized I'd seen this particular coin before. The cut on the cheek. That was the clue.

The man who had brought the coin into my shop was sitting opposite my desk. We were alone in my shop. I could feel his eyes upon me as I examined the coin.

"Yes, it's a very rare coin," I said, although he'd not asked for an opinion.

He'd simply handed me the coin in its plastic envelope, seated himself, and asked, "How much for this?"

"You know what it is?" I asked, looking up.

He looked at me indifferently. He didn't answer.

"It's a silver tetradrachm," I said. "Issued during the reign of Ptolemy I, King of Egypt. On the obverse is the head of Alexander the Great. The reverse is Athena, holding a javelin and shield. But the coin isn't in the best condition. There's an old cut on it. That hurts its value. You understand?"

He'd turned his shoulders and was looking around my shop, taking everything in with a rapid glance, his eyes pausing at the entrance, where he did a quick study of the security door and the wall area around the door. His eyes flicked back to me.

"How much?" he repeated. There was authority in his voice. Authority or contempt. I decided it was contempt.

Then I remembered.

I remembered where I'd seen the coin before. It had been almost two years ago, a day in later summer, in the month of September. I could recall the exact hour. I'd closed my shop early that day to make a few calls on my colleagues, dealers in the numismatic trade. That morning I'd got a telephone call from a close friend and competitor, Doc Parker, a specialist in ancient coins, who told me he'd just bought a small hoard of Greek and Cretan coins. "Come on over and take a look," he'd said. "There's some pieces here you won't be able to resist."

Doc's shop was located in a small shopping center at the other end of town. When I arrived he saw me waiting outside and reached under the counter to press the button that automatically released the security lock on the door. The buzzer sounded, and I heard the lock open. I went inside. There were two customers looking at some Roman bronzes in a display case. Doc came over and brought out a tray from underneath the counter and opened it. "Look through these," he said. "There's some nice coins here. But the best ones are back in my office. If you want any of these, pick them out and we'll settle up later back in my office."

He walked back to the two customers and talked about Roman bronzes. I took out several coins and studied them with the glass I always carry in my pocket. I was especially interested in an unusual Cretan coin. I guessed it had been struck in about the fifth century B.C., probably in Knossos. The design was one I'd not seen before. On the obverse was the head of the minotaur; on the reverse, a complicated pattern in the form of a labyrinth. I put it aside, intending to look at it again.

It was then I saw the silver tetradrachm with the head of Alexander the Great. I had a customer who'd been looking for this particular coin for years, but one only in a fine state of preservation. I focused my glass expectantly. When I saw the cut on Alexander's cheek my hopes faded. My customer for this coin was a finicky man. Difficult to please, you might say. He would quibble over the defect to beat down my price. I put the coin aside.

I walked around to the cash register. Doc nodded at me and I went through the turnstile and into his private office. He'd put two trays of coins on his desk for me to look at: "pieces you won't be able to resist," he'd said. Doc's private office was closed off from the rest of his shop, except for the door, and I'd closed that behind me. But there was a small one-way window that looked out into the shop. When you were seated at Doc's desk it was at the level of your eyes. From inside the shop, if you happened to look at it, surrounded as it was by a lot of framed coin displays, it looked like an innocent mirror hanging on the wall.

I looked down at the desk at the trays of coins. Doc hadn't exaggerated their quality. They were all excellent pieces. Good enough to consign to the best auction house in the trade. I got out my glass and turned on the high-intensity desk lamp. I vaguely remember hearing the buzzer and the automatic unlocking of the shop door. I was too absorbed in my study to pay any attention. But after a while, perhaps because of a kind of tension I sensed, I glanced up and looked through the one-way window.

Doc was standing in the center of the shop with his hands raised above his head. The two customers were down on the floor, spread-eagle fashion, a gun pointed at them. I looked at the man holding the gun. He was enormous. Almost a giant. I guessed he was well over six feet tall. With a powerful torso, massive shoulders, a neck as thick as a bull's. His head jutted out of that huge neck, arching and thrusting forward. He had a great mane of white hair, thick folds of it. His eyes were as brutal as the rest of him, fiery, the whites considerably inflamed or bloodshot. I guessed he'd weigh close to three hundred pounds. Middle thirties, you couldn't be positive. The white pullover sweater he wore emphasized his albino appearance. I fully expected, were I to see his eyes closely, that they would be pink. He held a .45 automatic in his hand.

I knew that Doc always carried a gun on his person during shop hours. He wore it in a small holster clipped to his belt, at the small of his back, concealed by his coat. He had a license. The first chance he got, Doc would reach for that .38 special of his. And he wouldn't hesitate to use it.

The man with the bull neck had opened one of the display cases and was dumping trays of coins into a canvas bag. With a sweep of his powerful arm, he gathered up the coins I had left on the counter top, including the two I'd removed from the tray. As he moved around the shop, Doc turned slowly, facing him. Doc's back was turned toward me. I noticed he'd dropped his right arm slightly, almost imperceptibly.

My first thought was to help Doc. I opened the desk drawers, looking for a gun. Nothing. I looked in the corner beside the desk. Doc had kept a shotgun there at one time. My own gun I'd left in my shop, in my top desk drawer. I never carried it on my person. Hoping that I was not too late, I reached for the telephone and dialed the police. I spoke softly, keeping my eyes glued on the window. He gave no sign he heard me. He was intent on his looting. When I'd reported the robbery in progress, I gently cradled the telephone and looked again for a gun.

Doc's right hand was now almost down to the level of his waist. He'd turned his body at an angle in an effort to conceal the movement of his right arm. The two customers were still down on the floor.

I racked my mind to think of something I could do. I realized if I were to open that door and enter the shop I might very well be shot down on sight. Perhaps I could create a diversion that might give Doc a chance to get his gun. Maybe, without actually entering the shop, I could stand behind the office door, give it a wild push forward, duck, and hopefully dodge the gunfire.

As I started toward the door I saw Doc reach his hand up underneath his coat. Before I could move, two shots rang out. The roar was deafening, the sound only a .45 makes. Doc was thrown back by the force of the impact, and crashed into one of the display cases. He was probably dead before he hit the floor. A .45 does terrible things to human flesh. A shot from a .45 can blow a man's arm off. Doc wasn't hit in the arm. He had been shot twice, in the chest and abdomen.

The man with the .45 was backing toward the door, carrying his loot. His eyes flashed. He was like a bull enraged, gathering his muscles for a ferocious charge. I knew then he was going through the security door. It could only be unlocked from inside the shop by pressing the button to release the automatic lock. He didn't have time to look for that button. He wheeled suddenly around, facing the door. It was a strong door. Steel frame with reinforced glass. He lifted one leg straight out, balanced himself on the other, then lunged forward, aiming at the frame with the heel of his shoe. The door popped out like a slice of toast from an automatic toaster. Didn't even break the glass. The force of the blow was so great it tore the anchor bolts out of solid concrete.

I ran out and grabbed Doc's gun. He'd at least got it in his hand before he was shot. The two customers were still on the floor, watching me. I leaped over the broken door and out into the mall of the shopping center. The parking lot was crowded with cars. Then I saw him lower his huge bulk into a blue Mustang, glancing back at the shop before he pulled his head inside. The engine started up with a roar. It was a hell of a thing I had to do—to take a shot across a parking lot crowded with cars. But I did. I hit the window on the passenger side as the Mustang swung out of the lot. I saw the glass shatter. But I'd missed him. I hadn't time to get another shot. And I couldn't see the license plate at that distance.

When I got back to the shop a crowd of people had gathered outside. Someone had telephoned for an ambulance. But Doc was beyond that. I went inside and looked at him. But there was nothing I could do for him. He had done a great deal for me. He'd helped me to get started in the business. He was twice my age. But I'd never thought of him as old. In the ten years I'd known him I'd never even noticed him aging. He had been given the name of Doc because there were a lot of us in the trade that respected him. Not only respected him as a man but because we respected his knowledge. He knew as much about ancient coins as anyone I'd ever met. He could read six languages. Knew as much about ancient history as most college professors. Maybe more. He had a memory for coins the way some people remember baseball scores, almost total recall. But he hadn't been one of those mousy antiquarian types. He'd been a big man, over two hundred pounds, robust, and he liked a good time. He'd liked hunting. One morning in the river delta we had watched a flight of geese very high up in the sky. So high you could barely hear their honking. Doc had liked that. Another time we had gone hunting wild boar in the Big Sur. We were in rough country when suddenly an enormous sow charged us. She was as large as a boulder and black as fury. With long white tusks that could disembowel a man. I shot twice from my hip, a tricky thing to do with a rifle. Hit her in the neck and snout. The momentum of her charge carried her right to my feet, where she had collapsed in a heap. Doc had hugged me like a bear, dancing me around. Now he lay dead at my feet.

When the police came, I gave them a full account. Every detail. One thing I hadn't mentioned before: when he'd shot Doc with that .45, the recoil hadn't even jerked his wrist up, the way it does with most people. The recoil of a .45 has quite a kick. It hadn't fazed him. I described him to the police. When I'd finished, they looked at me like maybe I was exaggerating. "That's the honest truth," I'd told them. "He's one of the biggest men I've ever seen. And he's as brutal as he looks. He has the body of a man, a powerful man, with the head of a bull." The last I'd heard, they'd not yet caught him.

I hadn't recognized him when he entered my shop. His appearance was changed. Not his huge bulk; nothing could disguise that. But his hair was now jet black, long and coarse. And, of course, his eyes weren't pink. They were dark green.

Early that morning I'd got a telephone call from a man who told me he had some coins to sell. I'd given him directions how to find my shop. When he appeared at my door I'd pushed the button underneath my desk to release the automatic lock. There was no help for it now. He was sitting opposite my desk in one of the big red-leather chairs I keep there for my customers.

He wore a black sweater over a sport shirt, open at the throat. I noticed the sweater was pulled down over his waist. A good place to conceal that .45, I thought. He reached into his pocket and pulled out another plastic coin envelope, and leaning forward, put it on my desk.

"How about this one?" he asked. His huge head jutted toward me. Then he settled back in the chair. There was an arrogance in his attitude, a kind of contempt. If not for me personally, then for everything in life. It wasn't a pose, you understand. That was simply the way he was.

I looked at the coin with my glass. It would give me time to think. I saw it was the other coin I had seen that day at Doc's, the Cretan coin with the design of the minotaur and the labyrinth. It was as though he'd handed me the final proof, and with a gesture of ultimate defiance and challenge, fantastic in its implications. But I was certain he hadn't seen me that day in Doc's shop. It just hadn't been possible. Not in the natural order of things. Even when he'd glanced back at Doc's shop, before pulling his head inside the blue Mustang, I was sure he hadn't seen me.

He was looking toward the corner behind my desk. To my right. I have a walk-in vault there. I leave it open during shop hours and lock it up every night. I keep most of my inventory in there. From where he was sitting he could see it was a vault and that the door was open, nothing more. I'd been working on a catalog to mail out to my customers and I had my book truck in there, loaded with reference books. The book truck is about four feet high, has a steel frame, and holds a lot of weight. It runs on rubber wheels, and when loaded it's plenty heavy. He kept looking at the vault and I guessed I knew what he was thinking.

I'd bought coins from a lot of people. Usually when people have coins to sell they keep their minds on business. Sometimes they try to exaggerate the value of what they have. Or if they don't know what they have, they try to pick your brains. Maybe get a free appraisal. Then use your own appraisal to go somewhere else and try to get a better price. He hadn't even been interested when I'd told him about the silver tetradrachm. But I was ahead of him. I knew he wasn't here to sell me any coins.

I continued to examine the Cretan coin, or pretended to, turning it over under my glass. I had to have time. Time to think. I knew I was no match for him. I hadn't the weight, not by half. He could break my bones with as little effort as it might take him to crack two walnuts in his fist. If he got his hands on me, I knew I hadn't a chance. When I have to fight, I want every advantage I can get. I'd been held up and robbed before. I've been pistol-whipped in my own shop. I've never stood still for it. But I've never done anything reckless, either. I'd never rush a man holding a gun on me.

"This is a valuable coin," I told him. "I'd like very much to buy it."

He turned his head quickly. He seemed somehow amused.

"I'm not sure I can really pay you what it's worth. But I'll go as high as I can." I put my glass down on the desk.

"Name a figure," he said. His mouth was forming a smile, of insolence.

"You see," I said, "right now I'm getting a catalog ready to mail out to my customers. I'd like a coin like this to feature in my catalog. It would create a minor sensation. My customers like to compete for really valuable coins. It gets their juices flowing, if you know what I mean."

He simply stared at me, cold but not withdrawn. I thought he acted as though he already owned everything I held of value. That I was an intruder in my own shop. He made you feel like that. That intimidation which radiated from him made you feel your dignity was in jeopardy. That your integrity as an individual was about to be destroyed. He said nothing. Just that cold stare.

"Not that I don't have some really valuable pieces in the shop," I said. "I do. I've been saving up some of the best things for my catalog." Then I tossed him the teaser. "I've got them in my vault over there," and I nodded toward it.

"Make me an offer," he said, and he seemed amused again.

"Oh, for the Cretan coin," I said, picking it up. "How about a thousand?"

He shrugged his shoulders. His face seemed to change. He'd got a figure from me, and he took it as a kind of victory. But more. He was looking at me as a victor might look at his victim. Now he was watching my hands, as I'd been watching his. I'd made sure during our conversation that my hands had always been in plain sight. My .38 automatic was in my top desk drawer, only inches away from my fingers. But I knew were I to open that drawer, even casually, he would probably go for his .45. He couldn't risk it. Not knowing what was in the drawer. Watching him, smiling at him, I understood that he'd always forced others to his will. That his lust for power had no restraints. He would make a sacrifice of anyone who opposed him. I knew I was in danger of my life. His or mine, I thought, smiling at him again, I knew that one of us would very probably die. He looked toward the vault again.

"I can go five hundred on the silver tetradrachm." I picked up the coin with the portrait of Alexander the Great and turned it over in my fingers. "Fifteen hundred for the two coins." I didn't want to lay it on too thick. Or be too obvious. "Would you prefer cash or a check? I think I've got that much cash in the vault."

He seemed contemptuous of me in that moment. A fool, he had taken me for. An easy mark. A piece of cake. It was written all over his cruel face. His eyes had an expectant look, like an animal contemplating its prey. Good, he had taken the bait.

I thought: in our age the ways of sacrifice have changed. We no longer slaughter younger boys and maidens to appease the gods or demons. Maybe we do symbolically. But not often literally. Sacrifice usually begins with intimidation. Today the threat of bodily harm is most often a means to an end, not an end in itself. There will always be those who demand sacrifice of others. Either through legislation or raw force. The end might not be the taking of life itself, not in the direct sense, though it had been in Doc's case, but rather the extortion of one's property. If an individual has invested knowledge and time in acquiring values and property, then what is extorted is life in its abstract form. When intimidation fails and the intended victim refuses to yield up what he values, the looter will resort to greater force. Threats, or worse. The victim, if he continues to resist, may find a gun pointed at his head. I wondered where on his person his .45 was concealed. Perhaps in a holster at the small of his back. Maybe strapped to his leg.

"You must have some interest in numismatics," I said, trying to keep a straight face. I stood up from the desk. I did it as casually as I could, keeping my hands in plain sight. He was watching me like a hawk. "Otherwise you wouldn't have these coins. Maybe you'd like to see some of my best pieces. The ones I've been saving for my catalog." I nodded toward the vault. "In any case, I keep my cash in the vault. The fifteen hundred I owe you, you know."

He stood up, drawing himself to his full height. He towered over me. I'd hoped to put an idea in his mind: that in volunteering to show him my most valuable coins it would save him the trouble of guessing which ones to rob me of. I hoped I hadn't overplayed it. He watched me, waiting for me to move.

"I'll go with you," he said. There was nothing in his face to suggest that he considered me a dangerous adversary. Only an amused look. And contempt.

I walked toward the vault. The door stood open. I paused at the threshold. He could now see inside the vault. His eyes flicked, taking everything in. He saw the trays of coins on the shelves. Stacks of silver dollars on the counter top. The book truck loaded with my reference books. I stepped inside.

He seemed to hesitate a moment. Then he looked at me and walked in. I said, "Over here is my rarest coin." I'd put on my best shopkeeper's manner. Chatty and confiding. "A really rare piece. A French twenty-ducat gold piece. On today's market it's worth at least ten thousand." That was some exaggeration. It wasn't a twenty-ducat in gold. Only a common one-hundred-franc gold piece, worth maybe eight hundred. I picked it up and set it on the counter, beyond his reach. As he moved toward it, I pivoted, got behind him and drove my shoulder into his back with all my weight. I'd taken him by surprise. I'd used the forward motion of his own body, when he was slightly off-balance reaching for the coin, to send him sprawling against the far wall of the vault.

As I leaped outside, grabbing for the steel door of the vault, I saw him struggling to regain his balance. I shoved against the heavy door, and almost had it closed when I felt him hit it from inside. The jolt shook me, but I only pushed harder. The door was about six inches short of locking position. I'd known I would have the advantage with the vault door. You understand: the door was balanced in my favor. Although it weighed over a ton, it was balanced so that it closed much easier than it opened, by at least half the effort. For a minute I gained nothing on him. But I didn't lose anything to him, either. The door seemed frozen there, motionless, as both of us pushed against it, from opposite sides, with all our strength. I felt sweat on my forehead. Neither of us spoke a word. I could feel my heart pounding against my rib cage.

We couldn't see one another. But suddenly I saw him

shove his hand through the narrow opening. I saw the .45. He tried to turn his hand to fire the gun where he guessed I would be. But he couldn't turn his hand in that small space, not without dropping the automatic. I summoned up all my strength. I knew that with one hand in the opening of the vault he had lost some of his leverage against the door. With a lunge that made my back and legs ache, I threw myself against the door. I pinned his hand. Or thought I had, when suddenly he jerked it free, the .45 disappearing inside. I lunged again and heard the lock catch. With my left elbow I spun the wheel, and then reached down and turned the combination lock.

I had him.

I turned around and leaned my back against the door. Sweat was dripping down my face. I took several deep breaths, making my body relax. Then I walked over to my desk, opened the top drawer, and got my .38. I picked up the telephone and called the police. They wanted to know all the details. I must have been on the line with them at least five minutes. I told them it was the same man who had robbed and killed Doc Parker two years ago. He'd tried to rob me today, I said. I had him locked in my vault. They said they would send over a squad car with three men. I told them I would meet the car outside.

I had good reason for telling them I would meet them outside. My shop is located in a large building. It covers an entire city block in the downtown section. Five floors. There are at least eight corridors on each floor, many of which intersect. Three stairwells connect all five floors. The building is rented out to shops and professional offices. Unless you're familiar with the building, or with a particular shop or office, you can easily lose your way. Some of my customers jokingly call the building "The Maze." But they know where to find me after one or two visits to my shop. One of my customers, a very charming young lady, once told me that I should carry a ball of string with me every day I entered the building. Meaning that if I played out the string on my way in, I would be able to find my way out again by retracing the string.

I locked my shop and started outside to meet the police. I

met them in one of the corridors on the first floor. When we got back to my shop, I explained the situation. "He has a .45 automatic. He'll use it. He's a big man, as big as any two of us."

They wanted to know if there were any vents into the vault. They thought they might even up the odds if they could shoot some tear gas in there.

"No vents," I said.

"Can we talk to him in there?" the older cop asked.

"No way," I answered. "It's a walk-in vault."

"Will he know it when we unlock the vault?" the fat cop asked.

"Yes," I said. "He will hear the combination and see the wheel turning when I unlock the door."

"I'd better go down to the squad car and get the tear gun anyway," the young cop said.

"Bring up the shotgun too," the older one said. "Then you wait outside in the squad car. Keep the front entrance covered. And phone in for an ambulance. We might need one before this is over."

The young cop left. The older one decided that I was to open the vault. Just a crack. Not more than an inch. That way the guy inside couldn't get the barrel of the .45 through the opening. The fat cop would help me with the door. I explained to them how the vault door was balanced in our favor.

"When we get it open just a crack," the older cop said, "I'll stand behind the door and tell him to throw out his gun. Or the clip. If he refuses, I'll tell him we're going to shoot tear gas in there. Actually, that might be a tricky thing to do. Especially if he won't give up the gun or the clip. But with two of us holding the vault door I think we can manage it."

The young cop came back with the shotgun and the tear-gas gun. "I loaded them both and called in for an ambulance," he said.

"If you hear any shooting," the older one said, "call in for another squad car."

I pressed the button for the security door and let him out.

The two cops drew their revolvers and took positions in front of the vault. I put my automatic in my waistband and wiped my hands with a handkerchief. I turned to the older cop. "Ready?" I asked.

"Okay," he said. "Easy does it."

The fat cop stood to my right, his weight against the vault door. I worked the combination and spun the wheel lock. We pulled the door open a crack. At first, for one wild second, I thought we had everything under control. Then I saw the flat end of a crowbar thrust into the opening. I had completely forgotten about the crowbar. I'd left it in the back of the vault two weeks ago when I'd moved some of the storage cabinets I keep in there.

He got terrific leverage with it. The door literally flew open. I hung on, but was lifted off my feet as it swung out. The fat cop was thrown against the older one standing in front of the vault. Then out of the corner of my eye I saw the book truck poised at the entrance of the vault. He was crouched behind it, like a runner, bracing himself, his bull neck arched forward. I cried out, but I was too late. The book truck shot out of the vault like a thunderbolt and hit the two cops. The older one went over backwards. The truck ran right over the fat cop's leg, making a sick crunching sound.

He burst out, .45 in hand. The whites of his eyes were red with rage. I saw his pocket bulging with my coins. In his left hand he had one of my canvas money bags, heavy with coins.

The older cop had struggled to his feet. He had lost his revolver. The fat cop was still on the floor, his leg broken. The bone had come clean through his flesh and trouser leg. It looked ghastly.

Seeing that the older cop was not armed, he looked around for me. His face was twisted with fury, his teeth clenched. I ducked behind the vault door. The older cop moved to grapple with him but he swung the money bag at his face and sent him reeling halfway across the shop. He seized the book truck and aimed it straight at the security door.

His back was toward me now. I leaned out and took careful aim at his right leg. He'd already sent the book truck crashing through the security door when I shot him. He didn't go down. He wheeled around and fired two shots at me. I ducked, and heard them ricochet off the vault door. He was limping out, still carrying the money bag, when I leaned out again and shot him in the other leg. He let out a terrific bellow, like a maddened bull. Then he went down. When he hit the floor in the corridor outside, the .45 fell out of his hand and slid from his reach. I walked out, keeping my gun on him.

Several people had run out of the other shops and were standing in the corridor. One woman raised her hand to her mouth, but she didn't scream. No one said anything. The air was so thick with tension you could have measured it with a barometer. He turned and looked at me. I'd never seen so much hate concentrated in a human face.

In a voice so low I could barely hear him, he said, "You should've killed me when you had the chance." Then he fixed me with his eyes, as if to say, "I'll never let you stop me. Nothing can. Nothing short of death itself." Then he rolled over and dragged himself toward the .45. His arm shot out, grasping for it. He grunted with pain, but I knew it was not for his life he was fighting. It was mine. He got his fingers around the butt of the .45. Someone screamed and I heard people running.

"Give it up," I shouted, my gun aimed at his heart.

He didn't say anything. He rolled over quickly, bringing the gun up with him, getting it into position to fire. He'd left me no choice. I pulled the trigger.

His eyes went blank, staring at some chaos known only to himself. He fell back heavily, firing the .45 twice into the ceiling, harmlessly.

In the distance outside I could hear the sirens of the ambulance and police cars. Several people began looking out of the shops, stepping timidly into the corridor. The dead man lay on the floor. I looked at him. His great mane of jet black hair almost obscured the features of his face.

There are men in this world, I thought, who live by the expected sacrifice of others. The mark of rage is upon them. You have probably noticed them. They intimidate and bully you. They are quick to fight over a card game. If they are jostled in a crowd they fly into a rage. You get the feeling that people like this expect you to apologize merely because you exist. Or that you owe them an apology simply because reality exists. Everything that happens to them is always somebody else's fault. In the moment of his death, when I'd seen that look of chaos in his eyes, I thought of his victims. I thought of Doc Parker, and of those victims unknown to me whose bones he had scattered in the wake of his lifelong rage.

The older cop staggered out into the corridor. He was dazed. I could tell by the slant of his mouth and chin that his jaw was broken. He pointed at the body on the floor and mumbled something to me that I couldn't quite make out. So I said "Dead?" just to make sure I understood what he was trying to say, and he said it again, nodding, and I answered, "Yes, he's dead." Then I volunteered something of my own. I said, "He had the body of a man, with the head of a bull."

(1976)

Layle Silbert

Layle Silbert is a freelance photographer. Her specialty is photographing celebrities, and in particular literary celebrities. Her photographic work has been exhibited in cities across the United States as well as in Mexico and Ecuador.

Her literary output is much less well known, though she publishes both stories and poetry. Making a Baby in Union Park Chicago *(1983) is a collection of her poetry illustrated by her own photographs.* Imaginary People & Other Strangers *(1985, Exile Press), which includes "A Hole in California," is her first collection of stories. Her fiction has appeared in many magazines, including* The Literary Review, The South Dakota Review, Salmagundi, *and* The Denver Quarterly.

Like Isaac Bashevis Singer, Silbert works with traditional Jewish themes, transforming them, adapting them to modern American urban existence. As I have said in my introduction to Grace Paley's "The Pale Pink Roast," Paley's work pushes past Singer; Silbert's goes behind Singer's, back into the folk traditions from which modern Jewish and modern Jewish-American writing both come. Silbert's carefully wrought fiction is the farthest thing from primitive. But it is beautifully, sensitively in touch with attitudes and characterological types that go back for centuries in an unbroken line. To re-create that long tradition in such supple prose, and with such taut control, is an accomplishment of a very rare order. Many other, more acclaimed American-Jewish writers have tried, and failed, to do what Silbert here does with deceptive ease.

A HOLE IN CALIFORNIA

"Hello."

"Did you say something?" Peter was startled. He looked at Ryah. How could she speak and give no sign of speaking? She knitted, a fall of green wool, a visitation from nature.

She didn't answer. She knitted, jerking at the green wool climbing into her needles.

He heard it again. "Hello," very soft, a whisper.

No, Ryah didn't speak. This time he had been looking at her, observing her more closely than he had in a long time. Whoever thinks to take a good look at his wife after so many years? You know how she looks at any time.

Peter looked up. Somebody in the ceiling? Ridiculous. Ridiculous indeed. He saw a hole. "Quick," he cried out, "the ceiling is falling."

Ryah languidly knitting looked at Peter as one looks around without thinking to see what's what. She began to count to herself, one, two . . .

The ceiling didn't fall. It was heaven itself which was revealing itself, not the people upstairs bending down and peering into the living room. But, no, impossible. There is no hole, nobody said anything, said Peter to himself, nor am I truly old. That could not be the reason I heard somebody say hello. Would the angel of death say hello like the laundryman coming to collect the laundry at the front door? Again impossible.

He picked up the paper once more, made himself read. The letters danced, mocked him, refused to make words.

"Oh Yudel," said the voice again, mocking him, teasing him.

Who remembers my name? Who calls me Yudel? Not even Ryah remembers any more.

"Yudel," the voice went on, "I'm coming down, through the hole. Now you remember what this hole is for, don't you?" still mocking, teasing.

Peter understood everything all at one time. He laid the newspaper on his knees and said. "That's not what it's for, you know that." He spoke sternly. "An *eyslechen*, a hole in the ceiling, is for you only and in particular in the special case of a man who is dying in great agony. Then you may come quickly and carry him off, oh angel of death," he added suddenly respectful, for it truly was the angel of death who had spoken. "You're making a mistake, a terrible mistake. Wrong house, wrong ceiling, wrong man," Peter cautioned. "The punishment is not even known to me. It must be awesome."

"It is," said the angel of death. "I cannot say the words to tell you about it."

"So," said Peter, "I am reasonable. Just go." As he spoke he found himself looking again at Ryah in her innocence, her trust and ignorance, counting stitches to herself, then frowning, absorbed in the tasks of life. She would never know. Like this, in no time at all, she would be taken from his side, out of his side again, leave him bereft, a tragic figure. He began to console himself at his loss, chilled with relief. What my mind thinks! Peter said in horror at himself, clutched his head with his hands on both sides and shook it from side to side in precisely the motions to use in case of a death in the family.

"You should be ashamed," said the voice of the angel.

"It is a measure of my tenacity. I am not ready."

"Are you offering me a substitute, your wife?"

"No, God forbid, heaven forbid. It's only an expression. In fact," Peter said, "I offer you nothing. I offer you goodby. Go, leave. Nobody wants you. You are an intruder."

"I am an intruder now. So that's it," landing lightly as from much practice, a young man came down through the hole. He could be the laundryman. He wore working clothes, his face was the face of a man outdoors during the day and he had a fine American smile. He also could be the man who drove the ice cream truck, white and sanitary, as large as an ambulance, tinkling mechanically through the neighborhood every day at dusk. No, lately old men dressed like boys wearing caps drove these monsters. Next year the truck would come by itself and deal the ice cream out by an intricate mechanical device, hands articulated like a man's. Then, only then, let the angel go after one of these old men. Nobody would want him. Why me? I am a quiet, orderly man. I never hurt anybody. I listen to what my wife tells me. I hurt nobody.

"Arguments, everybody tries arguments," said the young man.

Impossible to think he was the angel of death, the most savage of angels, the most heartless. He could be a man from the railway express coming for a trunk.

Suddenly Ryah dropped her knitting, the needles, the wool, and let out a short scream. "The ceiling's coming down," she said.

"I told you," said Peter.

"And who are you? What are you doing here?"

"Excuse me," said the young man. "I have important business."

"No, no, no." Ryah began to tremble. "Not here, not here." She turned to Peter and begged him as she had not begged him for anything before, for money, for love, to save her. "Save me," she cried out like a person overboard at sea, "save me, save me," even holding her hands up in the same way to the heavens which wished to take her.

He went to her. How sweet to live.

She flung herself against him, hiding like a child in his shirt. "No, no," she said sobbing. Was this the Ryah who had spent the money he earned all his life heartlessly, efficiently, with zest, and purchased property, making him a joint owner, a landlord, a stockholder, a who knows what, a man with a bank account?

"No danger," he comforted her. "No danger at all." He put his hand on her head, tried to stroke her hair, found he didn't know how, that he was awkward. All their differences were arranged from separate sites across long stretches of carpet, sometimes through a doorway, especially while Ryah was in the kitchen. She hated the kitchen and stayed there the most of all the places in the house to keep her hatred fresh.

Nevertheless he let her press her head against him and continued to stroke her hair. Naturally it was gray, but not as much as it could be. Now his hair, it had turned to white in no more than a year, so that people who hadn't seen him in those days for a while said, "What happened? A tragedy, an accident?" "No, it is my fate. My father was white as long as I knew him."

But even though they were gray and old the young man was making a mistake. No doubt.

See, Peter seemed to say as he turned indignantly to the young man. See what you have done. Out loud he said, "Now go. It's enough."

The young man stood where he had landed from the hole in the ceiling, awkward, not knowing what to do with his hands which hung at his sides. He resembled a man without a trade or more a man who had lost something, a big bundle of valuable furs on Seventh Avenue, a gold bar, the Mona Lisa, or a child.

"I can't," he said, all joy gone.

"No such thing," said Peter. "You made the hole in the ceiling. You came down through that hole. You scared my wife, didn't you? Go climb back into the hole and be sure you fix it before you finish. Do you hear?" he shouted. "Nobody is sick, nobody is dying, nobody wants you."

The young man stared at Ryah who had raised her head like a tear-stained child. He began to laugh while pointing a long arm at her. Ryah recoiled and, frightened, wept again. "You didn't know," he said in the same mocking tone he had used as he had called out, "Yudel, Yudel, I'm coming." "You didn't know. I know what you are thinking. It's a part of my equipment to expedite my work, saves time."

"She's afraid," said Peter and comforted Ryah with his new-found tenderness. "Be careful, please."

"She thought I was coming for you! She doesn't want to be alone." The young man laughed like a fool being tickled against his will. "Not for one minute did she think I had come for her."

Peter held her away from him the better to stare at her. "Is this true?" he asked.

With one hand in a motion to wipe him out, Peter said in scorn to the ice cream man, "You don't even know how to do it right. Would a self-respecting angel come like this in disguise, in masquerade? You should come as befits a man."

With the scruffy sounds in his ears of great feathered wings unfurling Peter went on, "In dignity and majesty, your head held high like a king, and four at a time, solemn in their great and noble task to remove a citizen of the world. Now what do they send? You." With another declining motion toward the floor as though giving the height of a pygmy, Peter belittled the inconsequential character of the ice cream man. "Vacant eyes, no chin, anyway a small chin, a crooked nose, a little to the side, yes? Football."

The ice cream man nodded and said, "No, a baseball right here," and hit his nose with his hand.

"Couldn't get into college, turned down by the draft, selling ice cream, and this is who they send to fetch me, like a pack of cigarettes from the corner. I used to send my daughter with a quarter to the corner in exactly the same way. At least they're doing it on an individual basis. Not carrying us off in loads wrapped in blankets, not yet, bundles of bones, bundles, bones, or—" and now Peter could speak no more. He had remembered extermination camps, pogroms and slave ships.

He rose suddenly, flew up like a startled rooster, all arms, and clucking, toward the ice cream man. "Out, out," he shouted as if he were dispersing a barnyard full of some domestic fowl.

The ice cream man did not move, would not move, in fact, couldn't and did not need to move. A higher power governed. He waited. Was it the moment for Peter to expend his last breath, his last thought, his last burden of love for Ryah, his last illusion of what he deserved, of the best in the world he deserved, and to revive one more memory? What should it be?

Like a movie, thought Peter. "They're making a movie. We're in the movies, Ryah," he said joyfully. "We're in the movies. That's what we came to California for, didn't we?"

"Sure, sure," she said in that half-mocking tone used to quiet children who one knows will not believe anyway, that they will keep on crying, crying for what? Probably the moon, why not? It's nearer than the stars.

"We crossed an ocean to come to the land of opportunity, and then they came, the opportunities, one after the other.

We got richer and lazier and older. Now here we are at the side of another ocean. No more oceans will I cross. You go alone.''

"Who's going anywhere?'' said Ryah. "Not me.'' She patted Peter's hand to reassure him, with her real old lady's hand.

"Here at last we're in the movies. We're actors. No stage, no audience. But everybody is looking at us out there.'' He pointed ahead to where an imaginary mirror hung, "and all around there and more there. I think they appreciate it. It's dark. They're eating candy or popcorn. They forget about everything else, and even when the movie is finished''—he gave a lost glance to the ice cream man—"when the movie is finished and they go outside with a couple of popcorns still tumbling down their front and they're blinking because the sun shines so hard here, especially after a movie in the afternoon, they will think, a good movie. I'm glad I went. But what was it about? Already they have forgotten.

"Up there. Up there he is, the man with the camera. He's pointed down at us.'' He looked up at the hole in the ceiling. "That's what it's for, the hole, for the camera man. How stupid. It took me such a long time to figure it out. I thought it was for him, that he could jump down from there.'' He glared and extended an accusing finger at the ice cream man, "for him to come down and take us. How do I look? Mr. Camera man,'' he smoothed his hair down, tugged at his shirt to straighten it. "Good, now I feel pretty good too. And doesn't she look fine? Look at her. Come closer.'' He waved the camera man to come down. "Look, she looks fine. Take her picture. Take us both together, like this.'' Again he put her face to his, close to crowd the both of them into the view from a camera lens.

"You think you can fool me, that you are touching my heart, that maybe I will go,'' offered the ice cream man. "I don't fall that easy, not like that.''

"I know,'' said Peter defeated, scrambling back to his own chair where he spread his arms out in a gesture of resignation. "It's over. Go ahead,'' he said. "To tell you the truth, I don't care. I don't care at all. Also I'm very tired. You have no idea.''

"Exactly, the idea. I have it."

"That's what I thought," said Peter.

"Such a nice young man," said Ryah vacantly. "Why didn't we meet you before?"

"No," said Peter, "don't say it."

"Don't you hear it? Do you hear it?" Without knowing how, he had again gone to Ryah and was standing close to her in her chair, with his hands on her bony shoulders. He had put his head again next to hers so that this time they were two people about to behold themselves in a mirror together, his head close to let her hear.

"What?" asked Ryah woodenly, not seeming to notice that Peter was that near to her, while automatically letting her cheek touch his, out of an old habit. "What should I hear? Nothing's happening. Just a nice young man."

"Don't you hear it? It's raining a little spring rain. It's night. The lights are on in the street. You can see the lights again, long and blinded on the wet pavement, on the puddles, on the drops falling from the trees, on the umbrellas going by. The automobiles are splashing like children through the street. We can hear it, but we don't have to pay any attention to it because we're in the house now. It's dry and comfortable and quiet with such a peace, such a peace. We should have brought it with us too."

She turned and gave him a quick smile, for encouragement which he knew well enough to know didn't mean she understood him at all. She was bestowing her good will, no more.

Peter went on. "On the corner we heard the streetcars coming, rain or no rain, clanging sometimes. You know how that was. Then they stopped and somebody got off, who knows, somebody to see us? and started again grinding like a machine in a factory. A rain factory maybe."

"Streetcars?" said Ryah. "Buses now. Where are there streetcars in America now?"

He answered. "In museums." To ride those streetcars, he knew from reading about it a long time ago, he would have to go to cities on other continents, South America, or to Calcutta, where he could again sit on a woven straw bench in an open streetcar that clanged as it went and made grinding sounds as a machine does in a factory. Otherwise there was only his head, his memory.

"I don't hear any rain," said Ryah sadly. "I can't remember it at all. It did rain though. It tracked up the carpets and spoiled the windows right after they were washed. I had to run down and take the laundry off the line. Here there's the laundromat and the dryers, so I don't have to worry. And it doesn't rain except like on order, certain months only."

Resigned, Peter pressed his head against Ryah, saying twittering sorrowing sounds. To this Ryah suddenly warmed and responded. She put a hand around Peter's head to keep him there as they continued to look ahead into the magic mirror, held perhaps by the ice cream man.

"You were always such a dramatist," she said wryly, "like Margolis. Always a five-act drama."

"One act only, madame," said the ice cream man. "One."

Suddenly Peter longed for the pleasure of a long rainy night in the city that came before California, to be back in life again with all its days still belonging to him, away from the garish whited environment in which they and appurtenances to stay alive with had been set, like the furnishings for a play surrealistically set in a desert. Walking among them or beneath a row of trees set like workmen, working trees, one then the next and the next, one expected to see ladders set against them for workers to harvest their fruit. Economic units. The design was not only total, including all vegetation but was also utilitarian, schematic, and a defiance of nature which in this part of the country wanted only to be desert. Were he to see a powdery white skull, a long bone at the foot of one of these trees it would have been as natural as ripe fruit.

Set down with chairs, automobiles, trees, carpets of lawn bought by the measure, houses seemed to be stage sets made without internal parts. Sometimes he looked and saw nothing but shimmer in the air as if what was there had a tenuous hold on being. At other times, it was as if he himself were not there either. He would hold his hand up to make sure that it still ran with blood. So also the blood, the vitality had disappeared from Ryah. She had become a figure nearly without substance. True, he could see her, hear her, even understand what she said, eat the food she put down on the table before him. But they were all part of the innumerable objects set down in a great planned order. When he heard her or looked, his heart did not stir any more, as if he didn't have one any more, and she spoke from a being also without such essential organs as a heart.

Now with the ice cream man in his disguise as the angel of death masquerading as an ice cream man they had become dummies still moving a little, without any connection one with the other or with anything in particular, sitting without strength to do anything else in their chairs, not even waiting, in a torpor, a muteness without sense or meaning. It had to end sometime, didn't it?

He opened his eyes, saw again the sterile, whited house standing open, saw the peopled, furnished desert outside through the open door, the open windows, without definite barriers between house and outside, and here was Ryah. With the sound of a quiet spring rain in his head and the ludicrous sight of his last home on earth he began to weep for Ryah, so empty, so distant, so lifeless, so foolish. He too was distant and ridiculous under a broken ceiling through which the angel of death trumpeting their names had descended.

"Good evening," said Peter in formal acknowledgement. "They used to call you *hamalach hanobis,* didn't they?"

"Yes, but I don't use the name now. I Americanized it."

Ryah overheard. "Americanized, you did? What was it before? What is it now?" She asked hospitably to make the stranger at home and also to acquire the information she craved, a craving that had been with her all her life and now seemed about to continue with her beyond.

"Ah ha, very nice," were Ryah's responses. "I understand, I see," as the angel explained in real American English.

She listened, forming part of a nice conversation in the living room under the place where the ceiling had broken through. Peter reflected. In the first place, he observed privately, a good thing if this had to happen that we moved to California. It doesn't rain very often. He looked over to where Ryah was listening and the angel explaining in that cozy relationship available to two people only when neither hopes to gain anything from the other, an exercise in friendliness, no sex, no sales, no honor. Had he forgotten what he came for? Well, wait, Peter cautioned himself.

He thought how many times a man considers his death and in how many ways. Well, two ways. One is death the end; there is nothing more. You close your eyes wherever you are and out, like this; he pinched off a candle flame. Sometimes it's faster—you don't have time or a chance to close your eyes. Somebody does that service for you, other services also.

That was when he began to consider the second way of looking upon his death, the aftermath, the afterlife of his own life as exemplified in wills, deathbed promises. No, I don't mean that hereafter. I mean—you gently separate yourself into two; one, the body, sits here—he slapped his bicep—and the other, the one who really dies does not go. He stands and takes a look at the window, her tears, his children, stunned, all swarming, coming in as they never came in life except in their childhood, the chair nobody dares to sit in for days as if left warm and mined with another death for the sitter, the tears everywhere, and pale faces, grieving faces, wringing hands. What would they be saying? A long and honorable life, a good man.

With relief, Peter thought then everything but the accolades would be forgotten, as is customary in the great forgiveness never granted to a man in life, as if now a judging was held and the verdict is innocent. Expunge from people's minds what wrongs, what failings, what failures there had been, the insults he had flung, the insects stepped on, the cat run over the first day he drove the old Maxwell. He turned from the sight, which had never left him. As he did so, he saw again Ryah sitting in her chair, her head turned up to the young man who was still explaining.

"And you like this work?" Ryah was asking comfortably like an earth-mother to a friend of her son, had she had one.

What was he telling her? That he was an ice cream man who drove an ice cream truck as large and white and glossy as an ambulance that rang his presence ahead of him in exactly the opposite purpose of the bell a medieval leper rang as he went abroad.

Just as well. Let him lie a bit, Peter decided. But what if

he is an ice cream man? and it is I who imagined this, that I have begun to invoke this separation of myself, first the myself in this chair—he sat more deeply and harder into his chair, the one nobody would sit in for a few days after he died—and then there will be the myself who will listen as the scene plays out, who also has a craving for information? What will they say? Has it begun?

I imagined the whole thing. Out loud, he said, "Bring us two. For me chocolate. And you, Ryah, strawberry? Ice cream now?"

"In the middle of the afternoon?" Astonished, Ryah swiftly changed her mind from no to yes. "Exactly," she said far more docilely than she had said yes to anything proposed by Peter in nine years, maybe ten.

The young man touched his cap, said, "Fine. Two. One chocolate. One strawberry. I'll be back."

"Yes, he'll be back," said Peter. "With ice creams?" He looked up. The ceiling had been broken through. No doubt. The plaster wept foolishly upon the wall-to-wall carpeting provided by the landlord. This is how it will happen. The angel of death will have no dignity, no presence, no mission; he will be doing his job, this single young American man brought up to do honest work by his parents in a state in the middle of the country, exactly halfway between the two oceans. A simple passing without dignity, respect, pathos or drama, a simple taking, for what? Two ice creams?

"We had a nice talk," said Ryah sitting back, a satisfied old lady.

"Don't sit back. Don't sit back," Peter called out. "Be careful. It's dangerous. He's coming back. We have to be ready."

"Should I comb my hair?" She smoothed her head, wet her lips as though getting ready for a photographer. "This dress. Oh well, I'm too tired to get up and change."

Exactly, thought Peter. He was not getting up either. I'm tired too.

They sat, each in a chair as if fixed for eternity and they were to be carried out in their chairs like people in fires. Was it happening? They were tired out and depleted each at exactly the same time, a piece of good fortune. No widows, no weeping. He would not be a widowmaker and, how much easier, it would be over with entirely at one time. Wiped out, cleaned out, nothing more. But ah, and he remembered. He would be there to observe, inspect and approve. He was sure this occasion would meet with his approval. He decided in advance, knowing no one would hear or even want to know that he approved.

(1977)

Jayne Anne Phillips

Jayne Anne Phillips was born and raised in West Virginia. She studied at West Virginia University and at the University of Iowa. She now lives in Boston.

Phillips published two limited-edition collections of stories, and stories in a wide variety of magazines—Redbook, The Atlantic Monthly, Rolling Stone, The Paris Review—*before* Black Tickets, *the 1979 collection which brought her acclaim and recognition very like that accorded Philip Roth, immediately after his first book appeared. And her novel,* Machine Dreams, *has allowed her to reach an even wider audience.*

But Phillips, very much younger than Roth, is a very different writer. Her specialty is a kind of machine-quick stiletto thrust, neither dispassionate nor truly cruel, but with hard and sometimes nasty meaning. The first story in Black Tickets, *for example, bears the romantic-sounding title, "Wedding Picture." But the first sentence informs us that romance is not what we are in for: "My mother's ankles curve from the hem of a white suit as if the bones were water." (R. L. Shafner's "Stop Me If You've Heard This," included here, uses very similar techniques, and with what seem to me very similar power and effect.) This is not—certainly not in the traditional sense—what is sometimes thought of as poetic prose. Rather, it is a sort of scalpelized prose, prose cut into the page, and fully intending to cut into the reader.*

Again, the almost instantaneous success of Phillips' work is the farthest thing from accidental. She beautifully represents basic trends in American life and American art.

SOUVENIR

Kate always sent her mother a card on Valentine's Day. She timed the mails from wherever she was so that the cards arrived on February 14th. Her parents had celebrated the day in some small fashion, and since her father's death six years before, Kate made a gesture of compensatory remembrance. At first, she made the cards herself: collage and pressed grasses on construction paper sewn in fabric. Now she settled for art reproductions, glossy cards with blank insides. Kate wrote in them with colored inks, "You have always been my Valentine," or simply "Hey, take care of yourself." She might enclose a present as well, something small enough to fit into an envelope; a sachet, a perfumed soap, a funny tintype of a prune-faced man in a bowler hat.

This time, she forgot. Despite the garish displays of paper cupids and heart-shaped boxes in drugstore windows, she let the day nearly approach before remembering. It was too late to send anything in the mail. She called her mother long-distance at night when the rates were low.

"Mom? How are you?"

"It's you! How are *you*?" Her mother's voice grew suddenly brighter; Kate recognized a tone reserved for welcome company. Sometimes it took a while to warm up.

"I'm fine," answered Kate. "What have you been doing?"

"Well, actually I was trying to sleep."

"Sleep? You should be out setting the old hometown on fire."

"The old hometown can burn up without me tonight."

"Really? What's going on?"

"I'm running in-service training sessions for the primary teachers." Kate's mother was a school superintendent. "They're driving me batty. You'd think their brains were rubber."

"They are," Kate said. "Or you wouldn't have to train them. Think of them as a salvation, they create a need for your job."

"Some salvation. Besides, your logic is ridiculous. Just because someone needs training doesn't mean they're stupid."

"I'm just kidding. But *I'm* stupid. I forgot to send you a Valentine's card."

"You did? That's bad. I'm trained to receive one. They bring me luck."

"You're receiving a phone call instead," Kate said. "Won't that do?"

"Of course," said her mother, "but this is costing you money. Tell me quick, how are you?"

"Oh, you know. Doctoral pursuits. Doing my student trip, grooving with the professors."

"The professors? You'd better watch yourself."

"It's a joke, Mom, a joke. But what about you? Any men on the horizon?"

"No, not really. A married salesman or two asking me to dinner when they come through the office. Thank heavens I never let those things get started."

"You should do what you want to," Kate said.

"Sure," said her mother. "And where would I be then?"

"I don't know. Maybe Venezuela."

"They don't even have plumbing in Venezuela."

"Yes, but their sunsets are perfect, and the villages are full of dark passionate men in blousy shirts."

"That's your department, not mine."

"Ha," Kate said, "I wish it were my department. Sounds a lot more exciting than teaching undergraduates."

Her mother laughed. "Be careful," she said. "You'll get what you want. End up sweeping a dirt floor with a squawling baby around your neck."

"A dark baby," Kate said, "to stir up the family blood."

"Nothing would surprise me," her mother said as the line went fuzzy. Her voice was submerged in static, then surfaced. "Listen," she was saying. "Write to me. You seem so far away."

They hung up and Kate sat watching the windows of the neighboring house. The curtains were transparent and flowered and none of them matched. Silhouettes of the window frames spread across them like single dark bars. Her mother's curtains were all the same, white cotton hemmed with a ruffle, tiebacks blousing the cloth into identical shapes. From the street it looked as if the house was always in order.

Kate made a cup of strong Chinese tea, turned the lights off, and sat holding the warm cup in the dark. Her mother kept no real tea in the house, just packets of instant diabetic mixture which tasted of chemical sweetener and had a bitter aftertaste. The packets sat on the shelf next to her mother's miniature scales. The scales were white. Kate saw clearly the face of the metal dial on the front, its markings and trembling needle. Her mother weighed portions of food for meals: frozen broccoli, slices of plastic-wrapped Kraft cheese, careful chunks of roast beef. A dog-eared copy of *The Diabetic Diet* had remained propped against the salt shaker for the last two years.

Kate rubbed her forehead. Often at night she had headaches. Sometimes she wondered if there were an agent in her body, a secret in her blood making ready to work against her.

The phone blared repeatedly, careening into her sleep. Kate scrambled out of bed, naked and cold, stumbling before she recognized the striped wallpaper of her bedroom and realized the phone was right there on the bedside table, as always. She picked up the receiver.

"Kate?" said her brother's voice. "It's Robert. Mom is in the hospital. They don't know what's wrong but she's in for tests."

"Tests? What's happened? I just talked to her last night."

"I'm not sure. She called the neighbors and they took her to the emergency room around dawn." Robert's voice still had that slight twang Kate knew was disappearing from her own. He would be calling from his insurance office, nine o'clock their time, in his thick glasses and wide, perfectly knotted tie. He was a member of the million-dollar club and his picture, tiny, the size of a postage stamp, appeared in the Mutual of Omaha magazine. His voice seemed small too over the distance. Kate felt heavy and dulled. She would never make much money, and recently she had begun wearing make-up again, waking in smeared mascara as she had in high school.

"Is Mom all right?" she managed now. "How serious is it?"

"They're not sure," Robert said. "Her doctor thinks it could have been any of several things, but they're doing X rays."

"Her doctor *thinks?* Doesn't he know? Get her to someone else. There aren't any doctors in that one-horse town."

"I don't know about that," Robert said defensively. "Anyway, I can't force her. You know how she is about money."

"Money? She could have a stroke and drop dead while her doctor wonders what's wrong."

"Doesn't matter. You know you can't tell her what to do."

"Could I call her somehow?"

"No, not yet. And don't get her all worried. She's been scared enough as it is. I'll tell her what you said about getting another opinion, and I'll call you back in a few hours when I have some news. Meanwhile, she's all right, do you hear?"

The line went dead with a click and Kate walked to the bathroom to wash her face. She splashed her eyes and felt guilty about the Valentine's card. Slogans danced in her head like reprimands. *For a special One. Dearest Mother. My Best Friend.* Despite Robert, after breakfast she would call the hospital.

She sat a long time with her coffee, waiting for minutes to pass, considering how many meals she and her mother ate alone. Similar times of day, hundreds of miles apart. Women by themselves. The last person Kate had eaten breakfast with had been someone she'd met in a bar. He was passing through town. He liked his fried eggs gelatinized in the center, only slightly runny, and Kate had studiously looked away as he ate. The night before he'd looked down from above her as he finished and she still moved under him. "You're still wanting," he'd said. "That's nice." Mornings now, Kate saw her own face in the mirror and was glad she'd forgotten his name. When she looked at her reflection from the side, she saw a faint etching of lines beside her mouth. She hadn't slept with anyone for five weeks, and the skin beneath her eyes had taken on a creamy darkness.

She reached for the phone but drew back. It seemed bad luck to ask for news, to push toward whatever was coming as though she had no respect for it.

Standing in the kitchen last summer, her mother had stirred gravy and argued with her.

"I'm thinking of your own good, not mine," she'd said. "Think of what you put yourself through. And how can you feel right about it? You were born here, I don't care what you say." Her voice broke and she looked, perplexed, at the broth in the pan.

"But, hypothetically," Kate continued, her own voice unaccountably shaking, "if I'm willing to endure whatever I have to, do you have a right to object? You're my mother. You're supposed to defend my choices."

"You'll have enough trouble without choosing more for yourself. Using birth control that'll ruin your insides, moving from one place to another. I can't defend your choices. I can't even defend myself against you." She wiped her eyes on a napkin.

"Why do you have to make me feel so guilty?" Kate said, fighting tears of frustration. "I'm not attacking you."

"You're not? Then who are you talking to?"

"Oh Mom, give me a break."

"I've tried to give you more than that," her mother said. "I know what your choices are saying to me." She set the steaming gravy off the stove. "You may feel very differently later on. It's just a shame I won't be around to see it."

"Oh? Where will you be?"

"Floating around on a fleecy cloud."

Kate got up to set the table before she realized her mother had already done it.

The days went by. They'd gone shopping before Kate left. Standing at the cash register in an antique shop on Main Street, they bought each other pewter candle holders. "A souvenir," her mother said. "A reminder to always be nice to yourself. If you live alone you should eat by candlelight."

"Listen," Kate said, "I eat in a heart-shaped tub with bubbles to my chin. I sleep on satin sheets and my mattress has a built-in massage engine. My overnight guests are impressed. You don't have to tell me about the solitary pleasures."

They laughed and touched hands.

"Well," her mother said. "If you like yourself, I must have done something right."

Robert didn't phone until evening. His voice was fatigued and thin. "I've moved her to the university hospital," he said. "They can't deal with it at home."

Kate waited, saying nothing. She concentrated on the toes of her shoes. They needed shining. *You never take care of anything,* her mother would say.

"She has a tumor in her head." He said it firmly, as though Kate might challenge him.

"I'll take a plane tomorrow morning," Kate answered, "I'll be there by noon."

Robert exhaled. "Look," he said, "don't even come back here unless you can keep your mouth shut and do it my way."

"Get to the point."

"The point is they believe she has a malignancy and we're not going to tell her. I almost didn't tell you." His voice faltered. "They're going to operate but if they find what they're expecting, they don't think they can stop it."

For a moment there was no sound except an oceanic vibration of distance on the wire. Even that sound grew still. Robert breathed. Kate could almost see him, in a booth at the hospital, staring straight ahead at the plastic instructions screwed to the narrow rectangular body of the telephone. It seemed to her that she was hurtling toward him.

"I'll do it your way," she said.

The hospital cafeteria was a large room full of orange Formica tables. Its southern wall was glass. Across the highway, Kate saw a small park modestly dotted with amusement rides and bordered by a narrow band of river. How odd, to build a children's park across from a medical center. The sight was pleasant in a cruel way. The rolling lawn of the little park was perfectly, relentlessly green.

Robert sat down. Their mother was to have surgery in two days.

"After it's over," he said, "they're not certain what will happen. The tumor is in a bad place. There may be some paralysis."

"What kind of paralysis?" Kate said. She watched him twist the green-edged coffee cup around and around on its saucer.

"Facial. And maybe worse."

"You've told her this?"

He didn't answer.

"Robert, what is she going to think if she wakes up and—"

He leaned forward, grasping the cup and speaking through clenched teeth. "Don't you think I thought of that?" He gripped the sides of the table and the cup rolled onto the carpeted floor with a dull thud. He seemed ready to throw the table after it, then grabbed Kate's wrists and squeezed them hard.

"You didn't drive her here," he said. "She was so scared she couldn't talk. How much do you want to hand her at once?"

Kate watched the cup sitting solidly on the nubby carpet.

"We've told her it's benign," Robert said, "that the surgery will cause complications, but she can learn back whatever is lost."

Kate looked at him. "Is that true?"

"They hope so."

"We're lying to her, all of us, more and more." Kate pulled her hands away and Robert touched her shoulder.

"What do *you* want to tell her, Kate? 'You're fifty-five and you're done for'?"

She stiffened. "Why put her through the operation at all?"

He sat back and dropped his arms, lowering his head. "Because without it she'd be in bad pain. Soon." They were silent, then he looked up. "And anyway," he said softly, "we don't *know*, do we? She may have a better chance than they think."

Kate put her hands on her face. Behind her closed eyes she saw a succession of blocks tumbling over.

*   *   *

They took the elevator up to the hospital room. They were alone and they stood close together. Above the door red numerals lit up, flashing. Behind the illuminated shapes droned an impersonal hum of machinery.

Then the doors opened with a sucking sound. Three nurses stood waiting with a lunch cart, identical covered trays stacked in tiers. There was a hot bland smell, like warm cardboard. One of the women caught the thick steel door with her arm and smiled. Kate looked quickly at their rubber-soled shoes. White polish, the kind that rubs off. And their legs seemed only white shapes, boneless and two-dimensional, stepping silently into the metal cage.

She looked smaller in the white bed. The chrome side rails were pulled up and she seemed powerless behind them, her dark hair pushed back from her face and her forearms delicate in the baggy hospital gown. Her eyes were different in some nearly imperceptible way; she held them wider, they were shiny with a veiled wetness. For a moment the room seemed empty of all else; there were only her eyes and the dark blossoms of the flowers on the table beside her. Red roses with pine. Everyone had sent the same thing.

Robert walked close to the bed with his hands clasped behind his back, as though afraid to touch. "Where did all the flowers come from?" he asked.

"From school, and the neighbors. And Katie." She smiled.

"FTD," Kate said. "Before I left home. I felt so bad for not being here all along."

"That's silly," said their mother. "You can hardly sit at home and wait for some problem to arise."

"Speaking of problems," Robert said, "the doctor tells me you're not eating. Do I have to urge you a little?" He sat down on the edge of the bed and shook the silverware from its paper sleeve.

Kate touched the plastic tray. "Jell-O and canned cream of chicken soup. Looks great. We should have brought you something."

"They don't *want* us to bring her anything," Robert said.

"This is a hospital. And I'm sure your comments make her lunch seem even more appetizing."

"I'll eat it!" said their mother in mock dismay. "Admit they sent you in here to stage a battle until I gave in."

"I'm sorry," Kate said. "He's right."

Robert grinned. "Did you hear that? She says I'm right. I don't believe it." He pushed the tray closer to his mother's chest and made a show of tucking a napkin under his chin.

"Of course you're right, dear." She smiled and gave Kate an obvious wink.

"Yeah," Robert said, "I know you two. But seriously, you eat this. I have to go make some business calls from the motel room."

Their mother frowned. "That motel must be costing you a fortune."

"No, it's reasonable," he said. "Kate can stay for a week or two and I'll drive back and forth from home. If you think this food is bad, you should see the meals in that motel restaurant." He got up to go, flashing Kate a glance of collusion. "I'll be back after supper."

His footsteps echoed down the hallway. Kate and her mother looked wordlessly at each other, relieved. Kate looked away guiltily. Then her mother spoke, apologetic. "He's so tired," she said. "He's been with me since yesterday."

She looked at Kate, then into the air of the room. "I'm in a fix," she said. "Except for when the pain comes, it's all a show that goes on without me. I'm like an invalid, or a lunatic."

Kate moved close and touched her mother's arms. "That's all right, we're going to get you through it. Someone's covering for you at work?"

"I had to take a leave of absence. It's going to take a while afterward—"

"I know. But it's the last thing to worry about, it can't be helped."

"Like spilt milk. Isn't that what they say?"

"I don't know what they say. But why didn't you tell me? Didn't you know something was wrong?"

"Yes . . . bad headaches. Migraines, I thought, or the

diabetes getting worse. I was afraid they'd start me on insulin." She tightened the corner of her mouth. "Little did I know . . ."

They heard the shuffle of slippers. An old woman stood at the open door of the room, looking in confusedly. She seemed about to speak, then moved on.

"Oh," said Kate's mother in exasperation, "shut that door, please? They let these old women wander around like refugees." She sat up, reaching for a robe. "And let's get me out of this bed."

They sat near the window while she finished eating. Bars of moted yellow banded the floor of the room. The light held a tinge of spring which seemed painful because it might vanish. They heard the rattle of the meal cart outside the closed door, and the clunk-slide of patients with aluminum walkers. Kate's mother sighed and pushed away the half-empty soup bowl.

"They'll be here after me any minute. More tests. I just want to stay with you." Her face was warm and smooth in the slanted light, lines in her skin delicate, unreal; as though a face behind her face was now apparent after many years. She sat looking at Kate and smiled.

"One day when you were about four you were dragging a broom around the kitchen. I asked what you were doing and you told me that when you got old you were going to be an angel and sweep the rotten rain off the clouds."

"What did you say to that?"

"I said that when you were old I was sure God would see to it." Her mother laughed. "I'm glad you weren't such a smart aleck then," she said. "You would have told me my view of God was paternalistic."

"Ah yes," sighed Kate. "God, that famous dude. Here I am, getting old, facing unemployment, alone, and where is He?"

"You're not alone," her mother said, "I'm right here."

Kate didn't answer. She sat motionless and felt her heart begin to open like a box with a hinged lid. The fullness had no edges.

Her mother stood. She rubbed her hands slowly, twisting her wedding rings. "My hands are so dry in the winter," she said softly, "I brought some hand cream with me but I can't find it anywhere, my suitcase is so jumbled. Thank heavens spring is early this year. . . . They told me that little park over there doesn't usually open till the end of March . . ."

She's helping me, thought Kate, I'm not supposed to let her down.

". . . but they're already running it on weekends. Even past dusk. We'll see the lights tonight. You can't see the shapes this far away, just the motion . . ."

A nurse came in with a wheelchair. Kate's mother pulled a wry face. "This wheelchair is a bit much," she said.

"We don't want to tire you out," said the nurse.

The chair took her weight quietly. At the door she put out her hand to stop, turned, and said anxiously, "Kate, see if you can find that hand cream?"

It was the blue suitcase from years ago, still almost new. She'd brought things she never used for everyday; a cashmere sweater, lace slips, silk underpants wrapped in tissue. Folded beneath was a stack of postmarked envelopes, slightly ragged, tied with twine. Kate opened one and realized that all the cards were there, beginning with the first of the marriage. There were a few photographs of her and Robert, baby pictures almost indistinguishable from each other, and then Kate's homemade Valentines, fastened together with rubber bands. Kate stared. *What will I do with these things?* She wanted air; she needed to breathe. She walked to the window and put the bundled papers on the sill. She'd raised the glass and pushed back the screen when suddenly, her mother's clock radio went off with a flat buzz. Kate moved to switch it off and brushed the cards with her arm. Envelopes shifted and slid, scattering on the floor of the room. A few snapshots wafted silently out the window. They dipped and turned, twirling. Kate didn't try to reach them. They seemed only scraps, buoyant and yellowed, blown away, the faces small as pennies. Somewhere far-off there were sirens, almost musical, drawn out and carefully approaching.

The nurse came in with evening medication. Kate's mother lay in bed. "I hope this is strong enough," she said.

"Last night I couldn't sleep at all. So many sounds in a hospital . . ."

"You'll sleep tonight," the nurse assured her.

Kate winked at her mother. "That's right," she said, "I'll help you out if I have to."

They stayed up for an hour, watching the moving lights outside and the stationary glows of houses across the distant river. The halls grew darker, were lit with night lights, and the hospital dimmed. Kate waited. Her mother's eyes fluttered and finally she slept. Her breathing was low and regular.

Kate didn't move. Robert had said he'd be back; where was he? She felt a sunken anger and shook her head. She'd been on the point of telling her mother everything. The secrets were a travesty. What if there were things her mother wanted done, people she needed to see? Kate wanted to wake her before these hours passed in the dark and confess that she had lied. Between them, through the tension, there had always been a trusted clarity. Now it was twisted. Kate sat leaning forward, nearly touching the hospital bed.

Suddenly her mother sat bolt upright, her eyes open and her face transfixed. She looked blindly toward Kate but seemed to see nothing. "Who are you?" she whispered. Kate stood, at first unable to move. The woman in the bed opened and closed her mouth several times, as though she were gasping. Then she said loudly, "Stop moving the table. Stop it this instant!" Her eyes were wide with fright and her body was vibrating.

Kate reached her. "Mama, wake up, you're dreaming." Her mother jerked, flinging her arms out. Kate held her tightly.

"I can hear the wheels," she moaned.

"No, no," Kate said, "You're here with me."

"It's not so?"

"No," Kate said. "It's not so."

She went limp. Kate felt for her pulse and found it rapid, then regular. She sat rocking her mother. In a few minutes she lay her back on the pillows and smoothed the damp hair at her temples, smoothed the sheets of the bed. Later she slept fitfully in a chair, waking repeatedly to assure herself that her mother was breathing.

Near dawn she got up, exhausted, and left the room to walk in the corridor. In front of the window at the end of the hallway she saw a man slumped on a couch; the man slowly stood and wavered before her like a specter. It was Robert.

"Kate?" he said.

Years ago he had flunked out of a small junior college and their mother sat in her bedroom rocker, crying hard for over an hour while Kate tried in vain to comfort her. Kate went to the university the next fall, so anxious that she studied frantically, outlining whole textbooks in yellow ink. She sat in the front rows of large classrooms to take voluminous notes, writing quickly in her thick notebook. Robert had gone home, held a job in a plant that manufactured business forms and worked his way through the hometown college. By that time their father was dead, and Robert became, always and forever, the man of the house.

"Robert," Kate said, "I'll stay. Go home."

After breakfast they sat waiting for Robert, who had called and said he'd arrive soon. Kate's fatigue had given way to an intense awareness of every sound, every gesture. How would they get through the day? Her mother had awakened from the drugged sleep still groggy, unable to eat. The meal was sent away untouched and she watched the window as though she feared the walls of the room.

"I'm glad your father isn't here to see this," she said. There was a silence and Kate opened her mouth to speak. "I mean," said her mother quickly, "I'm going to look horrible for a few weeks, with my head all shaved." She pulled an afghan up around her lap and straightened the magazines on the table beside her chair.

"Mom," Kate said, "your hair will grow back."

Her mother pulled the afghan closer. "I've been thinking of your father," she said. "It's not that I'd have wanted him to suffer. But if he had to die, sometimes I wish he'd done it more gently. That heart attack, so finished; never a warning. I wish I'd had some time to nurse him. In a way, it's a chance to settle things."

"Did things need settling?"

"They always do, don't they?" She sat looking out the window, then said softly, "I wonder where I'm headed."

"You're not headed anywhere;" Kate said. "I want you right here to see me settle down into normal American womanhood."

Her mother smiled reassuringly. "Where are my grandchildren?" she said. "That's what I'd like to know."

"You stick around," said Kate, "and I promise to start working on it." She moved her chair closer, so that their knees were touching and they could both see out the window. Below them cars moved on the highway and the Ferris wheel in the little park was turning.

"I remember when you were one of the little girls in the parade at the county fair. You weren't even in school yet; you were beautiful in that white organdy dress and pinafore. You wore those shiny black patent shoes and a crown of real apple blossoms. Do you remember?"

"Yes," Kate said. "That long parade. They told me not to move and I sat so still my legs went to sleep. When they lifted me off the float I couldn't stand up. They put me under a tree to wait for you, and you came, in a full white skirt and white sandals, your hair tied back in a red scarf. I can see you yet."

Her mother laughed. "Sounds like a pretty exaggerated picture."

Kate nodded. "I was little. You were big."

"You loved the county fair. You were wild about the carnivals." They looked down at the little park. "Magic, isn't it?" her mother said.

"Maybe we could go see it," said Kate. "I'll ask the doctor."

They walked across a pedestrian footbridge spanning the highway. Kate had bundled her mother into a winter coat and gloves despite the sunny weather. The day was sharp, nearly still, holding its bright air like illusion. Kate tasted the brittle water of her breath, felt for the cool handrail and thin steel of the webbed fencing. Cars moved steadily under the bridge.

Beyond a muted roar of motors the park spread green and wooded, its limits clearly visible.

Kate's mother had combed her hair and put on lipstick. Her mouth was defined and brilliant; she linked arms with Kate like an escort. "I was afraid they'd tell us no," she said. "I was ready to run away!"

"I promised I wouldn't let you. And we only have ten minutes, long enough for the Ferris wheel." Kate grinned.

"I haven't ridden one in years. I wonder if I still know how."

"Of course you do. Ferris wheels are genetic knowledge."

"All right, whatever you say." She smiled. "We'll just hold on."

They drew closer and walked quickly through the sounds of the highway. When they reached the grass it was ankle-high and thick, longer and more ragged than it appeared from a distance. The Ferris wheel sat squarely near a grove of swaying elms, squat and laboring, taller than trees. Its neon lights still burned, pale in the sun, spiraling from inside like an imagined bloom. The naked elms surrounded it, their topmost branches tapping. Steel ribs of the machine were graceful and slightly rusted, squeaking faintly above a tinkling music. Only a few people were riding.

"Looks a little rickety," Kate said.

"Oh, don't worry," said her mother.

Kate tried to buy tickets but the ride was free. The old man running the motor wore an engineer's cap and patched overalls. He stopped the wheel and led them on a short ramp to an open car. It dipped gently, padded with black cushions. An orderly and his children rode in the car above. Kate saw their dangling feet, the girls' dusty sandals and gray socks beside their father's shoes and the hem of his white pants. The youngest one swung her feet absently, so it seemed the breeze blew her legs like fabric hung on a line.

Kate looked at her mother. "Are you ready for the big sky?" They laughed. Beyond them the river moved lazily. Houses on the opposite bank seemed empty, but a few rowboats bobbed at the docks. The surface of the water lapped and reflected clouds, and as Kate watched, searching for a definition of line, the Ferris wheel jerked into motion. The car rocked. They looked into the distance and Kate caught her mother's hand as they ascended.

Far away the hospital rose up white and glistening, its windows catching the glint of the sun. Directly below, the park was nearly deserted. There were a few cars in the parking lot and several dogs chasing each other across the grass. Two or three lone women held children on the teeter-totters and a wind was coming up. The forlorn swings moved on their chains. Kate had a vision of the park at night, totally empty, wind weaving heavily through the trees and children's playthings like a great black fish about to surface. She felt a chill on her arms. The light had gone darker, quietly, like a minor chord.

"Mom," Kate said, "it's going to storm." Her own voice seemed distant, the sound strained through layers of screen or gauze.

"No," said her mother, "it's going to pass over." She moved her hand to Kate's knee and touched the cloth of her daughter's skirt.

Kate gripped the metal bar at their waists and looked straight ahead. They were rising again and she felt she would scream. She tried to breathe rhythmically, steadily. She felt the immense weight of the air as they moved through it.

They came almost to the top and stopped. The little car swayed back and forth.

"You're sick, aren't you," her mother said.

Kate shook her head. Below them the grass seemed to glitter coldly, like a sea. Kate sat wordless, feeling the touch of her mother's hand. The hand moved away and Kate felt the absence of the warmth.

They looked at each other levelly.

"I know all about it," her mother said, "I know what you haven't told me."

The sky circled around them, a sure gray movement. Kate swallowed calmly and let their gaze grow endless. She saw herself in her mother's wide brown eyes and felt she was falling slowly into them.

(ca. 1978)

Ivy Goodman

Ivy Goodman was born in 1953; she grew up in Harrisburg, Pennsylvania. She took a B.A. at the University of Pennsylvania and an M.A. at Stanford, where she was a fellow in the writing program. She has also been a fellow at the Fine Arts Work Center in Provincetown, Massachusetts, and has worked as a teacher, a bibliographer, a copyreader, and a bookkeeper. Her stories have appeared in many magazines, as well as in the O. Henry Award volumes for 1981 and 1982. Heart Failure *(1983), her first collection, made her the youngest writer ever to win the Iowa Short Fiction Award.*

Goodman's fictive world closely resembles the worlds of Barthelme and R. L. Shafner; it is not basically unlike that of Jayne Anne Phillips, though in matters of form and structure Goodman follows a distinctly more experimental path. The first story in her collection, "Baby," begins: "He shuttles from me, in Boston, to ex-wife and baby in Baltimore, to me, to baby." Two things fairly jump out at the reader. First, this is not going to be a pleasant tale of marital romance; neither is it to be a celebratory tale. And second, the mechanistic repetition of the prose beautifully, and importantly, matches the mechanistic repetitions in the characters' lives. This is a technique directly traceable to the remarkable innovations of James Joyce: it has radiated through a great deal of modern fiction, changing, evolving, as different writers have tried

*their hands at it. Goodman is thus quite directly in the line
extending from the father of modern fictional technique into
our own time; and the way in which she creates her fictions,
in her uniquely post-Joycean way, and in her shared post-
Joycean world, is both significant and impressive.*

LAST MINUTES

I was fifteen on the fifteenth. My father died on the first, my
grandmother on the twelfth, my boyfriend on the eighteenth.
"You're next," my mother said to me on the twenty-second.
She handed me a pack of razor blades and a blue revolver. "I
suggest the revolver," she whispered, "but either way, do
me a favor and crawl into a plastic bag first." She opened the
basement door and waved. "Good-by, Dena."

In the basement I used the laundry room phone and called a
friend of mine.

"She's not here," her brother said.

I dialed again.

"Didn't I just tell you she's not here?"

"I'm desperate," I said. "I'm going to kill myself."

"But she's not here."

I called my mother upstairs.

"Terrified?" she asked. "Just relax and get on with it."

"I'm too cold to."

"Hold on a minute."

She opened the door and threw down some blankets. "Better?" she asked when she picked up the phone again.

"I'm thirsty now."

"Well, there's running water right next to you, isn't there?"

"I don't want water. I want . . . ."

"You want, you want, you always want. Why don't you
kill yourself and leave me alone already?"

She hung up on me.

I called my sister at her college.

"She's in the bathroom," her roommate said.

"It's important."

"She'll call you back."

"No, I'll wait."

I waited ten minutes.

"What the hell do you want?" my sister asked. "How many times do I have to tell you that I call home on Thursdays. Don't call me on Wednesday when I'm calling home on Thursday."

"I need to talk to you."

"Does Mother know you're calling? It's such a waste of money. It's ridiculous. I should be studying."

"I'm going to kill myself."

"I can't believe this. Dena, if there hasn't been enough death this month, even that asshole you were going out with . . . ."

"He wasn't an asshole."

"He was an asshole. Asshole, asshole," she said, then disconnected me.

I dialed cousin Richard who once said I could depend on him.

"Forget it this time," Richard said.

I called his sister Brenda.

"Dena who?" Brenda asked.

I called my mother again.

"You mean you're still alive? Dena, I sent you down there hours ago."

I dialed Information. Information said to dial 0.

I dialed 0.

0 said, "Dial H-O-T-L-I-N-E."

I dialed H-O-T-L-I-N-E.

"Hello, Hotline."

"Help," I said. "I'm going to kill myself."

"Aw don't," Hotline said. "Aw don't. Aw don't. Aw don't . . . ."

I dialed my mother again.

"I knew it was you," she said. "Who else would wake me?"

"I'm sorry."

"Tell me one thing, are you in the bag yet?"

"No."

"Dena, what have you been doing with yourself? Get on with it. And if you expect to be noisy, turn on the washing machine first."

I undressed then stuffed my clothes and blankets into the washing machine. I sprinkled soap on top of them. I turned the knob and dropped the lid down.

After I found a plastic trash bag, I shook it open and crawled inside, taking the weapons and the phone with me. I picked the receiver up. "Daddy?"

"Listen to your mother," he answered. "I don't care what you do. Just keep your distance. After all, I died to get away from you."

"Is Granny with you?"

"Yes," she said. "What's that noise I hear? Is the washer running? And why don't you hurry up and slit your wrists or whatever? A woman my age can't put up with your nonsense. By the way, how's your sister doing?"

"Fine," my sister said. "And I miss you."

"Do it with the revolver," my boyfriend said. "Stick it in your mouth and point it toward the ceiling."

"Mother!"

"Dena, how many times do I have to tell you," my mother said.

"But it's so hot in here."

"You're hot, you're cold. What's wrong with you?"

"Don't tell me she's given herself a fever," Granny said.

"Dena, this is Mother. Does your head hurt?"

"Yes."

"Then keep her away from me," my father said.

"We were going to break up anyway," my boyfriend said.

"Did you twist the bag shut? Twist the bag shut," my mother said. "Or I'll have a mess on my hands. Bring the edges to the inside and twist the goddamn bag shut."

"But Mother, it's even hotter now."

"Breathe deeply, Dena, as if you felt nauseated."

"I can't. The walls are closing in on me," I said.
"The walls are closing in on her," they said.
"Please, the plastic's sticking to me."
No one answered.

(1978)

Susan Fromberg Schaeffer

Susan Fromberg Schaeffer was born in 1941. Educated in the New York City public schools, and at the University of Chicago, where she took a Ph.D. in 1966, she has been for many years a professor of English at Brooklyn College of the City University of New York. Her doctoral dissertation, at the time the first full-length critical study of Vladimir Nabokov, was later published.

Schaeffer's fiction, long and short, like her poetry, is distinguished by a limpid, lyrical, and flowing style. Cynthia Ozick said of the prose of Schaeffer's 1973 novel, Falling, *"This is wonderful and amazing. This is natural prose." Margaret Atwood said of Schaeffer's 1980 novel,* Love, *"It is both a song of mourning for life's brevity, elusiveness, and grief, and a celebration of its quirkiness and joy. It's also a family saga in the grand tradition . . ." Anne Sexton said of Schaeffer's 1974 collection of poems,* Granite Lady, *"These poems are completely original, associative and fascinating." And Jane Kramer said of Schaeffer's 1974 novel,* Anya, *"Schaeffer is a dazzling writer. Her kind of knowledge is rarely dared; when it is, it is rarely explored with anything like the necessary courage."*

The Queen of Egypt *(1980), the collection of shorter fiction from which "The Priest Next Door" has been taken, exhibits all of the virtues just noted, in addition to a driving sense of narrative and a sometimes breathtaking ability to keep the reader usefully off balance. Schaeffer has become a popular writer; her books sell well. But her critical reputation, particularly among academic critics, has yet to keep pace.*

THE PRIEST NEXT DOOR

In the old neighborhoods, where the houses hide as many as eighteen rooms under their packed and turreted roofs, silence falls as sweetly on the concrete sidewalks as sunlight; cars are not heard passing under the oak leaves, and it is the sound of wind and rain that people listen to. In neighborhoods like this, it is inevitable that everyone knows the rough lines and perspective of everyone else's lives, for the children belong to the same troops of Girl Scouts, and always have cookies to sell, so that the desperate mothers band together in threes and fours, each mother buying one box of cookies from the other two or three children so that their own child will not have to sell cookies to strangers and cross too many streets. So it is inevitable that not only the rough lines of a life, but the finer details, become common knowledge as well. Yet, on streets where the great tragedies are not deaths, which everyone chronicles in the ledger next to the births of the anonymous infants whose names the neighbors all carefully learn, but the falling of the great oak boughs from the trees in an ice storm, or the sawing off of branches by the telephone company, so they will not pull down the wires, where the truly remarkable event is the late frost aborting the crocuses and forsythias, or the early frost, cracking radiators of automobiles in their garages, themselves the sizes of houses, privacy is always respected.

For the people in the old houses have learned that a yard filled with oak leaves, cinder blocks, and damp cartons may mean the man of the house has had a stroke, and his wife must stay with him, or the woman of the house has been pregnant and confined to her bed and her couch. These events remain hidden, like shoots under leaves, while members of the family stand with their neighbor under an oak tree, admiring the solid ice coating, commenting on the tree's remarkable resemblance to glass. Therefore it is often easier to build a large spiked cedar fence around one's yard than discuss the condition of a neighboring fence with its owner, so that later, it is only possible to see the yard from a few upper windows of one's home, and soon the occupants' eyes learn to avoid the offensive cinder blocks and the thick black-brown sheet of leaves covering the adjoining lawn like a failed and terrible skin.

Still, strange attachments do begin to grow up. One house, which had long been known as the most beautiful on the block, fell into such savage disrepair that its yard was surrounded on two sides by high cedar fences. The neighbors had stopped visiting altogether, claiming the ice on the steps proclaimed the family's distaste for visitors, and no one would go where they were not wanted. In the summer, when everyone else's lawn had turned emerald green, the lawn of this house still blew with dry oak leaves, which would land on the other thick green carpets like dust tongues, each one bleating contempt for the block. So it was a surprise to no one when a *For Sale* sign went up over the door, for by now it was general knowledge that Mrs. Hills had had a heart attack, her oldest son having broken down in the local Catholic school after a month of misbehavior and blurted this out to Sister Grace. From that time on, there were rumors that considerably more of interest was taking place in the house, although no one attempted to find out what it was, since eventually, as is always the rule, the details would publish themselves in the very shingles of the house without anyone troubling to discover them.

The house was eventually sold to a young couple, who fortunately were not superstitious, for on the day they moved in, their baby's crib collapsed, and their own bed, when they sat down on it, fell to the floor in a splatter of splinters. It was a while before they had time to notice anything around them, surrounded as they were by what turned out to be seven truckloads of the Hills family's possessions: medicines abandoned in chests with the spoons beside them sticky, clothes of all sizes, dusty hangers, and, worst of all, in the basement, a trash can with an enormous decapitated doll's head, and, on an abandoned work table, a moose head, one eye torn loose, disgorging chalk powder through its socket, and above the entrance of the loft of the garage, a single leather boxing glove, cracked and peeling, hung from the rafters like a relentless old corpse.

Nevertheless, things settled. The baby who was one year old had stopped peering fuzzily around her new yellow room for the bookshelves of the study she had occupied, because the Zlotnicks' apartment had been much smaller; Mrs. Zlotnick, who was pregnant once again, began to feel the new baby kicking and was vomiting less and less frequently; it had been almost seven months since her last baby had begun growing in her left Fallopian tube, causing the blood explosion that sent her to the hospital for emergency surgery, and she would not be pregnant now if it hadn't been for God's Grace: accidents. Mrs. Zlotnick was beginning to open with the crocuses; less and less often, the emergency room climbed from its frame. Less and less often, she saw herself sitting in the receiving room; less often, she felt herself waiting for the real adults to come out of the cracks in the walls of the new house, although frequently, she did have a dream of a jagged lightning-shaped crack appearing on her stomach, a miniature doctor rising out of it as if on an elevator until he reached the level of her eyes, then menacing her with his stethoscope as if it were a hammer and shouting the names of various things that caused her to lose the baby; bananas! aspirins! antihistamines! turtles! stuffed rabbits! Edith Zlotnick often told her husband, Fred, and her closest friend, Susan, about this dream, carefully enumerating all the small changes in the doctor's list as if it were a grocery list, and always laughing, as if the dream were truly comical. Still, she had it more often than she would have liked.

"Look," Fred said one morning, as they were staring blankly out of their kitchen windows, both of them wondering whether the windows should have curtains or shades, for Fred was a champion of modesty and insisted they must have *something*. Had either of them known they had been thinking about the same thing, they would have been amazed, for, in fact, if they had begun to speak, each would have begun with a different subject. "Look," Fred said, "a fairy priest." "A fairy what?" Edith asked absently, inspecting the sludge of sugar at the bottom of her new china cup, trying to estimate the number of calories she was about to greedily consume. Fred had gone to the window and was staring with greater interest than he had shown in anything since the bathroom sink began its slow menacing leak. Edith got up, holding her stomach, and looked out the window also. In the backyard facing theirs, a priest was putting out paper plate after paper plate and cats were coming toward him through every bush and hedge. "God!" Edith thought, "our cats haven't had their booster shots." "She still hasn't had enough sympathy," Fred thought bitterly, his eyes carefully avoiding Edith, whose hands, he knew, would be supporting her mumpish stomach. "Look at that Persian cat; it's pregnant," Edith pointed, unconsciously adding, "Remember that time I was in the Emergency Room? I never thought a hospital could move so fast. I thought they just filled out forms while you wrote your will on the hospital walls." "The next obstetrician we get is going to give Green Stamps," Fred said absently; "look, he looks just like Mary Martin." "Mary Martin?" Edith echoed, studying the priest moving sideways in little dancing steps, his sharp elbow on his hip jabbing the air. "Mary Martin in *Peter Pan;* he looks like he's on a wire." "Oh." Edith considered politely. One of the cats the priest was feeding looked exactly like a kitten she had given away from her female cat's first and only litter. Zelda Cat had kept her other kitten, and still treated Ophelia as if she were a nursling. The cat Edith was intently watching was white and black patched, although even from a distance she could see he was a terrible mess. Edith assumed the cat was male. "That's a terrible mess," Edith said with more passion than she intended. "The Persian cat's beautiful!" Fred answered in a wounded voice; "it must have cost a fortune." "Anyway, the forsythias are out," Edith sighed. She had been married a long time. "A fairy priest!" Fred wondered out loud again, long after Edith had returned to the table and spooned up the rest of her sugar with her index finger. That night, Edith got into bed slowly and gingerly, not because she was pregnant, but because the shadows from the blinds fell across the floor in unaccustomed patterns, one in particular taking a shape she imagined to be that of a surgeon's knife. Fred was up very late, going over the year's forms, a habit he had developed since their move to the new house.

The next day, which was Sunday, Edith took Cara out into the backyard to rake leaves before the church bells of the neighborhood Catholic school had even begun ringing. The morning chill was beginning to leave the air, and the sky had turned from gray to slate blue and was now shimmering brilliantly at the edges. Her daughter was absorbed in a corner of her outdoor playpen, which resembled a zoo cage, pulling her doll's red wool hair, when a horrible cat voice sounded at Edith's feet just as she picked up a rake. The black and white cat she had seen from the kitchen was standing in a pile of last year's gray-brown leaves, angrily screaming up at her. It had a shocking pink mouth, a slightly coated pink tongue, and alarmingly shiny pointed teeth. "Good grief!" Edith thought, catching sight of his front paws with their long hooked claws. "I'm not supposed to touch you," she informed the cat defensively; "my husband says you'll give our cats germs." The cat screamed in outrage. "Are you hungry?" Edith asked guiltily. The cat screamed again. "If I feed you this *once*," Edith asked the cat, "will you go away?" The cat answered loudly. Oppressed, Edith went into the house. She listened carefully, but there was no sound. The cat was screaming his head off on the cement back porch. Edith decided to open his can of tuna with a hand opener, not the electric one, because she was afraid that otherwise Fred would hear, and come down and start a fuss. As she went back out, carrying the paper plate full of cat tuna, blocking her own large cat's exit with her calf, she looked through the window and thought she saw the priest's kitchen curtain pulling back, as if he were watching her.

"You are a terrible mess," she told the black and white cat's shoulders, as he hunched over the plate, gobbling his food. "I wonder how old you are?" she asked the indifferent back of his furry neck. She stopped, thinking what the neighbors might have named him. "Patches?" she whispered. The cat perked up his ears but didn't stop eating. Edith sat down on the step to watch him. The cat slid sideways, toward the edge of the porch, observing her, while chewing, from one large green eye. "Hmmm," Edith observed to the air. The cat raised his head and looked at her. "Nice cat," Edith sighed, getting up and going up to her leaves. Later, when she looked up, the priest's curtains were hanging naturally, and that night, through her kitchen windows, Edith saw him feeding the local army of cats.

The next morning, Edith woke up from a terrible nightmare in which her mother had her committed to an asylum after a violent argument over the decorating of her kitchen windows; she escaped to find her mother driving off with Cara in a purple Pontiac, and found a notice on the front door of the house saying it had been sold to her mother, Mrs. Picarillo, for sixty dollars. While she was trying to pull herself together over the baby bottle and the stove, which along with the rest of the house still belonged to her, an outrageous screaming began at the kitchen door. There was Patches, hanging onto the edge of the back door windows by his front claws. The priest's house had not yet opened for the morning, although two gray cats had taken up their stations on the railings of his porch like two cement lions. Mrs. Zlotnick flew to the back door with a full plate of tuna, then ran up the back steps with Cara's bottle, but as she was feeding her, she was preoccupied with the picture of Patches' desperate face, and her own desire, every moment more desperate, to go down and find him.

Although most of the tuna was gone, Patches was not in the backyard. Mrs. Zlotnick stood still, looking out of the back window, every minute more grimly depressed. When she heard the already-familiar grating scream from the windows of the front porch, and went into the dining room and caught sight of his infuriated face, Edith felt a hot flood of joy, utterly unlike anything she had felt in years. Upstairs, she could hear her daughter crying; she stopped, but only for a second, and went out in her bathrobe and slippers onto the glassed-in front porch. Patches took one look at her and jumped into Cara's red English carriage where, with his chin propped on its edge, he stared defiantly at her. The porch windowpanes rattled in and out in the white gale. "Cold," Edith said out loud, hugging her arms around her breasts; the nipples were cold and were standing up against the terrycloth. Edith sat down on the blue couch the old owner had left marooned against the wall. "I could get pneumonia out here because of this dumb cat," she thought without moving. She was getting colder and colder and more and more miserable, as if everyone in the world she loved had just been destroyed. "I could get pneumonia because of you," she said to Patches accusingly: "look, it's even snowing." Patches looked at her unimpressed, then stood up in the carriage, stretched, arching his back, jumped down and walked over to her. "Well?" Edith asked through chattering teeth as Patches regarded her like a miniature god from the floor. "You're very short," Edith informed him irritably. The cat regarded her without blinking. "You are a Terrible Mess," Edith said with emphasis, a fleeting cloud of guilt streaking across the gray world which held only the two of them; she would never call Cara a terrible mess, although she was, in fact, and most of the time. "A Horrible, Terrible Mess," Edith said loudly. The cat jumped up on to the couch. Joy clawed at Edith's throat. "We'll all get distemper," she warned herself; but without any genuine remorse or fear, her hand went over to him. Immediately, Patches' head twisted back on his neck and his teeth closed on her wrist. "No," she instructed, withdrawing her hand gently: "No. Hand," she said, holding it in front of his face. "Now it's here, and now," she said patiently, raising it over the tips of his ears, "it's here." Patches twisted his head back, but let her hand rest on his back. Edith repeated the lesson twenty times; by then, Patches was lying in her lap, emitting loud squeals, and kneading her swollen stomach. "My mother says cats can carry a virus that can blind a fetus twenty years later," she remembered. "Too bad," she cooed down at Patches, hugging him to her. The cat looked surprised, but did not resist. From a distance, with her head bent gently over the cat, her rapturous look shining through the March morning, Edith and the cat resembled nothing so much as Madonna and Child.

"I don't want that damn animal in the house," Fred told her; "our three cats don't have their boosters." "He doesn't have to come in the house," Edith insisted. "First he's on the porch; next he'll be in the house," Fred predicted unsympathetically. "No he won't," Edith fervently promised, although in fact that was exactly what she had in mind. "When our cats get shots, he can too," Edith sulked, her lower lip out, close to tears. "Do you know a vet who makes house calls," Fred asked sarcastically, "or should we just rent a van from the ASPCA?" "Well," Edith answered, "as a matter of fact, yesterday I was talking to Mrs. Campanella; her daughter dissects the animals? And she said her cousin was a vet who'd come to the house." "I don't want to hear about it," Fred shouted, slamming down his fork; "you'll wind up the crazy cat lady, that's just who Mrs. Campanella is going to tell the vet who makes house calls you are." "Also," Edith went on, more or less unperturbed, "that old lady next door who's always hanging out the laundry and feeding the squirrels? She said Patches used to live in this house. When the man moved, he left five cats." "That's nothing; he left seven truckloads of furniture." "The priest took the Persian," Edith finished. "I don't want to hear about it!" Fred shouted again, this time at the top of his lungs, and stomped up the back stairs to his study on the third floor. Edith tiptoed into the dining room, saw Patches asleep in her daughter's carriage, and with a lovely sense of satisfaction went back to the dishes. "Where's the cat?" Fred bellowed down to her. "Outside!" she shrieked back in an injured voice: "where you wanted him." A peaceable silence fell over the kitchen as Edith smiled to herself at the picture of Patches, stationed in Cara's precious package, and as she washed and rinsed the dishes, listening to the nipples jostle furiously in their sterilizer, she watched the priest dancing with plates of tuna among the chorus of neighborhood cats. It was obvious to her he was looking frantically about the backyard. "Too bad," Edith thought, pressing herself into a corner. The fairy priest was looking directly at her window, and she didn't want to appear either to notice or to gloat.

So the days went by, and if the high point of the day became Edith's early morning visits with Patches, who had taken up permanent residence on the couch under a huge canvasy moving cloth she had provided him with for the rest of the cold weather, she dismissed this oddity in her usual flip way, telling herself she was only meeting with neighbors, and Patches happened to be the only neighbor she liked. Meanwhile, she carried out a relentless war of wills with Fred. "Can't you at least come out and *look* at the poor thing?" she pleaded in horrendous tones. Fred came out and looked. "If your mother could see that, she'd be in the next county," Fred grumbled, watching Patches affectionately place his teeth around Edith's wrist; "God knows what he's picked up." "Do you want him to freeze?" Edith asked rhetorically. "Animal killer," she muttered. "Besides," she went on, "he chases all the other cats out of the yard, doesn't he?" Fred nodded with a bad grace.

"He wouldn't freeze to death," he said; "the priest takes care of him." "He only feeds him," Edith answered, cuddling the cat; "besides, he used to live here; the old woman said so." "She's moving, the old woman," Fred said, as if that canceled out her comment. "And stop calling me an animal killer." "We still need a door for the mail," Edith nagged him. The former owner of the house had put a lock on the porch door, but the bell itself was set into the house door so that daily mail was regularly returned to the post office. "Patches could come in the same door." "Patches can go to France," Fred exploded. "You'll scare him," Edith remonstrated; "will you do it?" "Yes, yes," Fred droned, "but he can't come into the house." Edith nodded. "I don't see what you like so much about that damn cat anyway." Edith kept quiet. "He's a toughy," Fred said with reluctant admiration. "I told you he chased away all the other cats," Edith reminded him, and then proudly began recounting Patches' heroic exploits for the fifteenth time. "And the scars on his nose are healing," she marveled, running her fingers along the long lines of caked blood on his nose, crossing each other in a tick-tack-toe pattern. "Disgusting," Fred said again, shaking his head; "the fairy priest's out in the backyard; he probably wonders where this thing is." "No, he doesn't," Edith answered; "the cat's too filthy to be a house cat. Don't worry; he stays out." "He stays on *our porch*," Fred corrected pedantically. There was the sound of a baby crying. "Who's going to feed Cara?" he asked. "You do it," Edith answered seraphically. Fred went into the kitchen, and on his third try had a warm bottle for Cara, having boiled the first so hard the plastic sack began leaking, and, having nearly melted the second bottle when he forgot to check to see if it was standing upright in its white enamel pan.

As the days went by, and Patches' visits became more regular, Edith found herself more and more preoccupied with the fairy priest. Did he live alone? Did he live with his mother? She never saw anyone else at the house. "What's he doing up there?" she asked herself from the corner of the kitchen where she often pressed herself and her swelling stomach to secretly observe him. The fairy priest was inching along on his bottom across the shingles of his roof, holding to the shingly surface with one hand and gingerly dipping the other into the metal gutter, putting whatever he fished out into a paper grocery bag. Then he slid onto the sharply inclined roof adjoining and repeated the performance. "Getting leaves out of the gutter," Edith mentally noted, filing this latest picture along with the one of the fake red felt lily she had gotten close enough to observe through the fairy priest's window by pressing her stomach so hard against the heavy diamond-shaped fence she wondered if she was doing damage to their unborn child. Edith now kept a pair of boots on the back porch solely for the purpose of walking around the muddy lawn with Patches, and although she told herself she tried to take Patches for walks when the priest was not home (he now followed her like a dog, jumping up into the air to reach the tips of her fingers) it somehow happened that she was invariably out with the cat when the priest was home, and she either saw his shadow move in the kitchen, or his curtains slowly pulling back until they were at a sharp angle to the sill. Occasionally, when she was balancing on one leg like a distended flamingo, tugging off one boot or gazing down on Patches in her bathrobe, she wondered what the fairy priest thought of her, and invariably she found herself blushing. "His Persian is pregnant," she thought to herself; "it looks like two fat skunks."

The Persian, who was evidently a friend of Patches', since she was the only cat Patches permitted in the yard, now also came to the back porch, but Edith righteously refused to feed her, reasoning she was definitely the priest's responsibility, although lately, the Persian had arrived shepherded by Patches, and Edith was weakening. Once, she arrived alone and Edith fed her in a fury, becoming even more enraged when the pregnant Persian finished the whole can, leaving nothing for Patches. The old woman had told Edith that the Persian, also, used to live in their house, but Edith was sure she was the priest's cat. "There'll be kittens all over," Fred warned her as portentously as he could, but nevertheless, he was making plans to acquire a jigsaw over the weekend and saw out a panel for both the mail and Patches. Domestic relations had become peaceful. "Look at what the fairy priest's doing now," Fred called, peering out the window, while Edith drank her Sanka, pretending not to be interested. She had noticed that lately the priest was always out in the yard wearing only his undershirt and jeans.

Then, one night, Edith who had gone to bed early after tucking Patches in for the second time on the porch, woke up to hear the loud crying of a cat. "Oh, it's Trembler," she thought, trying to move farther onto her side, falling back asleep as the crying continued. "Edith!" Fred was shouting in the middle of their dark bedroom; "Patches is in the house!" "Patches?" Edith asked groggily. "Patches! He's in the guest room." "Guest room?" Edith echoed; "pushy cat." And she attempted to go back to sleep. "Get up!" Fred thundered; "we have to get him out. Trembler won't let him out of the room." "Oh all right," Edith said, tying Fred's bathrobe around the shifting continents of her stomach. "Trembler," Edith said, addressing her giant calico cat in a firm voice. He blinked his eyes sulkily at her and lay down on the first step of the stairway to the third floor. "See?" Fred said; "you've upset all our cats." "I didn't let him in," Edith said, peering nearsightedly into the guest room. Patches shot by Trembler, down the stairs to the first floor. "Oh fine," Edith sighed, holding the rail, trudging down after him. "He's here," she announced, seeing Trembler's nose pointing under the couch. "Come on, Patches," she said, lying down on the carpet before the couch. Patches looked desperately in her direction. "Do you want me to get a broom?" Fred inquired helpfully. "Who'll carry him out if you scare him with a broom?'' Edith asked, inching forward like a worm on her side. ''Nice Patches,'' she cooed, scratching him under the chin. ''Just get him out,'' Fred said in an exhausted voice. ''That's what I'm doing,'' Edith answered, observing Patches, who was beginning to purr. Fred's loud sighs rose like dirigibles, bumping heavily against the ceiling. Edith caught Patches under the front paws, dragged him out from under the couch, and, with an injured stare at Fred, marched off with him toward the three doors leading to the front porch of the house, Fred running in front of her, frantically opening one after another. ''What are you doing there?'' she called a few minutes later, hearing Fred in the basement. ''Sealing up the gas vent to the old dryer; I think that's how he broke in.'' ''Enterprising cat,'' Edith thought with satisfaction, heavily climbing the steps, taking care to breathe rhythmically, going back to bed.

Two days later Trembler began sneezing and scratching his nose until it bled. ''I *told* you,'' Fred said; ''I *told* you.'' ''It's only a cold,'' Edith insisted, but Ophelia and Linda Cat were sneezing too. When Patches arrived in the afternoon, he was trembling all over; his nose was hot and caked, and his eyes were running. Edith locked him on the porch with a temporary kitty litter box made out of a grocery carton, some food and water, and went in to call Mrs. Campanella, and then the vet who made house calls. Meanwhile, Edith alternated her time between patting the three cats in the house and Patches on the porch, and staring out at the backyard of the fairy priest, which, like hers, was also empty. His shadow was moving about inside regularly and quickly. There were no plates of tuna on his porch. There were no cats in the yard.

''Distemper,'' Mr. Amadeo said, taking one look at the cats and writing out a prescription for chloromycetin; ''the house cats will probably be all right because they've got some immunity, but that black and white cat looks pretty bad.'' In the days that followed, Trembler, Linda Cat, and Ophelia began to stop sneezing and to eat more and more, but Patches, who had at first been fed through a dropper, now had stopped eating altogether, and lay trembling on the porch couch, his huge head on Edith's hand, looking up at her sadly from his electric green eyes. His breathing was labored. Edith thought about an electric blanket, but then worried that he might put his claws through it and electrocute himself. Edith herself had gone into a frozen panic, and Fred had taken over the care of Cara altogether. "He's toxic," the vet said on his second visit, and from her vigil on the porch, Edith saw him whispering something to Fred. She fell asleep with Patches' head on her hand, and when she woke up, the cat was rigid, and no longer breathing. "Get up!" she screamed, starting to shake him: "Get up!" And she pressed in and out on his furry chest as she had seen all the television doctors do. The cat lay there, rigid and staring. He was cold to the touch. Finally, Fred had to carry her to their room, where she cried so long she began running a fever. She heard Fred saying "psychiatrist" to her doctor in the hall, and then, "the vet took it away." "It!" Edith began crying, silently and steadily all over again. Her mother was called in; Edith barely noticed her. On the ninth day, she suddenly stopped; her mother began packing to go home and Fred began to look more cheerful. She still had no desire to go near Cara. From the bathroom, she heard Fred telling her mother that the vet had said there was no way of telling, that one of their cats might have picked something up from their clothes or shoes and given it to Patches. "It is my fault," Edith thought to herself, washing her face, rubbing it dry with a vicious terrycloth towel.

Evidently, the doctor had told them to leave her alone, for no one followed her out into the backyard when she wandered out that evening in her robe. As if she had expected it, the priest's door opened, and he walked toward her in his clerical clothes, although by this time of night he usually wore jeans and a blue sweatshirt. "Patches died," she told him. He had a jagged, bony face, red over the cheekbones. He looked at her and snapped a twig from his well-tended hedge, then stubbed it out against the wire fence as if it were a cigarette. "All my cats died," he said, "except the Persian." "Why?" Edith asked. "She had shots from before," he said, "when she lived in your house, and my aunt took her for a booster. She said she was too valuable a cat to take chances with." His bottom lip was chewed and blood-split. "She had five kittens," he added; "do you want one?" "No," Edith answered. "Good," he sighed; "how are your cats?" "They're fine." "That's good," the priest said sadly. They both looked desolately around the empty backyard. Edith thought she heard kittenish mews. "Well," he said. "Mmmmm," Edith murmured, and, supporting her stomach with her hands, she climbed the back porch steps. Just as she was going in, she saw the priest's back door still open, and then his hand carelessly reaching out for it, as if it no longer made any difference to the lives of the creatures on the block whether it was open or shut.

(1980)

Mark Helprin

Mark Helprin was born in 1947. He grew up in New York City, the Hudson River Valley area of New York State, and the British West Indies. He was educated at Harvard University and at Harvard's Center for Middle Eastern Studies; he has seen service in the British merchant marine, and the Israeli infantry and air force.

A Dove of the East and Other Stories *(1975) was his first collection. Six of the stories had already appeared in* The New Yorker. *The critical reception was extraordinarily favorable. John Gardner wrote: "A wonderful writer. He moves from character to character and from culture to culture, as if he'd been born and raised everywhere." Helprin's second collection,* Ellis Island and Other Stories *(1981), from which the story here printed is taken, only added to his reputation. He has also published two novels,* Refiner's Fire *(1977), which was praised but was not a success, and* Winter's Tale *(1983), which received strongly mixed critical notice but has been a considerable popular success.*

Again, the first sentence of the first story in his first collection, "A Jew of Persia," helps define Helprin's approach—and immediately exhibits his extraordinary mastery; "He had tried to explain for his sons the sense of mountains so high, sharp, and bare that winds blew ice into waves and silver crowns, of air so thin and cold it tattooed the skin and lungs with the blue of heaven and the bronze of sunshining rock crevasse." Helprin's world is neither cold nor pinched; it is filled with strangeness and with savagery, but also with wonder and beauty. Indeed, it is hard not to feel, reading prose like this, that Helprin is a writer who can do anything—and may very well end by doing just that.

THE SCHREUDERSPITZE

In Munich are many men who look like weasels. Whether by genetic accident, meticulous crossbreeding, an early and puzzling migration, coincidence, or a reason that we do not know, they exist in great numbers. Remarkably, they accentuate this unfortunate tendency by wearing mustaches, Alpine hats, and tweed. A man who resembles a rodent should never wear tweed.

One of these men, a commerical photographer named Franzen, had cause to be exceedingly happy. "Herr Wallich has disappeared," he said to Huebner, his supplier of paper and chemicals. "You needn't bother to send him bills. Just send them to the police. The police, you realize, were here on two separate occasions!"

"If the two occasions on which the police have been here had not been separate, Herr Franzen, they would have been here only once."

"What do you mean? Don't toy with me. I have no time for semantics. In view of the fact that I knew Wallich at school, and professionally, they sought my opinion on his disappearance. They wrote down everything I said, but I do not think that they will find him. He left his studio on the Neuhausstrasse just as it was when he was working, and the landlord has put a lien on the equipment. Let me tell you that he had some fine equipment—very fine. But he was not such a great photographer. He didn't have that killer's instinct. He was clearly not a hunter. His canine teeth were poorly developed; not like these," said Franzen, baring his canine teeth in a smile which made him look like an idiot with a mouth of miniature castle towers.

"But I am curious about Wallich."

"So is everyone. So is everyone. This is my theory. Wallich was never any good at school. At best, he did only middling well. And it was not because he had hidden passions, or a special genius for some field outside the curriculum. He tried hard but found it difficult to grasp several subjects; for him, mathematics and physics were pure torture.

"As you know, he was not wealthy, and although he was a nice-looking fellow, he was terribly short. That inflicted upon him great scars—his confidence, I mean, because he had none. He could do things only gently. If he had to fight, he would fail. He was weak.

"For example, I will use the time when he and I were competing for the Heller account. This job meant a lot of money, and I was not about to lose. I went to the library and read all I could about turbine engines. What a bore! I took photographs of turbine blades and such things, and seeded them throughout my portfolio to make Herr Heller think that I had always been interested in turbines. Of course, I had not even known what they were. I thought that they were an Oriental hat. And now that I know them, I detest them.

"Naturally, I won. But do you know how Wallich approached the competition? He had some foolish ideas about mother-of-pearl nautiluses and other seashells. He wanted to show how shapes of things mechanical were echoes of shapes in nature. All very fine, but Herr Heller pointed out that if the public were to see photographs of mother-of-pearl shells contrasted with photographs of his engines, his engines would come out the worse. Wallich's photographs were very beautiful—the tones of white and silver were exceptional—but they were his undoing. In the end, he said, 'Perhaps, Herr Heller, you are right,' and lost the contract just like that.

"The thing that saved him was the prize for that picture he took in the Black Forest. You couldn't pick up a magazine in Germany and not see it. He obtained so many accounts that he began to do very well. But he was just not commercially-minded. He told me himself that he took only those assignments which pleased him. Mind you, his business volume was only about two-thirds of mine.

"My theory is that he could not take the competition, and the demands of his various clients. After his wife and son were killed in the motorcar crash, he dropped assignments one after another. I suppose he thought that as a bachelor he could live like a bohemian, on very little money, and therefore did not have to work more than half the time. I'm not saying that this was wrong. (Those accounts came to me.) But it was another instance of his weakness and lassitude.

"My theory is that he has probably gone to South America, or thrown himself off a bridge—because he saw that there was no future for him if he were always to take pictures of shells and things. And he was weak. The weak can never face themselves, and so cannot see the practical side of the world, how things are laid out, and what sacrifices are required to survive and prosper. It is only in fairy tales that they rise to triumph."

Wallich could not afford to get to South America. He certainly would not have thrown himself off a bridge. He was excessively neat and orderly, and the prospect of some poor fireman handling a swollen, bloated body resounding with flies deterred him forever from such nonsense.

Perhaps if he had been a Gypsy he would have taken to the road. But he was no Gypsy, and had not the talent, skill, or taste for life outside Bavaria. Only once had he been away, to Paris. It was their honeymoon, when he and his wife did not need Paris or any city. They went by train and stayed for a week at a hotel by the Quai Voltaire. They walked in the gardens all day long, and in the May evenings they went to concerts where they heard the perfect music of their own country. Though they were away for just a week, and read the German papers, and went to a corner of the Luxembourg Gardens where there were pines and wildflowers like those in the greenbelt around Munich, this music made them sick for home. They returned two days early and never left again except for July and August, which each year they spent in the Black Forest, at a cabin inherited from her parents.

He dared not go back to that cabin. It was set like a trap. Were he to enter he would be enfiladed by the sight of their son's pictures and toys, his little boots and miniature fishing rod, and by her comb lying at the exact angle she had left it when she had last brushed her hair, and by the sweet smell of her clothing. No, someday he would have to burn the cabin. He dared not sell, for strangers then would handle roughly all those things which meant so much to him that he could not even gaze upon them. He left the little cabin to stand empty, perhaps the object of an occasional hiker's curiosity, or recipient of cheerful postcards from friends traveling or at the beach for the summer—friends who had not heard.

He sought instead a town far enough from Munich so that he would not encounter anything familiar, a place where he would be unrecognized and yet a place not entirely strange, where he would have to undergo no savage adjustments, where he could buy a Munich paper.

A search of the map brought his flying eye always southward to the borderlands, to Alpine country remarkable for the steepness of the brown contours, the depth of the valleys, and the paucity of settled places. Those few depicted towns appeared to be clean and well placed on high overlooks. Unlike the cities to the north—circles which clustered together on the flatlands or along rivers, like colonies of bacteria—the cities of the Alps stood alone, *in extremis,* near the border. Though he dared not cross the border, he thought perhaps to venture near its edge, to see what he would see. These isolated towns in the Alps promised shining clear air and deep-green trees. Perhaps they were above the tree line. In a number of cases it looked that way—and the circles were far from resembling clusters of bacteria. They seemed like untethered balloons.

He chose a town from its ridiculous name, reasoning that few of his friends would desire to travel to such a place. The world bypasses badly named towns as easily as it abandons ungainly children. It was called Garmisch-Partenkirchen. At the station in Munich, they did not even inscribe the full name on his ticket, writing merely "Garmisch-P."

"Do you live there?" the railroad agent had asked.

"No," answered Wallich.

"Are you visiting relatives, or going on business, or going to ski?"

"No."

"Then perhaps you are making a mistake. To go in October is not wise, if you do not ski. As unbelievable as it may seem, they have had much snow. Why go now?"

"I am a mountain climber," answered Wallich.

"In winter?" The railway agent was used to flushing out lies, and when little fat Austrian boys just old enough for adult tickets would bend their knees at his window as if at confession and say in squeaky voices, "Half fare to Salzburg!," he pounced upon them as if he were a leopard and they juicy ptarmigan or baby roebuck.

"Yes, in the winter," Wallich said. "Good mountain climbers thrive in difficult conditions. The more ice, the more storm, the greater the accomplishment. I am accumulating various winter records. In January, I go to America, where I will ascend their highest mountain, Mt. Independence, four thousand meters." He blushed so hard that the railway agent followed suit. Then Wallich backed away, insensibly mortified.

A mountain climber! He would close his eyes in fear when looking through Swiss calendars. He had not the stamina to rush up the stairs to his studio. He had failed miserably at sports. He was not a mountain climber, and had never even dreamed of being one.

Yet when his train pulled out of the vault of lacy iron-work and late-afternoon shadow, its steam exhalations were like those of a man puffing up a high meadow, speeding to reach the rock and ice, and Wallich felt as if he were embarking upon an ordeal of the type men experience on the precipitous rock walls of great cloud-swirled peaks. Why was he going to Garmisch-Partenkirchen anyway, if not for an ordeal through which to right himself? He was pulled so far over on one side by the death of his family, he was so bent and crippled by the pain of it, that he was going to Garmisch-Partenkirchen to suffer a parallel ordeal through which he would balance what had befallen him.

How wrong his parents and friends had been when they had offered help as his business faltered. A sensible, graceful man will have symmetry. He remembered the time at youth camp when a stream had changed course away from a once gushing sluice and the younger boys had had to carry buckets of water up a small hill, to fill a cistern. The skinny little boys had struggled up the hill. Their counselor, sitting comfortably in the shade, would not let them go two to a bucket. At first they had tried to carry the pails in front of them, but this was nearly impossible. Then they surreptitiously spilled half the water on the way up, until the counselor took up position at the cistern and inspected each cargo. It had been torture to carry the heavy bucket in one aching hand. Wallich finally decided to take two buckets. Though it was agony, it was a better agony than the one he had had, because he had retrieved his balance, could look ahead, and, by carrying a double burden, had strengthened himself and made the job that much shorter. Soon, all the boys carried two buckets. The cistern was filled in no time, and they had a victory over their surprised counselor.

So, he thought as the train shuttled through chill half-harvested fields, I will be a hermit in Garmisch-Partenkirchen. I will know no one. I will be alone. I may even begin to climb mountains. Perhaps I will lose fingers and toes, and on the way gather a set of wounds which will allow me some peace.

He sensed the change of landscape before he actually came upon it. Then they began to climb, and the engine sweated steam from steel to carry the lumbering cars up terrifying grades on either side of which blue pines stood angled against the mountainside. They reached a level stretch which made the train curve like a dragon and led it through deep tunnels, and they sped along as if on a summer excursion, with views of valleys so distant that in them whole forests sat upon their meadows like birthmarks, and streams were little more than the grain in leather.

Wallich opened his window and leaned out, watching ahead for tunnels. The air was thick and cold. It was full of sunshine and greenery, and it flowed past as if it were a mountain river. When he pulled back, his cheeks were red and his face pounded from the frigid air. He was alone in the compartment. By the time the lights came on he had decided upon the course of an ideal. He was to become a mountain climber, after all—and in a singularly difficult, dangerous, and satisfying way.

A porter said in passing the compartment, "The dining car is open, sir." Service to the Alps was famed. Even though his journey was no more than two hours, he had arranged to eat on the train, and had paid for and ordered a meal to which he looked forward in pleasant anticipation, especially because he had selected French strawberries in cream for dessert. But then he saw his body in the gently lit half mirror. He was soft from a lifetime of near-happiness. The sight of his face in the blond light of the mirror made him decide to begin preparing for the mountains that very evening. The porter ate the strawberries.

Of the many ways to attempt an ordeal perhaps the most graceful and attractive is the Alpine. It is far more satisfying than Oriental starvation and abnegation precisely because the European ideal is to commit difficult acts amid richness and overflowing beauty. For that reason, the Alpine is as well the most demanding. It is hard to deny oneself, to pare oneself down, at the heart and base of a civilization so full.

Wallich rode to Garmisch-Partenkirchen in a thunder of proud Alps. The trees were tall and lively, the air crystalline, and radiating beams spoke through the train window from one glowing range to another. A world of high ice laughed. And yet ranks of competing images assaulted him. He had gasped at the sight of Bremen, a port stuffed with iron ships gushing wheat steam from their whistles as they prepared to sail. In the mountain dryness, he remembered humid ports from which these massive ships crossed a colorful world, bringing back on laden decks a catalogue of stuffs and curiosities.

Golden images of the north plains struck from the left. The salt-white plains nearly floated above the sea. All this was in Germany, though Germany was just a small part of the world, removed almost entirely from the deep source of things—from the high lakes where explorers touched the silvers which caught the world's images, from the Sahara where they found the fine glass which bent the light.

Arriving at Garmisch-Partenkirchen in the dark, he could hear bells chiming and water rushing. Cool currents of air flowed from the direction of this white tumbling sound. It was winter. He hailed a horse-drawn sledge and piled his baggage in the back. "Hotel Aufburg," he said authoritatively.

"Hotel Aufburg?" asked the driver.

"Yes, Hotel Aufburg. There is such a place, isn't there? It hasn't closed, has it?"

"No, sir, it hasn't closed." The driver touched his horse with the whip. The horse walked twenty feet and was reined to a stop. "Here we are," the driver said. "I trust you've had a pleasant journey. Time passes quickly up here in the mountains."

The sign for the hotel was so large and well lit that the street in front of it shone as in daylight. The driver was guffawing to himself; the little guffaws rumbled about in him like subterranean thunder. He could not wait to tell the other drivers.

Wallich did nothing properly in Garmisch-Partenkirchen. But it was a piece of luck that he felt too awkward and ill at ease to sit alone in restaurants while, nearby, families and lovers had self-centered raucous meals, sometimes even bursting into song. Winter took over the town and covered it in stiff white ice. The unresilient cold, the troikas jingling through the streets, the frequent snowfalls encouraged winter fat. But because Wallich ate cold food in his room or stopped occasionally at a counter for a steaming bowl of soup, he became a shadow.

The starvation was pleasant. It made him sleepy and its constant physical presence gave him companionship. He sat for hours watching the snow, feeling as if he were part of it, as if the diminution of his body were great progress, as if such lightening would lessen his sorrow and bring him to the high rim of things he had not seen before, things which would help him and show him what to do and make him proud just for coming upon them.

He began to exercise. Several times a day the hotel manager knocked like a woodpecker at Wallich's door. The angrier the manager, the faster the knocks. If he were really angry, he spoke so rapidly that he sounded like a speeded-up record: "Herr Wallich, I must ask you on behalf of the other guests to stop immediately all the thumping and vibration!

This is a quiet hotel, in a quiet town, in a quiet tourist region. Please!'' Then the manager would bow and quickly withdraw.

Eventually they threw Wallich out, but not before he had spent October and November in concentrated maniacal pursuit of physical strength. He had started with five each, every waking hour, of pushups, pull-ups, sit-ups, toe-touches, and leg-raises. The pull-ups were deadly—he did one every twelve minutes. The thumping and bumping came from five minutes of running in place. At the end of the first day, the pain in his chest was so intense that he was certain he was not long for the world. The second day was worse. And so it went, until after ten days there was no pain at all. The weight he abandoned helped a great deal to expand his physical prowess. He was, after all, in his middle twenties, and had never eaten to excess. Nor did he smoke or drink, except for champagne at weddings and municipal celebrations. In fact, he had always had rather ascetic tendencies, and had thought it fitting to have spent his life in Munich—''Home of Monks.''

By his fifteenth day in Garmisch-Partenkirchen he had increased his schedule to fifteen apiece of the exercises each hour, which meant, for example, that he did a pull-up every four minutes whenever he was awake. Late at night he ran aimlessly about the deserted streets for an hour or more, even though it sometimes snowed. Two policemen who huddled over a brazier in their tiny booth simply looked at one another and pointed to their heads, twirling their fingers and rolling their eyes every time he passed by. On the last day of November, he moved up the valley to a little village called Altenburg-St. Peter.

There it was worse in some ways and better in others. Altenburg-St. Peter was so tiny that no stranger could enter unobserved, and so still that no one could do anything without the knowledge of the entire community. Children stared at Wallich on the street. This made him walk on the little lanes and approach his few destinations from the rear, which led housewives to speculate that he was a burglar. There were few merchants, and, because they were cousins, they could with little effort determine exactly what Wallich ate. When one week they were positive that he had consumed only four bowls of soup, a pound of cheese, a pound of smoked meat, a quart of yogurt, and two loaves of bread, they were incredulous. They themselves ate this much in a day. They wondered how Wallich survived on so little. Finally they came up with an answer. He received packages from Munich several times a week and in these packages was food, they thought—and probably very great delicacies. Then as the winter got harder and the snows covered everything they stopped wondering about him. They did not see him as he ran out of his lodgings at midnight, and the snow muffled his tread. He ran up the road toward the Schreuderspitze, first for a kilometer, then two, then five, then ten, then twenty—when finally he had to stop because he had begun slipping in just before the farmers arose and would have seen him.

By the end of February the packages had ceased arriving, and he was a changed man. No one would have mistaken him for what he had been. In five months he had become lean and strong. He did two hundred and fifty sequential pushups at least four times a day. For the sheer pleasure of it, he would do a hundred and fifty pushups on his fingertips. Every day he did a hundred pull-ups in a row. His midnight run, sometimes in snow which had accumulated up to his knees, was four hours long.

The packages had contained only books on climbing, and equipment. At first the books had been terribly discouraging. Every elementary text had bold warnings in red or green ink: "It is extremely dangerous to attempt genuine ascents without proper training. This volume should be used in conjunction with a certified course on climbing, or with the advice of a registered guide. A book itself will not do!"

One manual had in bright-red ink, on the very last page: "Go back, you fool! Certain death awaits you!" Wallich imagined that, as the books said, there were many things he could not learn except by human example, and many mistakes he might make in interpreting the manuals, which would go uncorrected save for the critique of living practitioners. But it didn't matter. He was determined to learn for himself and accomplish his task alone. Besides, since the accident he had become a recluse, and could hardly speak. The thought of enrolling in a climbing school full of young people from all parts of the country paralyzed him. How could he reconcile his task with their enthusiasm? For them it was recreation, perhaps something aesthetic or spiritual, a way to meet new friends. For him it was one tight channel through which he could either burst on to a new life, or in which he would die.

Studying carefully, he soon worked his way to advanced treatises for those who had spent years in the Alps. He understood these well enough, having quickly learned the terminologies and the humor and the faults of those who write about the mountains. He was even convinced that he knew the spirit in which the treatises had been written, for though he had never climbed, he had only to look out his window to see high white mountains about which blue sky swirled like a banner. He felt that in seeing them he was one of them, and was greatly encouraged when he read in a French mountaineer's memoirs: "After years in the mountains, I learned to look upon a given range and feel as if I were the last peak in the line. Thus I felt the music of the empty spaces enwrapping me, and I became not an intruder on the cliffs, dangling only to drop away, but an equal in transit. I seldom looked at my own body but only at the mountains, and my eyes felt like the eyes of the mountains."

He lavished nearly all his dwindling money on fine equipment. He calculated that after his purchases he would have enough to live on through September. Then he would have nothing. He had expended large sums on the best tools, and he spent the intervals between his hours of reading and exercise holding and studying the shiny carabiners, pitons, slings, chocks, hammers, ice pitons, axes, étriers, crampons, ropes, and specialized hardware that he had either ordered or constructed himself from plans in the advanced books.

It was insane, he knew, to funnel all his preparation into a few months of agony and then without any experience whatever throw himself alone into a Class VI ascent—the seldom climbed *Westgebirgsausläufer* of the Schreuderspitze. Not having driven one piton, he was going to attempt a five-day climb up the nearly sheer western counterfort. Even in late June, he would spend a third of his time on ice. But the sight of the ice in March, shining like a faraway sword over the cold and absolute distance, drove him on. He had long passed censure. Had anyone known what he was doing and tried to dissuade him, he would have told him to go to hell, and resumed preparations with the confidence of someone taken up by a new religion.

For he had always believed in great deeds, in fairy tales, in echoing trumpet lands, in wonders and wondrous accomplishments. But even as a boy he had never considered that such things would fall to him. As a good city child he had known that these adventures were not necessary. But suddenly he was alone and the things which occurred to him were great warlike deeds. His energy and discipline were boundless, as full and overflowing as a lake in the mountains. Like the heroes of his youth, he would try to approach the high cord of ruby light and bend it to his will, until he could feel rolling thunder. The small things, the gentle things, the good things he loved, and the flow of love itself were dead for him and would always be, unless he could liberate them in a crucible of high drama.

It took him many months to think these things, and though they might not seem consistent, they were so for him, and he often spent hours alone on a sunny snow-covered meadow, his elbows on his knees, imagining great deeds in the mountains, as he stared at the massive needle of the Schreuderspitze, at the hint of rich lands beyond, and at the tiny village where he had taken up position opposite the mountain.

Toward the end of May he had been walking through Altenburg-St. Peter and seen his reflection in a store window—a storm had arisen suddenly and made the glass as silver-black as the clouds. He had not liked what he had seen. His face had become too hard and too lean. There was not enough gentleness. He feared immediately for the success of his venture if only because he knew well that unmitigated extremes are a great cause of failure. And he was tired of his painful regimen.

He bought a large Telefunken radio, in one fell swoop wiping out his funds for August and September. He felt as if he were paying for the privilege of music with portions of his life and body. But it was well worth it. When the storekeeper offered to deliver the heavy console, Wallich declined politely, picked up the cabinet himself, hoisted it on his back, and walked out of the store bent under it as in classic illustrations for physics textbooks throughout the industrialized world. He did not put it down once. The storekeeper summoned his associates and they bet and counterbet on whether Wallich "would" or "would not," as he moved slowly up the steep hill, up the steps, around the white switchbacks, onto a grassy slope, and then finally up the precipitous stairs to the balcony outside his room. "How can he have done that?" they asked. "He is a small man, and the radio must weigh at least thirty kilos." The storekeeper trotted out with a catalogue. "It weighs fifty-five kilograms!" he said. "Fifty-five kilograms!" And they wondered what had made Wallich so strong.

Once, Wallich had taken his little son (a tiny, skeptical, silent child who had a riotous giggle which could last for an hour) to see the inflation of a great gas dirigible. It had been a disappointment, for a dirigible is rigid and maintains always the same shape. He had expected to see the silver of its sides expand into ribbed cliffs which would float over them on the green field and amaze his son. Now that silver rising, the sail-like expansion, the great crescendo of a glimmering weightless mass, finally reached him alone in his room, too late but well received, when a Berlin station played the Beethoven Violin Concerto, its first five timpanic D's like grace before a feast. After those notes, the music lifted him, and he riveted his gaze on the dark shapes of the mountains, where a lightning storm raged. The radio crackled after each near or distant flash, but it was as if the music had been designed for it. Wallich looked at the yellow light within a softly glowing numbered panel. It flickered gently, and he could hear cracks and flashes in the music as he saw them delineated across darkness. They looked and sounded like the bent riverine limbs of dead trees hanging majestically over rocky outcrops, destined to fall, but enjoying their grand suspension nonetheless. The music traveled effortlessly on anarchic beams, passed high over the plains, passed high over the forests, seeding them plentifully, and came upon the Alps like waves which finally strike the shore after thousands of miles in open sea. It charged upward, mating with the electric storm, separating, and delivering.

To Wallich—alone in the mountains, surviving amid the dark massifs and clear air—came the closeted, nasal, cosmopolitan voice of the radio commentator. It was good to know that there was something other than the purity and magnificence of his mountains, that far to the north the balance reverted to less than moral catastrophe and death, and much stock was set in things of extraordinary inconsequence. Wallich could not help laughing when he thought of the formally dressed audience at the symphony, how they squirmed in their seats and heated the bottoms of their trousers and capes, how relieved and delighted they would be to step out into the cool evening and go to a restaurant. In the morning they would arise and take pleasure from the sweep of the drapes as sun danced by, from the gold rim around a white china cup. For them it was always too hot or too cold. But they certainly had their delights, about which sometimes he would think. How often he still dreamed, asleep or awake, of the smooth color plates opulating under his hands in tanks of developer and of the fresh film which smelled like bread and then was entombed in black cylinders to develop. How he longed sometimes for the precise machinery of his cameras. The very word *"Kamera"* was as dark and hollow as this night in the mountains when, reviewing the pleasures of faraway Berlin, he sat in perfect health and equanimity upon a wicker-weave seat in a bare white room. The only light was from the yellow dial, the sudden lightning flashes, and the faint blue of the sky beyond the hills. And all was quiet but for the music and the thunder and the static curling about the music like weak and lost memories which arise to harry even indomitable perfections.

A month before the ascent, he awaited arrival of a good climbing rope. He needed from a rope not strength to hold a fall but lightness and length for abseiling. His strategy was to climb with a short self-belay. No one would follow to retrieve his hardware and because it would not always be practical for him to do so himself, in what one of his books called "rhythmic recapitulation," he planned to carry a great deal of metal. If the metal and he reached the summit relatively intact, he could make short work of the descent, abandoning pitons as he abseiled downward.

He would descend in half a day that which had taken five days to climb. He pictured the abseiling, literally a flight down the mountain on the doubled cord of his long rope, and he thought that those hours speeding down the cliffs would be the finest of his life. If the weather were good he would come away from the Schreuderspitze having flown like an eagle.

On the day the rope was due, he went to the railroad station to meet the mail. It was a clear, perfect day. The light was so fine and rich that in its bath everyone felt wise, strong, and content. Wallich sat on the wooden boards of the wide platform, scanning the green meadows and fields for smoke and a coal engine, but the countryside was silent and the valley unmarred by the black woolly chain he sought. In the distance, toward France and Switzerland, a few cream-and-rose-colored clouds rode the horizon, immobile and high. On far mountainsides innumerable flowers showed in this long view as a slash, or as a patch of color not unlike one flower alone.

He had arrived early, for he had no watch. After some minutes a car drove up and from it emerged a young family. They rushed as if the train were waiting to depart, when down the long troughlike valley it was not even visible. There were two little girls, as beautiful as he had ever seen. The mother, too, was extraordinarily fine. The father was in his early thirties, and he wore gold-rimmed glasses. They seemed like a university family—people who knew how to live sensibly, taking pleasure from proper and beautiful things.

The little girl was no more than three. Sunburnt and rosy, she wore a dress that was shaped like a bell. She dashed about the platform so lightly and tentatively that it was as if Wallich were watching a tiny fish gravityless in a lighted aquarium. Her older sister stood quietly by the mother, who was illumined with consideration and pride for her children. It was apparent that she was overjoyed with the grace of her family. She seemed detached and preoccupied, but in just the right way. The littler girl said in a voice like a child's party horn, "Mummy, I want some peanuts!"

It was so ridiculous that this child should share the appetite of elephants that the mother smiled. "Peanuts will make you thirsty, Gretl. Wait until we get to Garmisch-Partenkirchen. Then we'll have lunch in the buffet."

"When will we get to Garmisch-Partenkirchen?"

"At two."

"Two?"

"Yes, at two."

"At two?"

"Gretl!"

The father looked alternately at the mountains and at his wife and children. He seemed confident and steadfast. In the distance black smoke appeared in thick billows. The father pointed at it. "There's our train," he said.

"Where?" asked Gretl, looking in the wrong direction. The father picked her up and turned her head with his hand, aiming her gaze down the shimmering valley. When she saw the train she started, and her eyes opened wide in pleasure.

"Ah . . . there it is," said the father. As the train pulled into the station the young girls were filled with excitement. Amid the noise they entered a compartment and were swallowed up in the steam. The train pulled out.

Wallich stood on the empty platform, unwrapping his rope. It was a rope, quite a nice rope, but it did not make him as happy as he had expected it would.

Little can match the silhouette of mountains by night. The great mass becomes far more mysterious when its face is darkened, when its sweeping lines roll steeply into valleys and peaks and long impossible ridges, when behind the void a concoction of rare silver leaps up to trace the hills—the pressure of collected starlight. That night, in conjunction with the long draughts of music he had become used to taking, he began to dream his dreams. They did not frighten him—he was beyond fear, too strong for fear, too played out. They did not even puzzle him, for they unfolded like the chapters in a brilliant nineteenth-century history. The rich explanations filled him for days afterward. He was amazed, and did not understand why these perfect dreams suddenly came to him. Surely they did not arise from within. He had never had the world so beautifully portrayed, had never seen as clearly and in such sure, gentle steps, had never risen so high and so smoothly in unfolding enlightenment, and he had seldom felt so well looked after. And yet, there was no visible presence. But it was as if the mountains and valleys were filled with loving families of which he was part.

Upon his return from the railroad platform, a storm had come suddenly from beyond the southern ridge. Though it had been warm and clear that day, he had seen from the sunny meadow before his house that a white storm billowed in higher and higher curves, pushing itself over the summits, finally to fall like an air avalanche on the valley. It snowed on the heights. The sun continued to strike the opaque frost and high clouds. It did not snow in the valley. The shock troops of the storm remained at the highest elevations, and only worn gray veterans came below—misty clouds and rain on cold wet air. Ragged clouds moved across the mountain-sides and meadows, watering the trees and sometimes catching in low places. Even so, the air in the meadow was still horn-clear.

In his room that night Wallich rocked back and forth on the wicker chair (it was not a rocker and he knew that using it as such was to number its days). That night's crackling infusion from Berlin, rising warmly from the faintly lit dial, was Beethoven's Eighth. The familiar commentator, nicknamed by Wallich Mälzels Metronom because of his even monotone, discoursed upon the background of the work.

"For many years," he said, "no one except Beethoven liked this symphony. Beethoven's opinions, however—even regarding his own creations—are equal at least to the collective pronouncements of all the musicologists and critics alive in the West during any hundred-year period. Conscious of the merits of the F-Major Symphony, he resolutely determined to redeem and . . . ah . . . the conductor has arrived. He steps to the podium. We begin."

Wallich retired that night in perfect tranquillity but awoke at five in the morning soaked in his own sweat, his fists clenched, a terrible pain in his chest, and breathing heavily as if he had been running. In the dim unattended light of the early-morning storm, he lay with eyes wide open. His pulse subsided, but he was like an animal in a cave, like a creature who has just escaped an organized hunt. It was as if the whole village had come armed and in search of him, had by some miracle decided that he was not in, and had left to comb the wet woods. He had been dreaming, and he saw his dream in its exact form. It was, first, an emerald. Cut into an octagon with two long sides, it was shaped rather like the plaque at the bottom of a painting. Events within this emerald were circular and never-ending.

They were in Munich. Air and sun were refined as on the station platform in the mountains. He was standing at a streetcar stop with his wife and his two daughters, though he knew perfectly well in the dream that these two daughters were meant to be his son. A streetcar arrived in complete silence. Clouds of people began to embark. They were dressed and muffled in heavy clothing of dull blue and gray. To his surprise, his wife moved toward the door of the streetcar and started to board, the daughters trailing after her. He could not see her feet, and she moved in a glide. Though at first paralyzed, as in the instant before a crash, he did manage to bound after her. As she stepped onto the first step and was about to grasp a chrome pole within the doorway, he made for her arm and caught it.

He pulled her back and spun her around, all very gently. Her presence before him was so intense that it was as if he were trapped under the weight of a fallen beam. She, too, wore a winter coat, but it was slim and perfectly tailored. He remembered the perfect geometry of the lapels. Not on earth had such angles ever been seen. The coat was a most intense liquid emerald color, a living light-infused green. She had always looked best in green, for her hair was like shining gold. He stood before her. He felt her delicacy. Her expression was neutral. "Where are you going?" he asked incredulously.

"I must go," she said.

He put his arms around her. She returned his embrace, and he said, "How can you leave me?"

"I have to," she answered.

And then she stepped onto the first step of the streetcar, and onto the second step, and she was enfolded into darkness.

He awoke, feeling like an invalid. His strength served for naught. He just stared at the clouds lifting higher and higher as the storm cleared. By nightfall the sky was black and gentle, though very cold. He kept thinking back to the emerald. It meant everything to him, for it was the first time he realized that they were really dead. Silence followed. Time passed thickly. He could not have imagined the sequence of dreams to follow, and what they would do to him.

He began to fear sleep, thinking that he would again be subjected to the lucidity of the emerald. But he had run that course and would never do so again except by perfect conscious recollection. The night after he had the dream of the emerald he fell asleep like someone letting go of a cliff edge after many minutes alone without help or hope. He slid into sleep, heart beating wildly. To his surprise, he found himself far indeed from the trolley tracks in Munich.

Instead, he was alone in the center of a sunlit snowfield, walking on the glacier in late June, bound for the summit of the Schreuderspitze: The mass of his equipment sat lightly upon him. He was well drilled in its use and positioning, in the subtleties of placement and rigging. The things he carried seemed part of him, as if he had quickly evolved into a new kind of animal suited for breathtaking travel in the steep heights.

His stride was light and long, like that of a man on the moon. He nearly floated, ever so slightly airborne, over the dazzling glacier. He leaped crevasses, sailing in slow motion against intense white and blue. He passed apple-fresh streams and opalescent melt pools of blue-green water as he progressed toward the Schreuderspitze. Its rocky horn was covered by nearly blue ice from which the wind blew a white corona in sines and cusps twirling about the sky.

Passing the bergschrund, he arrived at the first mass of rock. He turned to look back. There he saw the snowfield and the sun turning above it like a pinwheel, casting out a fog of golden light. He stood alone. The world had been reduced to the beauty of physics and the mystery of light. It had been rendered into a frozen state, a liquid state, a solid state, a gaseous state, mixtures, temperatures, and more varieties of light than fell on the speckled floor of a great cathedral. It was simple, and yet infinitely complex. The sun was warm. There was silence.

For several hours he climbed over great boulders and up a range of rocky escarpments. It grew more and more difficult, and he often had to lay in protection, driving a piton into a crack of the firm granite. His first piton was a surprise. It slowed halfway, and the ringing sound as he hammered grew higher in pitch. Finally, it would go in no farther. He had spent so much time in driving it that he thought it would be as steady as the Bank of England. But when he gave a gentle tug to test its hold, it came right out. This he thought extremely funny. He then remembered that he had either to drive it in all the way, to the eye, or to attach a sling along its shaft as near as possible to the rock. It was a question of avoiding leverage.

He bent carefully to his equipment sling, replaced the used piton, and took up a shorter one. The shorter piton went to its eye in five hammer strokes and he could do nothing to dislodge it. He clipped in and ascended a steep pitch, at the top of which he drove in two pitons, tied in to them, abseiled down to retrieve the first, and ascended quite easily to where he had left off. He made rapid progress over frightening pitches, places no one would dare go without assurance of a bolt in the rock and a line to the bolt—even if the bolt was just a small piece of metal driven in by dint of precariously balanced strength, arm, and Alpine hammer.

Within the sphere of utter concentration easily achieved during difficult ascents, his simple climbing evolved naturally into graceful technique, by which he went up completely vertical rock faces, suspended only by pitons and étriers. The different placements of which he had read and thought repeatedly were employed skillfully and with a proper sense of variety, though it was tempting to stay with one familiar pattern. Pounding metal into rock and hanging from his taut and colorful wires, he breathed hard, he concentrated, and he went up sheer walls.

At one point he came to the end of a subtle hairline crack in an otherwise smooth wall. The rock above was completely solid for a hundred feet. If he went down to the base of the crack he would be nowhere. The only thing to do was to make a swing traverse to a wall more amenable to climbing.

Anchoring two pitons into the rock as solidly as he could, he clipped an oval carabiner on the bottom piton, put a safety line on the top one, and lowered himself about sixty feet down the two ropes. Hanging perpendicular to the wall, he began to walk back and forth across the rock. He moved to and fro, faster and faster, until he was running. Finally he touched only in places and was swinging wildly like a pendulum. He feared that the piton to which he was anchored would not take the strain, and would pull out. But he kept swinging faster, until he gave one final push and, with a pathetic cry, went sailing over a drop which would have made a mountain goat swallow its heart. He caught an outcropping of rock on the other side, and pulled himself to it desperately. He hammered in, retrieved the ropes, glanced at the impassable wall, and began again to ascend.

As he approached great barricades of ice, he looked back. It gave him great pride and satisfaction to see the thousands of feet over which he had struggled. Much of the west counterfort was purely vertical. He could see now just how the glacier was riverine. He could see deep within the Tyrol and over the border to the Swiss lakes. Garmisch-Partenkirchen looked from here like a town on the board of a toy railroad or (if considered only two-dimensionally) like the cross-section of a kidney. Altenburg-St. Peter looked like a ladybug. The sun sent streamers of tan light through the valley, already three-quarters conquered by shadow, and the ice above took fire. Where the ice began, he came to a wide ledge and he stared upward at a sparkling ridge which looked like a great crystal spine. Inside, it was blue and cold.

He awoke, convinced that he had in fact climbed the counterfort. It was a strong feeling, as strong as the reality of the emerald. Sometimes dreams could be so real that they competed with the world, riding at even balance and calling for a decision. Sometimes, he imagined, when they are so real and so important, they easily tip the scale and the world buckles and dreams become real. Crossing the fragile barricades, one enters his dreams, thinking of his life as imagined.

He rejoiced at his bravery in climbing. It had been as real

as anything he had ever experienced. He felt the pain, the exhaustion, and the reward, as well as the danger. But he could not wait to return to the mountain and the ice. He longed for evening and the enveloping darkness, believing that he belonged resting under great folds of ice on the wall of the Schreuderspitze. He had no patience with his wicker chair, the bent wood of the windowsill, the clear glass in the window, the green-sided hills he saw curving through it, or his brightly colored equipment hanging from pegs on the white wall.

Two weeks before, on one of the eastward roads from Altenburg-St. Peter—no more than a dirt track—he had seen a child turn and take a well-worn path toward a wood, a meadow, and a stream by which stood a house and a barn. The child walked slowly upward into the forest, disappearing into the dark close, as if he had been taken up by vapor. Wallich had been too far away to hear footsteps, and the last thing he saw was the back of the boy's bright blue-and-white sweater. Returning at dusk, Wallich had expected to see warmly lit windows, and smoke issuing efficiently from the straight chimney. But there were no lights, and there was no smoke. He made his way through the trees and past the meadow only to come upon a small farmhouse with boarded windows and no-trespassing signs tacked on the doors.

It was unsettling when he saw the same child making his way across the upper meadow, a flash of blue and white in the near darkness. Wallich screamed out to him, but he did not hear, and kept walking as if he were deaf or in another world, and he went over the crest of the hill. Wallich ran up the hill. When he reached the top he saw only a wide empty field and not a trace of the boy.

Then in the darkness and purity of the meadows he began to feel that the world had many secrets, that they were shattering even to glimpse or sense, and that they were not necessarily unpleasant. In certain states of light he could see, he could begin to sense, things most miraculous indeed. Although it seemed self-serving, he concluded nonetheless, after a lifetime of adhering to the diffuse principles of a science he did not know, that there was life after death, that the dead rose into a mischievous world of pure light, that something most mysterious lay beyond the enfolding darkness, something wonderful.

This idea had taken hold, and he refined it. For example, listening to the Beethoven symphonies broadcast from Berlin, he began to think that they were like a ladder of mountains, that they surpassed themselves and rose higher and higher until at certain points they seemed to break the warp itself and cross into a heaven of light and the dead. There were signs everywhere of temporal diffusion and mystery. It was as if continents existed, new worlds lying just off the coast, invisible and redolent, waiting for the grasp of one man suddenly to substantiate and light them, changing everything. Perhaps great mountains hundreds of times higher than the Alps would arise in the sea or on the flatlands. They might be purple or gold and shining in many states of refraction and reflection, transparent in places as vast as countries. Someday someone would come back from this place, or someone would by accident discover and illumine its remarkable physics.

He believed that the boy he had seen nearly glowing in the half-darkness of the high meadow had been his son, and that the child had been teasing his father in a way only he could know, that the child had been asking him to follow. Possibly he had come upon great secrets on the other side, and knew that his father would join him soon enough and that then they would laugh about the world.

When he next fell asleep in the silence of a clear windless night in the valley, Wallich was like a man disappearing into the warp of darkness. He wanted to go there, to be taken as far as he could be taken. He was not unlike a sailor who sets sail in the teeth of a great storm, delighted by his own abandon.

Throwing off the last wraps of impure light, he found himself again in the ice world. The word was all-encompassing—*Eiswelt*. There above him the blue spire rocketed upward as far as the eye could see. He touched it with his hand. It was indeed as cold as ice. It was dense and hard, like glass ten feet thick. He had doubted its strength, but its solidity told that it would not flake away and allow him to drop endlessly, far from it.

On ice he found firm holds both with his feet and with his hands, and hardly needed the ice pitons and étriers. For he had crampons tied firmly to his boots, and could spike his toe points into the ice and stand comfortably on a vertical. He proceeded with a surety of footing he had never had on the streets of Munich. Each step bolted him down to the surface. And in each hand he carried an ice hammer with which he made swinging, cutting arcs that engaged the shining stainless-steel pick with the mirrorlike wall.

All the snow had blown away or had melted. There were no traps, no pitfalls, no ambiguities. He progressed toward the summit rapidly, climbing steep ice walls as if he had been going up a ladder. The air became purer and the light more direct. Looking out to right or left, or glancing sometimes over his shoulders, he saw that he was now truly in the world of mountains.

Above the few clouds he could see only equal peaks of ice, and the Schreuderspitze dropping away from him. It was not the world of rock. No longer could he make out individual features in the valley. Green had become a hazy dark blue appropriate to an ocean floor. Whole countries came into view. The landscape was a mass of winding glaciers and great mountains. At that height, all was separated and re-fined. Soft things vanished, and there remained only the white and the silver.

He did not reach the summit until dark. He did not see the stars because icy clouds covered the Schreuderspitze in a crystalline fog which flowed past, crackling and hissing. He was heartbroken to have come all the way to the summit and then be blinded by masses of clouds. Since he could not descend until light, he decided to stay firmly stationed until he could see clearly. Meanwhile, he lost patience and began to address a presence in the air—casually, not thinking it strange to do so, not thinking twice about talking to the void.

He awoke in his room in early morning, saying, "All these blinding clouds. Why all these blinding clouds?"

Though the air of the valley was as fresh as a flower, he detested it. He pulled the covers over his head and strove for unconsciousness, but he grew too hot and finally gave up, staring at the remnants of dawn light soaking about his room. The day brightened in the way that stage lights come up, suddenly brilliant upon a beam-washed platform. It was early June. He had lost track of the exact date, but he knew that sometime before he had crossed into June. He had lost them early in June. Two years had passed.

He packed his things. Though he had lived like a monk, much had accumulated, and this he put into suitcases, boxes, and bags. He packed his pens, paper, books, a chess set on which he sometimes played against an imaginary opponent named Herr Claub, the beautiful Swiss calendars upon which he had at one time been almost afraid to gaze, cooking equipment no more complex than a soldier's mess kit, his clothing, even the beautifully wrought climbing equipment, for, after all, he had another set, up there in the *Eiswelt*. Only his bedding remained unpacked. It was on the floor in the center of the room, where he slept. He put some banknotes in an envelope—the June rent—and tacked it to the doorpost. The room was empty, white, and it would have echoed had it been slightly larger. He would say something and then listen intently, his eyes flaring like those of a lunatic. He had not eaten in days, and was not disappointed that even the waking world began to seem like a dream.

He went to the pump. He had accustomed himself to bathing in streams so cold that they were too frightened to freeze. Clean and cleanly shaven, he returned to his room. He smelled the sweet pine scent he had brought back on his clothing after hundreds of trips through the woods and forests girdling the greater mountains. Even the bedding was snowy white. He opened the closet and caught a glimpse of himself in the mirror. He was dark from sun and wind; his hair shone; his face had thinned; his eyebrows were now gold and white. For several days he had had only cold pure water. Like soldiers who come from training toughened and healthy, he had about him the air of a small child. He noticed a certain wildness in the eye, and he lay on the hard floor, as was his habit, in perfect comfort. He thought nothing. He felt nothing. He wished nothing.

Time passed as if he could compress and cancel it. Early-evening darkness began to make the white walls blue. He

heard a crackling fire in the kitchen of the rooms next door,
and imagined the shadows dancing there. Then he slept,
departing.

On the mountain it was dreadfully cold. He huddled into
himself against the wet silver clouds, and yet he smiled,
happy to be once again on the summit. He thought of making
an igloo, but remembered that he hadn't an ice saw. The
wind began to build. If the storm continued, he would die. It
would whittle him into a brittle wire, and then he would snap.
The best he could do was to dig a trench with his ice
hammers. He lay in the trench and closed his sleeves and
hooded parka, drawing the shrouds tight. The wind came at
him more and more fiercely. One gust was so powerful that it
nearly lifted him out of the trench. He put in an ice piton, and
attached his harness. Still the wind rose. It was difficult to
breathe and nearly impossible to see. Any irregular surface
whistled. The eye of the ice piton became a great siren. The
zippers on his parka, the harness, the slings and equipment,
all gave off musical tones, so that it was as if he were in a
place with hundreds of tormented spirits.

The gray air fled past with breathtaking speed. Looking
away from the wind, he had the impression of being propelled upward at unimaginable speed. Walls of gray sped by
so fast that they glowed. He knew that if he were to look at
the wind he would have the sense of hurtling forward in
gravityless space.

And so he stared at the wind and its slowly pulsing gray
glow. He did not know for how many hours he held that
position. The rape of vision caused a host of delusions. He
felt great momentum. He traveled until, eardrums throbbing
with the sharpness of cold and wind, he was nearly dead,
white as a candle, hardly able to breathe.

Then the acceleration ceased and the wind slowed. When,
released from the great pressure, he fell back off the edge of
the trench, he realized for the first time that he had been
stretched tight on his line. He had never been so cold. But the
wind was dying and the clouds were no longer a corridor
through which he was propelled. They were, rather, a gentle
mist which did not know quite what to do with itself. How

would it dissipate? Would it rise to the stars, or would it fall in compression down into the valley below?

It fell; it fell all around him, downward like a lowering curtain. It fell in lines and stripes, always downward as if on signal, by command, in league with a directive force.

At first he saw just a star or two straight on high. But as the mist departed a flood of stars burst through. Roads of them led into infinity. Starry wheels sat in fiery white coronas. Near the horizon were the few separate gentle stars, shining out and turning clearly, as wide and round as planets. The air grew mild and warm. He bathed in it. He trembled. As the air became all clear and the mist drained away completely, he saw something which stunned him.

The Schreuderspitze was far higher than he had thought. It was hundreds of times higher than the mountains represented on the map he had seen in Munich. The Alps were to it not even foothills, not even rills. Below him was the purple earth, and all the great cities lit by sparkling lamps in their millions. It was a clear summer dawn and the weather was excellent, certainly June.

He did not know enough about other cities to make them out from the shapes they cast in light, but his eye seized quite easily upon Munich. He arose from his trench and unbuckled the harness, stepping a few paces higher on the rounded summit. There was Munich, shining and pulsing like a living thing, strung with lines of amber light—light which reverberated as if in crystals, light which played in many dimensions and moved about the course of the city, which was defined by darkness at its edge. He had come above time, above the world. The city of Munich existed before him with all its time compressed. As he watched, its history played out in repeating cycles. Nothing, not one movement, was lost from the crystal. The light of things danced and multiplied, again and again, and yet again. It was all there for him to claim. It was alive, and ever would be.

He knelt on one knee as in paintings he had seen of explorers claiming a coast of the New World. He dared close his eyes in the face of that miracle. He began to concentrate, to fashion according to will with the force of stilled time a

vision of those he had loved. In all their bright colors they
began to appear before him.

He awoke as if shot out of a cannon. He went from lying on
his back to a completely upright position in an instant, a flash,
during which he slammed the floorboards energetically with a
clenched fist and cursed the fact that he had returned from
such a world. But by the time he stood straight, he was
delighted to be doing so. He quickly dressed, packed his
bedding, and began to shuttle down to the station and back.
In three trips, his luggage was stacked on the platform.

He bought a ticket for Munich, where he had not been in
many, many long months. He hungered for it, for the city,
for the boats on the river, the goods in the shops, newspapers, the
pigeons in the square, trees, traffic, even Herr Franzen. So
much rushed into his mind that he hardly saw his train pull
in.

He helped the conductor load his luggage into the baggage
car, and he asked, "Will we change at Garmisch-Partenkirchen?"

(1981)

Richard Yates

━━━━━━━━━━━◆━━━━━━━━━━━

Richard Yates was born in 1926. His first major publication was in the short-lived Scribners series designed to introduce new fiction writers; Yates was featured in Short Story 1 *(1958). His first novel,* Revolutionary Road, *appeared in 1961, and established him as a writer of great skill and exemplary patience. Critical reception was very favorable; popular acclaim did not follow.*

Yates has gone on to publish novels like Disturbing the Peace *(1975) and* A Good School *(1978), the latter perhaps his best-known book. After an epigraph from F. Scott Fitzgerald—itself a literary statement of some significance—*A Good School *opens:*

> *As a young man, in upstate New York, my father studied to be a concert tenor. He had a fine, disciplined voice that combined great power with great tenderness; hearing him sing remains the best of my early memories.*

This is neither the fictive world of Donald Barthelme nor that of Jayne Anne Phillips. In his stories, as in his novels, Yates has remained on the traditional pathway where he began his career. He walks it faithfully, powerfully, and with dedicated skill.

OH, JOSEPH,
I'M SO TIRED

When Franklin D. Roosevelt was President-elect there must
have been sculptors all over America who wanted a chance to
model his head from life, but my mother had connections.
One of her closest friends and neighbors, in the Greenwich
Village courtyard where we lived, was an amiable man named
Howard Whitman who had recently lost his job as a reporter
on the *New York Post*. And one of Howard's former colleagues from the *Post* was now employed in the press office
of Roosevelt's New York headquarters. That would make it
easy for her to get in—or, as she said, to get an entrée—and
she was confident she could take it from there. She was
confident about everything she did in those days, but it never
quite disguised a terrible need for support and approval on
every side.

She wasn't a very good sculptor. She had been working at
it for only three years, since breaking up her marriage to my
father, and there was still something stiff and amateurish
about her pieces. Before the Roosevelt project her specialty
had been "garden figures"—a life-size little boy whose legs
turned into the legs of a goat at the knees and another who
knelt among ferns to play the pipes of Pan; little girls who
trailed chains of daisies from their upraised arms or walked
beside a spread-winged goose. These fanciful children, in
plaster painted green to simulate weathered bronze, were
arranged on homemade wooden pedestals to loom around her
studio and to leave a cleared space in the middle for the
modeling stand that held whatever she was working on in
clay.

Her idea was that any number of rich people, all of them
gracious and aristocratic, would soon discover her: they would
want her sculpture to decorate their landscaped gardens, and
they would want to make her their friend for life. In the

meantime, a little nationwide publicity as the first woman sculptor to "do" the President-elect certainly wouldn't hurt her career.

And, if nothing else, she had a good studio. It was, in fact, the best of all the studios she would have in the rest of her life. There were six or eight old houses facing our side of the courtyard, with their backs to Bedford Street, and ours was probably the showplace of the row because the front room on its ground floor was two stories high. You went down a broad set of brick steps to the tall front windows and the front door; then you were in the high, wide, light-flooded studio. It was big enough to serve as a living room too, and so along with the green garden children it contained all the living-room furniture from the house we'd lived in with my father in the suburban town of Hastings-on-Hudson, where I was born. A second-floor balcony ran along the far end of the studio, with two small bedrooms and a tiny bathroom tucked away upstairs; beneath that, where the ground floor continued through to the Bedford Street side, lay the only part of the apartment that might let you know we didn't have much money. The ceiling was very low and it was always dark in there; the small windows looked out underneath an iron sidewalk grating, and the bottom of that street cavity was thick with strewn garbage. Our roach-infested kitchen was barely big enough for a stove and sink that were never clean, and for a brown wooden icebox with its dark, ever-melting block of ice; the rest of that area was our dining room, and not even the amplitude of the old Hastings dining-room table could brighten it. But our Majestic radio was in there too, and that made it a cozy place for my sister Edith and me: we liked the children's programs that came on in the late afternoons.

We had just turned off the radio one day when we went out into the studio and found our mother discussing the Roosevelt project with Howard Whitman. It was the first we'd heard of it, and we must have interrupted her with too many questions because she said "Edith? Billy? That's enough, now. I'll tell you all about this later. Run out in the garden and play."

She always called the courtyard "the garden," though nothing grew there except a few stunted city trees and a patch of grass that never had a chance to spread. Mostly it was bald earth, interrupted here and there by brick paving, lightly powdered with soot and scattered with the droppings of dogs and cats. It may have been six or eight houses long, but it was only two houses wide, which gave it a hemmed-in, cheerless look; its only point of interest was a dilapidated marble fountain, not much bigger than a birdbath, which stood near our house. The original idea of the fountain was that water would drip evenly from around the rim of its upper tier and tinkle into its lower basin, but age had unsettled it; the water spilled in a single ropy stream from the only inch of the upper tier's rim that stayed clean. The lower basin was deep enough to soak your feet in on a hot day, but there wasn't much pleasure in that because the underwater part of the marble was coated with brown scum.

My sister and I found things to do in the courtyard every day, for all of the two years we lived there, but that was only because Edith was an imaginative child. She was eleven at the time of the Roosevelt project, and I was seven.

"Daddy?" she asked in our father's office uptown one afternoon. "Have you heard Mommy's doing a head of President Roosevelt?"

"Oh?" He was rummaging in his desk, looking for something he'd said we might like.

"She's going to take his measurements and stuff here in New York," Edith said, "and then after the Inauguration, when the sculpture's done, she's going to take it to Washington and present it to him in the White House." Edith often told one of our parents about the other's more virtuous activities; it was part of her long, hopeless effort to bring them back together. Many years later she told me she thought she had never recovered, and never would, from the shock of their breakup: she said Hastings-on-Hudson remained the happiest time of her life, and that made me envious because I could scarcely remember it at all.

"Well," my father said. "That's really something, isn't it." Then he found what he'd been looking for in the desk and said, "Here we go; what do you think of these?" They were two fragile perforated sheets of what looked like postage stamps, each stamp bearing the insignia of an electric light bulb in vivid white against a yellow background, and the words "More light."

My father's office was one of many small cubicles on the twenty-third floor of the General Electric building. He was an assistant regional sales manager in what was then called the Mazda Lamp Division—a modest job, but good enough to have allowed him to rent into a town like Hastings-on-Hudson in better times—and these "More light" stamps were souvenirs of a recent sales convention. We told him the stamps were neat—and they were—but expressed some doubt as to what we might do with them.

"Oh, they're just for decoration," he said. "I thought you could paste them into your schoolbooks, or—you know—whatever you want. Ready to go?" And he carefully folded the sheets of stamps and put them in his inside pocket for safekeeping on the way home.

Between the subway exit and the courtyard, somewhere in the West Village, we always walked past a vacant lot where men stood huddled around weak fires built of broken fruit crates and trash, some of them warming tin cans of food held by coat-hanger wire over the flames. "Don't stare," my father had said the first time. "All those men are out of work, and they're hungry."

"Daddy?" Edith inquired. "Do you think Roosevelt's good?"

"Sure I do."

"Do you think all the Democrats are good?"

"Well, most of 'em, sure."

Much later I would learn that my father had participated in local Democratic Party politics for years. He had served some of his political friends—men my mother described as dreadful little Irish people from Tammany Hall—by helping them to establish Mazda Lamp distributorships in various parts of the city. And he loved their social gatherings, at which he was always asked to sing.

"Well, of course, you're too young to remember Daddy's singing," Edith said to me once after his death in 1942.

"No, I'm not; I remember."

"But I mean really remember," she said. "He had the

most beautiful tenor voice I've ever heard. Remember 'Danny Boy'?''

"Sure."

"Ah, God, that was something," she said, closing her eyes. "That was really—that was really something."

When we got back to the courtyard that afternoon, and back into the studio, Edith and I watched our parents say hello to each other. We always watched that closely, hoping they might drift into conversation and sit down together and find things to laugh about, but they never did. And it was even less likely than usual that day because my mother had a guest—a woman named Sloane Cabot who was her best friend in the courtyard, and who greeted my father with a little rush of false, flirtatious enthusiasm.

"How've you been, Sloane?" he said. Then he turned back to his former wife and said "Helen? I hear you're planning to make a bust of Roosevelt."

"Well, not a bust," she said. "A head. I think it'll be more effective if I cut it off at the neck."

"Well, good. That's fine. Good luck with it. Okay, then." He gave his whole attention to Edith and me. "Okay. See you soon. How about a hug?"

And those hugs of his, the climax of his visitation rights, were unforgettable. One at a time we would be swept up and pressed hard into the smells of linen and whiskey and tobacco; the warm rasp of his jaw would graze one cheek and there would be a quick moist kiss near the ear; then he'd let us go.

He was almost all the way out of the courtyard, almost out in the street, when Edith and I went racing after him.

"Daddy! Daddy! You forgot the stamps!"

He stopped and turned around, and that was when we saw he was crying. He tried to hide it—he put his face nearly into his armpit as if that might help him search his inside pocket— but there is no way to disguise the awful bloat and pucker of a face in tears.

"Here," he said. "Here you go." And he gave us the least convincing smile I had ever seen. It would be good to report that we stayed and talked to him—that we hugged him again—

but we were too embarrassed for that. We took the stamps and ran home without looking back.

"Oh, aren't you excited, Helen?" Sloane Cabot was saying. "To be meeting him, and talking to him and everything, in front of all those reporters?"

"Well, of course," my mother said, "but the important thing is to get the measurements right. I hope there won't be a lot of photographers and silly interruptions."

Sloane Cabot was some years younger than my mother, and strikingly pretty in a style often portrayed in what I think are called Art Deco illustrations of that period: straight dark bangs, big eyes, and a big mouth. She too was a divorced mother, though her former husband had vanished long ago and was referred to only as "that bastard" or "that cowardly son of a bitch." Her only child was a boy of Edith's age named John, whom Edith and I liked enormously.

The two women had met within days of our moving into the courtyard, and their friendship was sealed when my mother solved the problem of John's schooling. She knew a Hastings-on-Hudson family who would appreciate the money earned from taking in a boarder, so John went up there to live and go to school, and came home only on weekends. The arrangement cost more than Sloane could comfortably afford, but she managed to make ends meet and was forever grateful.

Sloane worked in the Wall Street district as a private secretary. She talked a lot about how she hated her job and her boss, but the good part was that her boss was often out of town for extended periods: that gave her time to use the office typewriter in pursuit of her life's ambition, which was to write scripts for the radio.

She once confided to my mother that she'd made up both of her names: "Sloane" because it sounded masculine, the kind of name a woman alone might need for making her way in the world, and "Cabot" because—well, because it had a touch of class. Was there anything wrong with that?

"Oh, Helen," she said. "This is going to be wonderful for you. If you get the publicity—if the papers pick it up, and the newsreels—you'll be one of the most interesting personalities in America."

Five or six people were gathered in the studio on the day my mother came home from her first visit with the President-elect.

"Will somebody get me a drink?" she asked, looking around in mock helplessness. "Then I'll tell you all about it."

And with the drink in her hand, with her eyes as wide as a child's, she told us how a door had opened and two big men had brought him in.

"Big men," she insisted. "Young, strong men, holding him up under the arms, and you could see how they were straining. Then you saw this *foot* come out, with these awful metal braces on the shoe, and then the *other* foot. And he was sweating, and he was panting for breath, and his face was—I don't know—all bright and tense and horrible." She shuddered.

"Well," Howard Whitman said, looking uneasy, "he can't help being crippled, Helen."

"Howard," she said impatiently, "I'm only trying to tell you how *ugly* it was." And that seemed to carry a certain weight. If she was an authority on beauty—on how a little boy might kneel among ferns to play the pipes of Pan, for example—then surely she had earned her credentials as an authority on ugliness.

"*Any*way," she went on, "they got him into a chair, and he wiped most of the sweat off his face with a handkerchief—he was still out of breath—and after a while he started talking to some of the other men there; I couldn't follow that part of it. Then finally he turned to me with this smile of his. Honestly, I don't know if I can describe that smile. It isn't something you can see in the newsreels; you have to be there. His eyes don't change at all, but the corners of his mouth go up as if they're being pulled by puppet strings. It's a frightening smile. It makes you think: This could be a dangerous man. This could be an evil man. Well anyway, we started talking, and I spoke right up to him. I said 'I didn't vote for you, Mr. President.' I said 'I'm a good Republican and I voted for President Hoover.' He said 'Why are you here, then?' or something like that, and I said 'Because you have a very interesting head.' So he gave me the smile again and he said

'What's interesting about it?' And I said 'I like the bumps on it.' "

By then she must have assumed that every reporter in the room was writing in his notebook, while the photographers got their flashbulbs ready; tomorrow's papers might easily read:

GAL SCULPTOR TWITS FDR
ABOUT "BUMPS" ON HEAD

At the end of her preliminary chat with him she got down to business, which was to measure different parts of his head with her calipers. I knew how that felt: the cold, trembling points of those clay-encrusted calipers had tickled and poked me all over during the times I'd served as model for her fey little woodland boys.

But not a single flashbulb went off while she took and the recorded the measurements, and nobody asked her any questions; after a few nervous words of thanks and good-bye she was out in the corridor again among all the hopeless, craning people who couldn't get in. It must have been a bad disappointment, and I imagine she tried to make up for it by planning the triumphant way she'd tell us about it when she got home.

"Helen?" Howard Whitman inquired, after most of the other visitors had gone. "Why'd you tell him you didn't vote for him?"

"Well, because it's true. I *am* a good Republican; you know that."

She was a storekeeper's daughter from a small town in Ohio; she had probably grown up hearing the phrase "good Republican" as an index of respectability and clean clothes. And maybe she had come to relax her standards of respectability, maybe she didn't even care much about clean clothes anymore, but "good Republican" was worth clinging to. It would be helpful when she met the customers for her garden figures, the people whose low, courteous voices would welcome her into their lives and who would almost certainly turn out to be Republicans too.

"I believe in the aristocracy!" she often cried, trying to make herself heard above the rumble of voices when her guests were discussing communism, and they seldom paid her any attention. They liked her well enough: she gave parties with plenty of liquor, and she was an agreeable hostess if only because of her touching eagerness to please; but in any talk of politics she was like a shrill, exasperating child. She believed in the aristocracy.

She believed in God, too, or at least in the ceremony of St. Luke's Episcopal Church, which she attended once or twice a year. And she believed in Eric Nicholson, the handsome middle-aged Englishman who was her lover. He had something to do with the American end of a British chain of foundries: his company cast ornamental objects into bronze and lead. The cupolas of college and high-school buildings all over the East, the lead-casement windows for Tudor-style homes in places like Scarsdale and Bronxville—these were some of the things Eric Nicholson's firm had accomplished. He was always self-deprecating about his business, but ruddy and glowing with its success.

My mother had met him the year before, when she'd sought help in having one of her garden figures cast into bronze, to be "placed on consignment" with some garden-sculpture gallery from which it would never be sold. Eric Nicholson had persuaded her that lead would be almost as nice as bronze and much cheaper; then he'd asked her out to dinner, and that evening changed our lives.

Mr. Nicholson rarely spoke to my sister or me, and I think we were both frightened of him, but he overwhelmed us with gifts. At first they were mostly books—a volume of cartoons from *Punch,* a partial set of Dickens, a book called *England in Tudor Times* containing tissue-covered color plates that Edith liked. But in the summer of 1933, when our father arranged for us to spend two weeks with our mother at a small lake in New Jersey, Mr. Nicholson's gifts became a cornucopia of sporting goods. He gave Edith a steel fishing rod with a reel so intricate that none of us could have figured it out even if we'd known how to fish, a wicker creel for carrying the fish she would never catch, and a sheathed hunting knife to be worn at her waist. He gave me a short axe whose head was encased in a leather holster and strapped to my belt—I guess this was for cutting firewood to cook the fish—and a cumbersome net with a handle that hung from an elastic shoulder strap, in case I should be called upon to wade in and help Edith land a tricky one. There was nothing to do in that New Jersey village except take walks, or what my mother called good hikes; and every day, as we plodded out through the insect-humming weeds in the sun, we wore our full regalia of useless equipment.

That same summer Mr. Nicholson gave me a three-year subscription to *Field and Stream,* and I think that impenetrable magazine was the least appropriate of all his gifts because it kept coming in the mail for such a long, long time after everything else had changed for us: after we'd moved out of New York to Scarsdale, where Mr. Nicholson had found a house with a low rent, and after he had abandoned my mother in that house—with no warning—to return to England and to the wife from whom he'd never really been divorced.

But all that came later; I want to go back to the time between Franklin D. Roosevelt's election and his Inauguration, when his head was slowly taking shape on my mother's modeling stand.

Her original plan had been to make it life-size, or larger than life-size, but Mr. Nicholson urged her to scale it down for economy in the casting, and so she made it only six or seven inches high. He persuaded her too, for the second time since he'd known her, that lead would be almost as nice as bronze.

She had always said she didn't mind at all if Edith and I watched her work, but we had never much wanted to; now it was a little more interesting because we could watch her sift through many photographs of Roosevelt cut from newspapers until she found one that would help her execute a subtle plane of cheek or brow.

But most of our day was taken up with school. John Cabot might go to school in Hastings-on-Hudson, for which Edith would always yearn, but we had what even Edith admitted was the next best thing: we went to school in our bedroom.

During the previous year my mother had enrolled us in the public school down the street, but she'd begun to regret it when we came home with lice in our hair. Then one day Edith came home accused of having stolen a boy's coat, and that was too much. She withdrew us both, in defiance of the city truant officer, and pleaded with my father to help her meet the cost of a private school. He refused. The rent she paid and the bills she ran up were already taxing him far beyond the terms of the divorce agreement; he was in debt; surely she must realize he was lucky even to have a job. Would she ever learn to be reasonable?

It was Howard Whitman who broke the deadlock. He knew of an inexpensive, fully accredited mail-order service called The Calvert School, intended mainly for the homes of children who were invalids. The Calvert School furnished weekly supplies of books and materials and study plans; all she would need was someone in the house to administer the program and to serve as a tutor. And someone like Bart Kampen would be ideal for the job.

"The skinny fellow?" she asked. "The Jewish boy from Holland or wherever it is?"

"He's very well educated, Helen," Howard told her. "And he speaks fluent English, and he'd be very conscientious. And he could certainly use the money."

We were delighted to learn that Bart Kampen would be our tutor. With the exception of Howard himself, Bart was probably our favorite among the adults around the courtyard. He was twenty-eight or so, young enough so that his ears could still turn red when he was teased by children; we had found that out in teasing him once or twice about such matters as that his socks didn't match. He was tall and very thin and seemed always to look startled except when he was comforted enough to smile. He was a violinist, a Dutch Jew who had emigrated the year before in the hope of joining a symphony orchestra, and eventually of launching a concert career. But the symphonies weren't hiring then, nor were lesser orchestras, so Bart had gone without work for a long time. He lived alone in a room on Seventh Avenue, not far from the courtyard, and people who liked him used to worry that he might not have enough to eat. He owned two suits, both cut in a way that must have been stylish in the Netherlands at the time: stiff, heavily padded shoulders and a nipped-in waist; they would probably have looked better on someone with a little more meat on his bones. In shirtsleeves, with the cuffs rolled back, his hairy wrists and forearms looked even more fragile than you might have expected, but his long hands were shapely and strong enough to suggest authority on the violin.

"I'll leave it entirely up to you, Bart," my mother said when he asked if she had any instructions for our tutoring. "I know you'll do wonders with them."

A small table was moved into our bedroom, under the window, and three chairs placed around it. Bart sat in the middle so that he could divide his time equally between Edith and me. Big, clean, heavy brown envelopes arrived in the mail from The Calvert School once a week, and when Bart slid their fascinating contents onto the table it was like settling down to begin a game.

Edith was in the fifth grade that year—her part of the table was given over to incomprehensible talk about English and History and Social Studies—and I was in the first. I spent my mornings asking Bart to help me puzzle out the very opening moves of an education.

"Take your time, Billy," he would say. "Don't get impatient with this. Once you have it you'll see how easy it is, and then you'll be ready for the next thing."

At eleven each morning we would take a break. We'd go downstairs and out to the part of the courtyard that had a little grass. Bart would carefully lay his folded coat on the sidelines, turn back his shirt cuffs, and present himself as ready to give what he called airplane rides. Taking us one at a time, he would grasp one wrist and one ankle; then he'd whirl us off our feet and around and around, with himself as the pivot, until the courtyard and the buildings and the city and the world were lost in the dizzying blur of our flight.

After the airplane rides we would hurry down the steps into the studio, where we'd usually find that my mother had set out a tray bearing three tall glasses of cold Ovaltine, sometimes with cookies on the side and sometimes not. I once overheard her telling Sloane Cabot she thought the Ovaltine must be Bart's first nourishment of the day—and I think she was probably right, if only because of the way his hand would tremble in reaching for his glass. Sometimes she'd forget to prepare the tray and we'd crowd into the kitchen and fix it ourselves; I can never see a jar of Ovaltine on a grocery shelf without remembering those times. Then it was back upstairs to school again. And during that year, by coaxing and prodding and telling me not to get impatient, Bart Kampen taught me to read.

It was an excellent opportunity for showing off. I would pull books down from my mother's shelves—mostly books that were the gifts of Mr. Nicholson—and try to impress her by reading mangled sentences aloud.

"That's wonderful, dear," she would say. "You've really learned to read, haven't you."

Soon a white and yellow "More light" stamp was affixed to every page of my Calvert First Grade Reader, proving I had mastered it, and others were accumulating at a slower rate in my arithmetic workbook. Still other stamps were fastened to the wall beside my place at the school table, arranged in a proud little white and yellow thumb-smudged column that rose as high as I could reach.

"You shouldn't have put your stamps on the wall," Edith said.

"Why?"

"Well, because they'll be hard to take off."

"Who's going to take them off?"

That small room of ours, with its double function of sleep and learning, stands more clearly in my memory than any other part of our home. Someone should probably have told my mother that a girl and boy of our ages ought to have separate rooms, but that never occurred to me until much later. Our cots were set foot-to-foot against the wall, leaving just enough space to pass alongside them to the school table, and we had some good conversations as we lay waiting for sleep at night. The one I remember best was the time Edith told me about the sound of the city.

"I don't mean just the loud noises," she said, "like the siren going by just now, or those car doors slamming, or all the laughing and shouting down the street; that's just close-up stuff. I'm talking about something else. Because you see there are millions and millions of people in New York—more people than you can possibly imagine, ever—and most of them are doing something that makes a sound. Maybe talk-

ing, or playing the radio, maybe closing doors, maybe putting
their forks down on their plates if they're having dinner, or
dropping their shoes if they're going to bed—and because
there are so many of them, all those little sounds add up and
come together in a kind of hum. But it's so faint—so very,
very faint—that you can't hear it unless you listen very
carefully for a long time."

"Can you hear it?" I asked her.

"Sometimes. I listen every night, but I can only hear it
sometimes. Other times I fall asleep. Let's be quiet now, and
just listen. See if you can hear it, Billy."

And I tried hard, closing my eyes as if that would help,
opening my mouth to minimize the sound of my breathing,
but in the end I had to tell her I'd failed. "How about you?"
I asked.

"Oh, I heard it," she said. "Just for a few seconds, but I
heard it. You'll hear it too, if you keep trying. And it's worth
waiting for. When you hear it, you're hearing the whole city
of New York."

The high point of our week was Friday afternoon, when
John Cabot came home from Hastings. He exuded health and
normality; he brought fresh suburban air into our bohemian
lives. He even transformed his mother's small apartment,
while he was there, into an enviable place of rest between
vigorous encounters with the world. He subscribed to both
Boy's Life and *Open Road for Boys,* and these seemed to me
to be wonderful things to have in your house, if only for the
illustrations. John dressed in the same heroic way as the boys
shown in those magazines, corduroy knickers with ribbed
stockings pulled taut over his muscular calves. He talked a lot
about the Hastings high-school football team, for which he
planned to try out as soon as he was old enough, and about
Hastings friends whose names and personalities grew almost
as familiar to us as if they were friends of our own. He taught
us invigorating new ways to speak, like saying "What's the
diff?" instead of "What's the difference?" And he was better
even than Edith at finding new things to do in the courtyard.

You could buy goldfish for ten or fifteen cents apiece in
Woolworth's then, and one day we brought home three of
them to keep in the fountain. We sprinkled the water with

more Woolworth's granulated fish food than they could possibly need, and we named them after ourselves: "John," "Edith," and "Billy." For a week or two Edith and I would run to the fountain every morning, before Bart came for school, to make sure they were still alive and to see if they had enough food, and to watch them.

"Have you noticed how much bigger Billy's getting?" Edith asked me. "He's huge. He's almost as big as John and Edith now. He'll probably be bigger than both of them."

Then one weekend when John was home he called our attention to how quickly the fish could turn and move. "They have better reflexes than humans," he explained. "When they see a shadow in the water, or anything that looks like danger, they get away faster than you can blink. Watch." And he sank one hand into the water to make a grab for the fish named Edith, but she evaded him and fled. "See that?" he asked. "How's that for speed. Know something? I bet you could shoot an arrow in there, and they'd get away in time. Wait." To prove his point he ran to his mother's apartment and came back with the handsome bow and arrow he had made at summer camp (going to camp every summer was another admirable thing about John); then he knelt at the rim of the fountain like the picture of an archer, his bow steady in one strong hand and the feathered end of the arrow tight against the bowstring in the other. He was taking aim at the fish named Billy. "Now, the velocity of this arrow," he said in a voice weakened by his effort, "is probably more than a car going eighty miles an hour. It's probably more like an airplane, or maybe even more than that. Okay; watch."

The fish named Billy was suddenly floating dead on the surface, on his side, impaled a quarter of the way up the arrow with parts of his pink guts dribbled along the shaft.

I was too old to cry, but something had to be done about the shock and rage and grief that filled me as I ran from the fountain, heading blindly for home, and half-way there I came upon my mother. She stood looking very clean, wearing a new coat and dress I'd never seen before and fastened to the arm of Mr. Nicholson. They were either just going out or just coming in—I didn't care which—and Mr. Nicholson frowned at me (he had told me more than once that boys of

my age went to boarding school in England), but I didn't care
about that either. I bent my head into her waist and didn't
stop crying until long after I'd felt her hands stroking my
back, until after she had assured me that goldfish didn't cost
much and I'd have another one soon, and that John was sorry
for the thoughtless thing he'd done. I had discovered, or
rediscovered, that crying is a pleasure—that it can be a
pleasure beyond all reckoning if your head is pressed in your
mother's waist and her hands are on your back, and if she
happens to be wearing clean clothes.

There were other pleasures. We had a good Christmas Eve
in our house that year, or at least it was good at first. My
father was there, which obliged Mr. Nicholson to stay away,
and it was nice to see how relaxed he was among my mother's friends. He was shy, but they seemed to like him. He got
along especially well with Bart Kampen.

Howard Whitman's daughter Molly, a sweet-natured girl of
about my age, had come in from Tarrytown to spend the
holidays with him, and there were several other children
whom we knew but rarely saw. John looked very mature that
night in a dark coat and tie, plainly aware of his social
responsibilities as the oldest boy.

After a while, with no plan, the party drifted back into the
dining-room area and staged an impromptu vaudeville. Howard started it: he brought the tall stool from my mother's
modeling stand and sat his daughter on it, facing the audience. He folded back the opening of a brown paper bag two
or three times and fitted it onto her head; then he took off his
suit coat and draped it around her backwards, up to the chin;
he went behind her, crouched out of sight, and worked his
hands through the coatsleeves so that when they emerged they
appeared to be hers. And the sight of a smiling little girl in a
paper-bag hat, waving and gesturing with huge, expressive
hands, was enough to make everyone laugh. The big hands
wiped her eyes and stroked her chin and pushed her hair
behind her ears; then they elaborately thumbed her nose at us.

Next came Sloane Cabot. She sat very straight on the stool
with her heels hooked over the rungs in such a way as to
show her good legs to their best advantage, but her first act
didn't go over.

"Well," she began, "I was at work today—you know my office is on the fortieth floor—when I happened to glance up from my typewriter and saw this big old man sort of crouched on the ledge outside the window, with a white beard and a funny red suit. So I ran to the window and opened it and said 'Are you all right?' Well, it was Santa Claus, and he said 'Of course I'm all right; I'm used to high places. But listen, miss: can you direct me to number seventy-five Bedford Street?' "

There was more, but our embarrassed looks must have told her we knew we were being condescended to; as soon as she'd found a way to finish it she did so quickly. Then, after a thoughtful pause, she tried something else that turned out to be much better.

"Have you children ever heard the story of the first Christmas?" she asked. "When Jesus was born?" And she began to tell it in the kind of hushed, dramatic voice she must have hoped might be used by the narrators of her more serious radio plays.

". . . And there were still many miles to go before they reached Bethlehem," she said, "and it was a cold night. Now, Mary knew she would very soon have a baby. She even knew, because an angel had told her, that her baby might one day be the saviour of all mankind. But she was only a young girl"—here Sloane's eyes glistened, as if they might be filling with tears—"and the traveling had exhausted her. She was bruised by the jolting gait of the donkey and she ached all over, and she thought they'd never, ever get there, and all she could say was 'Oh, Joseph, I'm so tired.' "

The story went on through the rejection at the inn, and the birth in the stable, and the manger, and the animals, and the arrival of the three kings; when it was over we clapped a long time because Sloane had told it so well.

"Daddy?" Edith asked. "Will you sing for us?"

"Oh, well, thanks, honey," he said, "but no; I really need a piano for that. Thanks anyway."

The final performer of the evening was Bart Kampen, persuaded by popular demand to go home and get his violin. There was no surprise in discovering that he played like a professional, like something you might easily hear on the radio; the enjoyment came from watching how his thin face

frowned over the chin rest, empty of all emotion except
concern that the sound be right. We were proud of him.

Some time after my father left a good many other adults
began to arrive, most of them strangers to me, looking as
though they'd already been to several other parties that night.
It was very late, or rather very early Christmas morning,
when I looked into the kitchen and saw Sloane standing close
to a bald man I didn't know. He held a trembling drink in one
hand and slowly massaged her shoulder with the other; she
seemed to be shrinking back against the old wooden icebox.
Sloane had a way of smiling that allowed little wisps of
cigarette smoke to escape from between her almost-closed
lips while she looked you up and down, and she was doing
that. Then the man put his drink on top of the icebox and
took her in his arms, and I couldn't see her face anymore.

Another man, in a rumpled brown suit, lay unconscious on
the dining-room floor. I walked around him and went into the
studio, where a good-looking young woman stood weeping
wretchedly and three men kept getting in each other's way as
they tried to comfort her. Then I saw that one of the men was
Bart, and I watched while he outlasted the other two and
turned the girl away toward the door. He put his arm around
her and she nestled her head in his shoulder; that was how
they left the house.

Edith looked jaded in her wrinkled party dress. She was
reclining in our old Hastings-on-Hudson easy chair with her
head tipped back and her legs flung out over both the chair's
arms, and John sat cross-legged on the floor near one of her
dangling feet. They seemed to have been talking about something that didn't interest either of them much, and the talk
petered out altogether when I sat on the floor to join them.

"Billy," she said, "do you realize what time it is?"

"What's the diff?" I said.

"You should've been in bed hours ago. Come on. Let's go
up."

"I don't feel like it."

"Well," she said, "I'm going up, anyway," and she got
laboriously out of the chair and walked away into the crowd.

John turned to me and narrowed his eyes unpleasantly.

"Know something?" he said. "When she was in the chair that way I could see everything."

"Huh?"

"I could see everything. I could see the crack, and the hair. She's beginning to get hair."

I had observed these features of my sister many times—in the bathtub, or when she was changing her clothes—and hadn't found them especially remarkable; even so, I understood at once how remarkable they must have been for him. If only he had smiled in a bashful way we might have laughed together like a couple of regular fellows out of *Open Road for Boys,* but his face was still set in that disdainful look.

"I kept looking and looking," he said, "and I had to keep her talking so she wouldn't catch on, but I was doing fine until you had to come over and ruin it."

Was I supposed to apologize? That didn't seem right, but nothing else seemed right either. All I did was look at the floor.

When I finally got to bed there was scarcely time for trying to hear the elusive sound of the city—I had found that a good way to keep from thinking of anything else—when my mother came blundering in. She'd had too much to drink and wanted to lie down, but instead of going to her own room she got into bed with me. "Oh," she said. "Oh, my boy. Oh, my boy." It was a narrow cot and there was no way to make room for her; then suddenly she retched, bolted to her feet, and ran for the bathroom, where I heard her vomiting. And when I moved over into the part of the bed she had occupied my face recoiled quickly, but not quite in time, from the slick mouthful of puke she had left on her side of the pillow.

For a month or so that winter we didn't see much of Sloane because she said she was "working on something big. Something really big." When it was finished she brought it to the studio, looking tired but prettier than ever, and shyly asked if she could read it aloud.

"Wonderful," my mother said. "What's it about?"

"That's the best part. It's about us. All of us. Listen."

Bart had gone for the day and Edith was out in the courtyard by herself—she often played by herself—so there was nobody for an audience but my mother and me. We sat on the sofa and Sloane arranged herself on the tall stool, just as she'd done for telling the Bethlehem story.

"There is an enchanted courtyard in Greenwich Village," she read. "It's only a narrow patch of brick and green among the irregular shapes of very old houses, but what makes it enchanted is that the people who live in it, or near it, have come to form an enchanted circle of friends.

"None of them have enough money and some are quite poor, but they believe in the future; they believe in each other, and in themselves.

"There is Howard, once a top reporter on a metropolitan daily newspaper. Everyone knows Howard will soon scale the journalistic heights again, and in the meantime he serves as the wise and humorous sage of the courtyard.

"There is Bart, a young violinist clearly destined for virtuosity on the concert stage, who just for the present must graciously accept all lunch and dinner invitations in order to survive.

"And there is Helen, a sculptor whose charming works will someday grace the finest gardens in America, and whose studio is the favorite gathering place for members of the circle."

There was more like that, introducing other characters, and toward the end she got around to the children. She described my sister as "a lanky, dreamy tomboy," which was odd—I had never thought of Edith that way—and she called me "a sad-eyed, seven-year-old philosopher," which was wholly baffling. When the introduction was over she paused a few seconds for dramatic effect and then went into the opening episode of the series, or what I suppose would be called the "pilot."

I couldn't follow the story very well—it seemed to be mostly an excuse for bringing each character up to the microphone for a few lines apiece—and before long I was listening only to see if there would be any lines for the character based on me. And there were, in a way. She announced my name—"Billy"—but then instead of speaking she put her mouth through a terrible series of contortions, accompanied by funny little bursts of sound, and by the time the words came out I didn't care what they were. It was true that I stuttered badly—I wouldn't get over it for five or six more years—but I hadn't expected anyone to put it on the radio.

"Oh, Sloane, that's marvelous," my mother said when the reading was over. "That's really exciting."

And Sloane was carefully stacking her typed pages in the way she'd probably been taught to do in secretarial school, blushing and smiling with pride. "Well," she said, "it probably needs work, but I do think it's got a lot of potential."

"It's perfect," my mother said. "Just the way it is."

Sloane mailed the script to a radio producer and he mailed it back with a letter typed by some radio secretary, explaining that her material had too limited an appeal to be commercial. The radio public was not yet ready, he said, for a story of Greenwich Village life.

Then it was March. The new President promised that the only thing we had to fear was fear itself, and soon after that his head came packed in wood and excelsior from Mr. Nicholson's foundry.

It was a fairly good likeness. She had caught the famous lift of the chin—it might not have looked like him at all if she hadn't—and everyone told her it was fine. What nobody said was that her original plan had been right, and Mr. Nicholson shouldn't have interfered: it was too small. It didn't look heroic. If you could have hollowed it out and put a slot in the top, it might have made a serviceable bank for loose change.

The foundry had burnished the lead until it shone almost silver in the highlights, and they'd mounted it on a sturdy little base of heavy black plastic. They had sent back three copies: one for the White House presentation, one to keep for exhibition purposes, and an extra one. But the extra one soon toppled to the floor and was badly damaged—the nose mashed almost into the chin—and my mother might have burst into tears if Howard Whitman hadn't made everyone laugh by saying it was now a good portrait of Vice President Garner.

Charlie Hines, Howard's old friend from the *Post* who was now a minor member of the White House staff, made an appointment for my mother with the President late on a weekday morning. She arranged for Sloane to spend the night with Edith and me; then she took an evening train down to

Washington, carrying the sculpture in a cardboard box, and stayed at one of the less expensive Washington hotels. In the morning she met Charlie Hines in some crowded White House anteroom, where I guess they disposed of the cardboard box, and he took her to the waiting room outside the Oval Office. He sat with her as she held the naked head in her lap, and when their turn came he escorted her in to the President's desk for the presentation. It didn't take long. There were no reporters and no photographers.

Afterwards Charlie Hines took her out to lunch, probably because he'd promised Howard Whitman to do so. I imagine it wasn't a first-class restaurant, more likely some bustling, no-nonsense place favored by the working press, and I imagine they had trouble making conversation until they settled on Howard, and on what a shame it was that he was still out of work.

"No, but do you know Howard's friend Bart Kampen?" Charlie asked. "The young Dutchman? The violinist?"

"Yes, certainly," she said. "I know Bart."

"Well, Jesus, there's *one* story with a happy ending, right? Have you heard about that? Last time I saw Bart he said 'Charlie, the Depression's over for me,' and he told me he'd found some rich, dumb, crazy woman who's paying him to tutor her kids."

I can picture how she looked riding the long, slow train back to New York that afternoon. She must have sat staring straight ahead or out the dirty window, seeing nothing, her eyes round and her face held in a soft shape of hurt. Her adventure with Franklin D. Roosevelt had come to nothing. There would be no photographs or interviews or feature articles, no thrilling moments of newsreel coverage; strangers would never know of how she'd come from a small Ohio town, or of how she'd nurtured her talent through the brave, difficult, one-woman journey that had brought her to the attention of the world. It wasn't fair.

All she had to look forward to now was her romance with Eric Nicholson, and I think she may have known even then that it was faltering—his final desertion came the next fall.

She was forty-one, an age when even romantics must admit that youth is gone, and she had nothing to show for the years but a studio crowded with green plaster statues that nobody would buy. She believed in the aristocracy, but there was no reason to suppose the aristocracy would ever believe in her.

And every time she thought of what Charlie Hines had said about Bart Kampen—oh, how hateful; oh, how hateful—the humiliation came back in wave on wave, in merciless rhythm to the clatter of the train.

She made a brave show of her homecoming, though nobody was there to greet her but Sloane and Edith and me. Sloane had fed us, and she said "There's a plate for you in the oven, Helen," but my mother said she'd rather just have a drink instead. She was then at the onset of a long battle with alcohol that she would ultimately lose; it must have seemed bracing that night to decide on a drink instead of dinner. Then she told us "all about" her trip to Washington, managing to make it sound like a success. She talked of how thrilling it was to be actually inside the White House; she repeated whatever small, courteous thing it was that President Roosevelt had said to her on receiving the head. And she had brought back souvenirs: a handful of note-size White House stationery for Edith, and a well-used briar pipe for me. She explained that she'd seen a very distinguished-looking man smoking the pipe in the waiting room outside the Oval Office; when his name was called he had knocked it out quickly into an ashtray and left it there as he hurried inside. She had waited until she was sure no one was looking; then she'd taken the pipe from the ashtray and put it in her purse. "Because I knew he must have been somebody important," she said. "He could easily have been a member of the Cabinet, or something like that. Anyway, I thought you'd have a lot of fun with it." But I didn't. It was too heavy to hold in my teeth and it tasted terrible when I sucked on it; besides, I kept wondering what the man must have thought when he came out of the President's office and found it gone.

Sloane went home after a while, and my mother sat drinking alone at the dining-room table. I think she hoped Howard Whitman or some of her other friends might drop in, but nobody did. It was almost our bedtime when she looked up and said "Edith? Run out in the garden and see if you can find Bart."

He had recently bought a pair of bright tan shoes with crepe soles. I saw those shoes trip rapidly down the dark brick steps beyond the windows—he seemed scarcely to touch each step in his buoyancy—and then I saw him come smiling into the studio, with Edith closing the door behind him. "Helen!" he said. "You're back!"

She acknowledged that she was back. Then she got up from the table and slowly advanced on him, and Edith and I began to realize we were in for something bad.

"Bart," she said, "I had lunch with Charlie Hines in Washington today."

"Oh?"

"And we had a very interesting talk. He seems to know you very well."

"Oh, not really; we've met a few times at Howard's, but we're not really—"

"And he said you'd told him the Depression was over for you because you'd found some rich, dumb, crazy woman who was paying you to tutor her kids. Don't interrupt me."

But Bart clearly had no intention of interrupting her. He was backing away from her in his soundless shoes, retreating past one stiff green garden child after another. His face looked startled and pink.

"I'm not a rich woman, Bart," she said, bearing down on him. "And I'm not dumb. And I'm not crazy. And I can recognize ingratitude and disloyalty and sheer, rotten viciousness and *lies* when they're thrown in my face."

My sister and I were halfway up the stairs jostling each other in our need to hide before the worst part came. The worst part of these things always came at the end, after she'd lost all control and gone on shouting anyway.

"I want you to get out of my house, Bart," she said. "And I don't ever want to see you again. And I want to tell you something. All my life I've hated people who say 'Some of my best friends are Jews.' Because *none* of my friends are Jews, or ever will be. Do you understand me? *None* of my friends are Jews, or ever will be."

The studio was quiet after that. Without speaking, avoiding each other's eyes, Edith and I got into our pajamas and into bed. But it wasn't more than a few minutes before the house began to ring with our mother's raging voice all over again, as if Bart had somehow been brought back and made to take his punishment twice.

". . . And I said *'None* of my friends are Jews, or ever will be . . .' "

She was on the telephone, giving Sloane Cabot the highlights of the scene, and it was clear that Sloane would take her side and comfort her. Sloane might know how the Virgin Mary felt on the way to Bethlehem, but she also knew how to play my stutter for laughs. In a case like this she would quickly see where her allegiance lay, and it wouldn't cost her much to drop Bart Kampen from her enchanted circle.

When the telephone call came to an end at last there was silence downstairs until we heard her working with the ice pick in the icebox: she was making herself another drink.

There would be no more school in our room. We would probably never see Bart again—or if we ever did, he would probably not want to see us. But our mother was ours; we were hers; and we lived with that knowledge as we lay listening for the faint, faint sound of millions.

                                                              (1981)

Blanche McCrary Boyd

Blanche McCrary Boyd was born and raised in South Carolina. Her two novels, Nerves and Mourning the Death of Magic, attracted little attention. But her third book, the collection entitled The Redneck Way of Knowledge: Down-Home Tales (1982), received a great deal of critical approbation and was reasonably successful with the public as well. The book's dedication helps explain why:

This book is for my mother, Mildred McCrary Corbin, who kept asking why I didn't write books people would understand, and for my sister, Patricia McCrary-Smith, who never questioned me about anything.

Boyd is an authentic redneck, and a female redneck. She is also a determined if genial rebel. Torn between her old and her new worlds, fully resident in each and yet fully comfortable in neither, she is also unsure about herself as a woman. The first story in the collection, "Aunt Jenny at the Rockettes," opens:

Last winter I telephoned my Aunt Jenny for the first time in eighteen years. "You probably don't remember me, Aunt Jenny," I said. "This is Mack's daughter Blanche."

"Why, Blanche," she said, as if it had only been a few weeks since she'd heard from me, "we'd been wondering when you would call."

Those same two worlds keep meeting, all through the book, and Boyd keeps trying to make sense of their juxtapositions, and to report back on her findings. She has a great deal to tell us.

SOUTH CAROLINA

When I was fifteen, I killed a black man on Yonges Island, South Carolina. He was lying in the road, drunk, late at night. I was not even driving the car, my friend Marla was.

The man was tangled under the left front wheel. The car was in the ditch. I twisted my ankle getting out of the car. I could see the man in the light from Harry's car, behind us. Harry shouted not to look, but I stooped down beside the black man. There was a lot to say, but I couldn't think of it till lately.

Now I say, Are you dead? I say, Please don't be dead, I don't want you to be dead. Please. I say, Go away, go away, go away. I say, Get out from under the car. What were you doing lying in the road? What kind of crazy thing was this to do?

Each time I say this the black man opens his eyes. He says, Get off me, get your big ugly self off me. You're hurting me. He says, You're cold and white, baby, and you weigh too goddamn much.

The black man says he can't breathe. He has a wife and three children. He says please, his chest hurts, he can't last much longer.

Then he shoves against the car, which has pinned his chest to the pavement. Okay, get off me, you motherfucker, you're killing me. He pushes at the weight crushing his heart and ribs.

He stops and laughs. I was just lying in the road. What the hell did you run over me for? Can't a man even lie in the road?

He fights again. Okay, crush me, I don't care. It hurts too much anyway, I just as soon die. I want to get it over with. I can't breathe. Please let me die.

The car's headlights slice the country dark. Now the car begins to talk. Hey, friend, you're stopping me. Get out from under me.

The black man doesn't answer.

Get out from under my wheel. What kind of asshole would lie down in the middle of the road? You're a crazy nigger and you're jamming my progress.

The black man opens his eyes. Well, he didn't mean to jam nobody's progress, he was just lying in the road taking a little rest. It's a fine thing if you can't even lie down to rest without some goddamn two-thousand-pounder laying down on top of you.

Well, look now, it's over. I'm very sorry. But I can't seem to move with you under my wheel.

I don't seem to be able to move much either. It's a little late, but you should be the one to move.

You don't understand. You are under my wheel, caught in my axle. I am, you understand, trapped here.

The black man says nothing.

I'm trying to be patient with you. Think of my wheel as an arm, my motor as my chest. You are like a knife in me and I can't move. I hate to mention it, but you hurt.

The black man says nothing.

I've been trying not to let you know, but I can't breathe either.

The black man says nothing.

The car begins to cry. Please. I'm trapped here. I can't move. You're a knife. I couldn't stop. I wasn't going fast.

The car begins to gag. The car begins to choke. Its eyes still slice the sky. Somebody put me here, somebody put you there. I didn't mean to do this. I didn't do this myself. Please, it hurts, it hurts.

I have been running up and down that asphalt road for twenty years, between the car in the ditch and Harry's car. I am screaming Harry's name but I don't know why, since he's as scared as I am. For twenty years Marla has been sitting behind the wheel of the car in the ditch, saying Hail Marys. I can only hail Harry, who can't help, and kneel beside the man, who is dead.

I see the man often, in the streets, in my dreams. He holds a silver knife. He says he'll kill me if he can.

(1982)

Bobbie Ann Mason

Bobbie Ann Mason, a native of Kentucky, made a sensational debut with Shiloh and Other Stories *(1982). Winner of the P.E.N./Hemingway Award for First Fiction, the book was also a finalist for three other major prizes, and was greeted by comments like this, from Robert Owers: "Bobbie Ann Mason is one of those rare writers who, by concentrating their attention on a few square miles of native turf, are able to open up new and surprisingly wide worlds for the delighted reader." Alice Adams, herself a distinguished practitioner, observed that "A gentle touch does not preclude exceptionally sharp observation; in her deft, witty and unobtrusive way Mason is amazingly acute."*

Mason's stories are not quite so straightforward as they seem. Her language is astonishingly easy: there appears to be no pressure, no hurry, just a succession of relaxed, calm notations. The title story of her collection, "Shiloh," begins: "Leroy Moffitt's wife, Norma Jean, is working on her pectorals. She lifts three-pound dumbbells to warm up, then progesses to a twenty-pound barbell. Standing with her legs apart, she reminds Leroy of Wonder Woman." Thirteen pages into the story, however, Norma Jean is saying, still in the same unobtrusive tone (and "without looking at Leroy"), "I want to leave you." There are two pages more to the story, but they simply allow the dust to settle on Leroy and help to emphasize the utter finality of Norma Jean's decision. "Norma Jean has moved away and is walking through the cemetery,

*following a serpentine brick path.'' Mason does not allow
herself many decorative touches like that brick path. And
anyone who knows the South knows how precisely right her
tone is, how beautifully she has caught, and compressed, and
transmitted the inner truths of her region. But this is not
regional writing, except as Flaubert's* Madame Bovary *or
George Eliot's* Middlemarch *might be regional. Mason is an
exciting new discovery.*

RESIDENTS AND TRANSIENTS

Since my husband went away to work in Louisville, I have,
to my surprise, taken a lover. Stephen went ahead to start his
new job and find us a suitable house. I'm to follow later. He
works for one of those companies that require frequent trans-
fers, and I agreed to that arrangement in the beginning, but
now I do not want to go to Louisville. I do not want to go
anywhere.

Larry is our dentist. When I saw him in the post office
earlier in the summer, I didn't recognize him at first, without
his smock and drills. But then we exchanged words—"Hot
enough for you?" or something like that—and afterward I
started to notice his blue Ford Ranger XII passing on the road
beyond the fields. We are about the same age, and he grew
up in this area, just as I did, but I was away for eight years,
pursuing higher learning. I came back to Kentucky three
years ago because my parents were in poor health. Now they
have moved to Florida, but I have stayed here, wondering
why I ever went away.

Soon after I returned, I met Stephen, and we were married
within a year. He is one of those Yankees who are moving
into this region with increasing frequency, a fact which dis-
turbs the native residents. I would not have called Stephen a
Yankee. I'm very much an outsider myself, though I've tried
to fit in since I've been back. I only say this because I

overhear the skeptical and desperate remarks, as though the town were being invaded. The schoolchildren are saying "you guys" now and smoking dope. I can image a classroom of bashful country hicks, listening to some new kid blithely talking in a Northern brogue about his year in Europe. Such influences are making people jittery. Most people around here would rather die than leave town, but there are a few here who think Churchill Downs in Louisville would be the grandest place in the world to be. They are dreamers, I could tell them.

"I can't imagine living on a *street* again," I said to my husband. I complained for weeks about living with *houses* within view. I need cornfields. When my parents left for Florida, Stephen and I moved into their old farmhouse, to take care of it for them. I love its stateliness, the way it rises up from the fields like a patch of mutant jimsonweeds. I'm fond of the old white wood siding, the sagging outbuildings. But the house will be sold this winter, after the corn is picked, and by then I will have to go to Louisville. I promised my parents I would handle the household auction because I knew my mother could not bear to be involved. She told me many times about a widow who had sold off her belongings and afterward stayed alone in the empty house until she had to be dragged away. Within a year, she died of cancer. Mother said to me, "Heartbreak brings on cancer." She went away to Florida, leaving everything the way it was, as though she had only gone shopping.

The cats came with the farm. When Stephen and I appeared, the cats gradually moved from the barn to the house. They seem to be my responsibility, like some sins I have committed, like illegitimate children. The cats are Pete, Donald, Roger, Mike, Judy, Brenda, Ellen, and Patsy. Reciting their names for Larry, my lover of three weeks, I feel foolish. Larry had asked, "Can you remember all their names?"

"What kind of question is that?" I ask, reminded of my husband's new job. Stephen travels to cities throughout the South, demonstrating word-processing machines, fancy typewriters that cost thousands of dollars and can remember what you type. It doesn't take a brain like that to remember eight cats.

"No two are alike," I say to Larry helplessly.

We are in the canning kitchen, an airy back porch which I use for the cats. It has a sink where I wash their bowls and cabinets where I keep their food. The canning kitchen was my mother's pride. There, she processed her green beans twenty minutes in a pressure canner, and her tomato juice fifteen minutes in a water bath. Now my mother lives in a mobile home. In her letters she tells me all the prices of the foods she buys.

From the canning kitchen, Larry and I have a good view of the cornfields. A cross-breeze makes this the coolest and most pleasant place to be. The house is in the center of the cornfields, and a dirt lane leads out to the road, about half a mile away. The cats wander down the fence rows, patroling the borders. I feed them Friskies and vacuum their pillows. I ignore the rabbits they bring me. Larry strokes a cat with one hand and my hair with the other. He says he has never known anyone like me. He calls me Mary Sue instead of Mary. No one has called me Mary Sue since I was a kid.

Larry started coming out to the house soon after I had a six-month checkup. I can't remember what signals passed between us, but it was suddenly appropriate that he drop by. When I saw his truck out on the road that day, I knew it would turn up my lane. The truck has a chrome streak on it that makes it look like a rocket, and on the doors it has flames painted.

"I brought you some ice cream," he said.

"I didn't know dentists made house calls. What kind of ice cream is it?"

"I thought you'd like choc-o-mint."

"You're right."

"I know you have a sweet tooth."

"You're just trying to give me cavities, so you can charge me thirty dollars a tooth."

I opened the screen door to get dishes. One cat went in and another went out. The changing of the guard. Larry and I sat on the porch and ate ice cream and watched crows in the corn. The corn had shot up after a recent rain.

"You shouldn't go to Louisville," said Larry. "This part of Kentucky is the prettiest. I wouldn't trade it for anything."

"I never used to think that. Boy, I couldn't wait to get out!" The ice cream was thrillingly cold. I wondered if Larry envied me. Compared to him, I was a world traveler. I had lived in a commune in Aspen, backpacked through the Rockies, and worked on the National Limited as one of the first female porters. When Larry was in high school, he was known as a hell-raiser, so the whole town was amazed when he became a dentist, married, and settled down. Now he was divorced.

Larry and I sat on the porch for an interminable time on that sultry day, each waiting for some external sign—a sudden shift in the weather, a sound, an event of some kind—to bring our bodies together. Finally, it was something I said about my new filling. He leaped up to look in my mouth.

"You should have let me take X-rays," he said.

"I told you I don't believe in all that radiation."

"The amount is teensy," said Larry, holding my jaw. A mouth is a word processor, I thought suddenly, as I tried to speak.

"Besides," he said, "I always use the lead apron to catch any fragmentation."

"What are you talking about?" I cried, jerking loose. I imagined splintering X-rays zinging around the room. Larry patted me on the knee.

"I should put on some music," I said. He followed me inside.

Stephen is on the phone. It is 3:00 P.M. and I am eating supper—pork and beans, cottage cheese and dill pickles. My routines are cockeyed since he left.

"I found us a house!" he says excitedly. His voice is so familiar I can almost see him, and I realize that I miss him. "I want you to come up here this weekend and take a look at it," he says.

"Do I have to?" My mouth is full of pork and beans.

"I can't buy it unless you see it first."

"I don't care what it looks like."

"Sure you do. But you'll like it. It's a three-bedroom brick with a two-car garage, finished basement, dining alcove, patio—"

"Does it have a canning kitchen?" I want to know.

Stephen laughs. "No, but it has a rec room."

I quake at the thought of a rec room. I tell Stephen, "I know this is crazy, but I think we'll have to set up a kennel in back for the cats, to keep them out of traffic."

I tell Stephen about the New Jersey veterinarian I saw on a talk show who keeps an African lioness, an ocelot, and three margays in his yard in the suburbs. They all have the run of his house. "Cats aren't that hard to get along with," the vet said.

"Aren't you carrying this a little far?" Stephen asks, sounding worried. He doesn't suspect how far I might be carrying things. I have managed to swallow the last trace of the food, as if it were guilt.

"What do *you* think?" I ask abruptly.

"I don't know what to think," he says.

I fall silent. I am holding Ellen, the cat who had a vaginal infection not long ago. The vet X-rayed her and found she was pregnant. She lost the kittens, because of the X-ray, but the miscarriage was incomplete, and she developed a rare infection called pyometra and had to be spayed. I wrote every detail of this to my parents, thinking they would care, but they did not mention it in their letters. Their minds are on the condominium they are planning to buy when this farm is sold. Now Stephen is talking about our investments and telling me things to do at the bank. When we buy a house, we will have to get a complicated mortgage.

"The thing about owning real estate outright," he says, "is that one's assets aren't liquid."

"Daddy always taught me to avoid debt."

"That's not the way it works anymore."

"He's going to pay cash for his condo."

"That's ridiculous."

Not long ago, Stephen and I sat before an investment counselor, who told us, without cracking a smile, "You want to select an investment posture that will maximize your potential." I had him confused with a marriage counselor, some kind of weird sex therapist. Now I think of water streaming in the dentist's bowl. When I was a child, the water in a dentist's bowl ran continuously. Larry's bowl has a shut-off button to save water. Stephen is talking about flexibility and fluid assets. It occurs to me that wordprocessing, all one word, is also a runny sound. How many billion words a day could one of Stephen's machines process without forgetting? How many pecks of pickled peppers can Peter Piper pick? You don't *pick* pickled peppers, I want to say to Stephen defiantly, as if he has asked this question. Peppers can't be pickled till *after* they're picked, I want to say, as if I have a point to make.

Larry is here almost daily. He comes over after he finishes overhauling mouths for the day. I tease him about this peculiarity of his profession. Sometimes I pretend to be afraid of him. I won't let him near my mouth. I clamp my teeth shut and grin widely, fighting off imaginary drills. Larry is gap-toothed. He should have had braces, I say. Too late now, he says. Cats march up and down the bed purring while we are in it. Larry does not seem to notice. I'm accustomed to the cats. Cats, I'm aware, like to be involved in anything that's going on. Pete has a hobby of chasing butterflies. When he loses sight of one, he searches the air, wailing pathetically, as though abandoned. Brenda plays with paper clips. She likes the way she can hook a paper clip so simply with one claw. She attacks spiders in the same way. Their legs draw up and she drops them.

I see Larry watching the cats, but he rarely comments on them. Today he notices Brenda's odd eyes. One is blue and one is yellow. I show him her paper clip trick. We are in the canning kitchen and the daylight is fading.

"Do you want another drink?" asks Larry.

"No."

"You're getting one anyway."

We are drinking Bloody Marys, made with my mother's canned tomato juice. There are rows of jars in the basement. She would be mortified to know what I am doing, in her house, with her tomato juice.

Larry brings me a drink and a soggy grilled cheese sandwich.

"You'd think a dentist would make something dainty and precise," I say. "Jello molds, maybe, the way you make false teeth."

We laugh. He thinks I am being funny.

The other day he took me up in a single-engine Cessna. We circled west Kentucky, looking at the land, and when we flew over the farm I felt I was in a creaky hay wagon, skimming just above the fields. I thought of the Dylan Thomas poem with the dream about the birds flying along with the stacks of hay. I could see eighty acres of corn and pasture, neat green squares. I am nearly thirty years old. I have two men, eight cats, no cavities. One day I was counting the cats and I absentmindedly counted myself.

Larry and I are playing Monopoly in the parlor, which is full of doilies and trinkets on whatnots. Every day I notice something that I must save for my mother. I'm sure Larry wishes we were at his house, a modern brick home in a good section of town, five doors down from a U.S. congressman. Larry gets up from the card table and mixes another Bloody Mary for me. I've been buying hotels left and right, against the advice of my investment counselor. I own all the utilities. I shuffle my paper money and it feels like dried corn shucks. I wonder if there is a new board game involving money market funds.

"When my grandmother was alive, my father used to bury her savings in the yard, in order to avoid inheritance taxes," I say as Larry hands me the drink.

He laughs. He always laughs, whatever I say. His lips are like parentheses, enclosing compliments.

"In the last ten years of her life she saved ten thousand dollars from her social security checks."

"That's incredible." He looks doubtful, as though I have made up a story to amuse him. "Maybe there's still money buried in your yard."

"Maybe. My grandmother was very frugal. She wouldn't let go of *anything*."

"Some people are like that."

Larry wears a cloudy expression of love. Everything about me that I find dreary he finds intriguing. He moves his silvery token (a flatiron) around the board so carefully, like a child learning to cross the street. Outside, a cat is yowling. I do not recognize it as one of mine. There is nothing so mournful as the yowling of a homeless cat. When a stray appears, the cats sit around, fascinated, while it eats, and then later, just when it starts to feel secure, they gang up on it and chase it away.

"This place is full of junk that no one could throw away," I say distractedly. I have just been sent to jail. I'm thinking of the boxes in the attic, the rusted tools in the barn. In a cabinet in the canning kitchen I found some Bag Balm, antiseptic salve to soften cows' udders. Once I used teat extenders to feed a sick kitten. The cows are gone, but I feel their presence like ghosts. "I've been reading up on cats," I say suddenly. The vodka is making me plunge into something I know I cannot explain. "I don't want you to think I'm this crazy cat freak with a mattress full of money."

"Of course I don't." Larry lands on Virginia Avenue and proceeds to negotiate a complicated transaction.

"In the wild, there are two kinds of cat populations," I tell him when he finishes his move. "Residents and transients. Some stay put, in their fixed home ranges, and others are on the move. They don't have real homes. Everybody always thought that the ones who establish the territories are the most successful—like the capitalists who get ahold of Park Place." (I'm eyeing my opportunities on the board.) "They are the strongest, while the transients are the bums, the losers."

"Is that right? I didn't know that." Larry looks genuinely surprised. I think he is surprised at how far the subject itself extends. He is such a specialist. Teeth.

I continue bravely. "The thing is—this is what the scientists are wondering about now—it may be that the transients are the superior ones after all, with the greatest curiosity and most intelligence. They can't decide."

"That's interesting." The Bloody Marys are making Larry seem very satisfied. He is the most relaxed man I've ever known. "None of that is true of domestic cats," Larry is saying. "They're all screwed up."

"I bet somewhere there are some who are footloose and fancy free," I say, not believing it. I buy two hotels on Park Place and almost go broke. I think of living in Louisville.

Stephen said the house he wants to buy is not far from
Iroquois Park. I'm reminded of Indians. When certain Indians
got tired of living in a place—when they used up the soil, or
the garbage pile got too high—they moved on to the next
place.

It is a hot summer night, and Larry and I are driving back
from Paducah. We went out to eat and then we saw a movie.
We are rather careless about being seen together in public.
Before we left the house, I brushed my teeth twice and used
dental floss. On the way, Larry told me of a patient who was
a hemophiliac and couldn't floss. Working on his teeth was
very risky.

We ate at a place where you choose your food from
pictures on a wall, then wait at a numbered table for the food
to appear. On another wall was a framed arrangement of farm
tools against red felt. Other objects—saw handles, scythes,
pulleys—were mounted on wood like fish trophies. I could
hardly eat for looking at the tools. I was wondering what my
father's old tit-cups and dehorning shears would look like on
the wall of a restaurant. Larry was unusually quiet during the
meal. His reticence exaggerated his customary gentleness. He
even ate french fries cautiously.

On the way home, the air is rushing through the truck. My
elbow is propped in the window, feeling the cooling air like
water. I think of the pickup truck as a train, swishing through
the night.

Larry says then, "Do you want me to stop coming out to
see you?"

"What makes you ask that?"

"I don't have to be an Einstein to tell that you're bored
with me."

"I don't know. I still don't want to go to Louisville,
though."

"I don't want you to go. I wish you would just stay here
and we would be together."

"I wish it could be that way," I say, trembling slightly. "I
wish that was right."

We round a curve. The night is black. The yellow line in

the road is faded. In the other lane I suddenly see a rabbit move. It is hopping in place, the way runners will run in place. Its forelegs are frantically working, but its rear end has been smashed and it cannot get out of the road.

By the time we reach home I have become hysterical. Larry has his arms around me, trying to soothe me, but I cannot speak intelligibly and I push him away. In my mind, the rabbit is a tape loop that crowds out everything else.

Inside the house, the phone rings and Larry answers. I can tell from his expression that it is Stephen calling. It was crazy to let Larry answer the phone. I was not thinking. I will have to swear on a stack of cats that nothing is going on. When Larry hands me the phone I am incoherent. Stephen is saying something nonchalant, with a sly question in his voice. Sitting on the floor, I'm rubbing my feet vigorously. "Listen," I say in a tone of great urgency. "I'm coming to Louisville—to see that house. There's this guy here who'll give me a ride in his truck—"

Stephen is annoyed with me. He seems not to have heard what I said, for he is launching into a speech about my anxiety.

"These attachments to a place are so provincial," he says.

"People live all their lives in one place," I argue frantically. "What's wrong with that?"

"You've got to be flexible," he says breezily. "That kind of romantic emotion is just like flag-waving. It leads to nationalism, fascism—you name it; the very worst kinds of instincts. Listen, Mary, you've got to be more open to the way things are."

Stephen is processing words. He makes me think of liquidity, investment postures. I see him floppy as a Raggedy Andy, loose as a goose. I see what I am shredding in my hand as I listen. It is Monopoly money.

After I hang up, I rush outside. Larry is discreetly staying behind. Standing in the porch light, I listen to katydids announce the harvest. It is the kind of night, mellow and languid, when you can hear corn growing. I see a cat's flaming eyes coming up the lane to the house. One eye is green and one is red, like a traffic light. It is Brenda, my odd-eyed cat. Her blue eye shines red and her yellow eye shines green. In a moment I realize that I am waiting for the light to change.

(1982)

William Wiser

William Wiser, born in 1929, was raised in the South. He lived for many years in France and did not become a fulltime writer until 1965. His first novel, K (1971), attracted little attention, but The Wolf Is Not Native to the South of France (1978) had an excellent critical reception. And Disappearances (1980), another novel, moved Edmund Fuller to exclaim, "a novel of real literary distinction." Anatole Broyard said, flatly, that it was "one of the most satisfying novels of the last several years. And Roberta Smoodin declared: "For such a book, hyperbole must be forgotten, the notion of exaggeration put aside: I must simply say that Disappearances is probably the best novel I have read this year, exquisite, spell-binding, beautiful. . . . Surely, this is what fiction writing is all about." Acclaim of other sorts has been forthcoming: in 1985–86 Wiser is the beneficiary of both a Guggenheim fellowship and an award from The National Endowment for the Arts.

Ballads, Blues & Swan Songs (1982), Wiser's first collection of stories, deserves equal praise. There is an ever-present sense of ease, of effortless seriousness, of deft storytelling. "Hitchhike Ride to Miracleville," for example, begins:

> Two Spaniards got in a fight over a woman and one got killed and his dead body threw under my viaduct where I used to go for lunch. Truckload of police came in from town.

As he so often does, Wiser here compresses a great deal of narratively useful information in a very short space. He also establishes a colloquial tone of genuine authority. And he impels us into the story with such deceptive, almost familiar gentleness that we hardly know what he has done. As Roberta Smoodin exulted, "Surely, this is what fiction writing is all about."

THE SNOWBIRD

He consulted with snowbirds and file cards in eight-by-fourteen feet of office space called A-1 Personnel & Employer Consultants: green metal army surplus desk and dented file cabinet, telephone, one single window looking out on a restaurant parking lot—the only consultant was Donald B. DeGraf himself, alone. He shared a washroom with Real Estate across the hall.

A big man, DeGraf got his clothes from Greater Miami Men's Comfortwear *(We "Suit" the Larger Sizes)*. He slit the sides and backs of his shoes for ventilation; he wore sponge pads in his armpits. One entire desk drawer was full of handkerchiefs. He tucked them one after another into his collar under the fleshy roll of chin, like napkins—and later washed them out himself, in the washroom, and hung them out the window to dry: a string of wet pennants flying over the tops of automobiles parked below.

For all the olive-drab scrappy officeware at A-1, DeGraf's swivel chair was a work of art: custom-made of airplane aluminum with contour padding, ball-bearing joints, an H-shift gear shift for the adjustable seat and rubber-shod wheels instead of rollers. During the snowbird season he seldom got out of it.

A-1 was ideally located, like a duck blind, across the street from Florida State Unemployment. Flocks of snowbirds flew across all summer. Florida Unemployment checked them in, classified them A through L, M through W—but a claim took maybe a month to process, and that first compensation check was weeks away; snowbird's prior home state might not even back his claim, or a hospital was where careless claimant last worked—hospitals did not qualify. Then DeGraf got them. Even a snowbird has to eat.

The decoy word was *Personnel,* a perfect bird call. Set yourself up as an employment agency, or use the crude word *job,* and you collect all the drifters, the dishwashers. Personnel Consultants brought down and bagged a slightly higher-class bird: waitresses, beauticians, and bellboys. And, with a name like A-1, you got listed first in the Yellow Pages.

One of these days DeGraf was going to put an air-conditioner in, but right now an electric fan with rubber blades stirred the scorched air while DeGraf sat tilted back in second gear watching the frosted-glass windowpane of the office door, waiting.

"Parakeets was when it all started collapsing down around us when I failed to cash in on the parakeet craze after Herbert warned me my own mother warned me and everybody said it was going to last and last but I wouldn't listen once I made my mind up and stocked dalmatians even after my sister-in-law came down from Chicago and claimed Chicago was wild over parakeets everybody wanted one and the pet shops couldn't keep up with the orders for one well Herbert said you're crazy if you don't stock parakeets and my own mother warned me hoop-skirts'll be back in style before dalmatians but do you think I'd listen to some sense once I make up my mind stubborn is my middle name and I figured parakeets would all of a sudden just die out or else the government would ban them for parrot fever but they didn't and it got so bad you couldn't *give* dalmatians away and everybody knows if you can't sell the pups pretty soon you've got full-grown animals on your hands to feed just after we'd built up to be the nicest well-known pet shop in Indianapolis till parakeets came in and ruined us and I think that's what finally aggravated Herbert's allergies to where I said all right you're a sick man and I'm a ruint woman let's pull up stakes but then Momma died and that delayed us I don't know if you know what

funerals cost anymore but after we sold the pet shop for
peanuts to what it was worth and buried Momma all that was
left to pull up stakes with was chickenfeed to come down to
Miami and start life all over again fresh at our age with
Herbert's allergies but I did have some of the cutest dalmatian
pups you ever laid eyes on before everything went bust.
Don't talk to me about parakeets.''

"Not parakeets," said DeGraf, "goldfish." He had selected a three-by-five index card from the file and dealt it to
the bird lady, face down, on the blotter. "Here's a fresh start
for you. Ninety-eight fifty a week. Includes a good hot meal
at the lunch counter."

"What kind of goldfish? I mean, what doing?"

"—just yesterday they had milk-fed shoulder of veal with
mashed potatoes and garden peas. I was there for lunch
myself, that's the kind of meals they serve. One of the nicer
higher-class ten-cent stores on Flagler, selling goldfish."

"I used to have my own store. Goldfish? I never . . . I
don't know."

"We never know till we try." DeGraf shifted gears and
settled deeper into the swivel chair. "To be perfectly frank,
and I make no bones about this, *if* you should be hired"—and
the word *if* hung there a moment between them—"*if* you
should be lucky enough to get this position you can count
yourself among the exceptional ones. One in a thousand."

"One in a what? I mean, lucky how?"

She was shaking her beak back and forth I-don't-know,
I-don't-know. She was a bird all right, he said to himself,
watching her pluck the lint from her blouse front; picking
nits, he thought, from her fine feathers.

"Let me be absolutely perfectly frank with you about how
the way things are down here. The employment situation. In
a nutshell, well, the employment situation, for people like
yourself, from somewhere else, from somewhere up north,
for people we call—rather, the residents down here call"—
and the word *residents* hung there a moment between
them—"well, the *residents* have got a name for those kind of
people. They call them, to be absolutely frank, snowbirds."

"Snow what?" She lowered her head until the great beak

sank out of sight. "I mean, I had my own pet shop. We came down here, like I said, for a fresh start."

They come down, DeGraf said to himself, calling themselves pioneers. *Pioneer* is the word they start out with, but when they get down here there's a colder word for them.

"Before," she said, "I was a resident myself, in Indianapolis. I mean, you can't be a resident till you live down here can you, right off the bat?"

But DeGraf was in first gear now, accelerating, and the chair shot across the brief splintery floor space between them. She was startled, fluttery, ready to fly—but trapped with the swivel chair between her and the door, as he rolled up to her with an A-1 contract form and a ballpoint pen in his hand. He was reminded of a cockatoo's crest when the pointed tufts of her dyed-orange hair appeared to curl forward in fear. Her bare arms in the cheap sleeveless blouse were suddenly pebbled with chicken flesh. DeGraf braked the swivel chair just short of the painted bird claws showing through a pair of open-toed huaraches.

She blushed under her feathers, but signed her foolish name, saying, "I just hope I don't have to wait on a lot of colored people."

He spun around in his chair at the sound: a young girl had slipped into his office through the door left open by the bird lady. Another snowbird, but that was nothing to be surprised about—this was the season.

Where do they come from? DeGraf asked himself, and the answer was: anyplace north, turning a little cold, looking a little grim in the first gray rain. Last summer was this girl's first summer to wear a bikini, and now she wants to wear one year-round.

A pretty thing, he thought, as he handed her an Address & Next-of-Kin card to fill out, and a Personal History form— but by now Personal Histories were all the same, and that form might as well be phased out. Twenty-two years in the swivel chair had given DeGraf a personal knowledge of Personal Histories. A Personal History form was for the birds; he never read them: he read faces, then shuffled index cards, consulting.

The girl was bent over her ballpoint. Nice little hand, DeGraf noticed, with a nice wristwatch her daddy probably rewarded her with at high-school graduation. Her legs were neatly crossed. Very nice legs, thought DeGraf, and he could see them in a drum majorette's saucy pleated skirt. They were sweet and tender cheerleader's legs: last year she was leaping up and down on those legs yelling riot songs to the football team. But right now the legs were tightly knotted together, and a strict job-hunting handbag lay in her lap.

She wore a gold chain around her neck, tucked in above the top button of her virginal white blouse. No doubt her high-school hero's gold football hung at the end of that chain, suspended between those twin delicacies: the doubtlessly perfect breasts that only her high-school boyfriend (and possibly one or two others on the team) had touched.

High school behind her, she had come to Miami to be an airline hostess, DeGraf decided—or a fashion model. The fledglings were all alike, looking for a share of glamour in this humdrum workaday world. But Donald B. DeGraf had long years of experience bringing teenage dreamers down to earth.

He waited for her to recite past failures and future hopes to him, but she sat silent with her unblinking owl eyes staring across the desk into his. Like a violinist, he replaced the sweaty handkerchief at his chin with a fresh one from the desk drawer, then sank back into the chair's reclining second gear, saying, "Well, I suppose you came down here to be a stewardess on one of our major airlines."

"No. No planes, please. I get airsick."

Strange, he thought, a snowbird unwilling to fly.

"Or maybe you left home with modeling in mind."

"Not me. I just want a job."

DeGraf sat up straight. Here was a bird of a different feather, she was a species apart. Her great green eyes stared innocence at him: they were limpid pools that maybe quarterbacks tumbled into—but not DeGraf.

"You want to go into television, I know what you want. You want to be an exhibition swimmer, or water-ski for a living. Maybe you think you'll manage an exclusive dress shop for wealthy matrons or interior-decorate seventeen-room

villas on Key Biscayne. Tell me, just what kind of *experience*"
—and the word *experience* hung there between them—"what
real *experience* have you had?"

"I never worked before."

"Exactly," said DeGraf. "No experience."

"To get a job you're supposed to have experience, but to
get experience you have to first get a job."

DeGraf smiled. Hearing the old sweet bird song, he re-
clined into second again. Idly he took up the deck of index
cards and shuffled through, searching the proper pigeonhole
for this pigeon. "Elevator operator," he announced, and
tossed the card out, face down on the blotter. "One of the
higher-class hotels on the beach."

"Elevator what?"

"—older-type, newer-rich clientele. You wear a snappy
little uniform with brass buttons and a bow tie. The tips, they
tell me, are something to write home about. These people
have got money to burn. Six-foot-six Texans who left their
wives home in Dallas, and Cubans who got their money out
of Havana before Castro snatched it. The famous inventor, I
forget his name, the one who found out how to make breakfast cereal out of seaweed, keeps a penthouse suite all season."

"Elevator operator? I get motion sickness."

"—*if* you should be lucky enough to get this position."

"I never said I wanted it. I'm thinking it over. I'm trying
to picture myself cooped up in an elevator all day."

When they start thinking it over, when they start shaking
their silly heads I-don't-know, it is high time to clip their
wings for them.

"Let me be absolutely perfectly frank with you," DeGraf
began—but Green Eyes was not listening.

She bent her fingers delicately to see what the bus ride had
done to her fingernails. She looked out of the narrow window
to where a string of handkerchiefs hung drying. She yawned.

She sat a firm perch, he had to admit; but he was, after all,
the almighty birdwatcher. It was DeGraf who held a full
house of index cards and rationed out the birdseed in this
world. Still, by the time he came to the word *snowbird,* he
was in a desperate sweat, and his voice was pitched higher
than he intended.

When he finished, she simply said, "You're the bird, if you ask me."

DeGraf went around in his swivel chair, a slow spin—contemplative, not stunned. When the chair stopped he closed his eyes to keep his head from spinning on. Then he reached a shaky hand into the drawer full of handkerchiefs.

Maybe he moved in too close, too slowly—or that last fumbling change of handkerchiefs had thrown his timing off—because her wide unblinking eyes surveyed the swivel chair's approach, and she was waiting for him when he got to her. His brakes failed and their knees bumped. She placed one firm hand flat against his heaving chest, and with the other hand yanked at the gold chain around her neck. A tiny gold cross dangled from the chain, instead of a football.

DeGraf threw the chair into reverse and scuttled backwards, crablike—like the vampire in a horror movie. Then he spun the chair a half-circle to the file drawer where he kept a bottle of rye whiskey wedged between the cards. As he drank he heard the purse go shut, and when he turned she was gone. Where she had been sitting an unsigned A-1 contract lay on the floor, a dirty sheet of paper at the bottom of his birdcage.

"Wellsir first the *first* retaining wall went and there went my garage foundations and I could've kicked myself for forgetting to remember to test your hillside first for drainage but I've learnt my lesson since believe you me and when the second wall went I swore on a stack of Bibles if ever I built anywheres on a slant someplace I want to know where the water comes through first and second if there's any highway referendums on the ballot because where I built the county voted yes and they put a road through that cut in above my house and I got the drain down my backlot which loosened up my underbeams till you couldn't cross across the kitchen for a drink of water without the whole floor shook but I'm a builder by trade a *builder* by damn a born builder if there ever was one and a crackerjack carpenter to boot and I'm a son of a gun if I couldn't build better than builders build nowadays if I do say so myself with your electric saws whatever became of good old-fashioned elbow grease and your solid so-called reinforcement concrete it may be solid but who wants to live in all-concrete unless it's a mausoleum or your prefabrications made out of sawdust either might as well live in a cardboard outhouse and I never got back a word of complaint in forty years building other people's houses but my luck seemed like it run out when I went and built one for myself for it washed right out from under me the first hard spring rain my two and a half retaining walls and all."

DeGraf was lying back in third gear, like a stretcher case, while Mr. Carpenter, a carpenter, confessed. That slug of whiskey had set off DeGraf's colitis: he felt unpleasant things happening inside him—also, he had changed three dripping handkerchiefs since Mr. Carpenter came in.

It was lucky the telephone rang, for DeGraf was not up to talking to a ruined carpenter right now. He reached out for the phone without sitting up, without looking.

"A-1."

"DeGraf? Blakey, over at the Chateau de Sable. That elevator job you had us down for? Forget it, we filled it already."

DeGraf sat up.

"Ten minutes ago this girl walked in the door, just right, just what we need."

"What girl?" DeGraf demanded, trembling.

"This *girl*, she just walked in, uniform fits her nice and everything. We hired her. So forget the elevator job you had us down for. What we need now is a night watchman."

"That girl. The one you hired. Tell me something. I'm curious. What were her legs like?"

"Legs? What do you mean, *legs?*"

"Was she wearing a wristwatch her daddy gave her for graduation?"

"What do you mean? What're you talking about?"

"And a gold chain. Did she have on this gold chain around her neck? I'm just curious, that's all. I was just wondering."

"I don't know what she had on for chrissake. She's wearing an elevator uniform right now is all I know."

"Listen, do me a favor. Take a look and tell me what color her eyes are."

"Green," said Blakey. "I don't have to take a look. Now

will you forget the elevator girl a minute and listen? What we need is a night watchman. One twenty a week and we pay his Blue Cross. You know, for the side door, for employees only. Check time cards and not let anybody in except deliveries. It can be an old guy—but *active,* you know."

"Night watchman," said DeGraf, distracted. "You need a night watchman."

"That's what I said. Jesus, you sound like you're under ether." And Blakey hung up.

He could take her to court. A nice little lawsuit would wipe that smile off her face. He'd put her in every blacklist in the book. She had turned up the index card on the blotter— nobody ever did that—and saw Chateau de Sable written on it.

Cheerleader? Graduation gift? She stole that wristwatch from her roommate. She never had a boyfriend on the football team, she was some gangster's gun moll. Vice queen, police informer, drug dealer, whore . . .

He could take her to court—but where did that get you? It only got you in deeper with those green eyes, maybe victimized again, maybe laughed at. Let Blakey have her. Blakey, the bell captain at the Chateau de Sable—he'd take her home with him tonight. A nice dose, that's what Blakey would get out of it. She'd take him and the Chateau de Sable for plenty, plenty. DeGraf could picture Blakey getting taken.

Well, surely, one mistake, at least, allowed in twenty-two years. But look at Mr. Carpenter. One mistake and there he sat cracking his big knuckles, nervous, waiting to hear the snowbird song. All his life was bad news now since his house washed down a hillside onto the Louisville & Nashville tracks. Not a contractor in all of Kentucky would trust him with a hammer again.

"Let me be absolutely perfectly frank with you," DeGraf began, "—*if* you should get this position . . ."

If? Mr. Carpenter pinched his red beak and blinked his watery blue eyes. A beer drinker, thought DeGraf, an old bird sliding downhill with his house. He wore a sporty tie knotted too thick for his denim workshirt collar, trying to look years younger than his stone-white hair. A railroad timepiece ticked like thunder in his shirt pocket. He planned to get back into the building trade, back on his feet—Florida was too flat for what happened back home to happen here. The old man had come down for a fresh start. A snowbird he was, and wanted to be a carpenter again—but suddenly, as if the force of gravity depended upon it, DeGraf needed to make a night watchman out of him.

(1982)

Tobias Wolff

Tobias Wolff grew up in the state of Washington. He has already published one collection of stories. In the Garden of North American Martyrs *(1982), which won the St, Lawrence Award for Fiction, and a short novel,* The Barracks Thief *(1984), which received the Faulkner Award for 1985. His stories have appeared in many magazines, including* Esquire, TriQuarterly, Vanity Fair, *and* The Atlantic. *The story here printed appeared in the collection,* Back in the World *(1985); its first appearance was in* Ploughshares, *in 1983. Wolff teaches in the writing program at the University of Syracuse.*

The quiet, immensely empathetic sensitivity of "Sister" is matched by the direct, carefully controlled prose. Wolff is not always so controlled or so direct. The story "Desert Breakdown," from his collection Back in the World, *for example, is distinctly overlong, far too confused in its narration, and irritatingly pretentious. "Sister" is none of these things. I know of no story written by a man which so deftly sets out both the traditional exclusionary tactics so often directed at women and, equally remarkably, haw a woman might feel about them.*

SISTER

There was a park at the bottom of the hill. Now that the leaves were down Marty could see the exercise stations and part of a tennis court from her kitchen window, through a web of black branches. She took another donut from the box on the table and ate it slowly, watching the people at the exercise stations: two men and a woman. The woman was doing leg-raisers. The men were just standing there. Though the day was cold one of the men had taken his shirt off, and even from this distance Marty was struck by the deep brown color of his skin. You hardly ever saw great tans like that on people around here, not even in summer. He had come from somewhere else.

She went into the bedroom and put on a running suit and an old pair of Adidas. The seams were giving out but her other pair was new and their whiteness made her feet look big. She took off her glasses and put her contacts in. Tears welled up under the lenses. For a few moments she lost her image in the mirror; then it returned and she saw the excitement in her face, the eagerness. Whoa, she thought. She sat there for a while, feeling the steady thump of the stereo in the apartment overhead. Then she rolled a joint and stuck it in the pocket of her sweatshirt.

A dog barked at Marty as she walked down the hallway. It barked at her every time she passed its door and it always took her by surprise, making her heart clench and then pound wildly. The dog was a big shepherd whose owners were gone all the time and never took it out. She could hear its feet scrabbling and see its nose pushed under the door. "Easy," she said, "easy there," but it kept trying to get at her and Marty heard it barking all the way down the corridor, until she reached the door and stepped outside.

It was late afternoon and cold, so cold she could see her breath. As always on Sunday the street was dead quiet, except for the skittering of leaves on the sidewalk as the breeze swept through them and ruffled the cold-looking pools of water from last night's rain. With the trees bare the sky seemed vast. Two dark clouds drifted overhead, and in the far distance an angle of geese flew across the sky. Honkers, her brother called them. Right now he and his buddies would be banging away at them from one of the marshes outside town. By nightfall they'd all be drunk. She smiled, thinking of that.

Marty did a couple of knee-bends and headed toward the park, forcing herself to walk against the urge she felt to run. She considered taking a couple of hits off the joint in her pocket but decided against it. She didn't want to lose her edge.

The woman she'd seen at the exercise station was gone, but the two men were still there. Marty held back, did a few more knee-bends and watched some boys playing football on the field behind the tennis courts. They couldn't have been more than ten or eleven but they moved like men, hunching up their shoulders and shaking their wrists as they jogged back to the huddle, grunting when they came off the line as if their bodies were big and weighty. You could tell that in their heads they had a whole stadium of people watching them. It tickled her. Marty watched them run several plays, then she walked over to the exercise stations.

When she got there she had a shock. Marty recognized one of the men, and she was so afraid that he would recognize her that she almost turned around and went home. He was a regular at the Kon-Tiki. A few weeks earlier he had taken notice of Marty and they'd matched daiquiris for a couple of hours and things looked pretty good. Then she went out to the car to get this book she'd been describing to him, a book about Edgar Cayce and reincarnation, and when she got back he was sitting on the other side of the room with someone else. He hadn't left anything for the drinks, so she got stuck with the bar bill. And her lighter was missing. The man's name was Jack. When she saw him leaning against the chin-up station she didn't know what to do. She wanted to vanish right into the ground.

But he seemed not to remember her. In fact, he was the one who said hello. "Hey there," he said.

She smiled at him. Then she looked at the tan one and said, "Hi."

He didn't answer. His eyes moved over her for a moment, and he looked away. He'd put on a warm-up jacket with a hood, but left the zipper open nearly to his waist. His chest was covered with little curls of glistening golden hair. The other one, Jack, had on faded army fatigues with dark patches where the insignia had been removed. He needed a shave. He was holding a quart bottle of beer.

The two men had been talking when she walked up but now they were silent. Marty felt them watching her as she did her stretches. They had been talking about sex, she was sure of that. What they'd been saying was still in the air somehow, with the ripe smell of wet leaves and the rainsoaked earth. She took a deep breath.

Then she said, "You didn't get that tan around here." She kept rocking back and forth on her knuckles but looked up at him.

"You bet your buns I didn't," he said. "The only thing you get around here is arthritis." He pulled the zipper of his jacket up and down. "Hawaii. Waikiki Beach."

"Waikiki," Jack said. "Bikini-watching capital of the world."

"Brother, you speak true," the tan one said. "They've got this special breed over there that they raise just to walk back and forth in front of you. They ought to parachute about fifty of them into Russia. Those old farts in the Kremlin would go out of their skulls. We could just walk in and take the place over."

"They could drop a couple on this place while they're at it," Jack said.

"Amen." The tan one nodded. "Make it four—two apiece."

"Aloha," Marty said. She rolled over on her back and raised her feet a few inches off the ground. She held them there for a moment, then lowered them. "That's all the Hawaiian I know," she said. "Aloha and Maui Zowie. They grow some killer weed over there."

"For sure," the tan one said. "It's God's country, sister, and that's a fact."

Jack walked up closer. "I know you from somewhere," he said.

Oh no, Marty thought. She smiled at him. "Maybe," she said. "What's your name?"

"Bill," he said.

Right, Marty wanted to say. You bet, Jack.

Jack looked down at her. "What's yours?"

She raised her feet again. "Elizabeth."

"Elizabeth," he repeated, slowly, so that it struck Marty how beautiful the name was. *Fairfield*, she almost added, but she hesitated, and the moment passed.

"I guess not," he said.

She lowered her feet and sat up. "A lot of people look like me."

He nodded.

Just then something flew past Marty's head. She jerked to one side and threw her hands up in front of her face. "Jesus," she said.

"Sorry!" someone shouted.

"Goddam frisbees," Jack said.

"It's all right," Marty told him, and waved at the man who'd thrown it. She turned and waved again at another man some distance behind her, who was wiping the frisbee on his shirt. He waved back.

"Frisbee freaks," Jack said. "I'm sick of them." He lifted the bottle and drank from it, then held it out to Marty. "Go on," he told her.

She took a swig. "There's more than beer in here," she said.

Jack shrugged.

"What's in here?" she asked.

"Secret formula," he answered. "Go for two. You're behind."

Marty looked at the bottle, then drank again and passed it to the other man. Even his fingers were brown. He wore a thick wedding band and a gold chain-linked bracelet. She held on to the bottle for an extra moment, long enough for him to notice, and give her a look; then she let go. The hood of his jacket fell back as he tilted his head to drink. Marty saw that he was nearly bald. He had parted his hair just above one ear and swept it sideways to cover the skin on top, which was even darker than the rest of him.

"What's your name?" she asked.

Jack answered for him. "His name is Jack," he said.

The tan one laughed. "Brother," he said, "you are too much."

"You aren't from around here," she said. "I would have seen you."

He shook his head. "I was running and I ended up here."

Jack said, "Don't hog the fuel, Jack," and made a drinking motion with his hand.

The tan one nodded. He took a long pull and wiped his mouth and passed the bottle to Jack.

Marty stood and brushed off her warm-ups. "Hawaii," she said. "I've always wanted to go to Hawaii. Just kick back for about three weeks. Check out the volcanoes. Do some mai tais."

"Get leis," Jack said.

All three of them laughed.

"Well," she said. She touched her toes a couple of times. Jack kept laughing.

"Hawaii's amazing," said the other man. "Anything goes."

"Stop talking about Hawaii," Jack said. "It makes me cold."

"Me too," Marty said. She rubbed her hands together. "I'm always cold. When I come back, I just hope I come back as a native of someplace warm."

"Right," Jack said, but there was something in his voice that made her look over at him. He was studying her. She could tell that he was trying to place her again, trying to recall where he'd met her. She wished she hadn't made that remark about coming back. That was what had set him off. She wasn't even sure she actually believed it—believed that she was going to return as a different entity later on, someone new and different. She had serious doubts, sometimes. But at other times she thought it had to be true; this couldn't be everything.

"So," she said, "do you guys know each other?"

Jack stared at her a moment longer, then nodded. "All our lives," he said.

The tan one shook his head and laughed. "Too much," he said.

"We're inseparable," Jack said. "Aren't we, Jack?"

The tan one laughed again.

"Is that right?" Marty asked him. "Are you inseparable?"

He pulled the zipper of his jacket up and down, hiding and then revealing the golden hairs on his chest though not in a conscious way. His cheeks puffed out and his brow thickened just above his eyes, so that his face seemed heavier. Marty could see that he was thinking. Finally he looked at her and said, "I guess we are. For the time being."

"That's fine," she said. "That's all right." That was all right, she thought. She could call Jill, Jill was always up for a party, and if Jill was out or had company then she'd think of something else. It would work out.

"Okay," she said, but before she could say anything else someone yelled "Heads up!" and they all looked around. The frisbee was coming straight at them. Marty felt her body tighten. "Got it," she said, and balanced herself for the catch. Suddenly the breeze gusted and the frisbee seemed to stop cold, a quivering redline, and then it jerked upwards and flew over their heads and past them. She ran after it, one arm raised, gathering herself to jump, but it stayed just out of reach and finally she gave up.

The frisbee flew a short distance farther, then fell to the sidewalk and skidded halfway across the street. Marty scooped it up and flipped it back into the park. She stood there, wanting to laugh but completely out of breath. Too much weed, she thought. She put her hands on her knees and rocked back and forth. It was quiet. Then, from up the hill, she heard a low rumble that grew steadily louder and a few seconds later a big white car came around the corner. Its tires squealed and then went silent as the car slid through a long sheet of water lying in the road. It was moving sideways in her direction. She watched it come. The car cleared the water and the tires began to squeal again but it kept sliding, and Marty saw the faces inside getting bigger and bigger. There was a girl staring at her from the front window. The girl's mouth was open, her arms braced against the dashboard. Then the tires caught and the car shot forward, so close that

Marty could have reached out and touched the girl's cheek as they went past.

The car fish-tailed down the street. It ran a stop sign at the corner and turned left back up the hill, coughing out bursts of black exhaust.

Marty turned toward the park and saw the two men looking at her. They were looking at her as if they had seen her naked, and that was how she felt—naked. She had nearly been killed and now she was an embarrassment, like someone in need. She wasn't welcome in the park.

She crossed the street and started up the hill toward her apartment building. She felt as if she were floating, as if there were nothing to her. She passed a gray cat curled up on the hood of a car. There was smoke on the breeze and the smell of decay. It seemed to Marty that she drifted with the smoke through the yellow light, over the dull grass and the brown clumps of leaves. In the park behind her a boy called football signals, his voice perfectly distinct in the thin cold air.

She climbed the steps to the building but did not go inside. She knew that the dog would bark at her, and she didn't think she could handle that right now.

She sat on the steps. From somewhere nearby a bird cried out in a hoarse ratcheting voice like chain being jerked through a pulley. Marty did some breathing exercises to get steady, to quiet the fluttering sensation in her shoulders and knees, but she could not calm herself. A few minutes ago she had nearly been killed and now there was nobody to talk to about it, to see how afraid she was and tell her not to worry, that it was over now. That she was still alive. That everything was going to be all right.

At this moment, sitting here, Marty understood that there was never going to be anyone to tell her these things. She had no idea why this should be so; it was just something she knew. There was no need for her to make a fool of herself again.

The sun was going down. Marty couldn't see it from where she sat, but the windows of the house across the street had turned crimson, and the breeze was colder. A broken kite flapped in a tree. Marty fingered the joint in her pocket but left it there; she felt empty and clean, and did not want to lose the feeling.

She watched the sky darken. Her brother and his friends would be coming off the marsh about now, flushed with cold and drink, their dogs running ahead through the reeds and the tall grass. When they reach the car they'll compare birds and pass the bottle around, and after the bottle is empty they will head for the nearest bar. Do boilermakers. Stuff themselves with pickled eggs and jerky. Throw dice from a leather cup. And outside in the car the dogs will be waiting, ears pricked for the least sound, sometimes whimpering to themselves but mostly silent, tense, and still, watching the bright door the men have closed behind them.

(1983)

Charles Barnitz

———————◆———————

Charles Barnitz was born in Pennsylvania, in 1949. He was educated at Saint Francis College, in Loretto, Pennsylvania. He has worked for National Geographic, for McDonnell Douglas' Computer Based Systems Training Group, and for I.B.M. His stories and articles have appeared in many magazines and newspapers. He has also served as an armorer in the National Guard, and as a mental health worker.

"Kemp's Homecoming" is adapted from a long novel, in progress for many years, entitled Mummers, a brilliant, complex treatment of the Vietnam era and the years immediately following it. In the novel, as in the story printed here, Barnitz manages to handle the irrationalities of his characters, and of their world, with great poignancy and yet also with uproarious wit. I know of no one in contemporary American fiction who can do these things better. His treatment of larger social issues, too, is polished and profound, but without any of the sense of strain that mars a good deal of recent fiction—and utterly without self-indulgence or pretentiousness.

The fusion of madness and humor, of sexuality and social conformism, of pathos and desperation, of brilliant prose and compelling narrative, makes "Kemp's Homecoming" an indelible reading experience. Mummers is full of such scenes. Like "Kemp's Homecoming," too, it is superbly crafted. Barnitz is a writer who works hard and with great success at being read: it is my expectation that he will go on being read for a long, long time.

KEMP'S HOMECOMING

The twin engine commuter flight from Houston banked into its final approach over the light-beaded grid of an oil refinery north of Port Arthur, Texas. Kemp was almost home. Except for the occasional flashes of energy behind his eyelids, it was dark inside Kemp's head. It was a trick he'd learned back at the Praesidio to avoid the long boredom of hospitalization, and he'd come to use it more frequently as he'd become more bored. It had other utility, though, and now he was using it to recharge himself after a particularly rough flight from Houston.

It had been a rough flight because he'd been seated next to a chartered accountant with ribs on his breath and a powerful thirst for knowledge about the southeast asian theatre of conflict, as he called it. This was not what Kemp had come home for, to trade foreign policy views with someone whose perspective was tainted by ribs and chartered accountancy, and so, as the plane was straining to leave the tarmac, he'd tried to short out the transmitter the CIA had implanted in his head. He let himself drift into contact with the unstable energy field of the plane, hoping to slip through a dilation in the electromagnetic pattern and short that transmitter out. Sparks had begun to drip from his ears, bounce off his shoulders and crackle toward the floor and onto the lap of the startled accountant beside him. The circuit breakers tripped as the plane left the ground and Kemp passed out.

When Kemp awoke, the accountant had removed himself from the row, disinclined to continue a conversation with someone suffering from a seizure disorder of such magnitude. That was alright with Kemp. Even if the transmitter was still intact, he'd gotten rid of the rib-breathed accountant: he'd take what he could get. So for the rest of the flight he sat alone, eyes closed, or just barely open, watching his brain idle. It was a good place to be, that dark place where synapses flashed randomly about him, like being safe at the bottom of the deep ocean where monstrous, blind, glowing things swam about while he watched them, warm and safe from their influence and ecology.

Kemp had convinced them at the Praesidio that he was ready for what they thought of as reality. He'd taken his thorazine and shut up about the Martians and they'd discharged him quid pro quo. It had taken Kemp a long time to get the point about Army psychiatry, the point being that getting well, whatever that was, wasn't the object of the exercise. The object was to convince them that well had been gotten. But it was a pyrrhic victory at best because, even as he was savoring the calm of his idling neurology, safe from intrusive accountants if not from eavesdropping Martians, the plane was dropping toward the last place on earth Kemp wanted to be: home. There were plenty of good reasons why Kemp didn't want to go home, and only one reason why he was there. It was the only way they'd let him out of the hospital; that, and weekly visits to the mental hygiene clinic at the Galveston VA hospital. Quid pro quo.

Down below, Kemp knew, his family was clustered around the Motorola color console watching *Laugh In*. He'd neglected to tell them about his discharge. After he'd told them about the Martians, communications had been strained. His plan was to take a room in town until he could get a job on an offshore oil rig under an assumed name. He knew the Martians were on his trail, their sunburnt noses to the ground, relentless in their vengeance. They wouldn't have too much trouble tracking him to Port Arthur; the best he could hope for was enough of a head start so he could lose them again. As long as the transmitter remained operational they'd always be there in the background of his reality like the remnant of a badly digested meal.

Kemp opened his eyes and blinked in the cabin lights. He leaned forward, gripping the armrests with clawed fingers, and noticed his reflection in the window, breathing heavily, sweat dampened, hair stuck to his forehead. Below he saw the grid of lights that was Port Arthur and home.

Kemp thought about his family. They were an embarrassment. He could understand their wanting to cover up about the Martians. He knew the idea of the Martians scared the hell out of them: it scared the hell out of him, too. But they could have said he'd contracted malaria or something. There were plenty of good diseases to be caught in Southeast Asia. This wounded hero horseshit was too much for Kemp's sense of proportion. He was glad he'd be incognito when the plane landed. He had it all worked out: he was going straight to the men's room to change into the new identity that lay folded up in his AWOL bag. Al Wolf, oilfield roughneck. He didn't think Wolf would mind under the circumstances. After all, he'd tipped Wolf to the two Martian hitters that were after him back at the Praesidio. He practiced thinking the thoughts of Al Wolf, oilfield roughneck. *Drink some fuckin Lone Star*, he thought, *knock offa piecea ass . . . Willie Nelson.*

The tires of the commuter flight shrieked on the runway and Al Wolf, oilfield roughneck, flexed his muscles inside Kemp's uniform. Kemp's family would never have recognized him. Not Kemp's mother, who was probably telling Kemp's little brother to put on a sweater; not Kemp's little brother, who was probably thinking about his zits; not Kemp's sister who was probably pulling her tee shirt tightly over her swelling Baylor boobs, the way she used to do when Kemp was at home; and certainly not Kemp's old man, who was probably dreaming up new ways to manipulate the spot oil market in Rotterdam. They would have walked right past Al Wolf, oilfield roughneck, without a second glance.

The plane rolled to a stop on the boarding apron near the terminal and Al Wolf, oilfield roughneck, unbuckled his seatbelt and stretched, wondering how long it would take him to find a room in town. He took his AWOL bag out from under the seat and opened it to check his new identity and wait for the deplaning of all chartered accountants. There it was, on top of the dirty laundry and crumpled clothing. He sat back and waited for the plane to empty.

The familiar hometown smell of Port Arthur, Texas, hit him in the face like a smoldering inner tube as he stepped onto the ground. Airport flunkies were chocking the wheels and unloading the luggage. He lingered beside the plane while the other passengers went inside to wait for their bags. He lit a cigarette and exhaled the smoke at the quarter moon, large in the damp night sky. He could see the curve of the earth's shadow arcing across the craters and lunar seas. He wondered how much time he had left. When the cigarette burned down to the filter he snapped it away and stooped to pick up his bag. He was going to have to switch brands: Al Wolf, oilfield roughneck, never smoked filters. He squared his shoulders and walked through the terminal doors to anonymity.

Flashcubes and noise exploded around him like direct hits on the fuel storage tanks at Da Nang, and Kemp froze, looking for someplace to hide. People were running toward him. He seemed to hear a song. More circuit breakers tripped inside his head as he recognized his parents and brother and sister in the vanguard of the assault. The AWOL bag slipped from numbed fingers as a mob of relatives, neighbors, friends of his parents', amused strangers, fellow travelers, and bored airport personnel came at him in a human wave, smiling maniacally, shouting their best wishes. He turned to rabbit back outside and saw the hand-lettered sign above the door. "Welcome Home Hero."

Kemp's mother blindsided him as he hesitated like a jackrabbit on the interstate; throwing her arms about him, she carried him against the ticket counter with her momentum, and his father stapled them both in place with even more widespread arms. Kemp's sister and little brother leaped on them from opposite sides.

Inarticulate fear collected in his guts and rushed up his spine like hot mercury, a barometer of the high pressure he suddenly found himself under. He thought chaotically of all the men who'd died in falling planes and choppers because he'd fallen asleep. Their faces transposed onto the faces around him, bloated and discolored, leering their greetings. His chest contracted in a silent scream for them to get away. Then his father was taking control, pushing everyone back, shouting: "Give the boy room to breathe."

The flashcubes continued to flare in his eyes. *Secondary burn*, he thought. His mother was a dead weight around his neck; he thought she'd fainted in the crush. His sister Cynthia was hugging his father, now, jumping up and down against him with her arms around his neck. Kemp's brother had been brushed aside and was pressed flat against the plate glass window.

Kemp struggled around and looked full into the twisted face of the American Airlines ticket agent, sleeves rolled up, shirt pocket full of pens, wilted in the collected bodyheat of the crowd and the humidity of the Port Arthur night, giving him thumbs up.

"Welcome home, son," Kemp's father said ostentatiously, boomed into his face. Kemp saw his father extend his hand, a gesture utterly alien and unexpected, and saw his own hand move to accept, but he didn't feel a thing. "It's good to have you back," his father said, the welcome home ambush neatly sprung.

The damage to Kemp's circuitry was extensive. All sensation was gone, nearly all gross motor coordination, anatomic reflexes were at 60%, sphincters were on the verge of surrender, the transmitter was surrounded by a blackened hedge of fused and smoking circuit breakers. He felt a scream begin to gather in his chest, starting so deep it felt like he was going to vomit it out, turn himself inside out in the utterance. THE MARTIANS ARE COMING FOR ME. THEY'RE WAITING ON THE OTHER SIDE OF THE MOON. An unexpected sequence of synapses flashed, and, instead of purging himself of this poisonous knowledge, he moved crablike against the counter facing his family and a girl they were thrusting forward who he seemed to remember vaguely from somewhere. He needed some Thorazine, bad.

Kemp's father took his gladhanding Texas millionaire face out of his inside coat pocket and put it on as he turned to confront the crowd.

"It's not easy waitin for your son in Veetnam," he began, "waitin for the phonecall or the visit from the army to let you know he's dead or worse. And you turn on the TV news and see what's goin on, see the damn hippies and the leftests riotin in the streets against the government, subvirtin the war with all that Jane Fonda bullshit, and you want to cry when you see what things have come to while your oldest boy is fightin to preserve our way of life; ours, not theirs, *ours* and he gets wounded savin a friend's life and lays in a coma in the hospital while they wipe their asses with the flag he was hurt defendin."

Kemp's father paused, momentarily overcome by his own rhetoric.

What an incredible run-on sentence, Kemp thought.

"I thank God he's home, now, safe and sound. It makes me proud to be an American to meet my oldest boy come home from war, not like we came back, to bands and parades, but home at least to his family and his friends and the girl he left behind."

Where did I fuck up? Kemp wondered.

The crowd began to applaud, and the girl he only thought he might know from somewhere stepped up to him and put her arms around his neck and kissed him hard on the mouth. She was crying and Kemp felt her wet eyelashes on his cheek. Her scent filled his lungs. Neural impulses feverously rerouted themselves.

Kemp knew a few things. He knew that he needed some thorazine, bad; and he knew that his father was full of gladhanding Texas millionaire bullshit; and he knew that the girl attached to his lips was not his girlfriend. Between college and the army Kemp had led a celibate, generally isolated existence, clinging like a limpet to the underside of the family fortune. He was certain the girl currently vacuuming his mouth had had no significant part in that life.

Kemp pushed the girl away in horror as he saw a local television crew pushing their way through the crowd. 'That's all I need,' he thought. 'Beam old Kemp's picture up to the Martians and give em an exact fix on his hideout. Beam a few minutes of footage up to the moon.'

He began to make his move for the exit, the girl struggling to return to his embrace, and Kemp's father sagging to the right to head him off, but even with the girl slowing him down, Kemp was too fast.

"Wait," the local reporter shouted as the cameraman wrestled with the cable that snaked back to the truck.

Kemp turned in the doorway. "I got to be alone," he said out of the bottom of his mouth as he tried to dislodge the girl.

"Soldiers," Kemp's father laughed knowingly. "He wants to be alone with his girlfriend Louann."

"Louise," she corrected him.

"Louise," Kemp's father said, louder.

"Louann," she faltered.

Kemp backed into the darkness and around the corner, out of sight of the mob inside, and tried to get a little space between himself and the girl. "Who the hell are you?" he demanded, ready to run.

"I'm Cynthia's friend," she said. "Louise Capulet. I know I'm not your girlfriend or anything, but your father was going on about how you didn't have anyone to meet you and how sad it was and I told him I'd meet you."

"What?"

"It meant so much to him," she finished.

"My father thinks I'm a queer," Kemp told her.

"I'm sure he doesn't think that," Louise said, moved by good breeding to try to protect him from the truth. "I went out with you once. I know you don't remember. It was four years ago, when Cyn and I were freshmen. We went out during the spring break."

Kemp was breathing deep, rhythmic breaths, trying to restore his vital signs to normal after the welcome home ambush. He didn't even try to figure out what she was saying. Lots of circuits were still fused, and he was running on emergency power.

"I knew it wouldn't work," Louise sobbed. "I told Cyn it wouldn't work. You don't think I'm pretty, do you? I told her." A half dozen stainless steel prisoner of war bracelets jangled on her wrists. Dark starbursts of mascara radiated from her wet eyes, making them seem enormous. Kemp noticed that her lipstick matched her opaque pantyhose.

"Why no," he protested. "It's not that. I was just startled. I had to get away from all those people is all. Please, I'm sorry."

Louise stood crying, unconvinced. Kemp took a step toward her. "Honest," he said. "Please don't cry." He put his hand on her shoulder, thankful his fingers were still numb and said, "I remember going to the movie."

"Really?"

"Yeah, I had a great time."

They stood there silently. Kemp looked into her eyes, or rather into the centers of the two dark spots on her face where her eyes were hiding, and then away at the plane they were refueling with some of his Daddy's aviation fuel.

"Was it bad over there?" Louise asked after a time, a sob lurking underneath her question.

"Where?" Kemp asked, not entirely sure what the popular story about his military career was.

"You can be modest," she said, "but I know it must have been terrible. I read all about the war in *Time* and *Newsweek*. Did you kill anyone? I'm sorry, I shouldn't have asked that. Did it hurt where you were wounded? Not where, when, when you were wounded."

But he was thinking of the falling planes again, after her question about killing, and not paying attention, except to notice that she had trouble shutting up once she got started. "I wasn't but cut on the arm," he said.

She had a metallic bronze Lamborghini, low and open to the glowing Port Arthur sky, and she gave Kemp the keys and lowered herself into the passenger bucket with a small wriggle of her tight Baylor ass. It was like the small spacers the Martians used to scout out likely young white girls. The leather upholstery was soft and comfortable.

Kemp eased behind the instrument panel and looked over the controls and the dashboard display: speedometer calibrated in miles and kilometers per hour; tachometer; oil, water and fuel pressure gauges; pitch and yaw stabilizers; ion drive monitor; oscilloscope; navigational telemetry. It was quite a vehicle, all right. Kemp buckled the seat belt and shoulder harness. His hair brushed the vanadium alloy rollbar. A pair of buff-colored kid driving gloves were thrown carelessly on the dash and he pulled them on, looking out of the cockpit at the moon hanging in the wet night sky with a loopy, idiot's grin.

After all, he thought, *she's nothing to me. Maybe I can buy them off. It's the young white girls they're really interested in.*

The engine rumbled to life and the Lamborghini vibrated about them. The trace line on the oscilloscope quivered at .7 as he began to draw power from the machine, restoring his fused circuits. Kemp was feeling like by-God Buck Rogers,

out to whup some interplanetary ass. He snapped on the
running lights with an insolent flick of the wrist. This was a
different Kemp than the one they'd ambushed an hour before,
Kemp was full of different Kemps that his family didn't know
about. He engaged the throttle, laughing aloud as the ions
sang about their ears. He threw the short stick forward and
the Lamborghini screamed across the pavement, leaped a
curb and fishtailed through a maintenance area toward the
runway. The tires smoked as torque and massive g-forces
pressed Louise firmly into the seat. Her eyes widened as the
effects of rapid acceleration manifested themselves. Kemp's
knuckles were white on the stick as he threw her into second.

"I think you were very brave," Louise shouted over the
transmission whine, "in the war and all."

Kemp favored her with a tight-jawed smile, one eye on the
oscilloscope and the other on the runway lights that were
flashing by on either side of the cockpit.

Louise tried to lean closer to him, but Kemp paid no
attention, watching the spasming oscilloscope, throwing her
into third, thinking: 'escape velocity.'

"Come on, baby," he growled to the engine, but Louise
misunderstood and smiled. She was torn between a primal
conviction that Kemp needed a woman like her to help him
reassemble the scattered shards of his former life and an
equally strong urge to scream. She felt giddy and moist. Her
fingers slithered like bamboo vipers through the shag carpet
that covered the transmission hump, and Kemp switched on
his force field. The runway began to elevate as he threw her
into fourth for the last thousand feet.

Louise looked at her lipstick smeared on Kemp's mouth
and felt her insides go watery, in the grip of tidal conflicts
involving sex and motherhood and the Methodist church. The
Lamborghini parted company with the runway as a terrified
businessman in a twin engine Cessna nearly pulled the stick
out of the floorboards to avoid landing on the hood. The
Cessna's landing gear wooshed by their ears as the Lamborghini, well short of escape velocity and subject to the laws
of terrestrial ballistics, began to level out over Texas Route
146 and nose toward the gently sloping ground beyond.

"Stand by for reentry," Kemp screamed.

Louise braced her feet against the firewall as the Michelines chewed into the soft earth beyond the road. Kemp fought to hold the Lamborghini upright as it cut an arc through what appeared to be a soybean field.

"That was wonderful," Louise Capulet shouted.

"That was nothing," Kemp said, struggling with the sluggish controls as the concrete ribbon of Texas 146 appeared ahead. "Vectoring at 108 degrees," he said clearly so the flight recorder could pick it up over the windblast. They left the rising ground and settled one wheel at a time onto the pavement.

"Would you like some music?" Louise asked. "I think Jefferson Airplane's groovy, don't you?" She slipped *Surrealistic Pillow* into the tape player and Grace Slick's voice flowed past Kemp's ears like it was made out of stainless steel and silk. Grace Slick was holding a wild, long note that even the windshear and the inadequate speakers failed to temper.

Kemp glanced at the compass and saw that random chance and Italian suspension had colluded to point him away from Port Arthur into that desolate land of salt marshes and petrochemical refineries between the city and the Gulf. Just the sort of place Kemp needed for another run at escape velocity.

The pressure in Kemp's head had returned to normal, normal, that is, for Kemp, the normal that kept the transmitter safe, but he knew that if he wanted to keep it normal he had to take steps. He reached into his jacket pocket and took out a brown plastic bottle of Thorazine, rattling it beside his ear like dice in a Martian crap game. "Got anything to drink?" he shouted.

Louise produced a bottle of Lone Star from behind the seat, secured it between her thighs and opened it. A plume of white froth shot straight up through the cockpit and sheared off into the slipstream. Kemp thumbed the top off the Thorazine and tilted the bottle up to his lips. Brown tabs dribbled out of the corners of his mouth and jammed against his tongue. He lowered the bottle and accepted the beer from Louise. It was warm and frothy but he managed to get the Thorazine down.

"What's the medicine?" Louise wanted to know.

"Malaria," Kemp told her.

*   *   *

Kemp's father was driving the Rolls down Memorial Boulevard toward the center of Port Arthur. His wife sat beside him and his daughter and younger son were in the back. The Rolls was so quiet that the only sounds were the sounds of the clock ticking and the strangled gurgle of his wife's crying.

"He looked so thin," she sobbed. "I knew they weren't feeding him."

"They fed him," Kemp's father said. "He looks just fine so long's he don't go round shootin his mouth off about goddam men from Mars." He was irritated by his wife's sobbing and angered by Kemp's sudden disappearance at the airport. "He never woulda started that crap if you hadn't coddled him," he snarled.

"Not men from Mars," his younger son corrected him. "*Mart*ians."

"You always let him do what he wanted to do. Let him go to highschool in town. Let him go to a shitty little college in goddam Minnesota that no one ever heard of."

"That's so easy and cheap," Kemp's mother shouted. "You have some responsibility, too."

"Me?" he yelped. "If I'd been allowed to raise him right, none of this woulda happened. The army might've helped him if you hadn't interfered."

"How did I interfere?"

"The same way you always interfered, sticking your nose in where it doesn't belong. Calling him all the time, sending him money and packages. Hell, they *pay* you for being in the army. It was the first time in his life he ever earned his own way. But you weren't content to let that happen, were you? When I was in the army we spent all our offduty time playin poker and chasin skirt, not getten money from mommie and talkin to men from Mars."

"I *told* you," his younger son said, "not men from Mars, *Mart*ians."

"Shut up you little asshole," his father roared. "You're going to a goddam military school next year. I'll not have both my sons turned into queers."

"He left with Louise in too big a hurry to be a queer, Daddy," said Kemp's father's little girl.

"That's the first hopeful sign I've had in years," he said. "That was a good idea, Cyn."

"Thank you, Daddy," Kemp's sister smiled, brushing at some lint that clung to the monogram on her sweater. "I think she'll be good for him."

"She's dumb as a brick," Kemp's kid brother sulked.

The Lamborghini was poised at land's end, pointed at a flaming offshore oil rig and, beyond, Cuba. Kemp sat secure in his forcefield and Louise stretched out in the seat, her eyes glowing and her cheeks flushed from the ride through the salt marshes. Kemp's hand was still clutching the six inch stick that rose from the transmission hump.

"I don't fool around unless I'm really serious about someone," Louise told him. "You know, go all the way I mean." She smiled at Kemp's handsome profile. "I do fool around a little, though." Her hand moved from her lap to Kemp's right arm, slipping through the forcefield like a laser scalpel through a cobweb.

Kemp's electronics were seriously confused as he sat rigidly under her hand. He could feel her fingertips curling around his wrist. He tried to shift more power to the forcefield, but too many circuits were still down. *No forcefield,* Kemp thought, *where's the fucking forcefield when you need it?*

Louise's fingers brushed softly up his arm. She knew that she had to go slowly with him, knew that months of battling infection had sapped his strength. She knew he was under a lot of stress and excited to be home: she knew she had to go slowly with him. She moved her hand from his arm and pushed the tape back into the player.

Kemp took advantage of the break in contact to throw the Lamborghini into reverse and whip it sharply around so they were facing down the road toward Port Arthur. The wrenching motion threw Louise toward the dash and then back into the seat, where g-forces kept her pinned until they were hurtling down the road at a steady 85.

> When the truth is found to be lies
> And all the joy within you dies
> Don't you want somebody to love?

Don't you need somebody to love?
Wouldn't you love somebody to
love?
You better find somebody to love.

She slipped her hand over the transmission hump, under Kemp's fist on the stick shift, through the weakened forcefield and onto his leg. Warning klaxons sounded inside his head as his telemetry indicated that the integrity of the reactor chamber was in jeopardy.

"This could be our song," Louise shouted, encouraged by his response to her fingers on his thigh. She knew Kemp was an honorable man because instead of stopping the car to take advantage of her in the desolation of the saltmarshes he was driving faster, eager to be home with his family. Her hand drifted to the metal door to the reactor chamber.

The skipper of the oceangoing tug *Seadog* took his eyes off the three barges of wood compost that he was nosing down the Intracoastal Waterway to glance at his watch. The waterway was empty and tideswollen. It was a warm night and he would be home in a few hours. The lights of the channel markers glittered on the crest of the long swell that cut away from the bow of the lead barge.

Kemp's parents led the parade of vehicles up the sweeping drive to their home. Outdoor lights bathed the side yard in an even glow that revealed the scattered tables and the buffet and the small band that was set up in one corner. Kemp's mother was out of the Rolls almost before it rolled to a stop, racing to the house where she hoped to get a grip on herself before facing the guests. Kemp's little brother followed her across the lawn, feeling as if he needed to get a grip on himself, too, after the ride from the airport in the back seat with his sister Cyn. Kemp's father and his little girl started to greet the guests. "He'll be along any minute now," Kemp's father told them as they disembarked and started across the lawn for the buffet.

Your eyes, I say your eyes may look like his
Yeah, but in your head, baby, I'm afraid you
don't know where it is

Don't you want somebody to love?
Don't you need somebody to love?
Wouldn't you love somebody to love?
You better find somebody to love.

Louise sang along with Grace Slick as her fingers approached the main control rod in the reactor chamber, and Kemp felt her radioactive fingers seize it, and a red light began flashing in the instrument panel.

"Reactor chamber integrity has been compromised," he said into the flight recorder microphone. The traceline on the oscilloscope was a blur and Kemp recalibrated it by a factor of three.

"Buckle up," Kemp told her as they both shifted into high gear. The marshgrass rattled beside the road as the car blasted toward the drawbridge that spanned the Intracoastal Waterway where the red lights were flashing.

Tears are runnin, they are runnin down your
  breast
And your friends, baby, they treat you like a
  guest

Grace Slick had never been in finer voice.

Kemp's father had never been more embarrassed. He'd promised his guests one returned war hero, less men from Mars, and a goddam psycho'd stepped off the plane and maybe kidnapped his little girl's school friend and stolen her fifty-seven-thousand-dollar Lamborghini. His wife was getting drunk and crying on the shoulder of anyone who'd stand for it, his younger son was holed up in the bathroom with last month's *Playboy*, and his little girl was teasing young corporate cock in front of the ornamental bamboo grove he'd had planted to set the mood for the party. His world was crumbling as the band began to crank up a dentist's office version of *I am the Walrus*. He looked at his rollex and saw that it was getting late. He was going to have to produce the wine soon, whether or not he produced a war hero guest of honor. He went over to the chief caterer who was standing beside the ice chests of wine.

Don't you *want* somebody to love?
Don't you *need* somebody to love?
Wouldn't you *love* somebody to love?
You better *find* somebody to love.

Grace Slick held the last note longer and harder than Kemp would have thought possible under ordinary circumstances, such as when no radioactive fingers were massaging the main control rod in the cockpit of the spacer as it approached escape velocity and the reactor approached critical mass and they all approached the rising drawbridge over the Intracoastal Waterway. The Lamborghini reached apogee exactly 2.8947 seconds after parting company with the drawbridge (according to the dashboard chronometer) and Kemp tensed as the nose dropped and he saw the mound of wood compost, a shadow, perhaps anything, perhaps coal, perhaps jello for all he knew, the way the evening had gone so far, and he swept his right hand off the wheel and pushed Louise into the seat where the harness would hold her on impact. Many questions strobed through Kemp's mind in the 2.0049 seconds between apogee and impact (by the dashboard chronometer) such as: what had happened to the ion drive? why wasn't the forcefield working? what was in the barge? how deep was the channel? who *was* this woman with her fingers around the main control rod?

In the .789 seconds before impact Kemp thought the thoughts of a pilot dropping toward the treetops, betrayed by a sleeping specialist in Da Nang and forces unknown; then the Lamborghini hit the compost heap, burying itself to the windshield in sawdust and shavings from a lumber mill 80 miles upstream and destabilizing the barge, loaded too full for its own good, causing it to rock on its keel toward the waterline, water pouring in amidships, breaking moorings fore and aft, buckling at the waterline, breaching, foundering, taking the next barge in line, rivets popping like stray rounds into the water, wood shavings spewing out.

Kemp, improperly buckled in, snapped toward the wheel, bounced off, both collarbones broken, struck the rollbar, loosing consciousness, slumped down in time to receive the full force of the seat, broken from the track, hurtling forward toward the steering column. His back made a sound almost as awful as the rending of metal as the barge broke in half and water wooshed over them. Kemp was headed toward a watery end, slipping into a sleep where the Martians couldn't follow, when he felt a great pain in his right ear.

Louise Capulet allowed herself a brief instant of wide-eyed surprise as the car went off the bridge, surprise because she hadn't been paying close attention to the driving, more interested in the main control rod, brief because she reacted to Kemp's protective hand by swinging her legs up and bracing her feet against the dash. She was still moving forward at better than sixty miles an hour when the car hit the compost, but her flexed legs and the harness decelerated her at an acceptable rate, leaving her with only a few cracked ribs and a hole in her lower lip from a slight overbite problem that she had never had corrected. She was stunned, too dazed in the few seconds when the barge quivered at the brink of capsizing to see that Kemp was being badly used by the Lamborghini, ping ponging around between seat and wheel, fracturing his collarbones and back.

But when she realized what was happening, when oily water washed over them, cold, bringing her to her senses, she disconnected the harness and reached for Kemp. The barge reared up behind them, threatening to roll completely over, burying them under a mountain of sawdust that would be impossible to swim through, and then changed its mind, tore in half and settled down into the channel. The next barge shot off toward the shore and went aground against the huge rocks that reinforced the bank. Louise grabbed at Kemp's hair, but it was too short to get a grip on, so she took his right ear in her fist and hauled him out of the car, swimming desperately up through water soupy with wood shavings, breaking the surface with a gasp as the tug sliced by and struck one of the bridge pylons with the loudest noise she had ever heard. The bridge started to buckle, dipped crazily to the right, then slowly the road surface entered the water, sending out a swell that lifted them clear of the clinging wood shavings and left them high above the surface of the canal on top of a rock.

Louise spat out some blood and wiped her hair out of her eyes. Kemp lay broken and unconscious on the rock beside her. The lead barge was adrift on the canal, still headed more or less out to sea, soon to run aground, the middle two were sunk, the bridge was out and the tug was caught in a tangle of steel superstructure. Louise Capulet began to sob; she had ruined Kemp's homecoming. She felt for a femoral pulse on Kemp's leg. He was breathing heavily. She was certain he had suffered lethal internal injuries. Banshee sirens wailed in the distant night and the screams and curses of the crew of the tug, imprisoned on the surface of the canal by the fallen bridge, were strident across the water. The moon reflected briefly in a patch of clear water and then winked out.

"Help," she cried. "Over here."

"Help your ass," came the answering shout from the tug.

"Help," she shouted. "He's dying."

"He'll be lucky if he dies," the tug shouted back. "If I get aholt of him it'll take him a year to die."

The sirens were getting closer. Cars, backed up on either side of the canal, their lights angled over the water, were disgorging humans eager to gawk at the damage and offer opinions about almost every aspect of the disaster.

"Help," shouted Louise Capulet.

"Ambulance is coming," they shouted back.

"Ooooohhh," Kemp said, returning to consciousness for a moment, long enough to realize that it was more comfortable unconscious, long enough to realize that something had gone seriously wrong with his second attempt at escape velocity.

"Are you alright?" Louise whispered in his ear, stroking the damp cords of hair at his temple.

"Oooohhh," Kemp repeated, monitoring his fractures and sprains. "Ooooohh shit."

"Help," Louise screamed. "Please help."

"Were you drinking?" someone shouted down from the side of the canal. "They were drinking," she heard the same voice say to someone else. "Damn fool kids."

"Ooooohhh," Kemp moaned softly, coming to the point on his inventory of pain where he realized he was lying wet on a hard rock beside the Intracoastal Waterway. "Louann," Kemp whispered.

"Louise," she corrected softly, playing out what she believed to be Kemp's death scene, the first big death scene of her life, the last for Kemp. She bent closer to him so she could memorize his last words, nearly overcome by the tragedy of his escaping the war to die after ramming a barge on the Intracoastal Waterway the night of his return. "What is it?"

"You got to keep your hands off the main control rod," Kemp told her. "You'll regret it if you don't."

Louise looked down at Kemp's pants and saw that his zipper was open and that he was lolling out, tumescent despite the crash and the swim through the sawdust. Gently Louise replaced the main control rod and zipped up his pants. "I'm sorry," she sobbed. "Forgive me."

"Ooooohhh," Kemp moaned as she replaced him in his pants. The moan had a quality that had been missing from previous moans; she took it as a good sign.

"Don't worry," she said. "You'll be alright. I promise." The siren of the first emergency vehicle was quite loud now, and she could tell it was forcing its way through the stopped traffic.

"Thanks," he whispered, glad for a more objective opinion because he felt like shit on a wet rock. He had his doubts. He passed out again.

First there was the falling with the earth not there and she knowing it, then there was the impact: hand on her breast, head on seat and dash while twisted Kemp flung about. Water struggling with sawdust to suffocate them; then the wave, the rock, the jackals that gathered. The police, the doctors, her father and now Kemp's. So many versions of the truth, where to begin? Louise stood at the door in the early morning light, wearing a neckbrace and looking at the wood grain.

Kemp's father was an asshole who affected not to know her name, and the year she had spent rooming with Cyn had been a learning laboratory in abnormal psychology. The little brother was not, at this point, a serious consideration, but, if pressed, she would have to admit that she had doubts in that quarter as well. Kemp's mother wasn't there at all: Tennessee Williamsing it out in the ozone since quite some time before Louise had arrived on the scene. But Kemp was something else: she'd locked onto him that time they'd gone to the movie that he couldn't remember, and she'd never forgotten. She thought he was the most beautiful man she'd ever seen, worth tolerating his family if she could make him love her, make him because he had to.

She didn't know what it was, biology maybe, some unexpected hormonal tide that resisted reason, young yet, not sure of the difference; but she knew that he was intelligent, more than her, probably, and she didn't sell herself short there: she knew she wasn't stupid. So she worried and waited in silence, not trusting anyone with the reality of things but herself. Surely no one in either of their families. And now that she'd met him again she knew that she'd been right not to resist it; the war had affected him a little but mostly she felt it had been just one thing too many for him to deal with. She knew he would snap out of it, emerge heroic, get a grip on himself: young then, not knowing the burden of a life choice once assumed. Soon to learn.

Louise Capulet followed the pattern of the grain on the door with her eyes, tired, terrified, hoping to hypnotize herself through the last task of the night. She saw her hand move forward and grasp the bronze knocker, lift it, and the slow fall to the striker plate echoed like death inside the house. It was all her fault; there was nothing for it. Now she had to face the Kemp family after a night without sleep while being kidnapped to Mars: if she'd known she would have told them. Fortunately she didn't know anything about the burnished aliens like elegant sheiks from red deserts far away. She had to fall back on something she knew about. The striker plate cracked hollow through the hallway and steps came. A black man with an expression of displeasure opened the door. His gray hair was cut close, his lips tight together and his eyebrows a chevron of irritation. "What?"

"Mr. Kemp, please," she said.

He looked at her clothes, soaked, wrinkledried and suspect in the early morning light. He knew who she was, alright, part of the plot to mindfuck Kemp home from the army alive. He didn't like it. "Is this important?"

"Yes," she said. "It's about Kemp."

"Come on in, then." VanBuren stepped aside and closed the door behind her.

He lets her in—she remembering houses like this house, empty, echoing as she walked through them with her father, Bubba Jim Capulet, gravely displeased now by the lost Lamborghini, insured but not yet paid for; by Kemp's injuries and the out of court settlement, anticipated but not yet negotiated; by the deals yet to be cut to reopen the Intracoastal Waterway. But all this vexation soothed by Louise alive and Kemp's heroic gesture as they fell toward the barge.

He leaves her at the door and slippers off down the hallway *shoop, shoop, shoop* to get Mr. Kemp from wherever, and she stands, then sits, neck braced, tired, wanting sleep after the visit to the hospital where Kemp drifts in Demerol and thickening Plaster of Paris.

Mr. Kemp strides down the hall, hardheeled on the carpet, and VanBuren stays long enough to look disgusted and shoops off to get some more sleep. Mr. Kemp, who may pretend to remember her name, worried she'd been snatched by his deranged son for God knew what purpose, now fearful of a story involving rape or sodomy, now worried again as he notices the neck brace, slipping into worry again and then fear like a silk shirt.

"Louise," he says, getting it right, "where's—"

"Mr. Kemp," she blurts, "I love your son and I want to marry him but he's in the hospital . . ." before she has to quit to cry full time.

"What happened?" Kemp's old man asks, eager to be occupying the high ground of paternity for a weeping woman, young maybe, and stupid, but in love with his faggot son.

"The car went off the bridge into the canal," she says through hiccoughed sobs.

"Who was driving?"

She hesitates, on the forking trailhead of truth, knowing down one fork waits the story of the main control rod and the blame that's hers for fooling around in the reactor chamber, and down the other the story that she liked it.

"He was, wasn't he?"

"Yes," she said, "but . . ."

"Say no more," he says. "I'll pay for everything."

"But . . ."

"Everything," he repeats. "I'll make it all good."

"But it was all my fault," she says.

"Don't try to protect him," Kemp's old man says. "We'll settle on any reasonable figure. I'm just thankful you're alright. How's your neck?"

"It hurts some," she says. "And my ribs are cracked, but I'll be alright. He's hurt pretty badly, though."

"How badly?" he asks with an interest she can't interpret.

"Pretty badly, but they said he won't die. His back is fractured, both his collarbones . . ." she has to cry some more here, and then it seems she's outside with his blessing and the promise of money to come. She goes home in the waiting taxi, and Mr. Kemp goes in to breakfast where he remembers to tell his family, after toast.

(1984)

R. L. Shafner

R. L. Shafner was born in Colorado, in 1953. She took a B.A. at the University of Colorado, Boulder, and an M.A. at the University of Denver. She has worked with publishing houses in New York City and with CBS Television News. Her stories have begun to appear in a variety of magazines. "Stop Me If You've Heard This," printed here, was a finalist in the 1983 Nelson Algren Short Story Competition. Shafner has also held grants and fellowships at Stanford, the Bread Loaf Writers Conference, Yaddo, and the Provincetown Fine Arts Work Center.

A poet as well as a writer of fiction, Shafner specializes in the chiseled delineation of character. Her prose is tightly controlled, as her characters' lives are not. Much of the power of her work resides in the tense contrasts between the irrationality of what is going on, of what is being done and said (like many younger writers, she makes consistent use of wonderfully realistic dialogue), and the carefully wrought prose which expresses these things. There is a hard edge to her work, distinctly familiar to readers of modern fiction. But as I noted earlier, this is not a dispassionate hardness. It is neither cruel nor cold, but simply the way Shafner sees her world and the people who share it with her.

Shafner has recently been extending her work into longer forms. She is currently at work on a novel.

STOP ME IF YOU'VE HEARD THIS

Janice looked up from her typewriter. She rubbed her eyes, moaned softly.

"I'm *sooo* tired," she said.

Wells opened up his assignment folder and looked through the different requests. One of his bosses wanted to know the name of the consulting firm in Washington that was advising foreign investors not to invest in American cities, that riots were expected. Another boss wanted a profile of Britain's unemployment situation: what was the alcoholism rate there now? Still another boss wanted some information on Tahiti—what was the cost of living, and what kind of land was for sale.

Janice lifted herself up from her chair, pressing both hands against her desk to get some leverage. Wells saw her out of the corner of his eye; she was struggling to get out of her chair. Her dress caught on one of the filing cabinets and she swore, jerking it away. Janice had worn the dress—a faded blue smock—almost every day for the past four months, ever since she had begun "to show." She was seven months pregnant.

"Wells?" Janice whispered.

He didn't know why she needed to whisper. There was no one else in this closet-sized room. No one else could fit in, even if they had wanted to. Not with the extra-large desks, the ceiling-high filing cabinets, and the bookshelves that sagged in the middle, weighted with computer manuals, dictionaries, and a wastebasket. There wasn't even any space for a wastebasket on the floor. Wells had typed at least a half a dozen memos in the course of the last few months, asking for his own office, and hadn't received a reply. He imagined that his letters were filed neatly in the bottom of someone's trash bin.

Janice walked over to Wells' desk. She didn't walk actually, Wells observed; her feet dragged against the linoleum.

The moccasins made it easier. The soles were thin, worn; there was little resistance. She had only three steps to take between her desk and his; he watched a bead fall off one of her shoes, roll across the floor.

"Did you have a nice evening?" Janice said.

Wells looked up at her. She wasn't a bad-looking woman. Short blonde hair with very short bangs. The sort of shortly-cropped hair that only flattered a woman when she had a slender face and small features, which Janice did, he had to admit. Sometimes, when she was speaking to him, he counted the different shades of her blonde hair. The last time he had come up with seven. It was the expression on her face that distorted her looks. A caricature of suffering.

Sara, on the other hand, was striking. A healthy glow to her skin and her eyes. Alert-looking eyes. Curious, expressive. A tall, thin adolescent boy's body—slightly hunched over, as if she were going to listen to someone, or as if she were ashamed. She had a different way of dressing—layers—of T-shirt, buttoned down cashmere sweater, tweed vest, denim jacket, and calf length skirt with different colored slips underneath. She dressed as if she had put on everything she owned, didn't know when she'd be back. Wells liked the way she smelled. She made her own perfume, never told him what it was. It was a light, clean smell. A gentle, kid kind of smell.

"Wells?" Janice said. "Did you have a nice evening?"

"I don't know," he said. He looked at the papers on his desk, reshuffled them, listened to her slurping her soda pop. He looked back at her. "Should you be drinking Coke?"

Janice frowned. She stirred her Coke with her straw, then lifted the straw out of the can. She licked the straw.

"I drink a lot of milk," she said. "But milk makes me tired." She seemed to yawn for emphasis. "Did I tell you that my husband went out and bought me a new mattress, that my back is so sensitive now?" She shook her head slowly. "The other pregnancies weren't this bad."

"I went out with some friends last night," Wells relented. "We heard some music."

"Oh." She looked down at the floor. "I wish I could go out sometimes."

"Why don't you?"

"My husband's always out of town. I have no one to go with."

"Mmmmm."

He turned on his computer terminal and dialed up, trying to get the system connected. The line was busy, and he put the receiver back in its cradle. He looked at the phone and thought about calling Sara. He knew the name of the company she now worked for: it was located only about two miles from Wells' office and he often wondered if he'd run into her on the street. At this time of year she'd probably be wearing her large down coat, a coat that appeared as if it had once been a sleeping bag. There might be a few wisps of down in her hair. Her shoes might be muddied, there might be mud on her tights. She often looked as if she were in a hurry, eager to assuage her boredom. "*Bor*-ing." She pronounced the word like the sound of a doorbell.

When Sara had worked at the same company as Wells she had often been bored, and she had often engaged in imitating people, sometimes to their faces, usually not. On the last occasion—two months ago—she had imitated one of the office managers. She had sprayed herself with the cologne he had kept in his desk, she had slapped people on the back whenever she had spoken to them, she had used words like "prioritize" and "familiarize" and "FYI" too often, and she had been fired.

Sometimes when she had gotten restless with office jokes or pettiness, she had put her head on her desk, feigned sickness, tottered to the restroom. She sat in one of the stalls, she had said, pulled a book out of her handbag. She had read all of Proust that way, she had claimed.

Wells hated going by the room where Sara used to work. An efficient-looking woman sat at her desk now—a cousin of one of the vice-presidents. She wore pin-striped shirts and black ribbon ties. She was cheerful.

Janice cleared her throat.

"Wells! You're not listening to me."

"Mmmm. What were you saying?"

"I was saying— I was saying that I *was* on the pill for a while."

"Uh-huh." He looked at her.

"Anyway," she looked back at him. "If I hadn't gotten that blood clot, I wouldn't have gotten off it. The pill. Nothing else is reliable." She finished her Coke, set the can on his desk. "Maybe I should have gotten an abortion. But that's not the way I was raised. But I knew that if I weren't pregnant, I'd—"

"I heard bluegrass music last night, Janice." He waited for her to be quiet. "Do you know what bluegrass is?"

She shook her head no.

"A lot of banjo. A steel guitar. Drums. A bass. A mandolin. A violin, but they call it a fiddle. A lot of twang. A lot of . . . *whoop* and . . . *kick*."

Janice looked at Wells quietly for a moment. "The thing about being pregnant—"

"It was great music, Janice," Wells said. "Absolutely great. Terrific in fact. Wonderful. Okay? . . . Think about it."

Wells swiveled back to his computer and Janice shuffled back to her desk. She sat down and turned on her typewriter. She sat there for several minutes, not typing, not doing anything while Wells dialed up the computer telex number again, and finally got the system connected. He typed in the necessary passwords, then sat back in his chair, watched the green lettering on the black screen. Janice laid her head on her desk.

"Wells?" she whispered.

"What?"

"Wells?"

"What?" He turned to look at her.

"Wells." She paused. "I used to listen to music."

On his way home from work that night Wells stopped to hide under an awning. It was raining, hard, and he didn't have an umbrella. Sometimes he bought one, but he always managed to lose it. He watched the people hurrying by, sunk into their collars, holding their umbrellas against the wind as if they were making some kind of offer or negotiation. Wells imagined how easy it would be to grab one of the umbrellas, and run. He hadn't yet read about that sort of robbery, and he supposed it was about time.

He thought about going into the bookstore he was currently leaning against, but the people who ran it often seemed as if they were standing on their toes, trying to look down on him. He looked in the window and his heart beat slammed. His face and the back of his neck got warm, he felt dizzy. A woman who was about five feet nine with medium length brown hair and a gray coat was standing inside the store. She was standing with her back to Wells and Wells pressed his hands against the store window, looked through the glass. Sara's hair was thick and curly—the kind of curls he could neatly slide his fingers through. The woman in the store could have had curly hair but because of the rain it was wet, tangled.

Wells pushed his own wet hair away from his face, cleared his throat, and walked into the store. The door had a bell on it, and it clanged when Wells opened it. Both the bookstore clerk and the woman turned to look at Wells and Wells stopped walking, tried smiling, then turned around, found another awning to hide under.

It hadn't been Sara. It had been nothing like Sara. The woman in the store had been about ten years older. She also had a look on her face as if someone had just spilled something on her. Wells walked down the block hating himself.

He continued walking, walked backwards, tried shielding the rain from his face. Other people were attempting to dodge the rain and each other, and several of them bumped into Wells, one man holding a suitcase over his head. Wells looked at faces, peered discreetly under umbrellas. It wasn't improbable that Sara would be in this neighborhood, on this block; she lived right around the corner. But if she saw him, she would, most likely, call out his name, from a speeding cab, or a tenth story window, then hurry on—to some new jazz loft, some new Russian cafe, some new book project she was working on with a bunch of her friends.

Wells forced himself to back away from the rain, and he climbed into a bus. The doors closed against his back and he couldn't move. A man who smelled as if he had showered in after-shave, and who appeared as wide as a doorway, stood one step above him.

Maybe Sara was not in her apartment right now, maybe she was not anywhere near her apartment. Maybe she was waiting for him, at his apartment. Once he had said good-bye to her for the night, saw her off in a cab, and then he went out for a quick dinner. When he returned home, he turned on the local news, and made himself a drink. Then he took a hot bath, read Proust, and dropped the book in the tub. Then he shut off all the lights in the apartment, and he turned off his radio, and he shivered inside his cold sheets. He had almost descended into sleep when he ascended. He had heard some noise in the apartment, and his body stiffened against his mattress, he listened. He turned on his bedside lamp, whipped the covers off himself, and looked down at the floor. There was a hand waving up at him and Sara was laughing.

Even now, when he entered his apartment, day or night, he checked his one closet, and he checked under his bed. She still had his key.

"I'm tired," Janice said. She lifted up her blouse, and looked at her belly, stroked it. "I did some Christmas shopping yesterday."

"Christmas shopping?" Wells said. "It's October."

"I have a lot of presents to buy. I have a big family. A bigger one soon." She patted her stomach.

"Oh," Wells said.

Janice sighed loudly, stretched her legs out in front of herself. Even with nylons, her legs appeared blue.

"Don't you like babies, Wells?" She sat up in her chair, got up, moved over to Wells' desk. She brought her can of Coke with her. "They're so cute. Don't you think?"

Wells began scanning the computer print-out for the exact locations of New Jersey's hazardous waste disposal sites. As an aside, the joker wanted to know where Richard Nixon lived in New Jersey, and why he had moved there. Wells smiled.

"Did you have a nice evening?" Janice said.

Wells shrugged. He opened up the envelope the office

messenger had left on his desk, and he took out the magazines. He opened up the *Fortune* magazine, perused the table of contents, turned to the article he needed.

"My husband," Janice said, "is in California now. First he said he was coming back in a week. Then he called last night and he said three more weeks." She sat down on Wells' desk. "He's never home anymore."

"Mmm. I know you have a lot of your own work to do but . . ." He handed her the magazine. "Can you Xerox this article? I'm really busy."

Janice looked at the article, closed the magazine, held it against her chest.

"My oldest son," she said, "is in trouble at school. He's at a funny age now, thirteen. He's been staying home or running around downtown. He was writing his own excuses and signing his own name to them. His name is the same as his father's, and for a while the school didn't catch on. Now they have. They act like it's my fault. . . . Why are you smiling?"

"It's funny. Don't you think it's funny that he—"

"Now he's really in trouble. He has a temperature of one-hundred. I had to stay up the whole night with him. His forehead was so damn hot, I just about burned myself on it. Then I had to help him to the bathroom and then he—"

"Janice." Wells made a smile at her. "I didn't go out last night. I've got nothing to report. Okay?"

"Then my other kids started crying. They were crying so loud the—"

"I stayed home last night, Janice. Home. I got caught in the rain and I got the chills and I took a hot bath and I went to bed. But everything's fine. I'm fine. And so are you."

"Why are you smiling?"

Wells shook his head, smiling, trying to hold back the smile. She was looking at him suspiciously. Angrily.

"Okay," he said. "Okay. I went to a Chinese restaurant last night with some friends." Janice sat down on a chair across from Wells' desk, took off her moccasins and rubbed her swollen ankles. He opened a desk drawer and looked at a menu from a Chinese restaurant. The other day a young boy had been passing menus out on a street corner. "Mu shu pork," Wells read from the drawer so Janice couldn't see. "Cold noodles with sesame sauce." He looked up at Janice. "Sweet and sour prawns. Egg rolls. Wonton soup. Japanese beer."

She stopped rubbing her ankles and looked at him. "I thought you said it was a Chinese restaurant."

Wells shrugged. "They have Japanese beer."

"I don't like Chinese food."

"I don't either."

Janice picked up her Coke can from the floor, and drank some of the Coke. She licked some of the Coke off her lips.

"I know," Janice said, "that if I went to college everyone wouldn't be treating me like I'm dumb."

"You know what?" Wells said. "I think I come here to work. I think that's why I come here. How about you? Can you Xerox that article for me?"

"I won't be treated," Janice shouted, "like I'm a child. I'm a grown woman. I am a grown woman! And you know it."

She scooted back to her desk, threw his magazine in one of her drawers.

Wells had started out the day in a good mood.

He had gotten up early and he had walked the entire three and a half miles to work. He had had enough time to take a fairly long detour and drop some boots off at a shoe repair shop. Someone—he couldn't remember who—had recommended this repair shop. The boots had been expensive, they needed new heels. He needed someone who could do a good job.

After Wells had slipped the shoe receipt into his wallet, he had loitered at a nearby newspaper stand, whistling at the flashy headlines, watching the thick flow of office workers pushing each other to work, or at least that's how it had seemed. The newsstand was located on the same block as the building in which Sara worked and Wells had inspected the faces, most of them looking distracted, or impervious. There had been a few times where he had thought he had seen her—not someone in the same ridiculously big gray down coat, but a woman in a faded denim jacket, another woman in a cape that appeared as if it had been made out of an army blanket. Neither of them, of course, were her. Not that he had really expected to see her. She was probably arriving at work right about now—at 11:00. She was always late.

After Wells had been elbowed away from the newsstand, he had stopped to peer at his reflection in a clothing store window. He had had the same expression on his face as the men he had often seen coming out of the welfare office, situated not too far from where he lived. In order to escape his reflection, all his reflections that would follow him along the long street of store windows, he had crossed over to the park.

The pathways in the park had been paved with leaves. A paint-thick fog had hung over the trees. The lake was so still it had seemed like ice. Perched on the water were birds, and they had shone like black oil. He wanted to be observant, and not think so much. He wanted to notice things. The way Sara noticed things. Like the white paint she had once pointed out to him, poured on the snow, and the kids giggling behind a parked car. Or, the peculiar way the cars in the city had been manufactured—the horns and the brake, she had said, were somehow wired together. When the drivers used their brakes, she had said, their horns went off. She had also pointed out that Wells bit his nails when he really wanted to say something offensive.

Wells had wanted to notice things on his long walk to work, but his mind had kept slipping to Sara. Too easily he recalled many of their conversations, the long pauses, the sighs, the look on her face—indecision, ambivalence. "Are you always like this?" he had asked her. "Yes," she had said, for once not hesitating. They had been standing in an elevator and Wells had kicked the soft metal wall, more than a few times. He had wanted to put his hands through her long, thick, clean-smelling hair, and pull.

Wells revised those conversations now—making himself appear more restrained, nonchalant. He imagined the conversations they would have. First, he would explain his past behavior—confusion, irritability—and attribute it to family problems. Then he would tell her all the *great* places he had been in the two months they hadn't seen each other, all the *great* people he had met. Wells would make them great. He would also be more spontaneous with her now, unpredictable, inconsistent. He would lie. He wouldn't make any mistakes.

He had enjoyed his walk through the park. As long as he had concentrated on the sound his shoes made against the paper-thin leaves, or the way last night's rain tore slowly off the trees, or the way the fog seemed to diffuse the sounds and the colors. For the most part, he had enjoyed his walk. Then he had stopped off at a deli, bought a steamy cup of chicory blended coffee. He remembered how carefully the cashier had placed the plastic lid over the styrofoam cup, how her hands had been moist with the coffee's steam. The coffee, however, was now cold; the milk had coagulated at the top.

"Darn," he whispered. "Darn."

Wells looked over at Janice who was sitting at her desk, rubbing her swollen ankles, moaning softly.

"Janice," Wells said, "would you do me a favor?"

She turned to look at him, warily.

"Would you," he said, "would you please shut up, Janice?"

Wells opened his assignment folder and began his morning work. He looked through the different requests, phoned the different libraries, and told them he'd send a messenger over to get some more periodicals. He was assertive and commanding. If only he could be that way more often, he'd save himself a lot of time. Janice appeared as if she were about to cry, and she staggered out of the room as if she were drunk. There now. See how easy things could be.

"Good morning," Wells said.

Janice looked more closely at one of her index cards. She wrote something on it, bearing down hard on her pencil, and she broke the lead. She pulled another pencil out of her desk, and continued writing. Wells sat down at his desk, and he looked at her. He folded his hands.

She had barely spoken to him in the last week and a half—answering him when she had to, avoiding his eyes—and he was disliking work even more now than when she had spoken to him. It was the white silence of a waiting room: the sound of pages being turned, but not read, or read, but not comprehended; a sporadic cough, a clearing of the throat and then: nothing. She spoke in a low modulated tone when she spoke. She spoke tersely. Wells was beginning to loathe the simple sounds of their chair springs creaking, the opening and closing of file cabinets.

"Mmm," he said. "Something smells good. Are you wearing perfume?"

She shook her head, not turning around to look at him.

"Must be the Xerox machine," he said.

He wanted her to laugh, but she didn't. Not that he always expected people to laugh when he joked. He did expect, however, that they would at least acknowledge his effort. Wells imagined getting up off his chair, tapping her on the shoulder, and when she turned to look at him, he would slap her face. Slap it loud. And clear. He would slap that face that appeared so disfigured with its exaggeration of pain and self-pity. "What do you have to feel so bad about?" he wanted to say. "Why don't you shut up?" But all he could do was look at her and feel uneasy.

"Janice," he said. "About the other . . . What happened last week. . . . Can you forget that I . . ."

She turned to look at him, waited.

"What do you mean?" she said.

"Well, you know," he said, exasperated, "when I got on top of my desk and took all my clothes off."

Janice swiveled her chair back to her desk.

Wells looked at his phone. He thought about calling Sara again. Not that he hadn't tried calling her in the more than two months now that they hadn't seen each other. He had called her several times at her home and had left messages on her answering machine. He had phoned her new job and she had apologized: for not returning his calls, for being so busy. But it was only temporary. She couldn't talk just now, she had said, but she wanted to talk to him, to see him. It was just that she was so busy with this new goddamn job. She'd call him, she promised.

About a week ago Wells had called her at her office once again. She had not recognized his voice, and he had had to tell her his name. "Oh," she had laughed, "oh, sorry." Then she had said nothing, and he had heard people talking in the background, but he couldn't hear what they were saying. "I gave at the office," she had finally said, and she had hung up.

Wells had wondered, was still wondering who Sara was speaking to, who she thought she was speaking to.

Did she mean to let her fellow workers know that it wasn't a personal call? Or, did she mean to let Wells know that it was?

Once he had told her that he didn't always know how to take what she said. She had shaken her head, slowly; she had sighed. "Sometimes I'm not sure myself."

Wells would like to put the whole thing out of his mind. The whole thing. He would like to.

He took a deep breath. He took another deep breath. He was not going to cry. He was not going to do that. He opened his assignment folder. One of his bosses wanted a listing of all the major bankruptcies in the last year in the U.S. Another boss wanted to know the last time a union had been formed in American business. Still another wanted more information about Tahiti. Wells closed the folder, put his hand over his mouth, squeezed his eyes shut.

"Wells?" Janice whispered.

"Mmmm?" He cleared his throat. "What?"

"Have you ever been to the horse races?"

"The horse races?" He took another deep breath. "No."

"I went last week."

He opened his eyes and looked at her.

"You should have seen those horses, Wells. They were going so fast you couldn't see them. You could only hear them. One was the color of a rusted beer can. But . . . with the sun on it. I mean," Janice said, "it was fun."

He nodded.

"And the weather. We were yelling so loud, the wind was louder. I mean," Janice said, "it was fun."

"Did you do any betting?"

"What?"

He cleared his throat. "Betting."

"I told you it was fun."

"Oh."

"I told you it was fun. We sat on the bleachers and the cheerleaders were jumping up and down so much I thought their clothes would fall off. Sequins. Silver ones. With purple fringe. I think I'd like the feel of fringe against my skin."

"Cheerleaders?"

"It was fun, Wells. I wouldn't do anything if it wasn't fun. I do things."

"Mmmm."

"There was a band. They had cymbals. Some drums. A tuba. Trombones. They looked so easy. It all looked so easy. Wells. . . . Why are you smiling?"

"Nothing." He turned his head away, shaking his head; he put his hand over his mouth. "I was thinking of something else."

Janice stared at him. She picked up her Coke can, put the straw to her lips, and drank from the Coke, staring at him. She stared at him until she finished her Coke. Then she got up. She came over to his desk. She sat down on his desk.

"Feel my ankles, Wells. They're swollen."

Wells felt an ankle. He nodded.

"My forehead. Feel my forehead."

He felt her forehead. He nodded.

"My back."

Wells touched her back.

"My back hurts," she said. "The other day I was trying to get the nursery ready. I washed all the windows and I washed the floor. I moved a dresser out of there. I'm strong, Wells."

Wells opened his assignment folder again.

"I washed the floor on my knees and now my back hurts when I lie down. My muscles hurt like when it's cold out. Even aspirin doesn't help. But I'm strong, Wells."

Wells nodded. He pulled one of the assignments out of the folder and began to read it more carefully.

"My back hurts," Janice said. "Feel it."

He touched her back again.

"You can't feel it," she said. She lifted up the bottom part of her blouse, put his hand against her back, holding it firmly against her skin. "*Feel* it."

He felt warm, soft skin. That was what he felt. He kept his hand there.

(1984)

Steven Goldleaf

Steven Goldleaf was born in 1953. He took a B.A. at Columbia University, an M.A. at Johns Hopkins, and a Ph.D. at the University of Denver. He also studied at Boston University, in 1978–79. In 1979–80 he served as movie critic for the Baltimore Jewish Times, *and subsequently as columnist and feature writer for a number of magazines in New York City. He has won many prizes, including the Cornell Woollrich Fellowship. His publications include fiction, poetry, criticism, reviews, and parodies.*

"The Duchess of Yzes" is a sustained tour de force, a carefully spun web of invention which is exceedingly difficult to sustain. Again, Goldleaf makes marvellously effective use of dialogue. Indeed, the colloquial tone is dominant, serving as a perfect foil to the horror of the denouement and the air of casual decadence which pervades the entire tale. Told in stiffly formal language, this would be about as attractive as the report of the Nuremberg Trials. Told lightly and even skippingly, as Goldleaf tells it, "The Duchess of Yzes" is able to swing from cheerful bumbling to barbarous torture, and then back again, without pausing for breath. The exuberant prose, too, makes the grim details astonishingly effective.

THE DUCHESS OF YZES

Like Saki's heroine, I specialize in romance at short notice. In other words, I'm a harmless but dedicated liar. The consquences of my lies are almost never great, but they often lead me into an interesting story.

When I was a grad student I was washing some linens in my building's laundry room when I happened to see, right by the dryers, two Arab women talking. One of them was the typical middle-eastern female: fat, sallow, thick-ankled, pregnant, large-nosed, gap-toothed, sprouting hair at every pore and dirt between each sandaled toe. But the other: she was nothing less than a beauty. When she smiled, four astonishingly deep wrinkles creased her dark cheeks. They were my only clue to her age; otherwise, I would have guessed she was a teenager. When her mouth opened, she flashed a cool-pink tongue and—rare in an Arab woman—dazzlingly white teeth.

I must have been paying closer attention to her mouth than I had realized, because she quite suddenly interrupted the conversation they were holding in Arabic to ask me, in English: "You spoke Arabic?" She pronounced it A-rah-bic.

"Some," I answered. As I said, I am a liar by instinct, and at that time, being in graduate school, one habitually claimed knowledge, however tenuous. Having spent one summer in Israel I had picked up a stray phrase or two of gutter Arabic, but I hadn't understood a syllable of their conversation, and that was plainly what she was asking. "I learned quite a bit when I lived in Jerusalem," I added.

"Yerushalem?"

"Yes," I compounded my lie, "I used to live in Jerusalem. I lived in the—do you know the city? Yes? I lived—"

"Do you spoke Franch?"

"French?" As it happened, my dissertation concerned Thoreau's research on the findings of some seventeenth-century French Jesuit missionaries; both Thoreau's journals and the missionaries' reports were written in a richly idiomatic French, and so my own French was, at that time, virtually fluent. "No. Sorry. Not a word."

She nodded and turned away and began conversing to her companion in rapid-fire French. I kept my eyes on my spinning laundry as I listened to her story:

It seems that in Beirut (or in some city that sounded, in her strongly accented French, like "Babe Ruth") there had been a man who lived in two worlds: Habib, the youngest son in a family of priests. Habib was bright, and he was lucky. The church of the city had sent him abroad for his education—right here to Los Angeles, in fact, where he studied finance, and accounting, and business administration. At the end of four years Habib was supposed to return home, but he persuaded his uncles, the high priests, that he could better serve the church by remaining longer in Los Angeles. Oh, yes, Habib sincerely wished to serve his uncles, but he also had grown to enjoy western life.

He was an amiable fellow, and his fellow-students at U.C.L.A. business school had liked him, had shortened "Habib" to "Bob," and had introduced him to western pleasures—like professional basketball (the Los Angeles team in those years featured a great many giants with Muslim names, and he would spend his evenings explaining the players' religious beliefs to his new friends), fast foods (including pork-burgers), and pornography. "Bob" developed an extensive Western wardrobe, designer eyeglasses, freeway driving habits, and an understanding of computers and accounting which he was to bring back home to help his native church's book-keeping. His uncles, having consolidated the religion's control over secular activities in recent years, had found that the traditional scribal methods of recording business holdings had become inadequate—this was the reason for Habib's western training.

So his feelings were mixed when he planned his return: he would be powerful beyond his years, but he would miss the West, where a man's ability to rise was controlled by himself only and not limited by priestly ritual. Habib would never have the opportunity to use most of his new business acumen, and he was sad. His native city had so much potential for business growth, there were whole areas completely unexplored, and he had ideas and plans for exploration which he knew his uncles would never permit. After three years of extra study, Habib returned home.

Habib had seen how the ripest field of all was pornography. It had existed in his city for ages, but it was restricted to the wealthy, since the cost of even a simple magazine was a week's pay for a peasant. And even these magazines were tame and ridiculously dated by western standards. Each privately printed issue featured five or ten poses of heavily bejewelled women performing stylized acts on jaded-looking older men. The peasantry, who needed pornography the most since for many years they could not afford even one wife, would go wild if Habib could print a magazine cheaply for them. And he would become wealthy beyond description. He could cull reprints from western magazines. He could translate the accompanying editorial copy into Arabic. He could find a friend to take original photos of local girls, perhaps. But he would also be running considerable risk. A newsdealer, some years ago, had operated a sort of peep-show, featuring western "whores" (all of whom were, by occidental standards, fully clothed—most of the peep-show consisted of reduced photos from *Vogue* magazine), and had had his right eye blinded on orders from Habib's uncles.

So Habib took great care. He removed himself utterly from the actual printing. His boyhood friend, Mustapha, ran his father's tea-importing company. They hid a small offset press in the basement's inner-most room. Mustapha was not terribly bright, and this was generally known, so he would be relatively safe from suspicion, and Habib, in addition to being in the trust of his uncles, never entered the tea-shop. He saw Mustapha socially, and would instruct him as they walked around the town. Mustapha, Habib thought, was just intelligent enough to do his bidding but not much more. Habib was pleased when the first two issues of the magazine, contrary to his own conservative projections, turned a fair profit. That was when Mustapha got greedy.

"We are risking a great deal," he said to Habib as they walked one afternoon. "We could lose our businesses any day now." [I am not sure if the girl telling this story meant "nos affaires" to mean literally *businesses*, or if she was using it in the slang sense to mean their sex organs.] "And for what? Why *not* raise the price? I only mean a little bit."

The low price of the magazine was intrinsic to its success—Habib had spent weeks fixing the best price, as a matter of fact, and had thought long and carefully about the exact point at which he could consider charging more. He explained this to Mustapha, and counseled patience. But when the third issue was printed, Habib found that Mustapha had doubled the cover price. The circulation dropped to one-tenth of what it had been.

"It will go up, Habib. You'll see," Mustapha grinned, as they walked amiably about the market-place. Habib had run a study on the computer, projecting how long it would take for the magazine to re-gain its readership if the price were reduced again, and couldn't yet tell whether he had the funds to support such a long-term project. He was considering waiting a year, maybe two, and starting again, without Mustapha. He said nothing. "Also I have an idea," Mustapha said. Habib grunted. "It will work."

"Stapha, I don't like your ideas," Habib told him. "Keep this one to yourself."

"A lottery," Mustapha said. "A raffle."

"What would you raffle?" Habib asked. "Your sister?" In his bitterness, he had given Mustapha just cause to slit his belly open, but Mustapha simply laughed out loud and shook his head Yes.

"Not quite, but close," Mustapha explained. "We will raffle off a woman. In the magazine. A prostitute. A European." Habib stared at him, hissed at him to keep his voice down. Mustapha whispered, "See? Hired by the night, she would cost us eighteen dollars or so, and by the month she costs five hundred, and by the year—"

"Six thousand. Which is all the money we can raise. I am a publisher, Stapha, not a pimp—"

"We offer six thousand to some prostitute, you understand, for a year's work, and we raffle her off in our magazine. The circulation will rise, and the lottery will no doubt pay for itself." To Habib's surprise, Mustapha's rude vision projected as he said it would, according to the computer in the church. The magazine's circulation climbed to a new high with the fourth issue, sold at the old price. The Duchess of Yzes, the last remaining daughter of a noble French house, was offered to the lucky winner of the lottery. Pictures of the young Duchess taken by Mustapha accompanied text by Habib, who watched the circulation climb further, to his amazement, in the fifth issue. He began to wonder whether in fact it would be necessary to hold the raffle at all. Wasn't the magazine's success sufficient? As the city buzzed with talk of the lottery, the church's effort to find out about the proprietors grew. Couldn't Mustapha leave well enough alone? Habib considered absconding with the lottery money, but Mustapha—taking most of the risk—kept the cash hidden in the basement underneath the printing press.

"We'll run a new lottery every month," Mustapha planned, "or maybe we can start producing a weekly magazine, Habib. Don't you like those sales figures? In two years, we'll have enough to retire."

Habib had enough money right now, if he could get his hands on it. He also had the motivation. His uncles were questioning peasants daily, and if some peasant were actually to know where the magazine was published, or by whom, no doubt he could be persuaded to tell. His uncles were very persuasive men, and the risk increased daily. But even more than this great fear, Habib had a higher motivation. His personal share of the risk was to hide "the Duchess of Yzes" until the lottery was to be held. She was actually a Turkic Arab girl with sufficiently western features to attract readers looking for the exotic, yet Arabic-looking enough so as not to alienate them. She was barely sixteen when Mustapha and Habib first saw her, and from the very first they knew she was the Duchess of Yzes—Mustapha just giggled and laughed, and Habib grew serious and sad. "You will cache the lottery money," he suggested to Mustapha, "and I will hide the girl." He was in love.

"Call me Bob," he told her when he showed her the spare bedroom where she would sleep. She asked him what kind of a name was this, "Bob"? "It is the name I will use when we two run off to a western City." She asked him when. She was a clever and ambitious young woman, who also yearned for the freedom of wealth. She admired Habib's western habits, and asked him questions about life in the West; that was why she was willing to endure serving some man for a year—with the six thousand, she would be able to run off to New York City.

"Los Angeles is better. Warmer," Habib told her. "But my uncles may look for me there, so maybe we will go to another city. I have heard nice things about Houston."

"Houston?" she said. He explained what he knew of Texas to her, and much, much more. He plotted his plans to escape with the lottery money, but she demurred. "First, I will get the six thousand," she insisted. "Do you suppose that the pig who wins me in the raffle will be horribly old? Do you suppose I can endure him for a year?"

"I can get four thousand, I think, from Mustapha. I'll tell him it's to promote the lottery some more," he said.

"But you said you would pay me six."

"No, no. This way, you will live with me in the West. Immediately. You won't have to be raffled. We wouldn't have to risk death another day."

She thought about it for a second. "Surely you can get six thousand for me."

Habib tried persuading Mustapha to cancel the lottery in return for having future lotteries to himself. Mustapha laughed, which made Habib very angry. "How can you not do me this favor? How can you sell her, Stapha?"

"How can I *not* sell her, now?"

"She is too beautiful to waste on pigs such as read our magazine."

"She is beautiful," Mustapha purred.

"Men of the world," Habib reasoned, "such as you and I know how to treat a woman."

"Oh yes, yes," Mustapha said.

"Who knows how a—" and here the girl in my laundry-room said an Arabic word which I didn't understand "—would treat her?"

"Oh, yes," Mustapha agreed. "Yes, indeed. Indeed. And let us say that he were to brutalize her physically, yes? Let us imagine that he were to—" and here followed a series of untranslatable Arabic words "—ha, then, Habib, let us say that word would get out among our readers. Can you imagine how the next issue would sell? And the next? I cannot.''

The girl slept all day long. When Habib returned from the church accounting offices, they would share a dinner lighted by one candle. Habib would fantasize, the girl would occasionally ask a question about places she had never been, or fine points about languages—English, German, French—which she was trying to learn. They talked almost exclusively about the future, but Habib was never certain that they were talking about a shared future; she always talked about herself, her plans, her coming ordeal, whether it would pass quickly or slowly, what she would do afterwards, when she was rich and free. Neither of them mentioned any more the danger that the future might hold.

Habib kept trying to siphon funds out of the lottery income, which grew more impressive every time Mustapha boasted to him about it, but each time he mentioned the subject Mustapha grew more guarded. Then not quite two weeks before the scheduled raffle, Habib's uncles called him in, and informed him they had new information as to the identity of the pornographers. They wanted Habib to tell them how much funding was available for bribes and tips and hiring "police." [This was the term the girl telling the story used, but it seemed to carry other, darker, connotations to the woman listening, who shuddered at the word.] Habib said he would check. They said they would wait, and he brought back reams of printout paper, explaining that there proved to be no money available for such things now. They waved away the printouts and scowled. Find the money, they ordered.

Instead, Habib went straight home, and told the girl that she would have to accept his four thousand and go with him now. She still refused: "Get the money," she repeated, "and we will go. You promised me six thousand."

"I can't get it."

"Then I must take my chances, dear."

She had never even called him "Bob" before—this "dear" was the first tangible sign that she regarded him with any affection, and Habib's face flushed. "I'll get the money," he promised.

That evening, he went to Mustapha's office to extort two

thousand from him. He was going to threaten to leave the
country that evening, and send a letter to his uncles implicat-
ing Mustapha, if he didn't give him the cash. He bought two
airplane tickets to Los Angeles along the way, as proof.
When he reached the office Mustapha was sitting behind his
desk, his hands clasped before him, his eyeballs cut out and
sewn to his cheeks, his testicles sewn to his tongue. Habib
didn't even bother to check whether Mustapha were alive or
dead, he ran to his bank, withdrew his whole account, and
telephoned the girl to meet him at the airport immediately. He
would leave a ticket for her at the gate for the next airplane to
Los Angeles. "Do you have the six thousand?" she asked.

"You don't understand," Habib said. "There is no lottery
any more. You must come now to escape with your life. If
we are fortunate, Mustapha told my uncles under torture that
I was not going to come to his office until tomorrow, so they
may yet be planning to kill us then, and not tonight. I will
leave you the four thousand in cash in the envelope with the
plane ticket, but you must come now. I will make the two
thousand up to you, I swear."

She found the money with the plane ticket exactly as he
had told her, but she did not find him. She boarded the plane.
Perhaps Habib had gotten an earlier plane, and would rendez-
vous with her later. Or perhaps he had plans to get the two
thousand and, when he had gotten it, would meet up with
her. Or perhaps, and the girl thought this the most likely, his
uncles had caught up with him at the gate to the airplane and
had mutilated him as they had his partner. Yes, she thought
that the most likely event of all.

The girl telling the story in the laundry room didn't say
what had happened. Her friend asked her a further question in
Arabic, and the girl looked my way, and apparently decided
that I couldn't pluck one word out of context, and replied in a
single Arabic word, and they both laughed hideously. Their
washing was done, and they left the laundry.

(1984)